Sweet Touch

Volume 1: Candy Hearts

Erica H Campbell

Sylifi

Chapter One

I stood in front of the building, looking up. It wasn't particularly grand, but it was four stories, and it had our name on the front. We weren't one of the stronger teams, far from it. From what I heard, one of the other girls aside from me didn't know *her* powers yet either, so the GGDS couldn't give us a full skyscraper like the Downtown Queens or a secret lair like the Rogue Hunters. Still, our deity was well know and widely worshiped, and her worshipers had made sure we at least got something worthy of her name. A lot of teams with lesser gods had to use office space, and a lot of solo Chosen were operating out of their apartments even after years of being heroes.

The part of the city we were in, section 247, was a quiet one. It was mostly abandoned, which meant the endless screens plastered all over the buildings in the other sections, blaring out ads for every-thing from breakfast cereal to church recruitment pitches were thankfully mostly absent here. If we helped to revitalize the area though, they'd show up here eventually, I was sure. As it was, the section was just filled with rows of small shops and old office build-ings, the walls plastered with a hundred years of posters and fliers, the cracked and neglected streets littered with no small amount of trash. Our building was the newest and most modern thing in the whole section, and it showed.

I stared up at the small tower in front of me, taking it in fully for the first time. The top floor was supposed to be our rooms, where we'd live. I'd never lived on my own before; even when I'd graduated I was still living at home, and it would be a new experience I was looking forward to. 'Crime never slept', so we needed to be ready for it any time, on call, and being able to live in the building was important. I would miss my family, but I was only an hour away from my mom's house, so I'd planned to go see her and my brothers when our team was on reserve call or we weren't patrolling.

The second from the top floor was a training room, a giant room full of all kinds of fun gadgets and training tools we were going to use to get stronger. That whole floor was windowless to hide our strategies, and jutted out from the other floors, making the building look slightly like a concrete mushroom. We'd get to help design the paint job on the outside walls of that floor once our team was more set in stone later. Until we had a 'brand' to put on there though, for now only the front wall of the building was decorated. It had tall silver script, flourished and pretty, reading "Lorgiaia's Angels". I wasn't happy about being called an "angel" already; we were just Chosen last month and hadn't earned the title yet. Our wings and glow did make the name at least kind of make sense in a historical context, if not a rank one. It was a minor frustration for me all the same, I needed to earn the rank of angel, and soon, so the building wouldn't be lying.

The next floor was more boring, it was a meeting room, a common area with inset sofas in a conversation pit, a kitchen, the rec room, things like that. I tended to spend most of my free time in my room at home, so I didn't see myself going there much unless it was for meetings or food.

The bottom floor was the public area. Our receptionist, our agents, and our marketing team would stay down there and make sure we were getting screen time in the talk shows and photo shoots if we wanted to do that kind of thing. It was open to the public, so there was a whole area for meet and greets for our fans, and a small cafe that was going to sell us-themed drinks and snacks in the lobby.

All that said, I hadn't actually been inside the building yet. I'd seen the blueprints and concept art, I even got a bit of input on the layout and amenities, but I'd never actually been to this part of Valley City before. I'd never even met my other teammates before for that matter; Lorgiaia had Chosen us from all over, plucked us out of the crowds across over a hundred mile radius to join her team. I had seen their emails over the last month, of course, as we discussed the team dynamics and helped plan the building, but I didn't have any faces to put to the names.

It was in a good location at least, or as good as it could get in section 247. There was a spa down the road, a pizza place called Stacie's that I hoped to get a lot of use out of, we were only a couple sections away from the good park with the ducks, and most of the shops along this stretch of road were actually occupied. Something that couldn't be said for most of the *other* streets in the section. There were diners and restaurants closer to downtown if you headed north, and even a few 'trendy' coffee shops I'd passed on the car ride over here, but the tape on the windows made me wonder if they'd just moved in when they saw construction on a new building. Hopefully they'd get business from the office workers we'd hired at least, places like that were the backbone of a section, at least until we got some retail stores to move in.

I stepped up to the double glass doors and took a breath. I was still a little early, but I wanted time to settle into my new room before our first meeting this afternoon. I reached out for the clean glass set of double doors, and one swung open in front of me. A short elven girl with dark skin and a mess of black curly hair held off her forehead with a black headband was holding one of the double doors. She wore a small blue dress with silver accents in lines around the edges, and black leggings. Her nose and ears were pretty long and pointed, so I knew she was at least fairly attractive by elven standards, but I never understood why long noses were 'attractive' to them. Still, she looked very cute, in a prim way. She smiled at me and stuck out her hand.

"Hello! My name is Alele! I'm an Angel of Lorgiaia! Are you one of my team members?"

I smiled and took her hand in mine. "Oh, hello! My name is Candy! I'm on the team too, looks like you're here early too!"

She nodded. "I have a lot of fragile things to unpack, so I showed up when the agents arrived at 8 to unlock the door for the movers. I saw you across the street from my window and thought I should head down to meet you. Come in?"

We stepped into the lobby and I was hit with the dry smell of plaster and slightly fresh paint. The walls were light pink with white deco designs on them, and the floor was white and gray marble. The big reception desk in the middle of the room was made of a white stone with black streaks. The whole place looked like someone was trying to design a traditional temple, but with more modern sensibilities, which, I supposed based on what I knew of Lorgiaia, was probably what had happened.

I saw the cafe and photo area to my right, with everything still covered in plastic, and to the left, the offices, where I could hear talking and laughter from the team of people that were going to manage us.

We walked around the desk to the elevator and got in, with Alele motioning for me to swipe my access card to open the door. It pinged a dark red, but opened anyway, meaning it was most likely colored to match my color theme, which was a nice touch. I thought for a second about if they would be using these to track our comings and goings, but I brushed the thought aside. If we got as popular as my mom seemed to think we would, the whole *world* would be tracking our comings and goings.

"Sooooo..." Alele said, leaning against the wall as we went up, "What's your power? Mine is time travel."

I blinked in shock. "Your power is *what*?! Gods, that's an S tier power, I'm so jealous... I haven't even found mine yet."

She laughed, proud of herself. "It's not that cool, it's a B tier power actually, according to the assessment. I can send my mind back in time a couple of seconds, that's all. I just skip back to where I was then, but with the memories from the next three-ish seconds, relatively speaking."

I shook my head. "Anything with time manipulation is a good power, that's like, a boss tier power if you could use it right I bet. You'd never get caught off guard or hit by an attack or anything..."

She tapped her lips with a slender finger. "Well, if I could use it on the fly it would make me basically immortal, but it still takes me a split second to remember I can do it in the first place, so it's not that handy. Anyway, you don't have a power yet? Have you been practicing your transformations?"

The door slid open on the top floor revealing a sitting area with a couple of chairs and a short table and vending machines along one wall. There were two rooms in each corner on either side of the sitting area, with walkways to the sides leading back to the area behind the elevator in the center of the building.

"Oh, uhh, yeah, I can transform pretty well, I'm getting pretty good at flying too, I live on the outskirts, so I had room to try it out. I couldn't figure out what my power was though, I might have to find out in combat."

"Ah, no, you *lived* on the outskirts, now you live next to me. I'm in the north-west room, you're in the north-east. That's you over there." She pointed at the room to the right of the sitting room.

"Oh, that's- ok! Is my stuff in there?"

"Yeah, they delivered it already, this morning. We got lucky, the three girls in the back have touching rooms, all in a row on the south wall. Ours are only touching the hallways and the outside, so no one can hear you if you get freaky."

I stumbled as we walked to the sitting area. "I thought this was like a special clearance only area or something, how would I even get someone up here to 'get freaky' with?"

She laughed demurely. "Well, you know according to studies, there's a 40% chance of teammates fucking in any team larger than 2 members, and that number goes up *exponentially* for each member you add. With four members, it's 60%, and with five, it's almost a certainty, and we have five *and* we all share a goddess…"

I suddenly felt a lot more nervous about being on this team. I wanted to be a hero of course, and a magical girl *especially*, but that…? Within the team? It just reeked of teenage drama. Speaking of…

"Um, how old are you, Alele?" I asked, trying to change the subject.

"Ok, wow, trying to see if I'm in your age range already, huh? What's the matter, can't you tell?"

I looked at her for a moment. Elves were… tricky to age correctly. They didn't really age in the same way most other people did, and they usually looked ageless to some degree, somehow both old and wise and young and innocent at the same time. That, mixed with their long lifespans meant I could be looking at a 20 year old or a 120 year old, with no real way to tell.

"I-I'm sorry, I can't tell…" I mumbled, blushing.

"Aw, that's ok, you'll learn. I'm 22, I just graduated college. I got my degree in architecture, then while I was job-hunting, bam, chosen by Lorgiaia. Waste of 4 years, by the gods… They didn't even let me design the building." She muttered.

"Oh, ok. I'm 23, my… um, degree is in agriculture…"

She raised an eyebrow and put on a country accent. "So ah rekkon y'all were a farmer, then, hun?"

I blushed again. "Well, yeah. We raised cows, and we grew peaches.

Me and my family, I mean. Kind of a small farm. Like I said, we're on the outskirts."

She opened the door to her room. "I take it you don't mind being teased, huh? That's good, thin skinned heroes have bad PR."

"Eh, I have 3 older brothers, so it doesn't bother me that much."

She turned back. "Oh yeah?" She said. "I have 5 older siblings, but they had already all moved out long before I was born, I don't even know them, really. One of the downsides of being long lived, your childhood ends up being like a tiny fraction of your life, so your birth family means less to you in the long term than it does to people who speedrun death like humans do. How was it, living with siblings?"

I thought about it. "Well, it wasn't bad. I had lots of protection growing up, and even though I got teased a lot, and we had fights, they were never mean. There wasn't any bullying, so I'd say it was pretty good. They showed me how to do fun stuff, and helped me with my chores."

I smiled smugly, remembering something from a couple of weeks ago.

"I got them back for the teasing though. Before I decided to go public with my identity, I hadn't told *anyone*, so I challenged them to arm wrestling, and I beat all three of them, back to back, in my base form, too. I let them think I'd been lifting weights for *months* to beat them for almost a full *week* before I told them I was a Chosen, you should have seen their faces! I think Jerry was trying to decide if he wanted to be proud or flip me off, and Henry just turned and walked off shaking his head, I was really proud of that..."

"Wait, you're public with your identity? Why did you give me a fake name then?"

I frowned. I took it my story hadn't landed if *that* was her take-away. "I didn't? I told you my name, Candy. Candy Clenson"

"...Huh, ok, I'm not judging, sorry. Listen, I have a lot to do, but it was nice to meet you, see you at the meeting later, Candy Clenson the farm girl."

She gave a small wave and closed her door. She was... Kinda rude, but still fun. I hoped all my teammates were as fun as her.

I turned to go to my own room when the elevator dinged and slid open. I looked to see a blonde girl wearing a black a-line dress over a full fishnet bodysuit step out. I stepped over to her, and noticed with slight surprise that she was visibly trans, seemingly early into her transition. I offered my hand.

"Hello, I'm Candy, I'm one of your teammates, what's your name?"

She flinched when I spoke, but relaxed after I asked her name. She reached out a fishnet covered arm and limply shook my hand.

"Uh, I'm Lucy, I just wanted to see if I could get my room set up before the meeting. My agent said that my stuff should be here already, so..."

Her voice was raspy, she was trying, but still not quite 'fem' yet. I felt bad for noticing, but I was still surprised that Lorgiaia was progressive enough to include a trans girl on a magical girl team. She was such an old goddess that she'd been around before *champions* were a thing, much less the Chosen, and we were her first ever Chosen after over 50 years of her refusing to pick anyone. I guess you can't judge someone's understanding of the world as a whole based on one or two old-time-y preferences though.

"Well your room is on the south wall, around the elevator to the back, I'm not sure which one though. Mine is there-" I pointed, "And our teammate Alele's is that one over there." I pointed again. "So, what's *your* power?"

She looked at her platform boots and shook her head. "Honestly, I have no idea. I haven't even tried to find out yet, I've just been enjoying the transformation. When I transform, I'm a real girl, so I just try to stay in my magical girl form as long as I can. I'm up to three hours a day so far."

"Ah..." I tried to find the right words. "I don't- I'm not trying to be rude, but I don't know that 'real girl' is the right way to say it? Um, if Lorgiaia chose you for a magical girl team, you're already a real girl; the gods say so right?"

Hopefully she wouldn't take it the wrong way, but if she had said that in an interview... I thought about what I had actually said and winced. "Oh, uh, no, even if she *hadn't* chosen you, you'd still be a girl, I'm just saying-"

"No, I get it." Lucy cut me off. She sounded like she'd heard this over and over by now. "I was just saying it's nice to be- I don't know, not cis, I guess, but. To have the right body." She crossed her arms. "Dammit, I was going to try to not bring this shit up..."

"I don't mind, it's ok, really." I said, awkwardly, "I asked about powers, it went from there."

We were quiet for a couple of moments. Then she glanced up from her shoes. "Well, just- Thanks, I gotta go. Don't bring this up, got it?" She said, trying to make her voice sound fem and forceful at the same time. She seemed to be going for the 'tough goth bitch' vibe, but her insecurities were getting in the way. I smiled at her, and nodded.

"Oh, whatever, do what you want." she said, giving up and stomping off.

She seemed like she could be fun, she just needed to come out of her shell more... I wasn't going to push her though. I hoped our other team members treated her well. It was usually more traditional for genderqueer Chosen to form their own teams in order to better support each other emotionally. It was only recently, the past 5 years or so, that trans heroes were starting to find their way onto more general teams, as public acceptance and understanding of them grew. Would her being on our team mean we'd be doing the stuff the queer teams did, like speak on diversity at schools and stuff? I hoped not.

I remembered back when I was a kid and the last wave of groups formerly known as "inhumans" or "monsters" were re-classified as just people groups, and I'd had to go to at least six after-school assemblies in one year. They'd been hosted by dryads, creeping ones, uruks, banshees, yokai, and faceless ones all telling us how they were 'just people like everyone else, and the horror movies we'd seen, and the names we'd heard them called, the laws that used to separate them from us, it was all just the result of misunderstandings and past mistakes'. I respected the people who could get on stage and say "look at me, I'm different, and that's ok!" but that person wasn't me.

I made a note in my commonplace book to ask my agent about it later, and finally headed to my room. There were 6 boxes stacked up in the middle of the room, with a kitchenette, a small couch in front of a tv, and two doors leading to a bedroom and bathroom with no shower. I supposed we'd be expected to use the ones in the training hall then? There were a couple of bookshelves in between the two doors, and a big window on the north wall that had a tall house-plant in front of it. The bedroom had a nice queen bed with red sheets and duvet that kind of matched my transformed self's dress, and had a desk in one corner with shelves above it.

It wasn't quite as small as a studio, but it was just big enough for one person. I was very happy for the kitchenette; I'd had to argue for them to be added to our rooms. It meant I'd be spending even more time in my room when we weren't on call, hopefully away from the noise and drama that I'm sure would pop up. Although... if my *other* two partners turned out to be mature, reasonable adults... It might not be so bad. I did like the two I'd met so far after all.

I rolled up the sleeves on my sweater and pulled my jeans up tighter. I had a lot to do, and the meeting was in less than 3 hours. There was no telling how long it'd go, and it'd be better to get as much unpacking done as I could now.

~~~

I sat in the dark room, Alele to my right, Lucy to my left, the other two girls to Lucy's left. They'd been in the briefing room when the three of us came down, so I hadn't had the opportunity to get their names yet. Across from us were our agents; the two people who were 'in charge'. Or at least, they had been hired to field the more tedious parts of being a Chosen; paperwork, settling contract disputes, getting us territories and patrol/on call slots in those territories, things like that. The first was a dwarf, bald, bearded, and wearing sunglasses indoors. His suit was pressed, and jet black. On his left was a brunette human woman, in an office skirt and white blouse. She had red framed cat eyeglasses and a giant smile on her face.

The table in front of us glowed blue, lighting up the room, and a message popped up in front of me on the glass of the table reading 'PLEASE PRESENT SECURITY CLEARANCE'. I tapped my card to the table, and a small desktop opened in its place. I poked around on the oval shaped screen, using the sidebar to scroll through files on myself, basic info on my team members and other notable Chosen, and some programs for taking notes. It turned out the other two girls were named "Galorna" and "Drizti", but there was nothing useful past that in their files, unless I needed to know factoids like Galorna's favorite food being hunan chicken for some reason.

The dwarf checked his watch and cleared his throat. We all looked up, and the other agent stepped forward.

"Hi! Gosh, we are SO excited to get to represent and support you girls, I just know we're going to have a wonderful time fighting crime and making fans!" she said, her voice high and chipper like a newscaster's.

The dwarf spoke up, his voice rich and full. "We will be taking care of everything behind the scenes, if you need something, let us know.
~~~

If a fan is bothering you, let me know. If you need to talk to someone about a personal or PR matter, let *her* know. We'll keep you up to date with everything *you* need to know about who you're fighting and where, what your patrols look like, and what's on your schedule in terms of public relations and outreach."

The lady picked up where he dropped off. "My name is Willa, and the tough guy is called Oori. Because Lorgiaia is very busy with her worshipers, and she's not used to having Chosen yet, we will be directly communicating with her for you, to save her time."

I heard Lucy grumble at that, and I couldn't help but echo her frustration. I know the more popular gods couldn't be expected to drop everything to talk to their Chosen, but we *were* still her Chosen, it stung that she was pushing us off onto someone else.

"That said..." Oori continued, "Because it's your first day, she did want to see you and meet you again to show you that you have her full support."

I smiled at that, at least I'd get to see her for a little bit, even if it wasn't a regular thing. Oori walked to the side of the room and knelt. An altar slid out of the wall, and torches lit alongside it. He held his hands out, and the markings on the altar glowed light blue.

"Oh goddess Lorgiaia, I call upon you to join us, and to give your blessings to these who are your Chosen." He quoted solemnly.

A glowing ball of light spiraled out of the center of a bowl on the altar, and shaped itself into solid form in front of him; a tall woman, stocky with six arms. She had white wings and a flowing white dress. There were a series of floating flowers where her face should be, golden hair flowing around her head from nowhere, and a light that filled the room like a sunrise.

"Hello, my Chosen." Lorgiaia said, her voice in layers and with a great power behind them. I bowed my head to her as Oori stepped off to the side, letting her walk up to the table.

"I have not seen you girls since I chose you, I take it you are finding your powers well? I had tried to fit the power to the girl, I think they should suit you all according to your strengths."

I stayed quiet, I didn't want her to know I hadn't found mine yet. I felt her presence intensify, and I knew she was looking into me, that she already knew.

"I see some of you have yet to bloom. No matter, you all shall be the seeds of my great garden. Your feats and deeds shall be great in number, and my followers shall sing your praises for generations. Tell me, do any of you wish to ask me a boon? Or to ask a question? I will attempt to be here for you if need me, but my times here in the waking world are short. I would ask that you present me your needs now, as I do not know when we will meet again."

I thought about it, a boon? Who could ask a goddess a boon the second time you met them? Was this a test? No one else was speaking either, so either they were as overwhelmed by her as I was, or they thought it was a test as well. A question though... I lifted my head, not quite looking at where her face would be, and spoke, trying to match her tone.

"My lady, I wanted to ask about our name. We are called Lorgiaia's Angels, and I think it is a lovely name, but none of us have earned the title of angel yet. What is the reasoning behind naming us that? I don't wish to steal glory from those that have worked so hard to earn it."

I felt her awareness caress me, and a chime sounded through the air, as if she was laughing.

"You are both brave and honorable, Angel Rouge." She said, her voice echoing around the room. "I named you that because I think you will rise to the title, I believe you will all become angels soon. In addition, for five Chosen, it cost me as much power to empower you as it would have taken to bless a single angel, so when the five of you are as one, you are as strong as an angel. Do you understand?"

I did, but it wasn't a good answer. It almost sounded like she just wanted us to sound more impressive to the other gods, but I couldn't say that, of course.

"I understand, my lady."

"Well, if that is all, then I shall leave you to your-"

"Hey, um, I have one too. A question." Lucy said. I suppressed a gasp, interrupting one of the gods? OUR goddess at that?

"Yes, my child?"

Lucy took a deep breath and spoke, her voice shaking as she did. "So, I wanted to know what you expected from me. I know I'm- not a traditional girl, and I'm the first trans girl to ever be on a magical girl team- which is huge for me, thank you- but I didn't know if you wanted me to use that? Am I supposed to be fighting for my rights and for trans visibility? Or am I just supposed to like, be token representation? Did you choose me to make a statement? To achieve a goal? I just... I don't understand my role as the first trans magical girl..."

Lorgiaia spoke softly and seriously, her echo almost gone. "Angel Sable, I chose you because you best fit what I was looking for. A Chosen that would reflect the colors of who I am. I chose you for the same reason I chose any of the girls, because I felt you were the best fit among all the people I considered. You being a traditional girl or not had no bearing or influence on my choice in any way, I chose you for you. As for what you should do with your position, that is your choice. You can forge your future in any way you want."

Lucy was crying, but she nodded. I couldn't tell if she was happy or sad, but the answer had been what she was looking for at least.

Lorgiaia looked at the other girls. "Anyone else?"

One of the other two, a very short girl with gray skin in an ankle length robe, half gnomish from the looks of it, raised her hand. "I- I wanted to know if we'll be getting m-more powers? I-I found m-mine, but it's, well, I don't understand how it'll help the team..."

"Ah, Angel Verdant. You are stronger than you know, put faith in your power, and remember that not all battles are won through brute force. I have put my trust in you. As for more powers, you will all find great utility in the powers you have. Master those, and when you receive your next blessings as full angels, we shall see if you still need any more."

She turned to the altar.

"I must go now, I am needed for a miracle in another part of the city. Be safe, and be blessed, my children."

With that, she streamed into mist, and snaked into the bowl, the glow fading and the altar sliding back into the wall. Willa stepped forward into the light and smiled again.

"Wow, the power of a god in the room with us, it never gets old! I'm so glad you all seemed at ease around her. Ah, I think now is a good time for introductions, clockwise if you please!" She pointed at Alele.

Alele stood and lifted her head.

"My name is Alele, I am known as Angel Cobalt, like the color not the rock, and I have the power to send my mind back in time a few seconds. I like to play the mandolin, and my hobby is drying flowers." She sat and looked at me expectantly. I stood and swallowed. I hated public speaking; when everyone was focused on me, it was oppressive and stressful.

"I'm Candy, my magical girl name is- um, Angel Rouge, and I'm still looking for my power, but I'm pretty good at flying so far? I used to be into life photography, but these days I really just like to make dioramas to photograph instead." I nodded at Lucy as I sat. She didn't stand and rushed through her introduction.

"Lucy, Angel Sable, no powers yet. I like to watch anime and play video games." She was quiet for a moment before the girl next to her, the one who had asked about powers, realized she was done, and stood up on her chair so we could see her.

"U-um, I'm Drizti, My code name is Angel Verdant, and my power is- well, I don't know, I can make little shiny lights, but they don't hurt anyone, they just feel warm and they tingle? I can't figure out what I'm supposed to do with them. Um, I like to go on walks, but I can't do it alone because I'm scared I'll get kidnapped, so hopefully...?"

She trailed off, leaving her request for one of us to join her unsaid. She looked down and sat, crossing her arms across her chest in embarrassment.

The final girl stood up; an ork-infernal mix? Or maybe a half ogre, I couldn't tell which. She had red skin and dark black hair.

"And my name is Galorna, or Angel Saffron in the field. My power allows me to use physical attacks at a range. In other words, I can punch the air in front of me, and still hit a guy 20 feet away. I'm still getting used to the quirks, but I really enjoy it so far."

She looked at me and Lucy.

"I'll help you two find your powers, I've been training my body for years, I know a couple of tricks. I'm into martial arts." She started to sit, the remembered something. "Oh, and I can make a mean meal if you don't mind spicy foods. I look forward to cooking for all you soon!"

Willa clapped her hands. "That was so great! I can tell we have such a great team of wonderful girls here, I think you'll all get along so well!"

She tapped on the table in front of her. My display changed to a calendar with dates circled. "Sooooo, this is what the next few weeks look like for us. The Angel Cafe officially opens next Wednesday, so that's the day we'll be having our first meet and greet for the fans! We'll need you signing pictures, shaking hands, and being your best self!"

She glanced at Lucy before continuing.

"Now... that doesn't mean you have to be someone you're not, if you're not a smiley person, you don't have to smile! Just don't be mean or rude, and the rest is up to you!"

Lucy raised her hand. Willa slumped slightly, like she'd expected this, and pointed to her, nodding.

"What if I want my brand to be 'the mean and rude one'? Can I be mean and rude then?"

Willa nodded slowly. "Yyyyes? But please tone it down until people like you, I understand a lot of teams will have a darker, moodier member for the... less chipper fans, but we are at our core a magical girl team! Just don't overdo it, ok? Anyway, that's the first thing we have planned, that gives you almost a week to get your team dynamics and presentation ready for your first public appearance, so-"

"Hey, Listen." Galorna said bluntly, "This is interesting, but what about the other stuff, the stuff we were Chosen to do? You know, fight crime? Battle the Chosen who went evil? Catch the bad guys and all that? The actually useful stuff."

Willa's smile grew a bit tighter. "I understand you want to get into that, but PR is 50% of being a Chosen these days, and the more popular you are, the more worshipers Lorgiaia gets! So this is every bit as important as fighting I assure you."

"Willa, I'll take this." Oori said, moving up to the table, "Girls, you've never fought before. A normal human with a gun can take out the average untrained Chosen, and aside from Galorna, none of you know what you're doing yet."

He pointed at the table.

"Now, that said, if you'll look at the calendar, you'll see that in just over two weeks, you have your first patrol. This is an underhand toss. It's in the main city square and the surrounding neighborhoods. It goes from noon sharp to around five. You'll be in your base forms most of the time, but dressed in uniform. We're making replicas of your transformed outfits for you to use while on patrol until you can all hold your transformations indefinitely to help sell the illusion you have more mana than you do. You'll be covered by two other teams on standby; a smaller support team called the Valley Nurses will be on location doing a pop-up clinic, and the Downtown Queens themselves have agreed to be on call for the area between those times."

He pointed at Alele.

"You are our early warning system on this patrol, you will use your power to press the call button on your bracelet *before* anything goes wrong, if it does go wrong. That said, we don't expect to see any combat or any kind of action on this mission. If all goes well, your job will be to spread out, be in public, make sure you're interacting with people, and be seen in your transformed state with your wings out at least once, preferably on camera. After, you will meet up with me and Willa at Lorgiaia's main temple off the main road for a charity dinner where your team leader will give a small speech."

He folded his hands behind his back.

"If, and *only* if, this goes smoothly, will we start easing you into actual patrols with actual danger. As far as I'm concerned, you're all still civilians for now and will be treated as such. Do any of you have any questions?"

I didn't, I was more than happy to let the PR side of things take over for us for now. We could still make it to angel if we got enough public attention and thought energy focused on us, it was a popularity contest at the core. We were a magical girl team for the gods' sake's, we were supposed to sell merch and inspire little girls to work hard so they could have a chance to be Chosen one day too. If we could leave the actual fighting to the *serious* heroes, I'd be perfectly ok to just trip purse snatchers and resolve civilian fights.

"Well, I think we have our game plan then girls!" Willa said, "Let's say we break up the meeting and meet back here same time Saturday? I'll be reaching out to you individually to go over some more specific details, so keep your phones on!" With that, she flipped on the lights.

I winced at the sudden florescent glow, and got up, following the other girls out of the room. It wasn't bad as a first meeting went, I learned a lot, and I had a game plan in mind. Avoid danger, get popular, and make angel as quickly as I could. I could do that, especially if the people managing us didn't even want us fighting. As we approached the elevators, Galorna turned to the rest of us.

"Hey, so, I know *why* they're doing it the way they are, I understand, I really do. It's dangerous out there, so cafes and easy promo patrols are normal for magical girls, MGs are usually Chosen to sell merch and get followers. That said, all of you are *weak* and still need to learn to defend yourselves, none of you could hold yourselves in a fight right now."

She eyed Drizti, who barely came up to her hip.

"Some of you could be beaten by a kid with a stick, if I'm being honest. But I can help. I know my stuff. I'm going up to the training room now to practice, and if any of you are serious about being a *hero* and not just a mascot for Lorgiaia's church, you'll meet me there."

Well... I looked around at the other girls and saw each of them had a look of determination, some more than others, but all of them clearly wanted to be more than a mascot. I wasn't sold on the idea of throwing ourselves into training this soon after our first meeting, but... I'd unpacked my gym clothes already, so I supposed I'd get a good workout in with them at the very least.

Chapter Two

I lay on the soft mat and groaned. It was like being hit in the stomach by a bowling ball, and it wasn't doing anything to help me find my powers. I sat up, holding my stomach and did my best not to glare at Galorna who was standing about fifteen feet away, her arms still up in front of her.

"How was that Candy, did you feel any powers trying to come out?" she called out.

I bit back a rude response and shook my head. "I'm- I'm going to see if I can help Drizti with *her* power for a bit, this isn't working..."

Galorna shook her head. "No pain, no gain, but fine, see if you can figure anything out. Alele, you're up, I want you to focus on dodging, alright?"

"I still get *hit*" she whined, "I can just send my mind back before the impact, it still hurts in the moment."

"If your body isn't damaged, the pain wasn't real, let's go."

I tuned them out as Alele shrieked and flew backwards much as I had, and walked over to Drizti on another mat. She was standing with her arms and legs spread apart, eyes closed and her traditional gnomish head covering discarded on the floor behind her, revealing ear length chalk-white hair that went well with her muted gray skin tone. Pink flushed her cheeks as she strained to focus on the twenty or so green lights that danced in the air around her, bouncing up and down.

"So, any luck figuring out what they do?" I asked.

She shook her head, eyes still closed. A few of the lights blinked out. "I-I can move them a little, b-but it takes so m-much energy..."

I watched them dance and waved my hand through one. My skin tingled, but nothing happened "Huh... What have you tried so far?"

She opened her eyes and half the remaining lights flickered out, leaving 6 around her. "Ugh, I've tried making a lot of them, throwing them, using them to block, I've even tried *eating* them, but they just phase through my mouth. I have no idea what they do..."

I whisked my hand through one, leaving a trail of green mist behind. It faded back into existence a moment later. "Maybe you can combine them? Maybe they're like bombs that need to be triggered to go off?"

Drizti looked at them and tilted her head. "Well they don't have mass, so an explosion wouldn't do much, and I don't think just making a bigger useless glow-y thing would be any better, but let me try."

She held out a hand and slid one into another, where it stopped, not moving any further.

"It's like a wall, I can't overlap them..." she said, "That's something at least, I know they can't pass through each other."

She slid them apart, and a thin green line hovered between them, connecting them.

"Hey, wait... That's new..." she muttered, looking up at it.

I reached out and poked the thread, and it was solid to the touch. I plucked it, and it made a twanging noise like a guitar.

"This could be cool, you could trip people with this, right?" I said, helpfully.

"Yeah, it's- ugh, it's still not right though, we're all supposed to have roughly equal powers, and this is *nothing* as good as time travel."

"Well... Maybe it's a weapon?" I asked, trying to grab one end, finding it immovable.

"No, you- I have to be the one to move it, here." she said, lowering it and grabbing the other end. Instantly my stomach felt better, like I hadn't been punched by an ogress in the gut 5 times. Drizti gasped in pain and fell over in the fetal position clutching her tummy.

"Oh GODS." she moaned, "I think my power gives people their period or something, this is horrible..."

Lucy glanced over at us from the sidelines. "Wait, what?"

"Ah, no, that's not- I think I gave you the pain I got from sparing with Galorna?" I said, unsure.

She stood shakily and rubbed her stomach. "Why in the wrath of the gods would I ever want to take people's pain? I'm the fragilest one already..."

"Well..." I said, thinking about it, "Hey Galorna, come here for a second."

She jogged over, stepping over a curled up Alele on the way. "What's up, did you figure it out?"

"Yeah I think so, grab this for me." I said, pointing at the green stick.

"Sure, what is it?"

"Ok, Drizti, grab the other end..."

She reached out for it, her hand shaking. "This had better not hurt." she said, still holding her tummy.

As soon as she touched the glowing green rod, Galorna flinched back, letting go.

"Whoah, ow, what was that?"

Drizti looked at the stick and her eyes widened. "Ohhhhh ok, yeah. This could be handy."

Galorna rubbed her stomach "What happened?"

I answered for her. "She can, um, send pain from one person to another?"

Alele stumbled over. "Can I send her *my* pain too? She hits hard..."

Galorna shook her head. "No, you need to keep it, otherwise you'll never get better. I was hitting you at least every two out of three shots, you *should* be impossible to hit considering that power of yours."

Drizti smiled. "So I'm actually useful! I can make a line to trip some-one, and if you guys get hurt, I just send your pain to the bad guys!"

"Uh, what if the bad guys are already hurt?" Lucy asked, "How do you know we won't get their pain instead?"

"Ummm..." Drizti said, still holding the stick, "I can kinda feel the flow of energy here, I think I should be able to move it at will?"

"Can you just go from one person to another, or does it have to go through you?" I asked.

Drizti looked at Alele. "Let's see, grab this?"

Alele grabbed it. "Seriously, if I don't get rid of these bruises, I'm going to my room for the afternoon, this is too much."

Drizti looked at the rest of us. "Ok, who want to try to take her pain?"

I shook my head. "Nope, I already felt the pain from being beat up by Galorna once today."

Galorna huffed. "That wasn't me beating you up, if I was beating you up, you'd know it."

"Ok, I- can you try to just send some of it? I know it's gonna end up being me anyway, Galorna still has Candy's pain, and I'm the only one who hasn't sparred..." Lucy said, dejectedly reaching out for the rod.

Drizti held out a hand and focused. "Ok... try grabbing it now..."

Lucy touched the rod, and hissed, cringing back. "Ow, yeah, ok, ok, gods, ok, fuck. That's all of it..."

"Yeah... I'm not feeling any pain anymore, sorry." Alele said, not sounding sorry at all.

"Shit..." Drizti muttered, the word sounding foreign to her small, high voice, "Well, I guess we'll need to keep practicing, I *think* I can do it..."

"In the meantime..." Galorna said, looking at me and Alele, "you two are fine again, so... two on one sparring?"

I groaned, but I nodded. I needed to find out my power soon, and if being beat up helped, I needed to try.

"Yeah, sounds good, we'll spar you." I muttered.

"Oh, I *hate* you for that, just so you know." hissed Alele as we walked back to the mat. I couldn't quite tell if she was joking.

~~~

Once I got to my room, I pulled off my robe from the showers and stretched, examining myself as I did. My new bruises were starting to color, but my stomach hadn't, which I supposed meant Drizti
~~~

actually could move injuries from person to person, not just pain. That could get interesting in the field, to say the least. It did sound hard to train around though.

I threw on some shorts and a hoodie and opened my last moving box, the one full of my miniature model making supplies. I pulled out the set I was currently working on and carefully put it on the table next to the kitchenette. I could eat on the sofa in front of the TV, so I planned on keeping the table as a permanent workspace, it'd be so nice to not have to pack everything up every day...

I pulled out the little boxes of terrain and popped them open. I was working on a cabin in a snowy forest right now, and the trees I had were plain, and not snowy yet. I dug through the box for my airbrush and changed the head. I'd spray a white coating of paint on the tops, then mix glue and baking soda for the snow clumps and spread them on. I had a long, relaxing night of work in front of me.

A knock on my door stopped me as I started to fit the small bottle of white paint to my spray head. I sighed and walked over to the door, opening it. Alele stood there in a long navy dress, with blue lipstick and a gold necklace.

"Really? You're wearing *that*?" she said, disdainfully looking me up and down.

I looked down at myself. "I'm just hanging out in my room, why do *you* care what I'm wearing?"

"No," she said condescendingly "you're going out with the team for a first day celebration at the nice restaurant down the street. I already made reservations."

"Wh- You didn't say anything about that..." I said, feeling lost.

"Yeah, I'm saying it now. Get dressed, something nice, and meet me in the lobby. I'll get the others."

With that, she closed my door.

I stood there. I had really wanted to work on my diorama, my body was aching from 'training', I didn't really have anything nice to wear... My stomach growled, and I remembered I hadn't gone shopping for food yet for my new place. I sighed again, and headed to my bedroom to find something to put on.

~~~

"I swear Candy, I say 'something nice' and you take that to mean a sweater? You have no idea what a fancy restaurant is like, do you?" Alele said as we walked down the street, the other girls in tow. "Even Galorna is wearing those cute slacks and puff sleeve top."

"Hey, what do you mean 'even Galorna'?" Galorna said, sounding annoyed.

"Yeah, that was rude, are you saying just because she's an ogre that she can't dress cute?" Lucy said, sounding like she just wanted to fuel the fire.

"Oh, for-, no." Alele snapped, "I was saying she's all tough and tomboyish and she still out-dressed Candy. You making it about her being an ogre is worse than what *I* said if you think about it."

"*I* think Candy looks cute." Drizti whispered.

"Oni, actually." Galorna said to Lucy.

"What about it?" she replied.

"I'm an oni, not an ogre. We *used* to be classified as ogres, but since yokai are considered full legal people now too, I'd like to make sure people know I'm actually an oni, which is technically a type of yokai."

I turned to look at Galorna. She did look less ogre-ish than even most half ogres I knew, and her horns were much taller. It also
~~~

explained why her skin was almost as red as a purebood deep infernal.

"Oh, shit... Sorry, I didn't mean to- I mean, me of all people should know better than to assume-" Lucy said, flushed.

"Nah, it's ok." Galorna shrugged, "Like I said, we were classified as a subtype of ogres until recently, just remember it from now on."

"You know..." Alele offered, "You *could* talk to the marketing team, try and see if they can get some eastern themes going for you in your promo art, maybe do a photo shoot in a kimono or something? That'd really sell it to the fans. Ogres are old news, but a yokai? On a magical girl team? You'd get almost as much attention as *Lucy* will."

"That sounds... like I'd be using my heritage as a way to be popular, like I'm selling out who I am to make money. I'm not going to do that." Galorna said firmly.

"Whoah..." Lucy said, staring up at her, "That's... that's super cool of you..." She looked down. "I... I kinda want to do that too, just be myself, not go after the attention. Just exist, I guess."

Galorna smiled at her. "Hey, I'm glad to hear it. We're here to save lives first, and you can still be a role model just by existing in the public eye."

Alele snorted. "Ok, yeah, fine, just throw away the two biggest novelties our team has, sure, it's not like we want to get attention and get popular or anything. Anyway, we're here."

"They're not a novelty, they're people." murmured Drizti

I hung back and patted her on the back as we walked in.

"You want to sit next me?" I offered

She looked up at me, searching my face before nodding. "Yeah, ok, for sure. I do like your sweater by the way; I like the dragonfly on it."

I glanced down and smiled. "Thanks, my brother Ted gave it to me for Yule, I like dragonflies too."

I looked at her outfit. She was still wearing a traditional gray gnome robe, but this one had gold hems and patterns sewn into it, and her matching head covering had two peaks instead of one, laying back in the modern fashion instead of sticking up, with one peak over each of her shoulders.

"I really like your outfit too, you look pretty good, I love how the patterns on your hat match the robe." I said honestly.

She blushed slightly "Well, this outfit is *supposed* to be for rituals, but it's the only thing I had that was 'nice', otherwise I wouldn't wear this outside a gnomeish cave cleansing ceremony. We- we should go shopping soon, for nice clothes, if that's ok."

I nodded. "Yeah, I'd love to! I never really go shopping, it could be fun!"

The waitress led us to our table, and we found our seats. Drizti could just barely see over the table from where she sat and I frowned.

"Hey, do you need a different chair? I'm sure they have different sizes."

She shook her head. "No, I'll be fine. Thank you. So are you-"

We were cut off by Alele clinking two pieces of silverware together.

"Ok girls, this is a celebration, and we're officially a team today, so this is officially a team meeting. That means the food and drinks will be charged to the team, so don't hold back!"

"Wait, do you have the authority to do that?" Lucy asked.

"Mm, I took the liberty of asking Miss Willa for the team's charge card, and she didn't seem to mind, so yes, I think I do." Alele replied smugly.

I looked down at the menu. The prices were outrageous, twenty blessings for a bowl of pasta? Seventeen for a drink? It's a good thing the team was paying for it. Even with my new paycheck and the full month's pay up front I'd gotten my account wouldn't have been happy.

The waitress stepped up to the table. "Hello, may I have your drink orders?" She asked quietly.

"I'd like your finest red, please. And a glass of water." Galorna said politely.

"Ooh, that sounds lovely, red for me as well! Maybe an aged Cabernet Sauvignon?" Alele said, perking up.

"Should we be drinking?... We're at a work meeting..." Lucy said nervously.

"Oh hush it's fine, everyone drinks at work meetings." Alele brushed her off.

"Ok... then... I'll have- um, cherry and vodka?" Lucy said, still unsure.

"Gosh, there's a difference between wine and vodka, girl." I laughed.

Lucy blushed and looked down.

"And for you two?" The waitress asked looking at me and Drizti.

"Oh, um, just a glass of tonic water for me, I'm only 20." Drizti said shyly.

"And I'll have... Whatever the sweetest wine you have is, and water." I finished for the group. The waitress nodded, and walked away.

"Seriously? You didn't have to *tell* them, Drizti..." Lucy said, leaning around me to see her, "I'm only 19 and they didn't card me at all, these fancy places don't do that."

Alele snickered. "Wow, day one as a superhero and you're already breaking the law, nice, Lucy."

Lucy blushed. "It's a stupid law..."

Galorna reached across the table and patted her hand. "It's ok, I think it's stupid too. I turned 21 like, a month ago, but my first drink was like, six years ago."

"ANYWAY." Alele said, "The reason we're here is to celebrate, but also, we have to discuss work stuff for this to be a work expense, so I'll start. When the bald guy-"

"Oori" I offered.

"...*whoever*, was talking he mentioned that the 'team leader' would be giving a speech at the charity event. He did NOT mention who that leader would be. This means I think *we're* supposed to pick a leader from among ourselves, and I would like to nominate myself, as I have experience with public speaking and I'll be heading up the strategies with my power already anyway."

She looked at the table and opened her hands. "Any objections?"

"Uh, I think Candy should be the leader, she's nice, and humans are the biggest demographic, and also I just would like her to be in charge..." Drizti said, starting out strong then fading into a whisper.

"Well, Galorna is obviously the *best* choice," Lucy said, "She's the strongest fighter, and she's not afraid to take charge either."

"Wait, I don't *want* to be leader, I'm flattered but I don't think I could ever lead a team, I'm literally just some farm girl." I said.

I couldn't imagine speaking in front of a crowd, or worse, having to give orders. If something went wrong, it'd be on my head, and I did *not* want to deal with that...

"I mean, *I* wouldn't mind being a leader, I learned a lot of discipline from my training, I could use that and I think I'd do ok." Galorna mused.

"Wait, no, listen, I'm saying I think *I* should do it." Alele said, "Look, *I* set up this dinner, *I* was the first person at the headquarters, *I* have the company card, *I* can time travel, and bald man gave *me* a special task for our first mission. I think it's a good fit, right?"

Lucy shook her head. "Nnnno, I think you seem like you'd make rash choices and stuff. Plus Galorna is cooler."

"I kinda think you're already being a bit bossy, too." Drizti offered.

"Ugh, no, bossy is *good* for a leader, and, *and*." Alele said, holding up a finger, "I wasn't going to mention this, I was trying to keep it a secret, but I'm *actually* born of noble blood, so like, I'm actually supposed to be called *Lady* Alele. I have a title, which means I was literally *born* to lead."

"I hate to say it, but aren't over half of all elves technically nobility?" I reminded her, "The way elven bloodlines work and the open marriages, I heard most elves have at least *some* claim to the elven throne."

She stamped her foot. "Ok, but I'm still nobility, so can we at least vote on it? And you can't vote for yourself, that's the rule."

I looked at Drizti, and she nodded back.

"Yeah, ok, let's vote. We'll make a group chat and all send our vote on three, ok?" I said, pulling my new phone out of my pocket to show everyone.

I'd just gotten it last week for my hero work, and it was very nice. I'd splurged on one with a touchscreen instead of a physical dial, and it had a see-through red back to show the electronics. I held it up to the table, the round, circular shape fitting perfectly in my palm. No one seemed impressed but Drizti, who was holding an ancient flip model, and I felt slightly embarrassed I'd assumed they'd care. I flipped the power switch and pulled up the bubble with texting in it, it was fine if no one was impressed; I got it to do PR stuff on, not show off, anyway.

We set everything up, and Lucy counted us in. "Ok, everyone has it typed? Alright, one... two... three."

All of our phones buzzed at the same time as we got the messages.

"Ok, one for- wait... Ugh, wait, really?" Alele muttered, "*No* votes? Really?"

She looked like she was going to cry.

"Looks like... three for Galorna, one for me, and one for Drizti." Lucy said, reading off from her screen.

"Wait, Galorna, you voted for *me*?" Drizti asked sounding surprised as she looked up from her phone.

Galorna grinned. "Yeah, you're the healer, and you didn't even consider being in charge, that's a good combo."

"Well, in any case, it looks like Galorna is the team leader." I said, tucking my phone into my back pocket.

"W-well. Good luck, if that's what the people want, I'll follow your orders, Galorna." Alele said, her head high, her eyes shiny.

"I don't know how many 'orders' I'll be giving, but yeah, thank you." Galorna replied.

"So I guess that's the business stuff done with, right? Work dinner achieved?" Lucy asked, "To change the topic before we start fighting over the vote, and because I want to, like, 'girl talk', who here is dating someone?"

"Oof, I'm not interested in all that right now, I just want to focus on work and stuff..." I said, shaking my head.

"I was betrothed, but the wedding was, uhh, kinda canceled when I was chosen?" Drizti said, sounding a lot happier about it than I'd have expected.

"Holy *shit*, are you ok?" Lucy asked.

"Oh, it was pre-arranged. I lived in a gnomish community until last month, and we followed allll the traditions, including selling your kids off to be married." Drizti said.

"That sounds horrible..." I murmured, "Ah! Oh, sorry, not to disparage your traditions, I just, gods, sorry..."

"It's fine, I still follow *some* of the traditions, I like feeling connected to my history, but, uh, most of them didn't age well."

"I'm guessing 'some traditions' means you'll be wearing those pointy hats everywhere?" Alele asked.

"O-oh, um, no, I'm not that strict, just- I'll get other hats too, but I *would* like to follow the head covering part of that tradition. A lot of gnome girls hate having to wear head coverings, so like, if I can make it look cool…" She blushed. "Um, anyway... What about the rest of you, any partners?"

Lucy shook her head. "Nope, I'm single as fuck."

"Elves don't really 'date', we just kind of fuck the people we like without worrying about 'partners', and then marry for power once we find someone who benefits us." Alele said aloofly.

"That sounds pretty elvish, yeah." Galorna said, "I *had* a girlfriend, but once I became Chosen, she got uhhh, I'll say 'jealous' and... it didn't end well."

"So *all* of you are single, that's very good to know." Alele mused, smirking, "You know, there's a 40% chance of-"

Seeing the waitress walking towards us, I spoke up, cutting Alele off. "OH HI, yes we *are* ready to order! I'll have the mushroom lasagna, thank you!"

The waitress frowned, but pulled out her pen and notepad. "Ok, and the rest of you?"

We made our orders, and she let us know our drinks would be out in a moment. I give Alele a narrow look as the waitress walked away. She lifted her hand and wiggled her fingers at me, blowing a kiss.

Lucy looked back and forth between the two of us. "Wait, are you two already starting something? On day one?"

"Ye-"

"*NO.*" I cut Alele off, "I just want to focus on work, like I said. I'm not really her type anyway, I wear *sweaters.*"

Alele pouted. "Hey, I never said I didn't *like* it, I just said it wasn't *fancy.* I think sweaters do wonders for making your farm girl body look good."

Galorna looked at me and nodded. "Ah, ok, farm girl, that makes sense. You took my hits a lot better than the others, I thought you must have had some kind of physical job."

Lucy rubbed her sore arms and torso and grimaced. "Yeah, I worked as a stock bo- uh, stock girl. The heaviest thing I lifted was a bag of flour. I have no muscle mass right now..."

"Don't feel *too* bad." Alele teased "Even if I have my natural elven strength, Galorna is an oni, and Candy picked up cows all day or something, at least you're still stronger than Drizti, right?"

"U-um, actually..." Drizti said. "I worked in the underground section of the community because I'm a grayskin? So I did a lot of mining and cave work, I'm- I think kinda strong for my size."

"Aww, never mind Lucy, I guess you *should* feel bad after all!" Alele snickered.

"Hey, you're still stronger than the average human, right? We have our buffs, and in your magical girl form, you'd be stronger than almost *any* human!" I offered.

Lucy nodded. "Yeah, but if my base form was stronger, my transformation could be as strong as... I don't know, an orc or something."

"Aw, I'll get you there, we'll do training, every day, ok? I still want to get stronger myself, I want to be able to one vee one a troll if I need to, and that's going to take work. We'll be workout buddies, got it?" Galorna said, giving Lucy a warm smile.

"Oh, uhh, every day?... Yeah, we can try that, I'll give it a shot." Lucy said. She sounded unsure, but hopeful.

"Ok, who had the ice wine?" A waiter asked, breaking in.

"What's an 'ice wine'?" Galorna asked, confused.

"That's Candy's. It's super sweet, it's *basically* the soda of wine." Alele said disdainfully.

He placed a chilled glass with a thin bottle of wine in front of me. As he passed out the other drinks, I poured and sipped. It was still wine, but it was a lot less 'wine'-y than a lot of other ones I'd had. I really preferred a nice spiced sweet ale, but this didn't seem like the place to carry that. I looked at Drizti who was up on her knees so she could reach her water.

"Hey, do you want to try a sip? It's pretty good, it's not too strong either."

She shook her head. "No thank you, but thank you! Maybe a different time."

I took another sip. I'd try to make sure I stayed sober, for her sake. It was no fun being the only sober person in a group. I didn't see any of the others getting *drunk*, but Galorna *had* just downed her first glass in one gulp, so it might pay to be aware.

~~~

"It-it-it- I jusht- I feel shho UGLY, allthetime..." Lucy said, sobbing into Galorna's blouse.

"Hey, it's ok, I get it, you're not ugly, you're lovely, it's ok..." Galorna said gently as she held her.

"Itsss not like that, im pretty for a *mmman*, nnot a GIRL, imma girl i just want to be a girl i just want to look like a regular person..." Lucy mumbled, her shoulders shaking with sobs.

"That's why we don't let the 19 year old drink..." I muttered. We
~~~

were still several blocks from home, and Lucy had stopped walking over a block ago. It was slow going.

"She had *three* drinks, Candy, that's NOT enough to get her this drunk." Alele snapped.

"She *is* a human, and a kid, I think three drinks would do it..." Galorna said, patting Lucy's back softly.

"This is terrible, w-what if we get stopped by the cops? And we all get arrested for giving an underage girl vodka..." Drizti said, clinging to the hem of my sweater with one hand.

"No, the restaurant gave her the vodka, not us. They might lose their license, but we'd be fine. Anyway, you're underage too, so they can't blame you for anything, right?" I said, patting her on the hat.

She fixed her hat, a few strands of white hair slipping out. "Y-yeah, I guess so."

We walked in silence for a few minutes before Alele spoke up. "How is she, still breathing?"

"Yeah, she's just passed out. She'll be fine. I'll make her something good to eat when she wakes up tomorrow and she'll be right as rain." Galorna whispered.

We arrived at the building, and I held the door open as the others walked in. I followed behind them to see Willa standing in front of the desk, her arms crossed and an angry look on her face.

"Girls, do you *know* what a public image is? Do you *care*?" she said, ice in her voice.

"I assure you, we do, this was a miscalculation, we won't be letting Lucy have any more alcohol from now on." Alele said primly, her hands folded in front of her.

"I assure *you*, you do *not*." Willa hissed, "I don't mind if you go out to eat, I don't mind if you drink even, but for the gods' sake's, if you're going to have more than one drink, *do it upstairs*. And if you go out to eat, do NOT go to a restaurant owned by a villain! I got a call from one of the agents that works for SpineSplit saying that his client saw *all five of you* while she was on an undercover mission there. I had to find out *from a solo rogue Chosen* that you were already *destroying* your reputations within *hours* of being briefed."

"In her defense, Alele didn't know it was a villain owned place, I'm sure." Galorna spoke up.

"That makes it *so* much worse." Willa said, glaring at Galorna. "It is *common knowledge*. It's in the *files on your desktops*. It is your *job* to look into everywhere you go to, know what you're supporting, who you're supporting. You are *lucky* your faces are only in the Chosen database right now and not plastered on a poster somewhere, because if anyone *other* than another Chosen would have recognized you? Your careers would be dead, right now. There would be photos, recordings, most likely an investigation, it's... I..."

She turned away, too upset to keep talking.

"Well, you should have told me this in the little meeting we had then." Alele snarked, "Or, gods, I don't know, asked where we were going out to eat when I got the card? It's not even my *fault*, this is on you."

"Um, I think it *is* on you, Alele. At least the restaurant part. The rest of us didn't even know where we were going." Drizti said.

"I admit none of us should have been drinking in public, and I think the fact that they didn't card any of us should have tipped us off to something being off about the location. I think we're all to blame." Galorna said diplomatically.

Willa turned back around, her eyes wet. "I have been working hard all month for you girls, and you throw it back at me on day one. That can't happen, we need to be a *team*. I need you to think, and I need you to be adults."

She pointed to Alele. "You are on probation, from now on you need to ask someone else before making *any* decisions or organizing anything, and you're not allowed to leave the building without approval."

Alele looked like she was going to burst with anger at that, but she just straightened her back and looked forward with her jaw clenched.

"And *you*." Willa said pointing at Lucy, "...Are on house arrest, no going out at *all* until next Wednesday. You need to give people who saw your face time to forget it. Understand?"

"Uh, she's... I'll tell her tomorrow." Galorna said, nodding.

"See that you do. As for the rest of you..." Willa continued, "the whole PR team is going to be having a serious meeting about this in the morning, so keep your afternoon free, because once we figure out what to do, I *will* be having a team meeting with you about it."

I felt sick, I just wanted to go to bed, but I felt like I needed to say something too. I opened my mouth, then closed it again, there was nothing to say. We'd fucked up. We weren't just regular people anymore. That was something I'd have to remember for the rest of my life, as long as I wanted to be a magical girl. As we rode the elevator up to the apartments, Drizti reached for my hand and gave it a squeeze. I looked down at her, and she gave me a sad, supportive smile. I gave one back, and wondered if I was up for the life I'd been pulled into, if any of us were.

Chapter Three

I lay in bed and looked at the ceiling. My body ached from the training, but I was also aching with guilt about what had happened last night. We had gotten lucky but I dreaded having to go to the meeting later anyway. Things had seemed like they'd be a lot simpler when Lorgiaia had shown up in my room that night and blessed me. I'd imagined flying around and smiling for cameras, high five-ing kids, maybe doing some fun photo shoots. But still just being me, overall.

This mess made me realize that I *couldn't* be me, not really, not without a filter. I had to be Angel Rouge, even when I wasn't. I wasn't a wild child or anything, but I was still a person, and people were jagged and rough. Angel Rouge couldn't be. If just going out to eat without thinking could almost cost us our whole lives as heroes, what would happen if we messed up on a job? Or even just at an event?

As far as I knew, all of us were public with our identities (not that Galorna and Lucy had a choice), so that meant that every time any of us went out in public, we would have to be representing Lorgiaia's church with whatever we did. I didn't even know the major tenants of her religion yet, I'd meant to look them up, but-

My phone buzzed, and I sat up, looking at the notification. It was a message from Drizti.

'hey, we're all down in the kitchen, Galorna is making us breakfast and then we're going to train to get our minds off the meeting later, plz join us?'

I thumbs-upped the message and got out of bed. I still needed to get food for my apartment or I may have stayed in my room, but as it was, I was getting hungry and breakfast sounded great. Maybe I'd get Lucy some groceries too whenever I did go out, seeing as she couldn't go to the store for now.

I didn't go down to the showers; no point if we were going to the training floor after breakfast, but I did change into clean gym clothes and brush my teeth. I put my phone in my armband and headed to the communal floor.

By the time I got there, Galorna had already finished cooking. It was fried rice with eggs, veggies, and a red sauce on top with some kind of grilled steak strips to go along with it. It didn't look much like a breakfast, but it smelled fantastic. The other girls were sitting around the counter at the kitchen while Galorna fixed the plates. I walked up to the kitchen, and Drizti waved at me.

"Hey Candy! I thought you'd be up way before us because you worked on a farm, guess not!" she said. It would seem that she was a morning person; she was way perkier than she had been yesterday.

"Well... At the farm I usually went to bed several hours before I did last night. I had a lot on my mind, so I lay in bed for a while after I woke up" I said, sitting in the seat in between her and Alele.

"We should all try and get up at around the same time, it'll make our schedules easier to coordinate that way." Alele said, taking the plate Galorna offered her.

"Uuuugh, I just want to go back to bed... My tummy hurts and I look like shit..." moaned Lucy from her position face down next to Alele.

"Hey, this will fix your tummy, I promise, just eat what you can and drink some water, ok?" Galorna said, passing her a plate.

Lucy lifted her head and saw she was wearing a mask over the lower half of her face. "I... I need to eat on the couch." She said. She took her food and sat behind us in the conversation pit, facing away.

I got my food and took a bite. The rice was spicy, but not overwhelmingly so, and the veggies were crunchy and fresh. I took a bite of the steak strips and found they were oddly sweet, like a kind of BBQ, but mixed with the spicy rice, they made a unique combination that I quite enjoyed.

"This is my go to training breakfast, girls." Galorna said proudly as she sat down where Lucy had been, "It's got carbs, fibers, vitamins, protein, it's all in one. Eat up, and once we're done, we'll wait like, thirty minutes to digest and then hit the gym. I wanna see if I can get Candy and Lucy's powers to come out today."

"Pleash don' hit sho hard thish time..." I begged, my mouth full.

"I'm going to see if I can get one of those training machines working, something that throws balls or something I can dodge. Being beaten by an invisible fist isn't helping my reaction times." Alele said.

"I'd like to practice with my powers more too!" Drizti chirped, "I was thinking if I could line up a few of the green lines, I could make a ladder!"

"Oh, good idea, I think your power is a lot more useful than we first thought, actually. Only you can move the bars, right? I was thinking about how you could use it to block doors or even pin people to the floor if you need to!" I offered.

She nodded, "Yeah, I really want to see what it can do!"

"So, Galorna..." Alele said. "Do you have any plans about what you'll make that speech on at the fancy dinner in a couple of weeks?"

Galorna shook her head. "I'll figure it out. I was in debate, so public speaking isn't a problem for me, I just have to find out what I'm supposed to be talking about. I'm guessing I'll talk about team plans, introduce you guys, and say some nice stuff about the church and the charity. It's a pretty easy speech all things considered."

"Wait, *you* were in debate?" Alele asked incredulously, "I honestly didn't see that coming."

Galorna fought off a frown. "I was in the anime club too, does *that* more closely fit your image of me?"

"Sorry, I just- Sorry. Yeah, I can see you being a closeted weeb, I just got different vibes from you I guess." Alele said sheepishly.

I focused on my food. I had gotten different vibes too, but to straight up *tell* her that…

"So... has anyone heard from Willa today?..." I asked, dreading the answer.

Everyone stayed quiet for a moment until Galorna spoke for the group. "No, we haven't. I'm guessing she's got her hands full to be honest. I was looking into that villain restaurant we were in yesterday, and the owner is really bad news. His code name is just "Homicide", and the fact that he's operating in the open with that name... It's not a good sign.

"He isn't even a fallen Chosen, he was one of the guys picked specifically to fight other Chosen by a rogue god, so he has the backing of a full church, but no one knows which one. He likes to pressure and lean on people for favors and money, so if he knows we were there, she's almost certainly in talks with him this morning making a deal."

"Oh, that sounds really bad..." Drizti murmured.

"You actually read up on this, I'm impressed!" Alele said, "You might be a good leader after all."

I was a little impressed too, I had just assumed Willa and Oori would explain it to us at the meeting. Looking it up on my own with our database honestly hadn't occurred to me.

"So what can we expect in terms of like, what she'll talk to us about?" I asked.

"No idea, it all depends on if he actually noticed us, or if he cared. I really have no clue." Galorna said, finishing her plate, "Hey, bring me your dishes after, I'll rinse up."

"Ah, no, I can do it," I said, shoveling rice into my mouth, "Y' coo'ed I don' mind."

"We don't talk with our mouths full, Candy." Alele said patronizingly.

I rolled my eyes and pushed the rest of the steak into my mouth. I walked over to the sink and turned on the faucet.

"It- ugh- it's no prob, you cook, I clean, it's ok." I said, swallowing hard.

"Hey, if you're offering, I'm not arguing." Galorna said, holding up her hands with a grin.

"Here's mine, I'm going upstairs, I'll be back down for training..." muttered Lucy, dumping her dishes in front of me with a clatter.

I washed the dishes quickly and thought about the team. From what I'd seen so far, it didn't feel like we really 'fit' together yet. There were little things I'd noticed that made me worried, like, I didn't like how Lucy automatically distanced herself from the meal just now. She didn't *seem* to be too antisocial other times, but that mood shift could be a problem if it wasn't just the result of her hangover.

Galorna seemed to be taking her role as leader seriously, and she was setting herself up as the 'mom' of the group with her cooking and casual comments. Having a team leader also be the team mom sounded nice, until she felt she couldn't make hard choices because it'd hurt her 'kids'. It may have just been her personality, but I could tell it was working on the others, even Alele.

Speaking of Alele... She placed her dishes next to me and gave a small nod as she walked past.

She was trying very hard to be the polite, prim one of the group. Almost a queen bee of sorts, but her tears at dinner and her snark were ruining the effect. Even so, I was getting more and more of an idea of her real personality. She did seem like a good person, just rude and selfish to a point. She'd dropped the leadership argument without complaint (well, without *too* much complaint), so she knew how to let things go, but the way she almost cried over it hurt my opinion of her a lot.

I took Drizti's plate from her as she handed it up and started washing it. Drizti was very sweet and I looked forward to getting to know her more than the others. I liked her a lot, but her powers themselves were weak; even if she got better at them, batons that transferred pain could only do so much, and she could end up being a serious liability in the field. I'd need more time with her to really understand how to work with her, or at least more time to be better friends. Out of all of them, I could see myself bonding with her the most.

Overall, everyone had problems, but they were... fine. I could see myself being friendly with half of them outside of this setting. I wasn't sure how we'd work together though, as a magical girl team or as a hero team. For one thing, we were wildly different sizes, there were a total of 2-3 group poses I could think of that would let us all share a spotlight. Trying to account for a three foot tall person and a six and a half foot tall person at the same time in any battle plan would be a nightmare. I hoped I wouldn't be expected to participate in planning the attacks or anything, I could hit a cue as far as I knew, but I had no idea where that cue would need to be in a theoretical fight. That sounded like something Oori would be good at, but he didn't mention training with us even once, would we just have to figure it out?

I put the last dish in the dishwasher and turned it on. I still had a good twenty minutes before Galorna wanted to meet, but I headed up to the training center anyway. I wanted to check out what kinds of gadgets we had available to us before I was subjected to Galorna's pummeling again...

~~~

I panted as I dodged the flashing lights that flew towards me from the hard light projector, my arm smacking into Alele as I ducked under a glowing trashcan.

"Hey, watch it!" she griped, just as sweaty and tired as I was.

"Shouldn't.... gods, shouldn't you have been able to dodge that?" I gasped, bending the other way to avoid a digital soda can aimed at my head.

"I can dodge the game, or I can dodge you, I can't dodge two things, Candy." she bit back.

"I still haven't felt *any* sort of pull from my power, are we sure I have a combat ability?" I backed out of the machine's field to catch my breath.

"Well..." Galorna said from behind me. "We already have a support, an attacker, and a tactical, so you and Lucy will most likely get one attack power and one tactical power between you, assuming standard team dynamics. It's just way easier to find a combat skill if you do have one, so we're focusing on that."

"Yeah, but... we're Lorgiaia's first team, does she even know about standard dynamics? We could end up both being support, with you
~~~

being our only attacker." Lucy said from on top of a freestanding ladder of green bars.

Galorna shrugged, "Maybe, if so, we'd just have to run missions as a full support team. It'd make me more useless, but we would get to meet a lot more of the big heroes that way, right?"

"Aren't we working with a support team next week?" Drizti asked. Her arms were out in front of her and she was collapsing the lower rungs on her ladder to make new ones up top, with Lucy climbing up step by step as she built the new rungs higher and higher.

"Aaagh, *gods*, I can't *focus* with all this, can you all shut up? We're training, not chatting." Alele snapped as a digital pencil hit her ear.

"Chatting is important, we need to know each other well enough to work together, just training won't do that." I said.

"Whatever, I'm going to go hit the showers, I'll work on activating my power *alone*, I can't think like this." Alele huffed.

She stormed away from us, pushing past Drizti on her way out. As she knocked into her, Drizti stumbled, and the whole ladder flickered out. Lucy screamed and seemed to hang in the air for a second before her whole body blurred. Galorna lunged forward, but before she could reach her, Lucy seemed to melt into a black mist. A second later, she was instantly on the ground, no falling, no sign she'd moved. The sound of her impact on the mat sounded out like a crack, and a wave of air blew out from around her. We all stared at Lucy lying on the mat unmoving. Was she ok? The tension was heavy, and I didn't know how to break it. Luckily, Alele did so for me.

"Oh, oh *fuck*, um, I'm so sorry, I didn't think- I-" she stammered, backing up. She flapped her hands, then turned and ran into the locker room on the far wall.

"Ok, nobody touch her..." Galorna said as she crouched next to Lucy. "Lucy, are you ok? That was a twenty foot fall right on your face, can you move?"

Lucy didn't move for just long enough to make me start to worry, then she slowly pulled her arms up and propped herself up on her elbows an expression between confusion and joy on her face.

"Uh, I... I think I'm fine, actually? It didn't hurt at all, I feel dizzy, but I'm fine... Did- did I do a power?"

"I think so?" Drizti said, a baton in her hand, "There was black stuff, and you were just on the ground, you didn't fall, but it sounded like you did? Do you need heals? I'm sure we can get Alele to take some of the pain, she sounded guilty..."

"No, no heals, I'm not hurt." Lucy stood up, "I think I can do that again now, I can *feel* that part of me, it's like, I was blind to it before, but now it's like I don't know how I *didn't* feel it?"

I looked into myself and tried to find a similar thing, something that i was blind to, but nothing presented itself. I'd try again later, in private...

"So what does it do? Is it like, invincibility?" I asked.

"Maybe it skips her past when she would have been injured?" Drizti offered.

"No, it's... It wants me to *move*, like, it wants to pull me back and let me go." Lucy mused. She looked around and pointed to a training dummy on the wall next to the elevators, twenty feet away. "I'm gonna try and get that guy. Let's see what this does..."

She braced herself against the floor and tensed.

"Hey, hold on, we-" Galorna said.

Lucy blurred, her body shaping into smoke, and hovered for a moment. Then, in a split second, she reappeared in front of the dummy, her fist out. A huge cracking noise echoed through the training hall, and the training dummy exploded back into the wall, splitting the drywall.

"Whoah, what was that?" Drizti gasped.

"Holy shit, you can teleport..." I muttered.

"Ok, come back over, let's talk about this, what happened?" Galorna called out.

Lucy jogged back over grinning. "Yeah, motherfucker! I found my fucking power!"

"Alright, but what *is* it?" I asked.

"Ok, ok, so, I started it, and everything got all gray, right? And everything was all slowed down, and I ran over to the guy, and punched him, and then WHAM everything snapped back and it knocked him super hard, way hard, it's fuckin' *great!*" Lucy crowed.

"So what does that mean?" Drizti asked, "I don't really understand..."

"Hmm, ok... Ok, I *think* she's soft teleporting, popping into the aether to move, but using the momentum as if she'd traveled the distance in the real world? I think it's a build up and transfer of energy to the target." Galorna said, studying the cracked wall from where we stood.

"Gods, I was *so* hoping I'd get a combat power... This is so fucking cool..." Lucy said. She was bouncing up and down and grinning, I could tell she wanted to go again.

"We need to fix the wall now I guess, did it hurt your hand?" Drizti said, still holding her baton.

"No, it's like, I couldn't even feel the impact until everything snapped back into place, it was great!" Lucy replied.

"Well, let's move the dummies out into the middle of the floor, and we'll do a bit more training with it, but we'll need to take it slow, ok?" Galorna said. "I don't want you getting power fatigue your first day."

As they trained, I sat on the sidelines. I was disappointed that I likely wouldn't get an attack power, but I didn't *mind* being a tactical hero, or so I told myself. Plenty of cool heroes *technically* had tactical powers. Grounded Mummy was tactical and he managed to use his earth threads to hold weapons instead of just using them as obstacles. Builder had found out that if she made her constructs with weaknesses or moving parts, she could literally drop buildings on her enemies. Lastly and *most* famously, Moonbug used his personal gravity manipulation to fly and to punch with as much force as a standard brick hero could. He was admittedly the exception to most tactical heroes though. He'd gotten lucky and his power had come with a secondary buff that increased his density as his personal gravity increased. That meant he could tank bullets and shrug off most attacks when he was using his power, even though he didn't have any combat based invulnerabilities.

I doubted I'd get *that* lucky, but I was creative, any power I got I could use somehow. I still considered Alele's tactical power to be practically S tier, despite her 'official' ranking, so at least Lorgiaia's tactical blessings were useful, unlike some of the unluckier heroes. I thought of Pea Soup, who could turn her body into a thick fog that made everyone in it (including herself) dumber for a while, or even *worse*, Rotten Fruit, who puked up a slime that made every one around them also start vomiting.

As a magical girl, I very much hoped to stay away from vomit as much as possible.

Tactical powers were a lot harder to discover, I'd need to just be in the right situation, or just happen to feel the pull of the power from inside. It could take weeks before I found out what I could do, and in that time, I'd slip further and further into the role of the 'useless' teammate. I watched Lucy flicker across the room, knocking the dummies away from her, the displaced air popping and snapping every time she came back into reality and I sighed. I would be ok with whatever power I got, for sure, but the security, the popularity, the feeling of being able to defend yourself... I'd really hoped I'd get an attack power.

"Hey, what's wrong? You look down, is everything ok?" Drizti asked, sitting down beside me.

I looked at her and tried to think of how to word it. She was a support, so she was in a similar boat, but supports were usually highly valued members of any team.

"I'm just... thinking about my powers." I said carefully.

She nodded. "Yeah, that's fair. I'm sure you'll find them soon though, we might just have to face off against some bad guys first or something, that would do it I think!"

She was trying to cheer me up. I should just be open about why I was upset, she'd get it I was sure, she'd had power insecurity yesterday herself.

"Yeah, I... wanted an attack power, so I'd feel safer and more important, but it looks like I'll be something tactical." I said.

"Oh, hm, I understand that..." She said, resting her chin on her knees. "I think it'll be ok though. Lorgiaia was getting a team of agents and managers together before she even chose us, so she was probably told what a team needed to function, I'm sure she wouldn't have make you useless."

"That's easy for you to say, you're a support, *and* you can injure the enemies if they injure us, that's really good, and very helpful." I said, poking her in the shoulder.

"I might not be a support, actually... I think I'm a tactical support, a blended class, those are getting more popular among the gods, right?" She asked.

I thought about it. "I heard about those, there's that one guy who could open doors to a maze from anywhere, and once in there you could eat the berries in the hedges to heal injuries in minutes, right? He was the first one?"

"Yeah, umm... Passkey or something, but after him, hybrid heroes are popping up more and more! You could be an attactical, or a tactical support like me!"

"That would be pretty nice..." I said, thinking. "And I would like to have a range of uses. Not to be rude, and I'm sure her power is very versatile, but Galorna's ability seems to just be hitting stuff, but farther away."

"*Hey*, watch it, I'll figure it out, it'll be 'versatile' or whatever." Galorna called out to me over her shoulder. I blushed, I didn't realize she could hear us from over there...

"Hitting stuff is what she's good at, she's trained for it, it's good for *her*. Lorgiaia said she'd fit the powers to us, so whatever she gave you, it's going to be good for you too, ok?" Drizti said, rubbing my arm.

I looked at her and tilted my head. "You're pretty smart, you know that?"

She grinned and poked out her thin gray tongue at me. "I just think a lot, I'm dumb as a box of rocks, I swear!"

We giggled at that, and were still laughing when we heard the locker room door bang open. A damp Alele with fresh clothes on stomped out, eyeing Lucy with a worried glance as she made her way to the elevator. She swiped her card, and waited on the doors to open, looking away from us. We all pretended to ignore her but her body language told us she knew we were watching anyway. The doors slid open and she turned to us as she got in.

"I'm not mad at you! I'm just sick and tired of my power not working when I want it!" she shouted.

The doors slid closed and took her up to the top floor.

"Well... I think that was her apologizing?" Galorna said, asking it like a question.

Lucy shrugged. "Eh, she got me my powers, I don't care too much."

As they kept sparring the dummies, I stood up. "I'm gonna hit the showers now that she's out," I told Drizti. "It's getting late, and I want to be clean and not stinky for the meeting this afternoon, whenever it is."

She grimaced, but nodded. "Yeah, me too." she turned to the other two, "Hey, let's hit the showers, it's after midday, the meeting could be at any time now!"

Galorna nodded and headed with us to the showers, stretching her arms as she went. "Good idea. Lucy needs to stop anyway or she'll get power fatigue soon."

"Uh, I'll... I'll just train a bit longer, I'll shower in a bit." Lucy said folding her arms.

"Hey, seriously, no, you should really stop," Galorna said gently. "I know it's cool to have a power, but-"

"That's not it, I just- Uhhh, I really need to just wait..." she muttered.

Drizti nodded, understanding "Oh, ohhh, yeah, no, it's ok Lucy, we don't mind if you're in there too, we're a team, all girls here!"

I realized why Lucy didn't want to join us and cringed. I hadn't noticed yesterday, but she *had* stayed behind when we all went to get cleaned up.

"Yeah, I get it, but there's private booths to shower in, it's not a problem, it'll be ok, Lucy." I offered.

"I just- I just started my transition, I haven't earned it yet, I- I don't know, it feels wrong..." she mumbled, her pale face flushed pink.

Galorna walked over and put a hand on her shoulder. "If you need to shower separately, I get it, but no one here minds, ok?"

Lucy shook her head. "Maybe sometime, but for now, *I* mind. I'm sorry..."

Galorna hugged her and patted her back. "I understand, how about you go first? We'll wait out here, and once you're out, then we go?"

Lucy shook her head. "No, I don't want you to wait, I'll wait. I really don't want to cause problems..."

Galorna nodded. "It's not a problem, but I get it. You're welcome to use the lockers and showers whenever you're comfortable, it's ok."

"I hope you feel comfortable around us soon..." Drizti said sadly, "Is there anything we can do to help?"

Lucy shook her head. "It's not that, I just- I'm not comfortable with myself, I'll get there."

"Well..." I said awkwardly. "I hope you can feel comfortable soon, either way. Let us know if like, we need to do anything different, ok?"

"Yeah, ok, will do..."

The rest of us headed into the locker room. I wanted to say something, to ask the others about their feelings with this 'situation', but somehow it felt wrong to talk about. I felt like if I brought it up without Lucy there to hear it, it'd be like we were treating her differently because of it, and that just felt gross. From the looks on the other two's faces, they were thinking hard about it too, but no one brought it up as we gathered our towels and soaps. I understood the reasoning behind Lucy's choice, of course, but I couldn't help but remember her eating on the couch, and wondered if she was distancing herself from the team subconsciously or on purpose...

~~~

For the second time in two days, I entered in the darkened meeting room on the second floor and took my seat. We were all in the same seats we'd sat in the first day, but the computers now had a glowing notification on the screens reading "URGENT MISSION PACKET
~~~

INFO". Something was wrong for sure, it wasn't asking me to swipe my card, and Oori and Willa weren't here to explain. I tapped on the notification, and a message marked as being from the agent team popped up on my screen.

~

"Emergency mission: neutralize or otherwise resolve the situation with Homicide.

The Chosen known as Homicide is currently attempting to blackmail Lorgiaia's Angels using footage taken from the security cameras in the "Petit Fleur" restaurant. This information, if leaked, would jeopardize the in-place deals we have with sponsors, as well as cast the church in a bad light. In order to preserve our organization and maintain our status, you will need to eliminate the target, or otherwise make it impossible to leak the information.

How you do this is up to you. This message will delete itself once closed, and all agents involved will deny all knowledge of it if asked. How you approach this mission is up to you, but the public cannot find out about it, remain covert.

Your deadline is tomorrow at noon."

~

I rocked back in my chair, my head spinning. I couldn't focus, they wanted us to do a *mission?* What was all that about 'you're all still civilians for now and will be treated as such'? It sounded like we were supposed to *kill* Homicide, or at least get into his base and destroy the footage. I didn't even have my power yet, could we even do this?

I looked to the other girls. I wasn't the only one who felt worried. I bit my lip and reread the message. It didn't seem to be optional, it was either take care of the problem, or we'd lose our jobs before we even had our first meet and greet. I tried to think of which of us could do things covertly, and the only one who came to mind was Alele. Lucy's power made a lot of noise, Drizti's glowed in the dark, and Galorna was massive enough that sneaking wasn't an option.

"Well, are we doing this?" Galorna asked, standing up.

"We- we don't even know where Homicide's base is, are we just going back to the restaurant?" Drizti asked nervously.

"Hold on, we're going along with this?" I asked. "This sounds dangerous, we could talk it out..."

"We don't have *time* to talk it out, Candy, we have like twenty hours to do this or we're fucked." Alele snapped.

"Was that a powers pun?..." Lucy asked.

"No. Maybe. Shut up, I can do puns, it's a thing heroes do." Alele grumbled.

"Ok, so, I have an idea about how to find out where his base is, I think." Galorna spoke up.

"Is it in the files?" I asked. I really needed to actually read those at some point...

"No, it's... remember I mentioned I had an ex-girlfriend? She's into this stuff. I think I can get her to give us some information. I'll see if I can get her to meet us. Lucy, do you have enough of your face masks for everyone?"

Lucy blinked. "Uhhh yeah, I guess, I got like a pack of them, they only cover your nose to your jaw though?"

Galorna nodded. "That's fine. Alele, get started on putting eye makeup on everyone, make them look as different as you can without drawing attention. Drizti, can you use your powers to make stilts? To look taller?"

"I- I could wear a longer robe and stand on a couple beams and just move them? It might look funny because I wouldn't be taking steps, but..."

"Ok, perfect, do that. I'll start making the call. Everyone needs to be in the most normal clothes you can, and try to wear something that covers your ear shape, makes it hard to see if you have horns, and above all, everyone but me *shut the fuck up* while we're there until we're done. Got it?" Galorna said, sounding like a drill sergeant.

"Um... What exactly are we doing?" I asked. It was sounding more and more dangerous by the second, and I'd be damned if I was going to die with weird makeup on.

"We're going to the place I met my ex." Galorna said grimly. "Valley City's number one fallen hotspot, The God's Taint."

Chapter Four

We walked along the road towards the bar as a group. Galorna hadn't told us where it was, but she knew how to get there herself. I pulled at my mask and used it to fan my sweating face, hopefully it wouldn't make me break out. Could I break out? I knew I had a slight healing factor now, would that fix acne?

I was wearing a hoodie and jeans, with a beanie under the hood to cover most of my features. My eyeliner was shaped into flared out feathers, and it looked very stupid. I was *never* letting Alele do my makeup again. The rest of the girls were dressed similarly, aside from Drizti, who was wearing a too-big hoodie she'd borrowed from Lucy over a long dress from Alele that dragged the ground as she floated forward on her bars, a slight green glow coming out from under it.

"That dress is going to be ruined, I hope you know that..." griped Alele as we walked.

"I'm sorry, I didn't have any robes long enough, I can get you a new one, I promise..." Drizti said apologetically.

"Ok, everyone shut up, stick close to me, and try and look bored, got it? If someone tries to talk to you, just ignore them." Galorna said, stopping in front of a wooden door on the side of a brick building.

I shuddered, what would a fallen bar look like? Would people be fighting? I couldn't imagine it'd be a nice place...

Galorna opened the door, and we filed in. It was a long corridor covered in posters, stickers, and graffiti leading to a set of double steel doors with a tall orc lady leaning against the wall. We made our way over to her and she looked us over, flicking a sucker from one side of her mouth to the other, the plastic stick bouncing over her tusks with a tapping noise as she did. Galorna pulled her mask down and looked at the orc for a moment, then the orc nodded, and opened the door. The noise hit me like a wave, and I cringed at the mix of chatter, yells, and a low, bass heavy soundtrack playing over shitty speakers.

We made our way through crowded tables and patrons and my eyes darted left and right, recognizing several of the Chosen in the bar. Mr. Manslaughter (no relation to Homicide) was drinking with Cancan, Papercut was arguing with a lady that looked like she was made of jello, and Nettizen was showing off their newest piece of tech to a very bored looking man dressed like a raccoon. There were a lot more, many I'd seen, but didn't know the names of, still more I'd never even known existed. With mild surprise, I saw Spacegirl standing in the corner, her silver dome helmet reflecting the bar's low purple and red lights as she listened to a man who was trying to give her a handful of cash. I had known she was a rogue without any real affiliation, but the thought of a heavy hitter like her taking jobs for fallen Chosen was still very concerning...

Galorna waved us into a booth, and I slid in first. Across from me was a human lady in an all black outfit, a bodysuit with leather straps over it criss-crossing down her limbs. She had a cloak and hood covering her head, black lipstick, heavy makeup around her eyes, and a tall dark wood staff with a circular top leaning against the wall beside her. I didn't recognize her, but she glared at me like she personally wanted to hit me as the other girls got into the booth around us. Galorna waved at the bar and held up four fingers, then sat down at the end of the booth in a chair she grabbed from another table. She pointed to the staff the lady had. The lady rolled her eyes and reached up, stroking the red, fleshy-looking crystal floating in the round part of the staff. Suddenly, the noise level dropped to almost nothing, and the table brightened up so we could see each other better.

"So, Lorna, these are your new... friends?" the lady said, shaking her head. "They look like children, I'm surprised Horach even let them in."

"This is my new team, Saara. I hope we can get along, despite our differences." Galorna said sternly.

"Whatever, we're broken up, so if you want a tip, you pay the rates everyone else does now. You do that, you're just another customer to me, no problem, no hard feelings." Saara bit back.

"Ok, that's all I can ask for, I guess." Galorna agreed. She pulled out a few hundred blessings and handed them over to her.

"So, what's so urgent that I needed to cancel on two other sessions just to get you in?" Saara asked as she grabbed the money.

"We need to know the location of Homicide's base, not the '*Petit Fleur*', his *real* base. We have a job we need to complete tonight at the latest, and we need to get to him to do it." Galorna said grimly.

"Ok, wow, that's not going to be easy. Getting to him, I mean. I can find his base easy enough though." Saara said, narrowing her eyes.

"Wait, no one knows what god chose him, won't you risk *your* god getting angry if they happen to be allies with his?" Lucy asked.

Galorna shot her a look to shut her up, but Lucy ignored it.

"I'm not a Chosen, dumbass, I'm a sorceress. I got my powers by sacrificing parts of my soul. I'm my *own* goddess, girly, and I've got no ties to that dumb fuck." Saara said. She reached up and held her staff again, and whispered a few words into the air. They took form, pouring out of her mouth and splashed onto the table, dripping upwards as they spread. A lady with an apron on set four beers on the table, and looked at the growing gray mass in front of Saara.

"Just clean it up this time, hun. That stuff stains, remember?" she said, putting a bottle opener down and walking off.

Galorna popped the tops off the beers, and passed them out to me, Alele, Saara, and herself. I didn't like beer much, but I sipped it anyway, pulling my mask away from my face and sliding the bottle under it.

"What, everyone gets one but me? Really? It's one bottle, come on..." Lucy complained.

"First off, you're still on house arrest from the last time you drank, and second off, we're going to need to be sharp for what's next. I only ordered these to blend in. Try not to finish them, anyone."

"Can I finish *mine* at least?" Saara said sarcastically as she waved her hands over the drips of gray lifting off the table.

"You can do what you want if you get us our information." Galorna said, "I really just want to get this over with."

I watched the gray slime ooze and separate as her hands moved. Once it took form more, I realized that it was actually a map of the city, the drips being the buildings, the gaps being roads. I tried to find our headquarters, but I wasn't familiar enough with the layout to pick it out off a map yet.

"Ok, so we're here..." Saara said, pointing to a spot on the map. "And the place with the most 'home energy' for Homicide is... here. That's an actual home though, it's in the 'burbs, so... the next most 'home' place is... here, about 23 blocks away, looks like it's..." she pulled out her phone and tapped away, "Some kind of gated warehouse. That's the place, I'm sure of it."

I nodded and jotted down the section number in my commonplace book. We could make it there only using major roads if we wanted, without even having to using the buses.

"23 blocks? That's like, almost three miles..." whined Lucy.

"Lucy I swear to Lorgiaia, shut up and sit still or I will *make* you shut up and sit still." Galorna growled, and turned back to Saara, "So, anything else jump out at you? Anything we need to be aware of?"

"You didn't pay for a reading, just a location divining, *that* costs extra, and you know it's not that specific anyway." Saara said wiggling her finger.

I dug in my pocket and pulled out a fifty blessing note I had brought along in case we needed to bribe anyone. "Will this cover it?"

"Hey, that's- No, it's not worth it." Galorna said, reaching for the money.

"Ah ah ah! Mine now!" Saara grabbed the cash and tucked it into the cleavage of her bodysuit. "Unless you want to try and fish it out, Lorna?"

Galorna crossed her arms and shook her head. "I'm not doing this, just do the reading, and let us leave. We've got a lot of ground to cover."

"That's what I *thought*, big girl. Ok, let me just..." Saara breathed in deeply, and exhaled, smoke pouring out of her mouth. It swirled and twisted on the table, and hovered in place as she studied it.

"Ok, hm. I'm seeing danger, but you knew that. Seeing death too, but that could mean anyone... I'm seeing fear, and... something new, the start of a thread that I can't follow without moving the focus, but I don't see any *failure* overall, just... a lot of muddied successes. You might lose someone though, just saying." she said, waving the smoke away.

"I will, um, keep all that in mind, thank you very much." I said politely, processing the reading. Death? Something new? That was vague and unhelpful, I'd just wasted fifty blessings on that bullshit. Lesson learned, I suppose, magic sucked.

"Listen, Saara..." Galorna started, then thought better of herself. "We're gonna go. I want- I'll let you know if we need anything else."

Saara snorted, and shook her head. "Whatever, just get out of here before someone notices a whole team of GFs in what's supposed to be a safe haven for the wicked."

"GFs? What does-" Lucy asked, but Galorna pulled her out of the booth and out of the quiet bubble Saara had made. I shuffled out behind the other girls, and waved goodbye to Saara with a light smile as we filed out the way we came. Once we made it back to the streets, we walked a full two blocks before Galorna slowed down and turned to face us.

"Ok, first up, I *really* meant it when I said to shut up. Those people would have actually killed you if they'd found out who you were. The only reason we even got in is because I used to fuck that bouncer, and once *any* promo material gets put out about us with my face on it? I'm banned for life, end of story." she pulled her hood off. "Secondly, I need everyone to shape up, and shape up *fast*. She mentioned 'death' in Candy's reading, and I know *she* said it's not a big deal, and to someone like her, it's not, but to *you*, it really is. It means that by the end of the night, one of us will have killed someone, or been killed *by* someone, or both. I know no one wants to kill anyone, but *please*, if it's you or them, do it. They're bad people, and they're paid very well for taking this risk, I should know, I used to do this kind of thing for a living."

"I really thought the reading would be more useful, I'm very sorry, I shouldn't have gotten it." I apologized.

"The reading was a lot more useful than you think, but in the future, please, if I say to shut up, *do*. I know these people." Galorna said firmly.

"So what's the plan now? Do we just, like, go there and start a fight?

Or do we wait until later to break in and try and erase the files?" Alele asked.

"We don't know anything about where the videos are, who has them, or if there's more than one copy." Galorna sighed "Really, we need to get to Homicide directly and make him talk, so we need to head out now. I'd say we should fly there, but we'll need to transform to fight, and I can only hold my magical girl form for about twenty minutes so far, so we'll have to walk."

"That's going to take hours..." groaned Lucy.

"*I* can run a mile in six minutes, I can get there pretty quick." bragged Alele.

"I can just float there, I think I can move faster on these sticks than I can by walking..." Drizti said, her voice muffled by her hood covering her face.

"No, we're all walking, we'll get there in less than an hour. No jogging or running, we'll still get there by midnight easily, and even if Homicide has gone home already, he'll come back once we make a scene. We need to keep our energy up, and our minds sharp." Galorna said firmly.

My heart started beating faster and I felt a chill. We were really about to do this, to take on a villain in his evil lair, fighting crime and putting our lives on the line. I hugged myself and watched the others as we walked at a brisk pace towards literally certain death, and I wondered if I'd still have all my teammates when the sun rose tomorrow.

~~~

A little after 12:30, we arrived at the warehouse. It was a nice place, with well lit docking bays, a clean parking lot, and a tall chain link fence around it. There were two guards next to the door to the left
~~~

of the bays, and they looked unarmed. Galorna walked us down a side road, and faced us.

"Alright, we're going in guns blazing, we all transform now, fly over the fence, and attack. I'll get the guy on the right, Lucy, you take the left. After that, we break down the doors and head in. I'll take point, Lucy, watch our backs. The other three stay in the center and only break out if there's a problem. Alele, you need to be ready to give us a warning as soon as you see something going wrong, can you handle that?"

Alele crossed her arms. "I'll do everything I can, I promise."

Galorna shook her head. "No, you'll do what you *need* to, even if you can't. Those guards don't have guns because they're outside and it'd draw attention, but the goons inside will be packing real heat. Even transformed, a bullet will still kill us, so *do not* let them get a good shot at you." she turned to Drizti, "You'll need to be on watch for when one of us does get shot, transfer the pain and injury if possible, as quick as possible, understand?"

Drizti nodded, and saluted.

"So, when you say 'take the guy on the left'..." Lucy asked,

"I mean hit him hard, into the wall. Avoid his head, but try to hit him with enough force to put him down. Your power is loud, so it'll make everyone inside alert, but that won't be an issue if we move fast."

I flexed my muscles and breathed deeply, trying to imagine what it'd be like to face down against a group of trained goons like this. I shouldn't be dealing with this, I should be at home cutting twigs into mini firewood for my diorama. I wanted to be a popular hero, of course, but was a little bit of bad PR worth *this?*

"Hey, I don't think I can do this." I admitted, "I'm not feeling like I know what I'm doing, and I really think it's going to go horribly wrong..." I wasn't lying, but I honestly just wanted to be anywhere but here, doing anything else.

"Candy..." Drizti said, "It's ok, we all have each other's back, it'll be ok."

"She's right," Galorna snapped, "we're going to be just fine. We can get through this safely, and all make it out alive. We'll go in hard and fast, and one of the goons might not make it, but it'll still be ok."

"I was wondering about that... Is our rep really worth someone's life?" Lucy asked, rubbing her arms.

"Yes. Absolutely." responded Alele automatically.

"It's not *about* that, it's about, I mean, if we can't do *this*, we can't do our *jobs*, and if we can't do our jobs, who knows how many more people will suffer? We could be the ones who stop a bombing, or a fallen attack, and we'll never get the chance to *do* that if we don't give ourselves a chance to *start*." Galorna said.

"I guess that makes sense... I don't- I don't want to kill anyone, though." Lucy mumbled.

"You might not have to, but we've wasted enough time, everyone, transform, and let's get our lives back, ok?"

I nodded, and focused inward, pulling at the red glowing part inside my chest, drawing it out over me like a blanket. I felt it wash over me and hug me, my clothes being replaced with a tight top and corset, a dark red bell shaped skirt blooming out of my waistband down to my knees. White tights covered my legs as puffed sleeves swirled into existence on my shoulders, my sneakers swapping out for Mary-Janes. My waist-long blonde hair flowing behind me on unseen wind, perfect and shiny, despite it being mussed up by my hood and beanie just moments before. My wings unfurled, and fluttered, framing me and lifting me up into the air a couple of inches. I landed, sighed in bliss to myself, the feelings of power flowing through my body.

"Ahhh, gods this feels so much better..." Lucy said, landing at the same time I did, her voice clear and bubbly, all traces of her former rasp gone.

I looked around, the rest of the girls were transformed too, all into the same outfit, but in our own colors. Alele was dark blue, Drizti was forest green, Galorna was a dark, almost burnt yellow, and Lucy was black and gray. I raised my eyebrows when I took a harder look at Lucy, her face was much softer, and she was a lot less rectangular than usual, with hips and her top being filled out a reasonable amount. I looked to the other members of the team, but no one else seemed to have any physical changes other than the wings. I suppose Lorgiaia really wanted to make sure Lucy was comfortable while she fought?

"Oh *no*..." Drizti gasped. "The dress, and parts of the hoodie- they weren't transformed with me, I ruined them, I'm so, so sorry..." she said, picking up the lower half of Alele's dress and the lower part of the sleeves on the hoodie.

"Hey, I've got like 6 dysphoria hoodies, it's fine, you can keep that one. It's you-sized now." Lucy said.

"My dress was ruined from you dragging it on the ground for twenty blocks, it's just *more* ruined now, it's whatever." Alele waved it off.

"Dresses aside, I only have twenty minutes before I revert, anyone else have a shorter transformation period?" Galorna asked.

We all shook our heads, and she continued.

"Ok, perfect. That means we get all the way in, clear the building, find Homicide, or get him to come here, twenty minutes. We ready?"

"I *think* I'm ready." Lucy said as she clenched her fists.

"Alright, on one, we take off, and go straight for the door. Three... Two..." Galorna counted.

I braced myself for launch.

"...one, GO GO GO!"

We all took off in a flurry of feathers, and flew over the fence on the other side of the street. I was leading the way, and I pulled back to let Lucy and Galorna pass me. They each sped towards their targets, and Lucy blipped out into smoke, popping back in a second later, slamming the guard into the wall so hard it crumpled around him. The other guard spun at the noise, his hand going to his belt for a radio. Galorna landed hard a few feet away, and swung, her power activating as she snapped her arm forward in front of the man's face. He lurched backwards, blood spraying out of his nose and ears, and he collapsed, unmoving.

I landed next to Galorna and stared at the man bleeding from every hole in his head in front of me. Lucy's man fell out of the divot on the wall in a heap and moaned, twitching, still alive, but this one, the one Galorna punched...

"Holy *shit*, you killed him in one punch..." I whispered.

"I- fuck, I didn't hit him that hard, it should have broken his nose, I didn't- FUCK." she whisper-yelled.

"One punch? At half power, max? I don't understand..."

"It- it looks like his brain is coming out..." Alele said, pointing to chunks bubbling out of his ears.

"Did- did you p-punch him in the b-brain?" Drizti asked, shaking and looking away, her face tinting.

"No, I just- I just punched him like I'd punch any bad guy, my power must have gone wrong..." Galorna said, her voice breaking. "Really, the *first* fucking guy, gods..."

"Hey, we knew this would happen eventually tonight, it's out of the way, right?" I offered.

"I don't- I've never killed before, fuck. This is- I don't know if I can do this, I'll kill everyone in the building..." Galorna moaned.

"Is *my* guy gonna be ok?..." Lucy asked in a small voice.

I looked over at the other man, he had passed out holding his arms around his chest, but he was still breathing.

"He looks fine, Lucy. You're way weaker, you should be fine. I guess you're on point now?" I said.

"No, I'm on point," Galorna said, wiping her eyes, "I'll just- I'm not going to use my power, I'll just fight like I always have, it'll be fine. We need to move, I can't look at him anymore, and the alarm is probably going up right now."

As if on cue, the door swung open and a man with a rifle stepped out.

"What the ever loving fu-" He started. He didn't get to finish, because Galorna's fist hit him in the side of the jaw, slamming him into the door frame. He tumbled down the steps in a heap. She knelt, and felt his neck.

"...Ok, this one's alive, let's move, same plan, we're on a timer, move, girls!" she barked.

We all ran up through the door. As I stepped over the knocked out man she'd just punched, I stopped, and reached out for his rifle.

"Candy, no!" Drizti said, "We can't be that, we can do it with our powers. If we do *that*, it's like saying we're not good enough to do it ourselves, and more people will die!"

Easy for her to say, she *had* a power. A *healing* power at that. I really wanted some kind of protection, but the girls were looking at me now, and I couldn't hide a whole rifle under my skirt, no matter how fluffy it was.

"Ah, yeah, no, sorry. I was just thinking about not leaving it in the open like this..." I said, stepping inside, "I guess that's dumb, it's inside the gate, right?"

No one answered, and I wondered if my excuse had landed. We ran along the bay doors towards the office area on the far side, looking down the aisles for anyone that might still be working, but no one else was in the warehouse. Getting to the door to the rest of the building, Galorna barely slowed down, planting a kick against the door right behind the doorknob. It folded in, crumpling, and swinging open with a bang, slamming into another guard who was standing on the other side.

He went down, but started to climb to his feet, grabbing at his gun as he did so. Galorna kicked him in the jaw, and he went down with a cracking noise. She looked at him to make sure he was moaning, then took off into the offices.

"He'll be up top, so look for stairs, bad guys always like being up high." Alele said.

I pointed. "There, there's an elevator, we can take it straight up."

"We're *not* taking the-" Galorna started, but the elevator opening cut her off. There were four guards inside, guns raised.

"Damnit, you have *one* job, Alele, warn us!" Lucy yelled as she blinked out.

"Oh, shit, I forgot I could- Ugh, just fight them!" Alele said as shots were fired.

Lucy popped back in, slamming the front two against the sides of the elevator, and flickered without disappearing as the remaining two re-aimed their weapons at her.

"Shit, I can't-" Lucy yelled.

Galorna tackled her as the spray of bullets exited the elevator, and they slid out of the doorway, leaving a trail of red behind them. I jumped up and kicked off the wall, flying as fast as I could with my arms out into fists, slamming into one's neck and crashing into the elevator. Drizti zipped in behind me, pinning the other one to the wall with her bars, holding his weapon down. The door closed behind us with a ding, and the elevator started to rise. I looked at Drizti, and she looked back, scared and crying. I punched my guy a few times until he fell over, and then started on the one Drizti was holding. By the time the elevator stopped moving, they were both unresponsive.

I hovered, my feet against the wall, ready to fly out and tackle anyone on the other side. When the doors opened enough to see out of, I saw it'd be useless to even try. Homicide stood across from me, two pistols in his hands, one pointed at each of us. His tan suit boldly clashed with his glossy, metallic-glass skin, and he had a smile on his face.

"Well, I didn't expect a personal call, but now that you're here, will you come with me to my office?"

~~~

I shuffled, the gun against my neck cold and filling me with an electric feeling of dread. I could really *die* here, just a twitch of his finger, and I'd be gone... I tightened my grip on his hand, the one on my shoulder pinning me to his body. It was slick, his skin inflexible and hard, but I could still feel his heartbeat through it somehow. I tried to think of a way to get out of the hold without the gun going off, but I couldn't, my wings were pinned in an odd angle, so I couldn't even open them without moving away first. I didn't *know* about combat stuff, I didn't even want to be here, and even if I *did* get out without being shot...

I looked over at Drizti, held upside down by her ankles by a man in a black suit, Homicide's right hand man, I supposed. He had a gun pointed at her head, and he was watching me closely. I swallowed hard. I didn't know how we were supposed to even get the videos deleted in the first place. We hadn't thought this through, it's not like we could just *fight* Homicide, everything from bullets to fire slid off his skin, even Galorna probably couldn't touch him.

The 'office' he'd brought us to was more of an evil lair than anything else I'd seen in my life. It was all brushed steel walls and furniture, with a wall full of rows of screens behind us, and a tall leather chair on the other side of the deck we were leaning against.
~~~

It felt very much like a spy movie set, except the guns had real bullets, and the air smelled like ozone for some reason.

The doors to the lair slid open and Alele, Lucy, and Galorna stood in front of us. Lucy was bleeding from a hole in her stomach and looked paler than usual, and Alele was crying. Galorna snorted and bared her teeth, showing off her short tusks usually covered by her lips.

"Let them go, you fucking monster." she growled.

"Really? *You* break into my workplace and kill my employees, and when I fight back, *I'm* a monster?" Homicide said. I couldn't see his face, but I could hear the grin.

"I will-" Galorna started, but Alele screamed.

"NO! No, stop, gods stop, that guy just killed Drizti! Or- he *will* kill-just- please, gods..." she choked out, her tears starting up again. Drizti started crying too, her whole body shaking with fear.

"Ahhh, a forewarning power, very clever!" Homicide said, "Well, less clever, and more cheating I suppose. As you just found out, you can only save *one* of them unless you listen to my demands, and I think you'll find them very reasonable. All I want is 25% of all proceeds your team makes, until you break up. That's all!"

"That's- We couldn't even do a fucking autograph signing without fueling crime, we'd never give you money!" said Lucy through clenched teeth.

"Oh, that's too bad... I suppose I'll just have to release the video of all of you partying in my establishment. Or... I *would* do that, if it weren't easier to just kill you here and now, now that you presented yourself to me on a silver platter." he said, his smile growing.

Fuck, fuck fuck fuck... Galorna must have gone for me the first time, which is why Drizti got shot. That was the stupid option, but I'm glad to have been picked. As much as I hated it, it made way more sense to get *her*, let me get shot, then have her transfer my wound before I died.

I met Galorna's eyes, and flicked them over to Drizti. Let me get hit, it'd be better than all of us dying, I willed her to understand. I tightened my grip on Homicide's hand. If I could pull him, yank him, the bullet might just graze me, it might not hurt so bad. I focused, and- I felt something. A buzz, inside him. A light that was just under the surface. I could feel it, I could touch it *through* him. My heart leaped, was this my power? What would it do? Would it even help? I looked back up to Galorna, and she looked back. I saw her determination.

"No? Still want to do this the hard way? Fine by me, Horatio, kill the-"

Galorna swung, her power crushing into Horatio's face, his blood and brains spraying out of his holes with far more force than the other man. At the same time, I used my power, I gripped the 'thing' inside Homicide, and I pulled. It felt like I was turning him inside out, his organs and skin folding in on themselves, spinning and churning as I pulled away from him. The whole thing happened in an instant and he was gone, the gun clattering to the ground. I spun back around and saw Drizti standing, her body shaking as she tried to move Lucy's gunshot to the now dead Horatio.

"It's n-not going, I-I'm s-sorry..." she wailed.

"It's ok, we have tons of other guys we left alive downstairs, and Homicide, too." Galorna panted, her transformation glowing and fading out, leaving her in what she was wearing earlier in the night.

She looked over to me. "Wait, where did he go? I wasn't watching, did he escape?"

I shook my head. "No, I- I made him fold up inside himself, I don't know what happened, it was my power. I don't know where he is."

"Uh, um, I was watching..." Alele said, her voice far away and empty.

"What happened then?" I asked.

"He, uh... He's..." she said, and pointed to my hand.

With a start, I realized that I'd never let go of him, and that I was still holding something in the hand I'd pulled him with. I looked at my hand, and was suddenly much more confused than before.

In my hand, looking perfect in every way, was a single slice of pumpkin pie.

Chapter Five

I stared at the piece of pie in my hand. I'd folded up Homicide, and... now I had pie? I held it up to my face and stared at it. Every part of it, from the golden brown crust to the dollop of whipped cream looked exactly like what you'd imagine a perfect piece of pie to look like. Where had it come from? Was it a reward from Lorgiaia for defeating a bad guy? Or was it... I looked around the room for any sign of Homicide, then back at the pie. I couldn't have actually... could I?

I looked over to Alele to ask what she'd seen, and her scared and sick expression told me everything I needed to know.

"Holy shit..." I whispered. "I think I can turn people into pie?"

"That's- that's not a real power, no. It's got to be something else, maybe he teleported or something, and swapped places with a piece of pie?" Galorna said, lifting Lucy up onto her shoulder, "We need to find someone still alive to transfer Lucy's wound to. You and Alele see about finding that video and deleting it."

I nodded, still looking at the pie.

"Yeah, we'll figure it out..." I said, distracted.

"Uh, Candy, I- I watched him turn into that piece of pie, I'm pretty sure that's him..." Alele's voice shook as the other three left the room.

"Uh huh, yeah, I know... I don't get it though, I *folded* him, why is he pie now?" I muttered, turning the pie left and right to see if there was anything odd about it.

"I'm going to look at the computers, just... help when you're ready, I guess." Alele said, her voice still scared and confused.

I picked up Homicide's gun and shoved it into my dress pocket. The pocket was underneath most of the fluff and much deeper than I expected, so the gun was hidden to anyone looking on. I didn't want him turning back and instantly grabbing his gun again. I found his right hand man's gun too, and tossed it away down the hall outside the room. I didn't think there'd be a reason for me to have two guns, but I didn't want *him* grabbing it either.

"Candy? I need you..." Alele called from inside the office

I stepped back in. "Yeah? What's up?"

"I can't even get past the log in screen, do you know computers?"

I shook my head. "No, I'm a farm girl, remember? I barely know how to use my cellphone."

"Uuugh, I was hoping it'd be like, me assuming stuff again, and you'd actually be great at computers..." she moaned.

"Well... I know who *can* help us..." I said, holding up what I was presuming was Homicide.

She wrinkled her nose. "Yeah, but how do we know he'll help us once you turn him back?"

"Because," I said, "if he doesn't, I'll just turn him into pie again, duh."

She nodded slowly. "Ooook, but if I say to stop, something bad happened, ok?"

"Got it, ok, let's just..."

I set the pie on the desk, and poked the side of it. I could *feel* the spark, the same something I'd found in him before, and I tried to grab hold of it. I pulled, and focused, but I just couldn't get a good grip. It was almost like it was inside a jello mold, and I could see it, but I couldn't reach through the goo, all I could do was paw at the sides, feeling the shape of the thing inside, but not reaching it. I tried harder, closing my eyes and straining at the tiny sparkling thing, if I could *touch* it, I could unfold it, and he'd be out, I just couldn't quite get to it...

"I... um... can't quite turn him back." I said, leaning back.

Alele's eyes widened, "What?! That's- that's not right, that's not a power someone would have, right? Just make people into pie without being able to make them people again?"

I shook my head. 'I mean, powerful magic users can turn people into rats and frogs and stuff, right?"

"No, that's *different*, they're perverting the mana flow, our powers come from the *gods*, and they manage that shit for us, Lorgiaia wouldn't just make *that* a real power..."

I frowned, and held my finger against the edge of the pie. "I can... I can still feel him, he's still there, still alive. It's just like he's coated in something thick that I can't reach him through..."

Alele pointed. "Yeah, he's coated in pie. He's a pie, Candy."

I blinked, thinking of something, "Oh... Oh! What if the reason I can't reach him *is* the pie?"

"And... what would that mean exactly?" she asked.

"It means... Ugh, I hope I'm right..." I picked up the piece of pie and held it in front of my mouth.

"Oh gods..." Alele whispered, "Oh that is *sick*. I'm not watching this..." She turned away and covered her face.

I didn't blame her... This was a risky move, and a little gross, but I needed to try. It's not like it'd kill him I'm sure, it'd just be a test, right? I opened my mouth and took a bite, the tip of the pie. I braced for something gross, and I chewed. It was... pie. Just pumpkin pie. Granted, it was the best pie I'd ever had, better than my grandmother's even, but it still just tasted like pie. I swallowed, and reached out to the spark again, trying to see if the shell around Homicide's soul had faded. It really hadn't, it was still just as thick, but the spark itself was going *crazy* now. Jittering, shaking, and flickering. I sighed, it was worth a try. Hopefully that bite hadn't done too much damage to him when he turned back, but even if it did, Drizti could fix it.

Alele turned around and uncovered her face. She was glaring at me. "You really should have told me it didn't work faster..." she said, crossing her arms.

"Really? Why?" I asked.

She pointed to the pie again, and I looked down. The pie was dripping blood from the bite, oozing and flowing out in sticky, thick strings to the floor.

"Oh, ew!" I yelled, "Why didn't you warn me?"

"I *tried*, this is round two, you told me it failed too late."

I groaned, "Uuugh, I don't- I don't understand... Why is it *bleeding*?"

"Uh, I don't know, maybe because it's a fucking person?" She snapped, "Now we can't get into the computer, AND we have a bleeding piece of human pie to take care of."

"No, there's got to be a reason why I have this power, it's gotta be... Something." I said, pacing back and forth, "Wait, let me see if I can guess the password, maybe eating him gave me part of his memory?"

She shuddered, "GODS, Candy, don't just talk about *eating* people like that. That's disgusting..."

"Well," I mumbled, "I already did it, so..."

I type away, trying the obvious words first, then the weird stuff that popped into my mind, then just typing at random. Nothing worked, I hadn't absorbed anything...

"Godsdammit..." I said, smacking the desk. It dented inward, and buckled. I stared at the indent of my palm in the metal and then back to my hand.

"What the *fuck* was that?" I asked.

"Could you do that before? You mentioned beating your brothers-"

"No no no, nothing like that. Here, you punch it now." I said, cutting her off.

"Ok, uhh..." She smacked the desk, and it made a clanging noise, but it didn't dent.

I hadn't been that strong during training, and I didn't think my power involved super strength, unless... I eyed Homicide sitting on the desk next to me.

"Alright, so, I'm going to take another bite-" I started

"Candy, NO. That's a person!" Alele squealed

"No- listen, ugh. I'll take a bite, and punch the desk again, then you rewind, and tell me what happened, ok?"

"Cannibalism still counts even if you time-travel it away, you know..." she said, but she didn't protest past that.

I took a breath, and lifted the pie to my lips again.

"Ok, ok stop!" she yelled, "The desk crumpled and was totally smashed, it's definitely eating Homicide that made you strong."

"Ok, ok... ok..." I said, thinking, "So now, what if *you*-"

"Candy, it is *bleeding*." she hissed, "I am *not* doing that."

That was fair. I wondered how my future/past self had handled the blood. The idea of biting into a bleeding, living thing made me want to gag just thinking about it. I still felt strong though, just from the one bite, if we couldn't get *into* the files we could still destroy them, right?

"So, I think... I think I'm going to start trashing the place, before my strength wears off, before he changes back, if it's on a timer or something." I said, flexing my arms.

"Wait, what if there's a backup somewhere? He could just-"

"He could just what? Try and cross the only girl in town who's power affects him? Once I turn him back, he'll be way too scared of me to try anything" I said smugly.

"Ok, fine, just... I'll be outside." she said, moving to leave.

"Hey, could you hold this then? I need both hands." I handed her Homicide.

"Ew, ew ew ew.... uuugh, fine, what if it *is* on a timer and he turns back? I can't fight him..." she said, her fingers splayed as she held him.

"Then you rewind time, and tell me he's coming." I said, annoyed. Gods, it's like she didn't remember she even *had* a power.

She left, and I set to work. I smashed the monitors first, tearing them off the walls, then started on the racks of data storage behind them, punching through them and ripping them out of the walls. The lights flickered, and the servers sparked as I tore through them, but it didn't seem to hurt me much. I moved to the other walls of the room, pulling the panels off and smashing the strange machines behind them too, before climbing on top of the desk and smashing my way into the ceiling, breaking the electronic boxes up there as well. I kicked through the ceiling in a different spot, and dropped down to the ground, right in front of an angry Galorna.

"Candy, what the *fuck*?" she asked.

"I, uh, broke the computers, now he can't leak anything when he turns back." I said, slightly unsure of myself now.

"What do you mean turn back? I *really* don't think he's that piece of pie you had, Candy." she said, shaking her head.

"Uhh, nooo? He's absolutely the pie, look at this..." Drizti said from behind her. I looked around Galorna to see her and Lucy standing by Alele.

The pie had bled all over Alele's fingers, and was dripping onto the floor. She was looking away, covering her face with her other hand.

"It's stickyyyyy" she moaned.

"Oh, what the fuck..." whispered Galorna, "Wait- there's a bite missing, Candy, what the fuck?"

I shook my head, "No! No, see, I could feel his soul inside it, so-"

"So you just chowed down, nice. I'd do the same." Lucy said, laughing. Her bullet wound must be better now, she wasn't in any condition to laugh last time I saw her.

"No, look, there's a shell around his soul, so I can't get through it to turn him back, I thought that meant I'd need to *eat* him to change him back, but- it didn't work..."

"It *did* make her crazy strong though, like, Galorna strong. If she ate more of it, she'd be like, full on troll strong or maybe more." Alele offered, pushing the pie back at me.

"I can't believe you just ate part of one of the city's biggest crime lords, that's..." Galorna shook her head.

"Well..." I said, "I was trying to fix him. I don't know what else to try at this point."

She sighed and looked around at the wrecked office. "We need to get out of here, I called an ambulance with one of the guard's phones for the guys we beat up and the one we gave the gunshot to, they'll be here any minute. We'll... bring Homicide with us, I guess? And try and think of something as we head home."

I nodded, and we headed out. I looked down at Homicide in my hands as we left the building, there had to be something I was missing, something I could change... He couldn't be stuck like this, right?

~~~

We walked down the street, all of us un-transformed. I had hoped Homicide would shift back once I did, but no luck there. It was past 2AM, and the streets were mostly empty, with the sounds of hero fights off in the distance. I was getting a creeping feeling of dread that I just might not be able to change him back to human form, and I was starting to feel a little sick about it.

"Hey, Galorna?" I asked, breaking the awkward silence, "Can I ask you a huge, *huge* favor? I understand if you don't want to, but-"

"What is it, Candy? I can't agree unless I know what it is." she said tiredly.

"Uh, well... Saara was a sorceress, and... they can turn people into things, right? So... I was wondering if maybe she could help me un-turn him from... this."

Galorna groaned, "Candy, I really don't want to see her. Or ask her for anything, seriously, can't you just try something else? Maybe like, you're doing it wrong?"

I shook my head, "No, my power is like, I can take hold of something, and fold it up. I *could* unfold him into a person if I could get a hold of him, I just can't get a hold of him. I think I need help."

She stared at me hard for a moment before answering, "...Fine, whatever. She seemed calm enough earlier, I'll see if she's still up." she dug in her pocket for her phone and dialed.
~~~

She held it to her ear for a moment, and then sighed as Saara answered.

"Yeah, it's me.

"No, I'm fine, it's-

"Listen, it's one of my teammates, the one who got the reading?

"No, she's still alive, gods...

"She had a problem with her power, it's a transformation power, and-

"No, she transformed Homicide, and she can't turn him back.

"...Uh, a piece of pie...

"Yeah, she did, he's bleeding now.

"I don't know, pumpkin or sweet potato I think? Is that important?

"Ok, yeah.

"Ok. We can do that.

"Thank you, baby- uh, Saara. I'll see you soon."

She slid her phone into her pocket, and stared at the ground. I waited, but she didn't say anything.

"Um... Are- are you ok Galorna?" Drizti asked.

"Yeah, I just really didn't want to do this," she said, "I really wanted to cut ties clean with all my past life stuff, and now it's getting mixed into my new life."

She looked up and gave us a once over. "This is a one time thing, alright? We're not using my connections and my ex for anything else after this, ok? I want to separate from all that."

"Well, if we have access to resources..." Alele said.

"No, I agree, we need this to be the last time, that's a good call." Lucy said, nodding.

"Yeah, anyway. Her apartment is this way, it's not too far." Galorna sighed, heading off down a side street.

We walked for about twenty minutes before coming to a nice brick building. Galorna walked up to the doors, and pressed a button next to them. A moment later, a ding sounded, and she pushed the door open.

"Alright, she's up a floor, room 207." she said resignedly.

"I wasn't expecting such a nice apartment complex..." I commented as we walked in.

"Well, crime does pay after all, and she caters to criminals."

We walked in silence until we got to her door and Galorna knocked. It swung open to reveal the same lady as before, but *much* less impressive. Gone were the leather straps and scary cloak, now she was just a sleepy woman in bike shorts and a t-shirt that was much too big for her (Galorna sized). She smirked, and waved us in. Her apartment was cozy; a big couch (also Galorna sized), a fluffy rug, browns and tans everywhere, and every square inch of the walls covered in symbols, cards, animal parts, and other magical items.

"That's not your shirt, Saara. I was hoping to get my stuff back while I was here, I can't do that if you're wearing it." Galorna said, sitting and folding her arms.

"Aw, well, if you want, I can take it oooooff?~" Saara teased, pulling the shirt up halfway.

"No, just- dammit, keep it. And stop flirting, *you* broke up with *me*." Galorna growled.

"I wasn't about to quit my job- the job that got you off the streets might I add- and move into a smaller, shittier apartment without you even *in* it, *just* so you wouldn't get in trouble for dating a 'villainess'."

"You didn't even *try* to find a compromise, you just dumped me as soon as I told you I got Chosen, before I even started the team, I *wanted* to make it work, *you* decided it couldn't." Galorna bit back. She looked embarrassed to be having this conversation in front of us, but it sounded like she'd wanted to say it for a while.

Saara shook her head. "I can *see the future*, Lorna, and we would have ended up broken up either way. I keep my business? You get called out for it when we're seen together and it ruins your life. I get brought on as an independent contractor for your team? It draws attention and I get targeted by the fallen who used my services because they assume I'm going to tell their secrets. I stop working fully, and just live on your pay? I end up depressed and lonely because you're never around and I can't do what I destroyed my soul to do. I *tried*, Lorna. I ran the predictions over and over for *weeks* before you told me. I already knew you were a Chosen, gods leave so much power behind it'd be hard to *not* notice one had been here. I waited until you admitted it before I said anything, hoping all that time that you'd reject it, that you'd choose *me* over some stuck up god. But I still *love you*, so, yeah, forgive me if I flirt a bit with the love of my fucking life, ok?"

I swallowed hard, I could see Galorna was trying her best to hide her tears. We shouldn't have been here for that, but this was probably the last time Galorna would ever see her again, so... If it had to be said, it needed to be now, in front of anyone around to hear it. Lucy reached out to touch Galorna's shoulder, but she tensed up, and Lucy lowered her hand again, and sagged. Some things just needed to be left alone.

"Well." Saara clapped her hands and took a shaky breath, "I want to move on to something else. Let's see this pie of yours. Come on, girl-friend stealer, into my kitchen."

I followed her in, and Drizti followed behind me. I set Homicide on the table, and sat down, Drizti climbing up on the chair beside me.

"I can feel his soul inside, and it's alive and moving, but I can't reach it to turn him back..." I offered as she looked closely at it, holding her hands over the top.

"Uh huh, yeah." she murmured, "I can see something under this pie... This is more like a magic curse than a Chosen power. Most Chosen use powers by using their *own* energy to draw off their *god's* energy, and have to keep drawing energy from both sources at a steady rate to use their powers."

Drizti nodded, "Yeah, that's why we can't hold our transformations, it takes something out of me, and it takes awhile to recharge."

Saara laughed, "No kidding, that 'something' is the entire source of my power, it's *magic*. Everyone has at least a little, and I've trained myself to have a LOT. I gave up a lot for my abilities, I don't recommend it."

She poked the pie on the bleeding part and licked her finger. "Oh, even the blood tastes like pie, interesting." she said, thinking, "*Any* way when, *I* use my power to start a change or fuel a spell, I put all the energy into it at once, and then it goes by itself, no more energy from me needed. That's how magic transformations *usually* work; you give the spell enough energy to do the change, and set it off. A Chosen, on the other hand, isn't 'using' magic past what it takes to channel their powers, they're just streaming energy from their god. It's just 'whatever their god is offering them in that moment'. That means you *should* have to be constantly putting power into whatever you changed to maintain the connection to your god, but there's no energy flow between you and this pie. It's fully stable, like a sorcery transformation would be."

I felt a bit sicker and shuddered. "Ok, so what does that mean? How do I undo it?"

"Well, hm." Saara said, "You're still connected to the person via a spiritual link, you can still feel them inside, right? There should be a trigger or catalyst to make the change. Can you feel any kind of fluctuations in them?"

I nodded. "Yeah, when I took a bite, the little spark went crazy, but the shell around it didn't move."

"I still can't believe you *ate* it..." Drizti said, "I can't imagine eating a pie I found in a bad guy hideout, even if it *wasn't* actually a bad guy."

"I thought it'd help me change it back..." I said, sadly.

"Alright, that aside, can you do me a favor?" Saara asked, "I want you to pick him up, and focus on the spark, ok?"

I picked up the pie and focused. The spark was still there, twinkling, sitting, not doing anything.

"K', *now*..." she said, "I need you to take another bite."

I shuddered, but if it would help, I'd try. I'd apparently already taken a second bite once, it couldn't be *too* bad. I lifted the pie up, and the spark inside went crazy again, flickering, shaking, and bouncing inside the shell. Just as the pie touched my teeth, Saara held up her hand.

"Ok, stop. Did anything change with the spark?"

"Uh, yeah, it got scared, or I guess Homicide did." I responded.

"Oh, *ew*, he's like, aware?!" Drizti said, recoiling.

"Sounds like it." Saara agreed. "That means one thing, he's not *actually* a pie. That's what I was worried about. See if he was *physically* turned into a pie, we just undo the magic and rewind so he's the same him as before. A piece of pie has no brain, no organs, nothing to support life, so that stuff is inside the magic spell, not the object. If *that* were the case, he'd be fully unaware of everything around him."

"But he can still see and stuff?" I asked.

"Yup, and that's because he's not *actually* a pie. How did it feel when you changed him?"

I looked for the right words. "Well, it was like I held his spark, and I pulled it, and turned it inside out, and folded the rest of him on top of itself?"

"And *that's* the 'shell' stopping you from getting to him. That 'shell' is him, his body and mind. You almost had the right idea about eating him, but you'd have to break him fully, body and mind to be able to actually reach the spark, and the pie isn't real."

"What? No, that's stupid, the pie is right there in front of us." Drizti said, pointing.

"Yeah, I don't understand..." I said.

"Ok, so like," Saara said, "you folded him in on himself, but not *really*, right? He'd die if you actually did that. So you just folded him *conceptually*, and now he's pie, right? So that means..." Saara looked at us expectantly.

"That... he's inside the pie?" I asked, more confused than before, "How does this help me turn him back?"

"No- ugh, I hate talking about magic with normies, look. He's not *inside* the pie, because there *is* no pie, there's just Homicide. What you did is to take him and his whole existence, and contain it within the *conception* of a piece of pie. You tricked the universe into *thinking* he's pie."

"But... she ate a bite, you can't eat bites of people like that, right?" Drizti pointed out,

"Ohhhhh, *gods*, ugh." Saara moaned, "Ok, so... He's contained within the conception of a pie, right? And pie is something we can eat, so if he's conceptually a pie, despite him *not* being a pie, as far as the universe is concerned, because remember, the universe thinks he's pie, he can be eaten."

"I have no idea what you're talking about, but how the fuck does that help me?" I asked, laying my head on the table.

"It *means* that he might still count as human for some things. Now, I'm guessing you have a healer on your team?"

Drizti lit up. "Oh! Me! I can heal him to normal!"

"Maybe! How does your power work?" Saara asked.

"I can transfer wounds from one person to another!" she said proudly, "Oh, wait... then someone *else* would be pie..."

"Well, does it have to be a person?" Saara tapped her chin thoughtfully.

Drizti shook her head. "I'm not sure, I've never tried it with anything but people, why?"

Saara got up and headed into the room off the kitchen. She came back a moment later holding a white mouse. "This is a feeder mouse, I was going to feed it to my snake earlier, but she wasn't interested. I want you to try transferring the curse to this mouse, ok?" she said.

"You feed your snake live mice?" I asked, "I thought that was bad or something."

"Nature is nature, she likes live mice, I provide." Saara dismissed me. She set the mouse on the table, holding it down with her hand. "I won't accidentally get hurt myself, right?" she asked.

"Just don't touch the green part..." Drizti said nervously.

She held out her hands, and formed a bar with her lights. She lowered one end to Homicide, and moved the other towards the mouse. If this worked, I could finally breathe easy. I wouldn't have doomed a person to life as a dessert. If it didn't, I might not have a place on the team anymore, and I cursed someone to a hell on earth. I really, *really* wanted it to work. I reached in my hoodie pocket for the gun I'd picked up in case he came back mad, not that it'd do much against him, but it wasn't there. I guessed it was stuck in my magical girl form's dress. I'd have to change later to get it out of my pocket, but for now, I braced myself.

The light touched the mouse, and it instantly squealed, kicking and shaking, writhing under Saara's hand.

"Oh- what the *fuck*?!" she bit out, moving her hand away. I gasped. The mouse's hind legs were missing and bleeding, and it shook and twitched as it tried to get away from us. I looked at Homicide, and saw that once again, the pie was perfectly whole, no bite missing.

"Well... shit." I said, feeling worse by the minute. I couldn't fix it, I'd ruined someone's life, I'd essentially killed him. I'd *bitten his legs off.* This was worse than killing him, I couldn't fix it, he was *like* this now, I could never-

"Yeah, I'm out of ideas. I got nothing, girls." Saara said, holding the mouse up by its tail. "But hey, if you ever decide you want to go fallen, I know a few people who'd *really* like to have that power on call. Good luck finding whatever triggers the change back."

"Yeah, t-thank you." I said, picking Homicide up. I was reeling, I felt like I was floating, and I couldn't think right. Was this what Galorna felt when she'd killed that guy? I walked back into the living room, and felt something being pushed into my other hand by Saara. It was a disposable plastic box for food. I put Homicide into it and closed it up. I heard Saara and Drizti talking to the others, and I felt Lucy pulling on my arm, leading me out. I walked behind the others, Lucy pulling my hand as we went home.

Somehow, I got back to the building. Willa wasn't waiting for us this time, and we all went upstairs to our rooms. Alele helped me to mine, and took Homicide from me. I was happy to see him go, I just wanted to not worry about him for a while. I walked into my bedroom to lay down on the bed, on top of the covers, closed my eyes, and tried not to think about my power.

~~~

I woke to my alarm going off, and I moaned. It was *Saturday*, why did I have an alarm on? We weren't even official yet. I dug my phone out and checked it. It was the alarm for the meeting this afternoon. The *meeting*... I rolled off the bed and looked up at the ceiling of my room. Everything was too dark in here. I know they
~~~

were trying to match it to my color, but deep red is a horrible color to paint the walls with. Whose idea was it to color code our bedrooms anyway? I tried to think back to the planning emails, but I hadn't know the girls then, so it was hard to remember who said what.

I stood up slowly. I had less than ten minutes to get to the meeting, the past me that set the alarm must have assumed I'd be out of bed long before now. Jokes on you, past self, I spent the whole night-

I got a chill as I remembered what I'd done, and I slowly exited my room, looking for the container with Homicide in it. It wasn't on my table, or in the kitchenette... I walked over and opened the fridge, and sure enough, sitting on the shelf, all alone, in a plastic box, was the piece of pie. I stared at it for a long while. Should I say something? I couldn't hear a response anyway, so would it even matter if I did say anything? Would talking to him make it weirder, or make him feel more human? Eventually, I did nothing. I closed the door, and left my apartment. I might as well head down to the meeting room, I was already dressed after all.

~~~

I sat in my seat, staring down at the screen but not really reading it. It didn't seem right, something was *off*, no one else had a power like that, why did I? I hadn't even heard of a power *like* mine before. There had to be a way to fix it... I heard my name and I looked up.

"Candy? Candy are you with us?" Willa was asking, looking as sharp and perky as ever.

"Uhh, yeah, I'm just- last night went really bad, I-" I didn't know what to say, I couldn't focus.

"I'm sure I don't know what you're talking about, but please try to stay focused, ok? We were talking about the big first day on Wednesday!" she said, smiling.
~~~

I looked around, and saw the other girls were in rough shape too. Galorna's eyes were puffy like she'd been crying, Alele looked scared, and the other two were quiet, not making eye contact. Oori looked frustrated, and he looked from girl to girl, leveling his stare at each of us in turn. Right, we weren't supposed to talk about the mission. That made things easier, I really didn't want to discuss that right now.

I looked at the screen in front of me, and saw sketches of cookies and sweets, colored like the other girls. A cookie that was red and yellow for Galorna with her face on it, a green and gray pastry roll for Drizti, a blue cupcake with gold and black sprinkles for Alele, a black and tan gummy sucker for Lucy.

All the girls but me, all sweets. Was this a prank? A collection of what they'd look like if I folded them? Who would play such a mean trick? Were they trying to make me think about what I'd done? Why would they do that? Didn't they *know* I was already freaking out?

Alele put her hand on mine. "Candy, we're designing our sweets for the-"

I felt her skin touch mine, I felt the connection, the energy activate, I felt her spark and tasted something wonderfully minty and fruity, and I screamed. I lunged back over the chair, backing away from her, from the girls, pressing myself against the wall.

"NO! No, don't touch me!" I screamed, "Gods, I *felt* it, I felt you, Alele, I almost did it, I can't, I can't, please, don't touch me..."

The tears gushed out of me, and I curled up, hiding my skin inside my hood, inside my pockets. I couldn't touch them, I couldn't touch anyone. I sobbed harder, I couldn't touch anyone *ever again*. I couldn't hug them, I couldn't kiss them, I couldn't even high five them.

Alele was crying too, and I heard her run out of the room, the door sliding closed behind her.

"Can anyone tell me what in Lorgiaia's beautiful glory is going on?" rumbled Oori.

"Fuck, it was *obviously* that stupid fucking mission you sent us on last night, dumbass!" yelled Lucy, "Galorna killed some guys, I got shot, and Candy turned a crime lord into a fucking *snack*, we're a little fucking upset, ok? And you have us talking about... about... fucking *junk food* like we're not all fucking broken over this? Gods, I'm surprised Candy was the only one of us to snap..."

She sat back down, hard. The room was quiet, until Oori spoke up, softer but angrier. "Lucy, what mission are you talking about? I didn't send you on any missions, you're not even close to ready. Did you girls really go out and fight crime last night?"

"Oh, for- Seriously?" Galorna asked, frustrated, "I know we weren't supposed to mention it, but it's *very clear* that we need to talk about it. Candy is a gibbering mess, Alele is traumatized, and I'm still trying to reconcile the fact that I punched two people so hard their brains sprayed out their ears, we clearly are *not* ok."

I lifted my head and looked around my chair. Willa's eyes were wide, and her smile forced. Oori took off his glasses and shook his head. "Girls, I honestly would never have sent you out yet, no matter what. I'd hire a team of fallen for-hires before I did that. Now tell me, where did you get the mission from?"

"From..." Drizti pointed. "From the screens, from yesterday's meeting?"

"We didn't have a meeting yesterday, who called the meeting?" he said coldly.

Drizti slowly pointed to Willa. "She- she did? It was about us accidentally eating at a villain owned restaurant..."

Oori nodded, and asked again, gently, "And the mission was to?..."

"We were supposed to get the video Homicide had of us at his place, and destroy it. It had me getting drunk in it..." Lucy said, embarrassed.

"Ok. I see. Thank you. I'd like you to all return to your rooms, get some rest. I think I know what happened, and I'll take care of it." he said, his voice calm.

I followed the girls out of the room, trailing behind so I didn't bump into them. I looked back at Oori as I walked out the door to see if he was angry with us. He *was* angry, but not at us. He was glaring at Willa, who was hyperventilating and shaking her head.

"I was acting in the best interest of the girls, Oori, I was just-"

The doors slid closed behind me cutting them off. I took a deep breath, and headed to my room. I took the stairs behind the elevator, to make sure I didn't run into the other girls. I couldn't risk them touching me. I couldn't risk *anyone* touching me ever again.

Chapter Six

I focused as I painted the interior walls of the cabin on the open side, the darker brown wash seeping into the textured cracks to give depth and imply shadows. I dipped my brush into the watered down wood stain again and start on the woodpile, trying to make the bark stand out more, giving the twigs I'd cut up more of a 'log' appearance. I'd been working on this for hours, the trees were coming along nicely, I'd painted them, finally, and they were drying, awaiting snow on top once they dried. I couldn't stop thinking about what I was trying to avoid thinking about though...

I glanced over at the fridge to my left, should I take him out and like, let him see the outside world or something? It had to be inhumane to keep someone in a cold, dark box like that. Would it be a security risk if he saw too much of my downtime? It's not like he could do anything about it now, but if he ever *did* turn back it'd be a danger. It was honestly easier for me to not have to see him, too. Slightly easier to not think about him, to just work on my little snowy forest scene. It was long past dinner, and I hadn't eaten anything since the night before when Galorna made us stir fry before our mission. Somehow though, I just couldn't manage to get up an appetite, even if I *did* have anything to eat. Well, anything except-

I put my brush down. I couldn't sit around like this anymore. If nothing else, I needed to get my custom dessert designed for the big opening Wednesday. I could probably still access the files and do something quick, and we were supposed to have had that done today. I dug through my clothes and found some winter gloves and slid them on; I wasn't taking any chances. I went to my door and glanced back at the refrigerator. I'd try to change him back again later, once my mind was clearer.

I left my room, and stood in the hall, listening for any noises; anyone around I might accidentally bump into. I didn't hear anything, so I went to the stairs, and jogged down them to the common floor, and went to the conference room. To my surprise, the wall on one side had opened up into windows, and the whole place looked much less serious and a lot more inviting now. Was this how it looked when we weren't having meetings?

I sat at my spot and swiped my card, opening the screen where I'd left off and clicked through the meeting notes. It was nothing too interesting, just advice and rules on how to act, how to pose with the kids, what not to say, and a basic training exercise we were supposed to do. It looked like we each took turns pretending to be customers, and the rest of us would do a fake photo shoot with the 'customer'? It seemed like Willa had put a lot of work into the meeting, and we hadn't even gotten a chance to do any of it but design sweets before my meltdown.

Speaking of, I pulled out the stylus and drew a quick sketch of a red velvet chocolate chip cake with white icing on it. Simple, but still something people would buy a slice of. I'd buy it at least. Red velvet was my favorite kind of cake aside from my mom's brown sugar cake, but *that* was only my *favorite* favorite because it was my mom's cake, not because it was particularly special. Red velvet just seemed fancier to me.

I heard sirens bloop outside the building for a moment, and I walked to the window to peek out. Outside on the street, Willa was being led to a GGDS vehicle in cuffs. It looked like she was crying, or maybe yelling? It was hard to tell from all the way up here. If *she* was being arrested, what about the rest of us?

I considered running, taking the stairs to the roof and flying home to my mom, but I needed to face the music. I'd done something horrible, and if anyone could set things right, the GGDS would. I pulled my gloves back on and went to the stairs, heading down slowly, anticipating my fate. Once I got to the lobby, I braced myself, and walked into the open area in front of the desk. There were three GGDS agents talking to Oori, and another next to the door. I walked up to the group, and nodded to the agents.

"Oh, Candy, I'm glad to see you're more stable now." Oori said, stepping away from me slightly.

I didn't *feel* stable; I felt like I was laying on top of the ocean with no way to anchor myself. "Yeah, I just needed some alone time, sorry about my outburst."

"Miss Candy, was it? I understand you were part of the unauthorized mission?" one of the agents asked.

I took a breath. "Yes, I was." I looked at Oori, but his expression was near unreadable with his beard covering his mouth and his sunglasses over his eyes.

"I'm sorry to hear that Miss Candy. Am I to understand that there were three fatalities during that mission?"

"Well... kind of, depends on what you mean." I said reluctantly. Homicide might as *well* be dead, but it wasn't a sure thing.

"We have one body outside the building, one in the office, and one report of a death through the use of an unknown power, is that accurate?"

"Oh, uh." so they *did* mean it like that. "Homicide isn't *dead*, he's just... I can't recover him."

"I understand, powers can be difficult. Is there a chance he will come back in the future?"

I looked at the ground. "I'm trying my best, but I don't know how to bring him back, I'm sorry. If you know of a way to reverse powers, maybe you could help?"

"This is just for our records, and no, powers work on a case by case basis, we can't dedicate resources to any one individual's power because the time and labor wouldn't apply to any other cases." the agent said curtly

"Ah, Miss Candy," Oori said "I wanted to let you know that we'll be getting a new PR agent soon. Miss Willa has been let go from our service. Please pass that along to the other girls, won't you?"

I look from him to the agent that had been talking to me. "Wait. Wait, I'm still on the team? I'm not in trouble?" I was sure I'd be sent to Lorgiaia's temple to be stripped of my powers and shipped off to the moonbase for the rest of my life...

A different agent spoke up. "No, we have been over the computer records and been through the deleted meeting notes. We also got a full confession from Miss Willa herself. As far as you knew, you were acting in the best interest of your goddess, at the behest of the church. No charges against you will be filed, it's all on Miss Willa."

"I- We don't-" I felt shocked, but relieved. "We honestly aren't in any trouble?"

The first agent shook his head. "No ma'am, we *will* require this team to update and reinforce security measures, and require direct communication on missions, but you were all acting within your rights as Chosen given the threat level of the organization in question."

"Ok, wow..." I said, "I guess I'll go tell the others?"

"Thank you, Candy," Oori said, "and let them know the grand opening is postponed until a week from today, to get the new PR agent caught up and to make sure all of you are in top form."

"Yeah, ok, yeah." I said, still stunned

"We'll be out of your hair soon sir, we just need to ask one or two more questions, and we'll be gone." The last agent said, pulling a clipboard out from under his arm.

"My... hair?" Oori said, running his hand over his bald head. Despite my mixed mood and emotional stress, I had to try not to smirk as I walked towards the stairs.

I headed up to the common floor and sat on the couch, thinking. I had almost *wanted* to get punished for it, to make it real somehow. As it was, the agents didn't even care if he was alive or dead, they just needed a number to put down. Chosen law was weird and murky compared to civilian law as it was, but this seemed like a bad way to handle it. Not that she'd meant to or had a choice, but Galorna was *literally* going to get away with murder, and I was getting away with condemning someone to a life *worse* than death.

My phone buzzed and I pulled it out. It was in the team's group chat, the one we'd voted on a leader in, with a new message from Lucy.

'hey, I'm ordering delivery. I was going to get pizza, anyone want in?'

I responded to her

'I'll share whatever you guys get, I'll pay you back. Everyone meet me in the middle floor though, I need to talk'

I got a thumbs up from Lucy, then one from Drizti a second later. Galorna requested meat lovers, and they chatted about how to pay Lucy back for it before deciding on just using cash. Alele was noticeably absent from the chat... Was she still upset? I know *I* would be if my teammate almost erased me just because I touched her hand... I couldn't imagine the fear she must have felt. I know the fear *I* had felt as soon as I touched her spark, and it'd taken hours of working on my diorama to calm down. I imagined her in her room, playing her mandolin and crying, and I felt sick to my stomach.

The elevator dinged open behind me and I looked around to see the others minus Alele. Lucy and Drizti stepped out, and Galorna stayed behind, the elevator taking her down. She must be on Pizza duty, I assumed. I put my hood on to make sure as much of my skin was covered as possible, and stood up.

"I'll pay you back later, Lucy, my money is in my room, ok?" I said, walking to the counter to set out plates for everyone.

"Yeah, it's whatever. I have more money than I've ever had right now, and my medical stuff and rent is covered by the church, so I'm not sure what I'm going to do with it all." she responded offhandedly.

"So Candy, are you alright?" Drizti asked, "I know it hit you really hard once you realized- last night I mean."

"Uhh, no?" I said, "I feel horrible, and I can't fix it, and I can't ever touch people ever again, and-" my voice cracked. "I don't want to think about it."

"Oh... well, here, hold still." Drizti said. I froze, and looked at her, puzzled. She climbed up on a stool and leaned forwards on her knees, hugging me around the torso, burying her face in my ribs. I gasped and lifted my arms up.

"Drizti *no!*" I said, "It's dangerous, I just said-"

"All you girls need lots of hugs, and you're wearing that big hoodie anyway! You can still be touched, you just need to be careful! I just want to make sure you know I can give you hugs still." she smiled at me.

"That's kinda gay, not gonna lie." Lucy said, watching us as she leaned against the back of the couch.

"Hey, that's not- wait, can you say that?" Drizti asked, "Is it like, you're allowed to call things gay and it not be rude because you're trans?"

"Nnnno, trans and gay are like, different things." Lucy said, "but... I *am* also gay, so yeah. I totally did mean it in a rude way though."

"Well, it's just girl stuff..." I said, unsure of how much Lucy knew about female bonding, "It's just, like, normal? Girls usually hug more than other people, it's just a thing, saying girls need hugs isn't inherently gay."

"I think I *am* actually gay though." Drizti said, thinking, "Or something like it? I think about girls and others the same way I think about guys, like I want to get hugs from *everyone*."

"Is that a gnomish euphemism?" I asked, "Wanting to 'get hugs' from people?"

"N-no!" she squeaked, "Gosh, Candy, I just like hugs, don't be rude."

"Drizti, that's just... normal?" Lucy said, raising an eyebrow at her, "Almost everyone feels like that."

"Oh, is it? I'm sorry, I thought we're only supposed to be attracted to people we can make kids with... That's what my clan taught at least." Drizti said, confused, "Sorry, I wasn't trying to like, take the gay for myself."

"No, outside your clan, it's not quite as, uh, 'restrictive'." Lucy said, "Like, no real gender preference is the norm, only liking people you can reproduce with is pretty rare, and 'gay' is only when you like specifically *only* the same general gender presentation as yourself."

"Oh, gosh, I didn't mean to steal your terms, I feel terrible..." Drizti said sadly, clutching her hands.

"I straight up do not care," Lucy sighed, sounding bored, "I know that I only like fems and I *do* be a fem tho, so I'm gay. Past that, other people can call themselves whatever the fuck they want." She must have had *this* conversation a few times too many as well.

The elevator dinged, and we all looked over. Instead of the pizza being here though, Alele stepped out, her hands gloved and her usual leggings replaced with thick camo cargo pants. She stayed close to the wall, and looked down at the ground.

"I don't need any pizza, I just wanted to hear the news Candy had to tell us..." she said, barely audible,

"Ok, I'm waiting on Galorna, but once she's back up, I'll tell you all at once." I said.

"'K." she muttered, and leaned against the wall.

"Hey, I don't think I really did almost change you." I lied, "I think I just was jumpy and overreacting to being startled, you weren't in any danger."

She looked up at me and glared. "Then why are you wearing gloves?"

I looked for an excuse, I couldn't exactly claim it was because I was cold. "Even if it was an overreaction, I want to be safe until I understand my powers more." I said, trying to downplay her fears.

"Ok, sure." she said shaking her head, unconvinced.

I'd have to be careful, she'd just openly called me out on bullshit, if that happened too much, I'd be other-ed in the group even more that I already would be for having a useless power.

The elevator dinged again, and this time it *was* Galorna with the pizza. "Hey, so like, there's a GGDS car parked right outside." she frowned, "Should I be concerned about being brought in?"

"Oh, no, that's what I wanted to talk about actually." I said, "It turns out, we're all cleared. They're pinning all three deaths on Willa, and they said we were 'acting within our rights' as Chosen so... yeah, it's all good."

"Holy- wait, three deaths? Did the guy we gave the bullet wound to die?" she asked, setting the pizza down.

"Ah, no... Homicide was declared unrecoverable, and, uh, dead." I said.

That hung in the air for a moment.

"Was that all?" Alele asked.

"No, Oori told me to tell you that we're bumping the opening to Saturday to give the new agent time to get brought up to speed, and that's all I know."

"Ok, well, I'll be in my room then." Alele said, swiping her card.

"Won't you take some pizza with you?" Drizti asked, pointing to the two boxes on the counter, "We can't finish all this with just the four of us."

"No, I need some time, ok?" she said, turning away.

We watched her go, I felt bad, and I really hoped she'd come around to being friendly again, she was hard to please, but she was still a team member and we needed to get along. Galorna opened the top pizza box and pulled out three pieces onto a plate.

"Well, *I'm* going to eat, I'm starving." she said, sitting at the bar.

"So are *you* doing ok? You seemed upset earlier." I asked her as I took off a glove to get myself a slice.

"...I'm just rethinking my strategy is all." she said, "Like I said, those people were paid well, and the union wouldn't have put them in a location with guns if they weren't willing and ready to die."

"Tha's kinda cold, Lorna." Lucy mumbled around a mouthful of pizza.

"...Don't call me that, ok? And I know it's cold, but it's the only way I can tell myself that what I did to that guy outside the door was 'ok'. The other one, the one who was holding Drizti, he deserved it, he'd already killed her once, but the first one, I mean, I just have to tell myself that he knew the risks."

"That's... one way to see it." I said. I wished I could do that, rationalize it away, make it all seem like it wasn't a big deal.

"How about you?" Galorna asked me, eyeing my bare hand, "You holding up ok?"

"Well I almost cried when Drizti asked me that a few minutes ago, and I have a man in my refrigerator upstairs." I shuddered, "I'm just trying to think about how I'm even going to be a part of the team now. I can't use my power without-"

I looked at her, remembering. "Oh, yeah, I guess you have the same problem..."

"Uh, actually," she said, not quite looking at me, "I figured it out. I can project my punches, right? So when I'm training, I'm not trying to really hurt you guys, so the fists appear in *front* of you and get pushed into you. When you're fighting someone for real though, you're supposed to try and aim *behind* them, to get more power in your punch, so..."

"Oh gods you really *were* punching them in the brains!" Lucy said, "That's *so* cool."

"It's not 'cool', Lucy, I killed two people." Galorna said sternly, "This is why we needed much, much more training. I can still hit people, I just need to control my projection distance better."

"So I'm the only one who can't use her power." I muttered, putting my crust in the trash, "I'll be the 'lame' one, I'll never get any fans or ad deals, this is just *great*."

"You could be the fast one?" Drizti offered, "You're way better at flying than the rest of us, you could make that your power and just pretend it's the only one?"

"That's a lame power, especially since the rest of you will catch up soon and I'll just be plain old powerless Angel Rouge again." I said as I replaced my glove.

"No no no, it's like, a marketing gimmick, like, we make promo materials about how fast you are, and how good you are at flying, and like, really push it?" Lucy said, "And the people will just buy it, they don't care. Some nerds will look at videos and say 'hey she's not *that* much faster', but like, who cares about some dumbass nerds? We're MGs, we're supposed to appeal to kids first and foremost."

"Wow, that's pretty well thought out..." Drizti said, surprised.

"I've seen it before in other teams, I used to be a huge Chosen fan before I decided it was too masc of an interest." Lucy said sheepishly, "I used to know alllll the teams and the secrets and who was dating who and what their favorite foods are, that stuff is big in the Chosen drama magazines."

"Oh, so *that's* why we had to fill out those stupid personality charts." Galorna said, "Shit, I hope everything I wrote was kid friendly."

"So, you know all about Chosen, right? Like, obscure ones?" I asked Lucy, "Are there any with a power like mine?"

She thought about it. "Uhh, well there's not many Chosen that have powers that last indefinitely, and even less who have transformation powers... There's Gorega, she can kinda turn people into stone? But you can chip off the top layer and they're fine, just kinda sore. Other than that, hm."

She took another piece of pizza.

"Oh, I know, there's, uh, what's his name, Binder? He can merge people with existing items and seal them into it, body mind and soul, but if the item is damaged, they just pop back out, so not really the same after all, now that I think on it."

"Well, huh." I slumped, "I guess I really am on my own here."

"We'll figure it out, Candy it's ok!" Drizti said, giving me a thumbs up, "You'll be fighting bad guys full strength in no time!"

I didn't really want to fight at all, I just didn't want to be useless or seen as 'less cool' by the fans and marketers. "Thank you, Drizti. Until then" I looked at my puffy winter gloves, "I'll need to find ways to cover my skin."

"Oh, oh!" she said, "We're supposed to go shopping soon, we can go tomorrow! We can look for cuter hats for me, and gloves and stuff for you! It'll be fun!"

"Right, um, ok, sure, tomorrow?" I said, thinking. I really wasn't feeling up to it, I just wanted to stay in my room and work on my model, maybe watch a period drama. I couldn't risk the others falling away from me though if I wanted to be 'valuable', I needed to be a 'main character' to all of them. "That sounds good to me, I'll have to be really careful in public, but... I guess I'll have to go in public to get the stuff I need to go in public eventually"

"Perfect! We should invite Alele too! I bet with Willa fired, she's not grounded anymore!" Drizti said, clapping, "She needs cheering up, and she'd know all the best stores! Plus I kinda owe her a dress..."

I really hoped Alele would say no. Her fear of me, the way she was processing all this, it just made me feel guiltier and guiltier. I smiled wide. "Oh, of course! That's a good idea, I'll text her tomorrow morning!" I pointed upstairs, "I have to go now though, I was in the middle of a project, and I want to get back to it. Lucy, I'll pay you tomorrow, ok?"

As I went up to my room with a couple leftover slices of pizza wrapped in paper towels, I wondered if it'd be rude of me to keep them in the refrigerator...

~~~

I stood by the front doors, a sweater, gloves, and a scarf on. It wasn't even close to cold enough for any of this, but being around civilians would be dangerous, so I needed to be prepared. I couldn't use my phone with my gloves on, and I hadn't heard back from Alele if she'd be joining us. Drizti was *supposed* to have been here five minutes ago, but she was nowhere to be seen. I looked outside, a group of teens were looking at me from the other side of the glass.
~~~

One pointed to the door and mimed me opening it. I sighed, and swung it open from my side.

"Yes?" I asked.

"Hey, uhhh..." A goblin boy asked, "Are you one of the heroes who's going to be working here?"

"Not officially until Saturday. Right now I'm just some lady." I said. These must be clout chasers, trying to get into our fanbase before we were cool.

"So can we get a pic with you? We won't post it until after Saturday, if that matters." A tall dryad girl said, holding up her camera.

"I don't- You *know* we're a magical girl team, right?" I said, "We're expecting the fans to be between eight and fourteen. I'm not sure how cool it'll be to have a picture with me."

"Hey, I'm fourteen, I totally fit that range." One of the human kids said, finger-gunning me.

"Ok, fine, just don't post it until we come out as heroes, and whatever you do, don't touch me." I relented, opening the door open all the way.

"Wow, rude much?" The dryad said, growing her arm out longer to get all the teens in the shot with me behind them.

"No, I have an issue with being touched, I-" I started to make an excuse.

"Smiiiiile!" she said, and I plastered a fake smile onto my face as her camera clicked.

"Ok, was that good?" I asked.

She checked her camera. "Yeah, that's fine, thannnnks!"

I waved to the group as they headed further down the street.

"Who were *they*?" Alele said from behind me. I jumped and turned around.

"Ah, just some kids trying to get a picture with me. I just did it to get them to keep moving."

"That was sweet of you!" Drizti said, giving me a thumbs up, "Not even official and already making fans happy!"

"Yeah, whatever. You want gloves, right?" Alele asked, "We'll need to go downtown to the shops. There's a couple of places that sell what you're looking for, opera gloves. They'll cover your arms as well as your hands."

She still seemed prickly, but she wasn't as shaken up as she was yesterday. She seemed moody and grumpy, but not afraid.

"Sorry again about yesterday." I said, "I freaked out, I don't know how to turn the power off or anything, or how to really trigger it, so I was scared I'd-"

"Just stop, ok?" she cut me off, "I'm over it, just don't touch me with your skin ever again, and we'll pretend you didn't almost condemn me to your tiny fridge for the rest of my life."

"Well, you might not have had to live in the fridge." Drizti pointed out, "We don't know it's pie every time, it could be other stuff too, the only thing is we know it's edible, so she can get the power boost."

"Stop stop STOP. I don't want to think about it," Alele shivered, "I want to think about *shopping* and getting tea later, and how jealous I am that Candy got the first fan-photo instead of me."

"Sorry, I didn't know you wanted that honor?" I said.

"It's *fine*. It'll just be put on fan sites and in magazines as the first time you were seen in street clothes, and most likely dominate the gossip scene about us for *weeks* because of how suspiciously bundled up you are in the middle of spring, taking spotlight away from me and the grand opening. It's *fine*."

I really hadn't thought it was that big a deal. I wanted to be popular as much as she did, but hearing the thoughts that had run through her head in the moments since the picture, I felt outclassed in my understanding of what that meant.

"Weeeeell, let's just not worry about that, it'll be the new **PR** person's job!" Drizti said, "I want to go shopping, I've never been before, and I'm really excited!"

"Wait, you've never been *shopping*?" Alele asked her, shocked.

"No, in my clan clothing was assigned," Drizti said, "and we didn't really have any opportunities to go into the city proper unless we were on the outreach team."

"Outreach team?" I asked, holding the door open for them as they came outside, "I thought clans were gnomes only, are that many gnomes without clans that you need an outreach team?"

"Well, as you know, not all gnomes are in a clan, and that's getting a lot more popular these days, and we also wanted to get gnomes from *other* clans to join ours." Drizti explained, "We'd just try to reach any gnome we could, really. I did it for a while as a teen but it was really scary talking to people like that. And we never went to the shopping places, mostly we'd go around where the other gnomes were, like the parks and the tunnels."

"Ok, so, like," I said as we started for downtown, "how do they feel about you being in the city now?"

She shook her head. "When I was chosen, I had to collect my stuff and sneak out, I left a note telling them I was leaving and breaking off my engagement. They'd have said that me being chosen was 'proof' I wasn't worshiping the earth enough. If I was a *true* gnome, no god would ever consider me as a Chosen."

"That sounds terrible, I'm glad you left." Alele said, shaking her head

"Mmm, well... I really miss my family and my friends, but once I realized I had a chance to actually *be* someone, to do something with my life, I started to feel trapped, and I *had* to leave. Still I'm super lonely these days compared to a couple months ago..."

"Well you have us, right?" I offered. "I'll be here for you if you need anything at all."

I hoped that'd get me brownie points with Alele too, make her think of me as less scary. I *did* want to be there for Drizti, but I wasn't sure I'd be the best at making her feel any less lonely.

"Yeah, like, we're a team or whatever, right?" Alele said. "This is your new clan, we got you. Hit me up sometime, we can cuddle, even." she gave a wink and stuck out her tongue a little. I rolled my eyes, of *course* that's where her mind went when someone complained about being lonely...

"Aw, girls..." Drizti said, smiling, "That means a lot to me. I was always around someone at home, even sleeping we all shared a bed. I've never felt as alone as I did sleeping in the hotel room for those few weeks while I waited for the building to be finished. I appreciate you being willing to be there for me."

I thought about what she'd said. That made it sound like she'd want to be around someone constantly now, too. It'd be better to ease her away from needing that than to just always have someone be around her. I thought of what made me feel less lonely when I was alone; talking on the phone, playing games online with my brothers, watching my shows, stuff like that.

"So, did you have TVs in your clan?" I asked, picking the only thing I could think of that didn't require other people.

"Umm, yeah? But they were in the rest halls." she replied, "We'd turn them on once a week or so and watch a movie, or sometimes videos about safety, or stuff like that."

"Well, personally, TV makes me feel less lonely." I said, "I love turning on a show set a couple hundred years ago, back when everyone wore fancy clothes and you weren't allowed to marry people from other churches, and just soak in all the personal drama."

"I know about stuff like that." Drizti said, thinking, "I tried to watch something on the TV in my room at the hotel, but it was... indecent."

"Driz, no, that was-" Alele started, "Listen, we're going to have a watch party, ok? We'll each pick something to watch, and we'll meet in Candy's room to watch it. We'll show you what stuff is cool, and you can watch it when you feel lonely. Got it?"

"Wait, my room? Why my room?" I said.

"I only let people into my space who I'm planning on sleeping with." Alele said as if it was the most obvious thing in the world.

"I'd really rather spend time with you girls than to replace people with a television, but I'd *love* to have a party!" Drizti said.

"We'll need to get creative with the seating, or like, make sure Candy is burrito-ed in a blanket." Alele said. "For obvious reasons."

I felt bad again. I couldn't even have a simple get together without having to think about my power. Not that I really *wanted* to throw a party. The girls were fun though, and I didn't mind, I just would have rather had it anywhere else. The common floor had a TV, *that* would be the better option, but being vulnerable and letting people into my home would be endearing and make me 'the hostess' of that kind of thing, which would be points towards be being a valued member of the team. It was a fair trade off in the end.

"I'm sure we can work it out. Let's do it Wednesday night, ok?" I offered, "It'll be like, since we're not having the big opening that day, we'll still have something to look forward to."

"Ok, yay!" Drizti said, pumping her fist, "I *do* look forward to it!"

"Anyway, that aside, we need to apply to have a bus stop set up closer to our headquarters." Alele said, "We shouldn't have to walk this far just to get to a bus. We've got stuff to do."

"Oh, are we taking a bus? I thought we'd just walk downtown..." Drizti said.

"I was going to walk, yeah, but I just realized I'll have bags on the way back. How close *is* the closest bus stop?" I asked, "To be honest my mom dropped me off in front of the building in our truck, I've never taken a bus before."

"Three more blocks. Fuck it, we'll be in the same 4 block part of the city give or take all day, we only need the bus to get there. I'm ordering us a ride share." Alele pulled out her phone and I noticed it was the same kind as mine.

"Well, I won't say no to a free ride." I said.

"I'm not really sure what that is, but I can guess, I'd like that too. You guys are hard to keep up with on foot if I'm being honest..." Drizti said.

"Ah, yeah, fair." I said. I hadn't thought of how much shorter her legs were, she must have been jogging this whole time to stay with us.

"It'll be here in like, fifteen minutes. Let's stop here and go ahead and get tea now while we wait, 'k?" Alele said, jutting a thumb at the cafe behind us.

"Oooh, tea... I love tea!" Drizti said.

I pulled at my scarf. Tea was the last thing I needed, I was already sweating... maybe they'd have an iced coffee or something instead.

~~~

I sipped my mango slush and flipped through a rack of clothes. I wasn't seeing anything that stood out to me. I would wear plain clothes every day if I could, and if I needed to make a public appearance I could just transform, but Alele insisted I have at least two or three pieces of formal wear. They needed to be long, I'd need pantyhose under them, and they needed to look good with opera gloves, so our options were kinda limited. I'd found one evening
~~~

dress with a flared skirt and three quarter sleeves that worked pretty well, it was red so it even fit my color scheme, but I was having trouble finding anything else.

"Hey, Driz, did you see this?" Alele called out from across the store. I glanced over to see her holding a gray beret that was pretty close to Drizti's skin tone.

"Oooh, it wouldn't be too same-y?" Drizti asked, trying it on.

"No no no, your hair breaks it up, it looks fine." Alele assured her.

This had to be the fifth hat Alele had convinced her to get, between the beanie, the sunhat, the fedora, and something called a 'cloche' that looked 80 years out of style, it was hard to imagine a situation that could come up where she wouldn't have a hat ready. Once we were done here, we'd head over to the alternative shops to find Drizti some street clothes that didn't make her look like a priestess or a nun, and more than likely, more hats. I sighed and grabbed a skirt and blouse out from under a display. They looked good together in the advertisement, so it was probably fine, and the blouse was long sleeve. In a perfect world, I'd get fitted for a cute dark red suit, but that involved being measured, and therefore touched.

"Hey, I'm ready when you are." I said to the girls, holding up my findings.

"Oh, um, ok, are we going to another store?" Drizti asked, "I got a cocktail dress, but it's not something I want to wear a lot."

"Oh, we *absolutely* are." Alele said, "We have to make you even cuter than you already are, and loose robes are *not* your look."

Drizti looked down at herself. "They- well, I don't really have curves, so it's-"

"Driz, *I* barely have curves," Alele snapped, "there's tricks for that, and we're going to help you find casual clothes to sell that illusion, got it?"

'Oh, really? Ok!" she said, "Do you use those tricks too, Candy?"

"Uhhh, no, I just, uh, actually have curves, or some at least. I never really had to try for that."

"Uh huh, says the girl that lives in sweaters and high waisted jeans, I see you." Alele said, raising an eyebrow.

I blushed. "Well I didn't start dressing like that because of my shape, I just like cozy sweaters, and short jeans make me nervous."

"Sweaters and high waisted jeans, hmm..." Drizti said, "I don't want to steal your look, but I'll remember that."

We checked out, and headed out onto the street, the bright, flashy screens that covered every building playing different ads and church recruitment videos, the droning noise of the videos making a dull background ambiance. Alele was getting frustrating. I really wasn't dressing like this to accentuate my body, but the fact that she called me out on it made me unsettled, like she could see straight through any walls I put up. She was observant and smart, and I'd need to make extra sure I stayed aware of what I did and said around her.

"Oh, look! A Chosen!" Drizti gasped, pointing.

I looked across the street to see Lady Lunge of the Downtown Queens crawling across the sidewalk in her odd, lurching way, her limbs stretching and distorting as she pulled herself along at inhuman speeds. She slammed into a man with a stroller and pinned him to the ground with one hand, her fingers and palm blurred and warping as space shifted to try and contain her non euclidean form.

"Please, please, I'm the father, I just want to see my kid again, please..." The man sobbed.

"Kidnnnnapping issssss kidnnnnapping, peon." Lady Lunge hissed in her echoed, slurred voice.

Another member of the Queens, Miss Missile landed beside them with a boom and a thud, and pulled a crying child out of the stroller.

"I'm sorry Mr Calahan, but you lost custody, you'll need to go through the courts if you want to see little Emily here again, and this little stunt? Did *not* help your odds." she hugged the girl and rocked back and forth. "Lady Lunge? Bring him back to HQ, I'll get *this* little cutie back to her mom, Queens, move out!"

As Miss Missile flew into the sky with a blast and Lady Lunge crawled away with the wailing man twisted in her blurry and unknowable limbs, I couldn't help wonder about the story behind it all. Was the man abusive? Did the courts just side with his wife because she was the mother? Was the kid safe flying through the air like that?

"Whoah..." Drizti breathed, "I've never seen a Chosen fight before..."

"Driz, we were *in* one two days ago." Alele said, "And what we saw just now was *hardly* a fight"

"Well, I didn't *see* the fight we were in, I was a part of it." Drizti said, frowning, "And it's still cool to see famous Chosen do stuff, I've even *heard* of those ones."

"I mean, soon we'll be doing stuff just like that. In, what, two weeks?" I said, thinking of our first patrol.

"Do you think we'll get to save a kid too?" Drizti said, "I'd love to save a kid, I think it'd feel really nice…"

I sighed. I hoped we wouldn't have to save *anyone*. I hoped we'd just be minding out own business the whole time, but this *was* the area we'd be in that day, and we'd been here less than an hour and already seen Chosen doing their jobs. The odds of us not having at least something to do were pretty low. Saving a kid though, it took a special kind of person to put a kid in danger.

"Well, even if we don't," I said, "at least you'll still get to meet the fans, right?"

"Oh, yeah! I wonder if I'll recognize anyone from the first event on Saturday on patrol the week after!" she smiled.

"Just keep in mind, if you *do*," Alele said, "make sure to let them *know* you remembered them, that level of personal interaction is key in building audience and a strong fanbase."

I thought about the meet and greet, and walking around the city with my arms exposed all day. There was no way I'd be able to go all day without accidentally touching someone unless I wore my new gloves, and if I did, it'd throw our whole costume cohesion off. If I wanted to make fans I'd need pictures and handshakes and to not be afraid of turning a child into an edible treat if they got too excited and touched my face. This was going to be hard. Luckily, I had a while to think about it, the next store looked pretty goth-y. Far more suited to Lucy than me. I'd have plenty of time to plan what to do while the other two poked around in there.

Chapter Seven

"Ok, so that makes any kind of marketing a problem." the new head of PR said, tapping on her tablet.

"Well, yeah. I can't really use my power, so it's going to look like I don't have one." I agreed, taking a mint out of her bowl.

"Mm, just make sure no one finds out about the power no matter what. Powers like this are usually not used by the good guys. Did you have any ideas about alternative marketing?" She pulled her black hair out of her face as she looked back up, her no-nonsense expression somehow intimidating and comforting at the same time.

"Well Lucy was saying I could just pretend my power is flying fast? I am pretty good at flying, and if we can install a wind tunnel in the training room I can get-"

"Too expensive." she snapped, "But I do like the 'fast' idea. We can work with that. We'll need to fix your look though, you don't really look fast."

I glanced down at myself. "Ah, well, I look less heavy when I'm not wearing sweaters, it's-"

"The hair." she said, "Your hair is too long, it's going to catch the wind and whip around, making you look slow, we need to cut it, make you look streamlined."

"Now, Miss Debbie, I really don't think we can demand any of our girls cut their hair for a marketing gimmick, that's too far." Oori said, speaking up at last.

"No, I- I can do it." I said, butterflies in my stomach. My hair was special to me, it was almost long enough to sit on, and I took very good care of it. If it was slowing me down on my path to fame and glory or just slowing me down in general though, I'd cut it off. "How- how short does it need to be?" I asked.

"Mm, well, I'd prefer it to be a pixie cut, but a bob should do the trick." Debbie said, chewing on her stylus and flipping through photos on her screen.

"Oh... Ok, I can do a bob." I said. My stomach was tight and I felt nervous, a *bob*?! It'd change my whole look for the worse.

"And the color too." she said, pointing, "Lucy's already a blonde human with a dark dress, and it makes the two of you look too similar at a distance."

"W-what?!" I said, "What color would you want me to dye it?"

"Miss Debbie, really, I-" Oori said.

"I think you should do a vivid dark red, like your outfit, it'd make you pop, which you'll *need* if you're not using any real powers."

"..." I ran my hands through my hair and pursed my lips. I needed to do this, I needed to be a valuable member of the team, this was my life, my career. "Ok, yeah, red is good, we can do red."

Oori frowned and sat back, his arms folded. He looked at me sadly, and shook his head, like he was disappointed in me. I ignored him. He was a good person, and he seemed to know what he was doing when it came to tactics, but this wasn't his field, and I'd be making the calls for my own life.

"Now, I see in your post mission report that you've been wearing gloves since the whole ordeal, correct?" she asked me, pointing to my hands.

"Ah, yeah, these are opera gloves, I wear them at all times, unless I'm sleeping or showering or something." I said, nodding.

She popped her back and sat down in her chair, fixing her skirt as she crossed her legs. "So, that's going to break up costume cohesion with all the other girls, unless- Mhh." she drew on the pictures with her stylus.

"Unless what?" I asked, "I'm pretty sure Drizti can't use her power effectively if she can't connect her rods to people's skin, so everyone else wearing gloves makes *her* job harder..."

"We're going to give you all accessories." she said, distracted, "The gnome girl has a hat already, we just need something for the other three... maybe a kabuki mask for the oni?"

"Well, I don't think she'd want-"

Debbie looked up and shook her head. "I have what I need from you, Candy, you can go. Send in..." she looked at a list. "Uh, 'Galorna', next."

I stood up, pulling on my hair as I left, my heart pounding. I felt like I was making a huge mistake, but I needed to do this if I was going to be a team member, even if I didn't want to. I just had to keep telling myself that...

~~~

I carefully moved Homicide into the new refrigerator and slid him onto the top shelf. I had a small speaker in there that was set to play the radio for 12 hours a day at a low volume, and a dim LED that came on at the same time. It wasn't... perfect, but it was better than a dark box without anything to do forever. I cranked the tempera-
~~~

ture as low as it would go, just above freezing, so he wouldn't get mushy, and looked at his new home. It was a small mini fridge, it fit in the corner of my kitchenette away from my usual stuff, and more importantly, it had a lock. It was a simple combination lock, but that was all it took to make sure no one accidentally went in and- I shuddered, imagining someone eating him without realizing.

"Um, so I'm closing the door now." I announced to the pie, "I'll check on you in a week or two... I have the radio set to a channel that plays the news in the mornings and evenings, and music during the day. I don't- I don't know what to do about this, so I hope it's not too bad?"

I looked at the unresponsive piece of pie and slumped. "Ok, uh... bye then."

I closed the door and latched the lock, shuffling the combination. I looked back at the pile of groceries I'd brought in with me a few minutes ago; now that I had my fridge back, I could put it all away. It'd taken a few days for the new locking one to be delivered, and I was worried that I wouldn't get it in time for the 'party' tonight for Drizti, but it'd worked out with half a day to spare.

I slowly put away the party food and soda away into my old refrigerator and looked over at the tiny prison in the corner of my room. I couldn't hear the radio going through the door, but the light on the cord snaking out of the bottom of the fridge let me know it had power at least, hopefully Homicide didn't hate top 40 hits...

I pulled the last things out of the last bag, the things I was dreading the most, and set them on my counter. A set of hair scissors, a bottle of dye, and disposable gloves. If I was going to do it, it might as well be now. We had three days 'til Saturday, so I could touch it up over the next few days if it ended up looking bad, right? I collected the items, and slowly walked to the small bathroom to do what needed to be done.

~~~
~~~

I sat on the couch in my footie pajamas and a scarf, staring straight ahead. If I didn't move, I couldn't tell, if I didn't move, I couldn't tell, if I didn't move-

Someone knocked on my door, causing me to jump. Were they here already? I looked at my phone, it was still twenty minutes before they were supposed to arrive, but I *had* been sitting and staring off into space for over two hours it seemed. I sniffled, wiped my eyes again, and stood, fluffing my hair and ignoring the pit in my stomach, and went over to the door.

I swung it open with a fake smile on my face and glanced down. Drizti was standing in front of me with her mouth gaping open, her eyes wide. I pretended I didn't see her shock and waved her in.

"Hello Drizti, welcome to the party! I see you brought something?"

She blinked and looked at the basket she was holding. "U-um, yeah. These are some scones my mother used to make, I thought I'd share them?"

She looked back up at me as she walked in. "Candy, are you ok?... You've been crying, and- gods, I don't-"

"Haha, well, it needed to be done." I said, my voice trailing off, "Does it look bad?"

She winced. "Well... The color is nice, but... Um," she looked for a nice way to say it, "...if I'm very *very* careful not to touch your skin, can I fix a few things?"

I felt my hair and looked at Drizti, thinking. Was risking her life worth having nicer hair? Obviously not. But maybe... If she was careful, it should be fine.

"...Let's go into the bathroom, just tell *me* what to fix, ok?"

We went into the bathroom and I stared in the mirror at my ugly, jagged bright red hair. It didn't do the 'bob' thing at all, it just stuck out at the bottom and looked funny. I teared up and hugged myself, if I didn't have such a *stupid* power I could have just gone to a fucking *salon* or something, I didn't know how to cut hair, what was I thinking? Drizti gently guided my gloved hands, keeping away from my face and pointing out areas that needed work, she showed me how to twist up my hair and layer it by cutting the twist. After a few minutes, my hair looked... still a mess, but at least it was pointing in the right directions. It had lost a couple more inches during the repair though, putting it in between a bob and a pixie cut. Debbie would be happy at least.

"You'll need to put something in it every day, some kind of volume or something, to give it fluff. That will hide the harder to touch up stuff and puff it out, making it look like you have more hair than you do." Drizti said as I brushed the hair off and stood up.

"Thanks. I take it you did hair cutting in the clan?" I asked as we headed into my living room.

"Ehh, sometimes, off and on. I know enough." she said. She looked around. "So what needs to be done?"

"What do you mean?" I asked, "We're just going to be watching TV, I figure I'll get the snacks out, and we'll just, like, watch TV?"

She nodded. "Oh, ok. Usually when we had get-togethers back home, we were supposed to show up early and help with getting ready. I guess that's not a thing here? Or are the others just really bad guests?"

"Oh, uhh, no that's not a thing, it sounds nice though." I said, "We can get out the snacks I bought and put them on plates though?"

"Ok, yeah, we'll need somewhere to put them though..." she said, looking at my table covered in diorama making materials.

"Sorry, I was thinking just on the coffee table or the counters?" I said, pulling out a bag of chips and a bowl, "I was trying to make the table my permanent workplace."

"You made this little house?" Drizti asked, climbing up on a chair to see better, "Like, with bits of wood and stuff?"

"It's not done, but yeah!" I said, glancing over, "I use foam board, polymer, clay, and plaster a lot for things too, but I really like using actual wood for wooden structures. I have a whole box of painting sticks and chunks of pallet wood that I stain and cut up to use!"

"I feel so big looking at it... I never feel big, it's a nice feeling!" she said, looking closer, "Do you have any finished ones?"

I peeled the plastic off of a tub of dip and licked it. "Mm, mm, yeah, let me show you!"

I walked to my bedroom door and swung it open, and she walked over. "I put them up in here, let me get the light." I said.

I stepped over to my desk and flicked on my lamp, pointing it upwards. The red walls absorbed most of the light, but it was still enough to see the rows of tiny scenes I'd displayed on the shelves over the desk. Drizti made a couple of bars and sat on them, floating them up so she could see better. She made cooing noises as she tilted her head left and right, admiring my handiwork. Her favorite piece seemed to be a small koi pond I'd made, with a small boy fishing in it off of a stone bridge. She looked at the resin water and ran her finger along the flat side of the base that let you look 'into' the pond from the side.

"That was a fun one to make," I said, "I was so nervous I was going to fuck up the water look after so much work, but aside from a few little bubbles, I think it turned out well!"

"I can tell you worked really hard on them, how long do they take?"

"Ah, it differs. Some take a week or so, but others can take up to a few months." I said. I pointed to a small house with cherry trees around it "This one took almost four months, it was a nightmare to get the trees right. I couldn't find cherry trees in the hobby shops, so I ended up having to buy sakura branches and making my own trees on top of them."

"Wow, you're really dedicated!" she said, "I need to find something like this. Back home I'd just walk around the compound, just watch nature and see people and move around, *that* was my hobby, but here? It's scary out there, and I'm small enough for some of the people in the city to just pick me up and take off with me."

"Is that something that happens?" I asked, "Gnomes just getting kidnapped?"

"Well- I don't actually know? It might have been the elders making up stories to keep us from leaving the clan, but it's still-"

A knock on the door made me jump. I glanced over and shouted out. "It's open!"

The door opened, and Galorna and Lucy walked in each holding food in their hands. I walked out of my bedroom, and Drizti followed, closing the door behind her.

Lucy gave us a smug look. "Oooh, alone in the bedroom, I see, trying to see how close you can get to playing without making physical contact?"

"No! She was showing me her tiny stuff, the stuff she makes." Drizti protested, blushing.

"Uh, Candy, your *hair*." Galorna said, frowning, "Are you having a crisis or something still? That's pretty drastic."

"I wasn't going to say anything, but like, you look like a fully different person, yeah." Lucy chimed in.

"It was Debbie's idea." I muttered, "It's- I'll get used to it. It makes me stand out."

"That's putting it lightly." snickered Lucy.

"It's going to take a while to get used to, but I *think* I can see how it'd look good with your costume?" Galorna said helpfully, "Here, I brought some dumplings, I steamed them downstairs a few minutes ago, they're super hot."

She set the round container on the counter next to the chips, and cracked the lid, showing me the round white shapes inside. An amazing smell wafted up out of the steamer basket and my mouth started watering. Homemade scones, fresh steamed dumplings, my store bought chips and cookies were looking pretty sad now...

"I brought something too, it's brownies." Lucy said, holding up a box of brownie mix.

"Oh, thank you? I don't know if we can make those, I don't have eggs and stuff. Or a stove, just an air fryer." I said, looking around.

"Ah well, I tried." she said, and set the box down, "So, what are we watching?"

"We're supposed to all pick something to show to Drizti, she's never seen TV before." I explained.

"Yeah, I was thinking about that," Galorna said, "Do we show her like, the first episode of each, or our favorite episodes or...?"

"Just whatever you think is the best introduction." Alele said. "Hi, by the way. Door was open."

I looked at Alele's empty hands. Well, at least my snacks were still in *third* place then. She was wearing a strange blue wrap that went around her limbs and looped loosely, with skin showing in between the fabric. Did she sleep in that?

"I like your... pajamas?" I asked, pointing.

She glanced down. "Yeah, traditional elven sleeping clothes. Loose and soft, with lots of 'access'."

I wrinkled my nose. "There will be no 'accessing' happening at this party thank you very much."

"Whatever, I'm still dressed hotter than the rest of you. Footie pajamas? Really?"

I crossed my arms. "They're my Yule pajamas, in my family we'd all wear them and cuddle up by the fire before the feast. I wore them so *you* guys would be safe around me, they cover a ton of skin."

"That's thoughtful of you, I just wore my old sleeping robes. I don't have anything else." Drizti said.

"Didn't you buy like, a billion bags of clothes two days ago? You should have at least *one* fun thing to wear to a pajama party." Lucy pointed out. She was wearing flannel pants and one of her 'dysphoria hoodies', not really one to talk.

"Those were all *regular* clothes, you can't sleep in regular clothes." Drizti explained.

"I mean, *I* do." Galorna said, pointing at her tank top and workout shorts, "I wear these to the gym *and* to sleep in."

"I think gym clothes and pajamas are already the same concept." Alele said, "They need to be comfortable, sexy, easy to move around in, breathable..."

"I never thought of it like that, but yeah, I guess so." Lucy said.

"I do *not* want to think about working out in this outfit." I said, picking at mine, "I would drown in sweat, this thing is half fuzz."

"Well, it's not *universal*." Alele said, rolling her eyes, "I'm just saying, I'd work out in these clothes. I mean, I *have*, depending on your definition of 'working out'. I've 'gotten a workout' in them at least."

"I don't want to talk about that, shouldn't we start figuring out what we're going to watch?" I said as I turned on my TV.

We all settled in, I grabbed a few dumplings and scones and sat on the far left closest to the door, making sure I had a 'pillow wall' between me and the other girls. Lucy sat next to me with Alele on her other side, and Galorna sat on the floor with Drizti leaning against her. The first show started; Lucy's pick. It was a strange animated show about a magical girl who fought off bad guys with the power of music. It was... odd, and very old. Almost 40 years old, and the concept of 'magical girls' as a unique classification of Chosen hadn't *really* taken off yet when it was made, so the dynamics of the character were unusual, but it was still a cute, fun experience.

I savored the hot dumplings and sweet flaky scones and looked over at the other girls, thinking. Aside from the pillows blocking me from them, they seemed pretty at ease around me, Even Alele was her normal self again. If they were this relaxed, maybe I really *could* just be a normal member of the team? It was comforting to think that. I only had a few more hurdles to get over before I really knew how my life looked from now on; the grand opening, and the first patrol... If I could make a good impression at those two, it wouldn't matter if I had powers I could use or not.

~~~

I adjusted the skirt of my dress and tried to make sure it was staying down. Despite *looking* identical to my actual transformed outfit, the fake one the church had made for us just didn't fit as well. The skirt didn't want to stay put, the tights kept bunching up, the sleeves slid up my arms if I moved too much. Whatever magic Lorgiaia had put into our real outfits was working *hard* to keep us looking good while we moved around.

"Angel Rouge, did you sign the photo release form for Magi G Hotspot yet?" Debbie asked, flipping through a stack of papers, "They're saying they're missing two release forms for their article, and they won't show up unless they can get a group photo."

"Ugh, damnit, let me see..." I ducked behind the desk and picked my phone out of the lockbox to look through my emails.

"Language, Angel Rouge, there'll be kids here soon." she admonished me.

I found the email buried in a sea of other releases I'd already signed and signed it with my elbow, taking the gloves on and off was a pain, and the signature didn't need to be perfect or anything.

"Yeah, I got it. The kids will be told not to touch me, right?" I confirmed, putting my phone back in the box.
~~~

"Yes, you can high five and shake hands if you want with the gloves on, but I made it very clear hugs are off limits for *all* our magical girls. They'll be reminded again when they come through the doors to get in line."

"Aw... I really wanted hugs..." Drizti said as she floated past us on her green bars to get to the cafe, "Uh, sorry, Candy, I know why we *can't*, I just like hugs."

I felt bad screwing up everyone's big moment like this, and I felt even guiltier about everyone else having to wear dumb accessories to 'match' my gloves. Galorna had said hard no to the kabuki mask, as I'd assumed, but she was still wearing a white headband tied in the back, and boxing tape on her hands. Drizti had her hat of course; today she'd gone with a traditional single point gnome hat, green, and folded over back onto her back. Lucy... she'd demanded she be allowed to use a *katana* as her 'accessory', but had been talked down to having throwing knives strapped to her upper arms for now, until the church could train her to actually *use* a sword. Alele had argued hard against *any* accessory, she said it'd make her look too 'busy', and that she preferred the plainer, classy look her unaltered costume had. In the end, Debbie had gotten her to wear gold bracers instead of her bracelet with the alert ping in it, and while she wasn't happy about it, she was still wearing them.

I sat down at one of the tables in the cafe and looked at the shadows outside the paper-covered windows. Kids, their guardians, creepy guys with a thing for women with powers, all in line to meet us, to get to see us for the first time. I was ready for it, I'd run through the training with Debbie and the girls every day this week, but actually *being* here, I couldn't help but be afraid something would go wrong.

My stomach hurt, and I couldn't tell if it was nerves, the tight dress, or just a tummy ache, but whatever the cause, it was making the whole situation worse. I looked over at the menu above the cafe, looking for something to settle my stomach, but it was all sweets. The foods we'd designed were on display, with little cartoon us-es next to them to show who's treat was who's, and they'd added a series of drinks themed like us as well. Looking at the pictures, mine was a carbonated cherry slurpie with cream swirled in and a red candy straw sticking out of it. It looked way too sweet, and I would *rather* have had Galorna's spiced pineapple mango smoothie, but I probably needed to be seen drinking my 'signature drink' when the guests were let in.

I went up to the counter and ordered the drink, getting a small just in case it made my stomach worse. The shaggy young man behind the counter didn't ask for payment, and I wondered in the back of my head if we could just get free stuff from the cafe whenever, not that I'd take advantage of that. I sipped the sticky sweet slush up through the candy and rocked back and forth as it helped my stomach slightly, the sugar making my head buzz pleasantly. There was nothing for me to do but wait, why had they made us come down so early? I'd been waiting around for hours, and I couldn't even see the time to check how long we had left. Of *course* the handy pockets my *real* magical girl outfit had weren't in the dummy outfit, so I didn't even have my phone on me to pass the time. Not that the screen worked with gloves on anyway.

"Ok girls, Debbie will be off to the side if you need anything, I'll be next to the photo set looking for any trouble." Oori announced, "We need all of you to make your way to your places, we're doing full group photos now, then after three o' clock, once the crowds die down, we'll let them take individual photos with you. Do not, I repeat, do *not* let any of the customers pressure you into one on one time past a few sentences until the designated time, we need to get them in and out; we've got a line out there."

"We have 5 minutes until the doors open, remember to direct them to the cafe, the information booth, or the merch booth after they get the photos. Smile big, remember your lines, and try to really sell it, ok?" Debbie said, leveling a look at us as we scrambled to get to the big white sheet that was hanging on the far wall.

We'd practiced our poses so, so many times. We had 5 different group poses, depending on the size of the person taking the picture with us, but in all of them the general order from left to right was Galorna, Lucy, me, and Drizti and Alele in front of us. We stood in loose formation as the church's workers unstuck the paper from the windows, letting in light and finally allowing the line of people to see us. I beamed and waved at them through the glass, and they cheered and clapped as they finally got a glimpse at the heroes they'd been waiting in line for. I looked in the crowd for my mom or brothers, I'd told them about the opening of course, but I didn't see them at all. I wasn't upset though, I hadn't told my mom about my hair yet, and I wasn't really prepared for her to find out about it; her tears alone would send me spiraling, even if she didn't *say* anything.

The doors opened, and the lobby filled with cheering kids and their parents. Most of the people here today were already a part of the church, and had been told by the leaders to 'come see their brand new heroes!' but the rest were just regular people who heard 'Chosen event' and showed up to meet a Chosen, any Chosen. As a result, instead of a good mix of different types of kids, I was only seeing two kinds; ones who were Chosen nuts with hero shirts and autograph books, and ones who were only here because they (or their parents) wanted to support the church. The second group was pretty easy to recognize, they all had the little white ribbon Lorgiaia's followers wore somewhere on their bodies, and a lot of them even had the traditional worship face paint on too. I tugged at the ribbon around my own waist, and idly wondered if we'd need to paint the lines and flowers on *our* faces for events sometimes.

I set my drink on a table next to the photo set and turned my attention to the front of the line. A light pink kid with blonde braids and gray horns was beaming at us from behind the velvet rope, her mom standing behind her with a camera. I gave her a little wave, and the attendant opened up the rope, letting her and her mom in. She dashed up to us and jumped up and down excitedly.

"Hi! I'm *so* glad to meet you, I heard about you during group meet and I got *so* excited, I've never had a Chosen in my church before!" she said, looking from one of us to another. She saw Galorna and pointed to her horns. "Are you an infernal too? My mom said most gods won't choose infernals, but they're starting to sometimes!"

"Ah, sorry, I'm an oni, but I like your horns a lot! I love how they look with the ribbon going back and forth between them." Galorna said, smiling, "You know, oni used to be considered monsters too, just like infernals were back in the pre-Chosen days! But *I* was still considered a monster back when I was just a little girl, so even if I'm not *exactly* the same, I think we're kinda similar."

The girl's mother, a human, stepped forward and put a hand on her daughter's shoulder. "I'm sorry, she's just excited, can we get a picture?"

"Of course, if you can stand on the dot... What's your name?"

Galorna went through the process of setting up the photo, and I watched the child with a strange feeling in my chest. She was *very* excited about this, we hadn't even done anything publicly yet, she'd just heard we existed, and somehow that made her happy? My church growing up *did* have a Chosen, we worshiped a local god, with a local chosen. The god we'd followed had been in charge of the farmlands where we owned property, and his Chosen was just a glorified strongman with a weak weather control power. He wasn't anything special, I saw him every week joking with the dads at our church's meetings. But to *these* people, the people in Lorgiaia's church, we were something new, something they'd never seen before.

Sure, there were Chosen all over the city. There were *thousands* of gods across the world, maybe more, and many of them had multiple Chosen. Seeing a Chosen wasn't that big of a deal, but when it was *your* Chosen, someone worshiping the god you followed, a god who had tens of thousands of other followers... The weight and pressure to be perfect for these kids amped up, and I forced my grin to be a hint more cheerful as the camera snapped.

"Thank you SO much for coming to visit us, and don't forget to check out the snacks!" Drizti said, making a heart with her hands the way Debbie had showed her.

"There's a snack based on each of us, I designed the big cookie! It's strawberry lemon!" Galorna offered, pointing at the sign.

"Thank you so much! I'll come see you again too!" the girl said, waving as her mom led her over to the cafe.

"Well that was nice..." Lucy said, nodding. "I feel good about that."

"Yeah, just keep that feeling for another 300 kids and we'll be doing ok." said Alele, gesturing for the next one to come up

It went smoothly, we hit our marks, we said the things Debbie asked us to say. We told the kids from the church to go to the cafe, the hero nerds to go to the information booth, and we told the adults to go buy a shirt with our logo on it. I could see how it'd get exhausting though, I was putting on a front the whole time, and I was getting tired less than an hour into the meet and greet. I took a big sip of my drink, making sure not to mess up my lip gloss and turned to beckon the next kid. To my surprise, I recognized her; it was the dryad girl who'd taken my photo last week. I waved at her and put my drink back down.

"Hi! I know you!" I said.

"Oh wow, you don't even look like the same lady, does your transformation do that?" she asked, pointing to my hair.

"Mm, no, I got a haircut to look better in the group, do you like it?" I asked, trying to engage her on a more personal level. She was one of the older kids we'd seen today, and she *did* have a picture of me ready to post that she could frame in a bad light if she wanted. I needed her to like me, or at least not see me as a dick.

"That's dedication..." she said, ruffling the leaves on her head, "I'd never do that for a job, any job. But uh, you look good?" she sounded unsure.

"I didn't know you had a fan, Angel Rouge!" Lucy said, trying to break up the conversation and keep the line moving.

"Oh, well, not yet, but if I can get traction with her, I'll be her number one, it just depends on what my followers want." The girl explained, "I'm MagicalCl0ut on CirNet, with a zero instead of an oh, I take pictures of magical girls and post them."

"Well, you're in the right place." Alele said, trying to hide her annoyance.

"Oh, yeah, sorry. Here..." she handed her phone to the attendant and posed, leaning in closer to me and giving a thumbs up.

She *could* be the one to help me get more famous, if her page was big enough. She could also be my first internet fan, and start a real fanpage. I wanted her on my side. I put on a more casual, friendly smile; one that said 'hey, it's just me and my friend', and gave my own thumbs up, bumping my fist to hers as the photo took. As she got her phone back, she grinned and nodded.

"Oh, perfect, thanks a ton. Hopefully the fans like you, I def wanna cover more of y'all!" She waved and jogged over to the information booth to get pamphlets to share with her followers.

I glanced at Alele, who was glaring at me. "...Sorry..." I said, "She knew me, and she's got followers, I had to."

"I didn't say anything." she snipped back, and called up the next kid

Chapter Eight

I lay on the sofa munching donuts and scrolled on CirNet with my fancy new professional account and I frowned. I was seeing so, so many photos tagged with "Lorgiaia's Angels", but almost no actual discussion. The ones that *did* have comments were almost always from the relatives of the child in the photos talking about how cute they were, or how they were 'so grown up now'. I gave each of the posts and comments a sparkle though, I needed to make my presence online known, and from what I could tell, Alele had already sparkled the posts herself with *her* account. I was even seeing her leave comments on some of the photos, making comments about having fun, or being happy to meet the kid. I was falling behind in the social world already and it was only a day after our debut.

I needed to fix that, with my lack of powers, popularity was the only way to stay relevant. I bookmarked my place in the chronological scroll, and tapped in the search bar. What was it? Magical-some-thing, I knew that much, it had numbers in it... I looked through the results for 'magical' and recognized the green and orange leaves of the dryad who had my photo, this had to be her, MagicalCl0ut. I opened her page, and sure enough, pinned at the top was the group photo of us, posted last night just before dinner time. I gave it a sparkle, and scrolled down. Below it was a two photo post; one picture was a cropped version of the group one, zoomed in on me and her, and the other was the picture the girl had taken with her friends last week. The post read:

"Angel Rouge is dedicated to her job! I got an exclusive photo with her last weekend, before she finished getting into her role, and you can tell she gave up a LOT to be the best magical girl she can be! I'm impressed, what do you guys think, is that much dedication a good sign?"

I sparkled that post too, and opened the comments section, nervous about what I might find. They were about what I expected, with most of the users talking about how I haven't seen action yet, so it was impossible to tell if I was any good at my job or not, with a couple comments about how 'it looked like I'd lost weight' since the older picture was taken. One comment though stood out to me, it was of an account without a profile picture and just a bunch of numbers for the name. It stated:

"I think she's going to be very, very interesting to watch. I heard she's already been out 'practicing' unofficially..."

I frowned and wondered if there was any leaked info of my first mission, or if anyone had gone to the press about it. I couldn't imagine any of the girls would, and everyone *else* who knew was either in jail, in the church, or working for the GGDS. I tried to shrug it off and scrolled up to the top to friend MagicalCl0ut, and my eyes widened in surprise. She had over 100,000 followers on this account?! I looked back at the pictures and saw each of them had tens of thousands of sparkles. This was an *amazing* platform for my popularity, I'd beat Alele in no time. I went back to the post about me, and commented:

"It was so nice to see you again! I'm going to do my best and work hard to keep everyone safe! Fun fact about the hair; I actually cut it because it was slowing me down! My skill is flying extra fast, so I wanted to streamline my form to get even faster!"

I bit my lip. Was that too much?... It needed to come off as genuine... I couldn't take it back now, though. I went back to the chronological scroll and kept going through photos. Most of the kids hadn't interacted with me too much. Alele had been the most vocal one of the group, so I wasn't seeing many that I recognized well enough to comment on. Aside from one guy who went for a side hug right before the picture took, but I was NOT about to give him the satisfaction of interacting. He was lucky I ducked away before he actually touched me, *that* would have been a messy end to the day.

A notification popped up, and I opened it. It was a reply to my comment on the picture, from MagicalCl0ut herself:

"It was nice seeing you too! I look forward to seeing more of you in the future, we should get brunch some time! I know this great place not too far from your head-quarters, maybe Saturday?"

I raised my eyebrows, that was a lot of interaction to give just a random fan. Was I going to go have a meal with this girl I'd only spoken to for a couple of seconds? Would that set a precedent? Saturday was out anyway, we had our first patrol then. I got a personal message popup and a new follower notification at the same time, both from her. I opened the message.

"Hey, so like, I want to meet up again, for one to get more pics of you, but for another, I want to talk strategy. I think we can do something here, build each other up, I've done it before, it's where my followers came from. If we're 'friends', then it makes you more grounded, and me seem cooler, so I want to talk about how that looks when we meet up."

I thought for a moment, I should really talk to Debbie about this, but... I typed out a reply.

"Well, I can't do Saturday, but maybe some time during the week? And just you, if I see a crowd, I'm leaving."

"Ok, chill, no problem, Wednesday at 10 ok for you?"

"It should be, yeah. I'll let you know if anything changes."

"Perfect, and hey, try to be more normal when you reply to the message on the post, ok? You kinda sound 'corporate' in your first one."

She sent me the address and I marked it in my maps app. It wasn't too far away, about a 20 minute walk, or a 2-3 minute fly, I could do that. I went back to her post and replied:

"I'd love that! My week is up in the air though, let's chat, and try to work out an earlier date, I look forward to it!"

I nodded, and closed my phone. My first comment already had six likes, and I had two new followers. This was going to work out great, I could tell.

~~~

Candy, I'm just saying, you might be all super powered, but you're still human..." Galorna said as I put my satchel on the ground and stepped away from it.

"Relax, she's a kid, and I'm transforming now, so even if she *is* trying to trick me, I'll already be powered up." I said shaking my head.

"Honestly? I think this is stupid of you." Debbie snapped at me, "PR is my *job*, and you're teaming up with some fan instead? Give me time, your follower count will *dwarf* hers."

"Hey, if she thinks *cheating* will help her, I say let her do it." Alele said, shrugging.

"Gods, it's one brunch with a fan, just relax, ok?" I said, starting my transformation. Once the glow faded, I pulled my gloves out of my bag and slid them on. "I'll be fine, and I won't do anything to jeopardize the team."

"Just be careful..." Drizti said.
~~~

"I don't know why me going out needed everyone to come see me off..." I grumbled, "I'm a grown woman."

"Yeah, but you're *our* grown woman." Lucy said pointedly, "Or-wait, that sounds creepy. Uhh..."

"What she *meant* is that after what happened last time we 'just went out', people died, *and* we're public now, so we have a lot more on the line." Galorna said firmly.

"Ok, well, thank you, I appreciate your concern, but I looked this place up, I even went there yesterday to scope it out, I'm *fine*." I said

"Just please be careful about getting close to anyone." Galorna said, "Try and stay away from the other customers."

So *that's* what this was. They were worried about me using my powers accidentally or something. I fought back a feeling of anger and frustration and gave a wry smile instead, pretending to be unhurt.

"Hey, it's ok, I gotta get used to living a normal life sometime, right?" I said, trying to look wistful and slightly sad. The other's faces fell at that, even Alele's, and I turned away to lock in that emotion.

"I'll be back soon, I'll be safe, I promise."

The other girls and Debbie stayed in the lobby as I walked out. I wasn't doing anything wrong, I was *pretty sure* I wouldn't endanger anyone, I wish they'd leave me alone. Once I was clear of the building, I pumped my wings and shot into the sky, letting the world fall away from me. The people all dwindled to dots, and the buildings just looked like gray squares on a chessboard. I tilted my angle, and dropped face first, letting my wings guide and slow me as I neared my target, a small diner on a street corner with a view of a major intersection.

As I approached, I saw MagicalCl0ut on the sidewalk, looking around. I whistled to let her know I was coming, and she looked up, stumbling back. She quickly pulled her phone out and started snapping pictures as I fluttered to the ground, landing a couple of feet in front of her.

"Holy *shit*" she said "You look way more impressive than you did before, are you *glowing*?"

I nodded "Yeah, just a bit. And thanks, this is the 'full transformation', or that's what **PR** is calling it."

"Ok, so you have different tiers of transformations?" she asked, putting her phone away and pulling out a notebook

I wasn't supposed to let on that the fake costumes were just us untransformed or we'd be targeted in them. I hated to start our relationship off on a lie, but I needed to keep me and the other girls safe.

"Yeah, We have a base form, then one where we have powers and outfits, and then one where we get wings and glow-y." I think that was what we were supposed to tell people at least. Debbie's meetings were boring and I had a hard time keeping track of anything that wasn't a direct order.

"Ok, damn, so you wanted to go full on magical girl for this?" she asked, looking up from her writing

"I didn't want to walk for 20 minutes or ride the bus." I said honestly.

"Cool, cool, relatable, that's good. Hey, my name is Forica, do I just call you Angel Rouge? Or...?" she said, opening the door for me. I folded my wings and stepped inside.

"My name is publicly listed in the hero registry, you can call me Candy, but I'd prefer it if you used my actual hero name in the posts, for branding."

She nodded, making a note. "Ok, ok. I *may* wanna drop your real name in there, after a few months, just to like, humanize you, make it look like an accident."

We took our seat, and I tried to ignore the looks and stares I was getting from the other patrons. I ordered a stack of pancakes and a glass of OJ, and Forica ordered mineral water and some eggs. As I waited for my food, I asked her something I'd been wondering about since she agreed to meet me at this time of morning.

"I gotta know, how old are you? You don't look old enough to be graduated, but you're here on a weekday, so..."

She nodded. "Yeah, I'm 16. I dropped out to be a full time social media star. I have an account that's just pics of me, and the one where it's magical girls. I get a good amount of money, people donate to me on my main one, and news outlets buy the rights to the pics on the MG one."

"Oh, ah, well." I felt bad, this girl dropped out of high school just to take pictures of people like me? "Maybe you should still get a certificate? I had to do that because I worked on a farm most of my high school years and I kept missing classes, but it wasn't too hard to get."

She shrugged. "I make more than my parents, I think I'm ok." she put her notebook on the table. "So a farm, huh? Rags to riches story?"

"Nnnno, we were doing ok, we had ok sales, and our stuff grew well, it was just a lot of work. I had brothers though, so the work got split up."

She asked me more questions about my 'backstory' until our food arrived, and I dug in, cutting the pancakes into bites and eating them with a fork. I glanced at Forica to see her giving me a funny look.

"What?" I asked, patting my face with a napkin, "Did I smear my makeup? I didn't think magical makeup *could* smear."

"No, it's..." she said, "Your gloves, they'll get all greasy, why not take them off?"

I looked at my gloved hands. Was it really that odd? "Oh, it's a branding thing, I need to be seen with them so they're a part of my character design." I said smoothly, "I never take them off!"

"Ok, well, it's weird to eat with gloves on is all. Anyway, I was going to post some pics this afternoon, one of us, maybe one of you alone, and then drop the ones of you flying in over the next couple days, get extended engagement, is that ok?"

"Um, yeah, I suppose so?" I finished my plate, "I'm not the one who knows this stuff, before I joined the team I only used CirNet to look at memes and catch up with family."

"Great, I'll get those edited and scheduled later then, perfect." she made a mark on a checklist in her notebook. "Ok, so what's a good opportunity to get more pics?"

I thought about how to say it. Just telling her we'd be on patrol Saturday could be bad, and could trigger an attack from fallen who saw the area as an easy target due to our low experience if she talked, but it *would* be a good spot, and we *were* supposed to be seen while there...

"Ok, so it's a secret, buuut..." I looked around dramatically and leaned in. She leaned in closer, and I whispered. "We'll be making a public appearance this Saturday in city square, but don't tell anyone!"

She narrowed her eyes at me. "Okayyy... 'Don't tell anyone' don't tell anyone? Or '*Don't tell anyone*' don't tell anyone?"

"No, like, actually don't tell anyone." I clarified.

"Ok, damn, thanks for the tip then, I'll be there!" she said, smiling, "Inside information already, I can tell this team up is going to go very well."

We finished up, and left the diner, with her taking a few selfies with me as we left. I tried to pay for hers, but she said it would 'look like a bribe', and refused. I waved goodbye to her, and took off to the sky at top speed as she snapped pictures of me flying away. I flew around a building out of sight and slowed down to a stop. I needed to take it easy, that much grease in me was making me feel sluggish. I stretched, and lazily headed back to headquarters, I'd check in with the girls, get a little training in, and relax with-

A powerful force slammed into me from behind, knocking me out of the sky and onto a nearby rooftop. I clambered to my feet and spun around to see my attacker thud into the roof behind me, her own wings flared. She was tall, a foot taller than me, and her *head* was... it almost reminded me of Lorgiaia's except where *her* head had been a series of flowers, this woman's was a series of glowing rings, covered in darting eyes and spinning slowly, a golden light inside them. She was dressed in white robes, and her six alabaster wings curled around her body like the legs of a spider, making her even more imposing as she walked towards me drawing a long, thick silver sword covered in odd runes.

"Where do your wings come from, red one? Have you been granted the power of the heretics?" Her voice slid out of the rings in echos and waves, and I fell to my knees, shaking.

I thought fast, was this a fight? Was I going to have to use my power on this bitch? I thought of any other solutions, and remembered I'd never taken the gun I took from Homicide out of my pocket. It wasn't *much* better than using my power, but if came down to it, a gunshot was slightly less fatal than being turned into an inanimate object.

"I- I'm a Chosen!" I said waving my hand "I'm not a heretic, I work for a goddess!"

Her sword came to rest under my chin, and she tilted my head up to look her in the face as the rings where her head should be slid back in on themselves, showing her actual face behind them. Golden wavy hair, amber eyes, and her forehead and mouth wrapped up in bandages. What was left of the rings wove themselves into an upside down crown, floating over her head, the eyes still looking every way at once.

"What goddess do you serve?" she said, her mouth unmoving under the wrappings.

"Lorgiaia! I serve the church of Lorgiaia!" I said, my mind racing. Was this woman a fallen? A sorceress? Or- she had more presence than any hero or fallen I'd ever seen, was she something more?

"Are..." I said, leaning back from the sword slightly, "Are you a new goddess?"

She looked me over, surprised, and lowered her sword, keeping it between us. She stepped closer, the eyes on the joints of her wings following me as she moved, and pulled at one of my own wings, causing me to flinch. I tried to reach out to her spark as she touched me, but there was no connection through the wing, the feathers must block the power, I'd remember that.

"I am *not* a goddess, I am sent by my master to hunt down what is rightfully his." Her voice was strong and clear, ringing like a bell in my head. "Hm, how many wings does the goddess 'Lorgiaia' have?"

"Uh, j-just the normal amount, two." I said standing up and slowly reaching into my pocket for the gun.

"Unfortunate. Do you know of any goddesses who have more?" she asked, turning away from me.

I stopped going for the gun. Was she not actually after me? Was I just knocked out of the air by *mistake*? Who *was* this lady?

"No, I don't think so? I think most goddesses just have two, if any... most don't have any, thinking about it."

"I see..." she mused, "This will not be as straightforward as I'd thought it would be upon seeing you, red one."

I could regain control of this, she seemed less intimidating now, and she wasn't as sure of herself as she'd been at first. I held my hands out and gave her my best magical girl smile. "Let me see if I can help you. Um, who are you exactly?"

She looked at me with golden eyes, open wide, but harsh and cold. "I am a Sister following the only true god in existence. That is all."

"So," I rubbed the stinging place on my chin where the sword had pricked me. "no name? You try to attack me, ask me weird questions, and not give me anything?"

"I gave up my name when I took on the task of tracking down the heretics. I am nameless until re-named." she said, drawing herself up to her full height.

"If- If I give you a new name, will you tell me what's going on?" I asked.

She looked at me, then around at the city. "Are you native to this place?"

"Well, I lived on the outskirts, but yeah a little, why?"

"...Very well, you may name me according to your customs."

According to my customs? Like, as a hero? Or as a magical girl?

"Ok, well, you're obviously *some* kind of Chosen, so it'd need to be a hero name..." I thought out loud, "Uhh, We can go with something old school, back when the gods used created constructs to talk to people? You look like some of those things, kinda. You could be... Throne? No that's stupid, uhh, some were called Seraphim? That sounds like a name, how about that?"

She sneered and laughed. "My kind devoured the last of the seraphim ages ago in my homeland, but I can see that it may fit well. I shall adopt it. Thank you, red one."

"Angel Rouge" I corrected her, "Or Candy, if it's just us."

She walked to the edge of the roof and looked down, arms folded. "Very well then, Candy, I will tell you what I can, and in exchange, I expect you to provide me with an understanding of this place I find myself in."

"An understanding?" I asked. Of what, the city? Was she really that out of her element? She must be from the northern wastes. "Yeah, ok, whatever I guess."

"I am from a far off land, beyond even the veil of time itself." she said dramatically "My lord has sent me to track down and find those that stole his power, and to slay them. One fled here, and I will find her and reclaim what was lost. I am at a loss as to what I should do however, I have never seen the wonders that fill this city; the lights, the moving and talking pictures on every building, the carriages, the foods. Cursed ones still walk the streets here, and monsters mix with people as if they *belonged* together."

"Uh, we try not to call people 'monsters' anymore. If they can communicate somehow, they're supposed to just be 'people'." I said, frowning, "Monsters are specifically creatures that can't talk or anything."

So *not* the northern wastes; even *they* had accepted the non-humans as people by now. 'beyond the veil of time' made me think of the folded lands. Could she be from so deep in a fold that they hadn't seen the outside world in the past 75 years? That seemed unlikely, given how many rescue efforts went into getting people out. And what was a 'cursed one?'

"This land is very different than mine," she said, placing her hand on my shoulder, causing me to flinch, "and I would ally myself to one such as yourself who would name me and provide me with information. Would you be amenable to that?"

"Like, help me do hero stuff and stuff?" I asked, "I mean, yeah, we can be in an alliance, as long as your god isn't enemies with Lorgiaia."

She laughed at that, her mouth stretching the cloth over it. "My dear Candy, my god is at constant war with everyone. I do not believe *your* goddess knows of his existence yet though. He is starkly absent from this place."

"Okayy…" I said. I didn't get it, but if she wasn't going to tell me her god, then I wasn't going to push it. There were a couple Chosen who had 'mystery gods', Homicide had been one, and if she wanted to be one too, then so be it. It'd be on her when she ran out of funds and couldn't get any marketing deals.

"I need to get home... Can I have your phone number? Or your CirNet name?" I asked her, pulling my phone out.

She looked at it without recognition. "My name is Seraphim, Candy, you know this."

"Fine, well, I guess I'll see you in the sky then." I muttered. If she was going to be like that, I didn't need her alliance anyway. She was weird, and the way she moved and spoke made me think she was used to being treated like a princess, even more so than Alele was. I didn't need that in my life right now. I waved goodbye, and her crown split into rings again as she watched me leave, her face once again obscured.

As I flew back home, I tried to figure out what that was all about, was she trying to shake me up? Was she a mentally unstable Chosen? Could her powers have messed her up when she got them? That wasn't unheard of, most people claimed to notice a difference in people's personalities after they were chosen. Some were fully different people, but psychologists claimed it was just because of 'lifted inhibitions', and not actual changes to the brain. Still, seeing her made me think they might be wrong...

~~~

I shifted uncomfortably in the thinly padded seat and leaned forward, looking out the front window to see if traffic was letting up.

"We're not there yet, if you were wondering." Lucy said from her seat across from me in the van.
~~~

"No, I was just wondering if we'd be moving soon, we're supposed to be at Queen Tower in less than twenty minutes, we should have just flown at this point." I said

"Even if you all flew, Debbie and I would *still* have to take the vans." Oori pointed out from his seat up front next to the driver. "We still need to get the t-shirt and info booths set up, so we'd need the equipment, and in case you forgot, Candy, Debbie and I can't fly."

I sighed and leaned back. I hated long car rides, I always felt like I was wasting time I could be using for something interesting. The windows in the van were blacked out too, so I couldn't even see out of them to people watch or to see landmarks. We were only an hour walk from city square, but in a car on a Saturday, it was a 45 minute drive. I started to pull off my right glove to grab my phone to look at so I could at least pass the time that way, but Alele slapped my hand.

"Candy, I am literally almost touching you as it is, one bump and our arms rub, I am *not* going to let you risk my life so you can add sparkles to posts about you." she said, scooting further away.

I groaned. "I need to at least let my person know I'm going to be there setting up in a few minutes, she wanted to do photos."

"Now, we're not going there just for photos." Oori said, "This is an actual mission as much as it is a publicity stunt, and we need to take it seriously. the city square is the safest area to patrol, yes, but that's *only* because the Downtown Queens are stationed there full time."

He rotated his seat to face us.

"Actually, this is a good time to go over what we need you to do and what to expect today."

"Didn't we go over that like, twice already? And we have *so much* public relations training now that Debbie made us work with her every day." Drizti said, looking up from her phone. She'd been talking to a lot of fans herself since she'd been taught how to use CirNet, and she was slowly getting known online as a Chosen who would respond to any and all mentions of her. I'd tried to explain that people would abuse her interactions, but she needed to learn for herself it seemed.

"We can always use a touch up on mission specifics, Oori, go ahead." Galorna said, patting Drizti on the knee.

"Today, our mission is to be seen in the area, and show that you're 'actual heroes' and not just 'mascots for the church'." he gave Galorna a wry look and she blushed. "Lorgiaia wants you to fight crime in her name, this is how we build up to that. Alele, you're on point, you'll rewind time to let us know if something happens, Galorna, you need to be seen chatting with kids, seem approachable. Lucy, like you requested, you can stay transformed the whole time, but *please* don't act too 'edgy' with the civilians. Candy, you need to stay in open areas, and do fly overs of the area every few minutes, be seen, fly fast, and do tricks if you can. Sell the idea that you're the best flyer on the team, like you and Debbie talked about, ok?"

I nodded.

"And lastly, Drizti," he continued, "I heard you'll be doing tricks for people?"

"Yeah!" she said, smiling, "I'm getting good with my power, I can connect the lines into 3d shapes if I combine them the right way! I thought I'd do that, maybe take requests, or let people help me design shapes, since I'll be over by the support team most of the time anyway."

"That sounds good, just don't let anyone touch your power." Oori reminded her, "If you accidentally transfer someone's terminal illness or chronic ailment to someone else, trying to fix it would destroy our reputation."

"So you *do* know about PR! And here I thought Debbie was the only one." Alele said, smirking.

"I know enough, and I have common sense." he said firmly, "Now, as for the support team, you'll be working with the Valley Nurses, they're pure support, and they'll be offering a walk up clinic during your patrol, but they're working for you as well. If you need them, let them know, and they'll be there."

"This sounds like it'll be boring and a pain." Lucy complained, "I want to go somewhere with actual crime and stuff, like, the area around our base?"

"Wait, there's crime around our headquarters?" Drizti asked, alarmed.

"No, she's being dramatic," Galorna assured her, "there's just currently no overlapping hero teams that patrol it, so there's random gaps in the day that are un-patrolled. It's still pretty safe."

"Is that why we built our building where we did?" Alele asked.

"As far as I know, yes. Once we are finished with all the paperwork, we'll apply for patrol rights for an 8 block radius." Galorna confirmed.

"Wait," I asked, "why haven't we applied yet? We've been an official team for like, a week."

"Well, Miss Candy," Oori said, "As a full team, we need at least one documented group mission under our belt before we can apply. I'll actually be taking the paperwork over to the GGDS office while you patrol, to get a head start on it."

"I just want to be pointed at what I need to do, and let go." grumbled Lucy "I'm tired of like, all this dumb stuff about rights and PR and stuff, I just want to go off, you know?"

I couldn't relate. I wanted to do as little fighting as I could, but I knew I was mostly alone in that. I leaned back and tried to think of cool poses to do at me and Forica's photoshoot, I wanted to make them look natural, and she *did* say she'd be following me around and trying to get candid shots too. I didn't need to think too hard, but since she posted her pics of me in the air, I'd gotten just over 11,000 new followers, bringing me up to a grand total of... around 11,000 total followers. She really was the main force growing my presence online, I needed to find a way to thank her somehow.

Lost in thought, I snapped back to the present when we parked and the back doors opened, letting the cacophony of voices from the dozens of advertisement screens playing in the main square into the van. I looked up and saw a slightly disgruntled and off looking Debbie on the other side. She waved her hands at us and motioned for us to get out. From the looks of where we were, we'd parked right next to the square in the 'no parking' zone. The vans would move once we unloaded I was sure, but it was still a nice perk to have.

"Gosh, Miss Debbie, are you ok? You look rough." Drizti said, as she got out.

"I get carsick, I'll be fine." Debbie said, glaring at her, "You girls are officially on patrol in 15. That gives us 10 minutes to let up the booths and introduce ourselves to the support team, if you let the workers get started on the booths, I'll bring you five over to them."

As I watched a couple of people from the office climb out of the other van with bags, I felt guilty I wasn't helping them. I'd set up my family's booth for the yearly fair over and over, I *could* help, but the way I was dressed and the publicity of one of Lorgiaia's Angels 'having to do manual labor' stopped me from giving them a hand at all. I sighed and hopped out, following the others to a closed tent on the other side of the square. It was sealed up, but I assumed it'd be opened up with signs out around it once the time hit.

I ducked inside, and saw the other girls sitting around a small table. They glanced up at us when we walked in, and one waved. She was wearing pink scrubs with a white domino mask and matching medical face mask. She had a pillbox hat on her head with a large pink and white cartoon pill busting open on it; the Valley Nurses logo.

"I'm guessing you're the Angels?" she said, "I'm Trauma Response, this is my team."

"Yep, we just wanted to get to know you before we broke out and started the patrol, it's nice to meet you." Galorna said, shaking her hand.

"I can't believe you guys are calling yourselves 'angels' already..." said one of the girls at the table. She was wearing a white plague doctor's uniform that had a corset and skirt attached, with a pink cape over her shoulders down to her knees. Her logo was on the side of her 'beak', and she was holding a rod with flowers on one end. "I had to work for like 6 years before I made angel, do you know how many lives I saved? How many nights I slept in a hospital chair to earn that title?"

"I- I'm *so* sorry." I said, "I asked Lorgiaia about it, but she said she wanted the name, I'm not trying to steal any glory or anything..."

"Don't mind her, that's Field Dress, she's been bragging about her title since she got it, she's the only one of us who cares." Trauma Response said dismissively.

"And who are the rest of your team?" Alele asked, "I didn't read the file thingy."

"My name is Sterile, and this is Ice Pack." one of the remaining two said, pointing at the other one. She had an open shoulder cropped blouse and her hair up in a bun. Her logo was pinned to her top, and from what I could see under the table, she was wearing something very short that showed her whole legs. Ice Pack, on the other hand, was bundled up, with a blue and pink parka, white fur trim hiding most of her face. Her logo was on her right shoulder, and she had some kind of white padded leggings on.

"That's an unfortunate name," Lucy pointed out, "It makes it sound like your power is not being able to have children."

"Well, no foreign microscopic life can survive in or around my body, so... I can't get pregnant. I thought it fit." Sterile said, shrugging.

I glared at Lucy for her stupid comment, but she didn't notice.

"I'm going to be hanging out with you guys!" Drizti said, "I look forward to working with you, I'm a healer too! Kinda."

Ice Pack laughed, the sound muffled by her parka. "Yeah, 'kinda' a healer is about the closest anyone gets to being a healer these days, all the good powers are gone by now, welcome to the club, kid."

I smiled politely at the other group. "I have to step out for a second and meet someone before we're on duty, so it was nice meeting you, but I'll have to catch up later!"

I ducked out as Drizti asked them what their powers were and scanned the area for Forica. I wanted to get some shots in while we were in the main square, but I also planned on heading over to 'patrol' the park the next street over for some pics by the water, maybe in a tree? I had an idea for a low angle shot I saw in a magazine once, with my leg blocking anything important, but in a tree or on top of a building, crouching down? I saw her on the other side of the square, talking to Debbie. I jogged over just in time to hear the tail end of the conversation.

"...and if I see so much as a piece of *trash* with an unapproved brand on it, we're suing your ass, do you understand?"

"It's just going on CirNet, it's not a big deal, but fine, no branded anything, no panty shots, and nothing with fighting in it. I got it."

"Um, wait" I said, jumping in, "Were you going to be taking-?"

Forica shook her head. "No, I wouldn't do that, she's just being dramatic."

"I'm not being 'dramatic', Candy, this is my job." said Debbie firmly, "I need you to be on top of this, I don't like this, but if you *insist* on going outside the church's resources, then we need rules."

"Well it sounds like it's all set up then, and I have two minutes to go before we start, can I have her now?" I said.

"It's your funeral, but get out of here." Debbie said, waving me away.

We walked away and Forica looked at me nervously. "So, should I be worried? She mentioned suing me..."

I rolled my eyes. "I'll deal with her, just... Let's go get some photos by the statue of Lady Guillotine, we can use her blade for me to stand on and look off into the distance or something."

As we walked over to the statue of the tall orc lady in question, I scanned the square for any danger; a quick once over to make sure that I could at least claim I was doing my job. The booth for checking and healing minor ailments was open, Drizti was trying to build a replica of Queen Tower, Alele was actively chasing a group of teens down, waving at them, and Galorna and Lucy were in the sky, doing circles around the center of the square. They were all getting attention in their own way, so I couldn't feel *too* bad, right?

Chapter Nine

I hopped off the statue and stepped over to Forica. She was flipping through the pictures she'd taken and frowning.

"Any good ones?" I asked, peeking at them.

"Mm, yeah, a few. Nothing groundbreaking though. Where to next?"

I looked around. "Well I'm *supposed* to be doing air patrol, and it looks like Lucy and Galorna are done with their fly-over, so I guess I'll head to the park. I'll be doing tricks and stuff on the way, you follow on foot and try and get some action shots, alright?"

"It's hard to focus on a moving object like that, is it ok if I just get a video of you and cut it into clips?" she asked.

"Yeah, that's fine. Let me know when you're filming, I'll do a cool takeoff?" I offered.

She nodded, and when she gave me the thumbs up, I crouched and took off, flaring my wings and rocketing up into the sky. I didn't need to flap them as much as I would if I was a bird, lift and momentum were built into the power, but it *did* help give me a little extra speed and control. Honestly, watching the other girls, they pretty much never used their wings while flying, which may be why I was so much faster than them. I did a spiral, and shot towards the ground, snapping up at the last minute. I heard a whistle, and I grinned, someone had liked that. I did a loop de loop into a barrel roll and blasted forward, beating my wings. The air streaked around me, and I felt the familiar tunnel of protection around me as I neared my top speeds. I arced my flight, going up higher and further until I was over the park, then I twisted around, letting myself fall, speeding up until I was almost to the ground. Just before I hit, I beat my wings backwards, making a shockwave, and settled onto the ground.

I panted for air, it had only been a short flight, but I'd put a lot into it, and turning and moving midair took a lot more energy than just flying straight, and I'd done a *lot* of moving. I was getting better though, when I first started flying on the farm last month, I'd eaten dirt several times trying to land, I was just glad I was steadier in the air now.

"Holy- aaagh, holy *shit*." gasped Forica as she ran up, sap beading on her wooden skin like sweat, "You flew too fast, I didn't- I didn't get the landing"

I shook my head, annoyed, but I *had* gone pretty fast. It was supposed to be my signature after all. "Yeah, that's fine, I'll do another one later. Can we get some shots around the lake though? I want to be seen in the air again soon, so Debbie doesn't get mad."

We took photos around the park for a while, getting a few with fans, as well as some of me flying over the water. Soon it was about time to head back to the square for the midday check-in.

"Hey, let's get one shot down there by that big storm drain outlet before we go" I said, pointing, "I can pretend I'm looking into it about to fight something."

"Uhh, I *guess* that could work?" Forica said, "It sounds kinda cringe, but we can try."

I bit back a comment at the usage of the word 'cringe'. I was supposed to be connecting to fans, and making fun of modern slang would just make me look old. I jogged down the hill to the mouth of the pipe and posed.

"How's this?" I asked over my shoulder.

"Yeah, let me just- oh, shit, fuck, *shit*" she gasped. I looked back to see her backing away from the opening. I frowned and peered in. She must have better eyes than me, I didn't see-

Three glowing yellow eyes glinted at me from the darkness and I drew my breath in with a hiss. A monster attack? A mutated fallen? A set of sharp, brilliantly white teeth bloomed into view as the eyes drew closer. I fumbled on my belt for my communicator to call for help, to let them know I was under attack. I braced myself for an attack as the thing stepped out of the darkness, large shapes unfolding around it, white and long, like legs or wings, or-

I blinked, and relaxed my guard. "Oh, um. Hi, Seraphim. I wasn't expecting you to be in a storm drain?"

She smiled, her sharp, pointed teeth clean and dangerous, and started re-wrapping her face with white cloth she'd been wearing last time as she walked over to me. Had she always had three eyes? She covered the one on her forehead with the bandage and I realized she must have been hiding it for some reason when we'd met a few days ago. It *was* pretty uncommon to see stuff like around here, up north it was a little more common, but *no* one went up north these days. Maybe she was from the wastes after all?

"Hello, Cand-" Her eyes flicked to Forica. "...Angel Rouge. I see you're out and 'in the air' today, I've been looking for you, and you found me instead. I wanted to discuss this place more with you."

"Uh, Candy do you know this scary homeless lady?" Forica said, keeping her distance.

"Yeah, kinda, she's... fine." I said. I didn't really know if she *was* fine, but I wasn't about to say that in front of *her*, she had a sword.

"What did you want to talk about?" I asked Seraphim, turning back to her.

"This place has inadequate woodlands, I was forced to take refuge in this strange round building. I wanted to ask, is there a place to set up my home for the time being while I conduct my search?"

I frowned. "Like a homeless shelter? We have a lot of those, you can-"

"No, someplace to *stay*, not to take shelter in." she said, correcting me, "I have... 'items' that need to remain stationary."

"Well, if you won't tell me what god you're following, I don't know of anywhere. I'd say you could stay at your god's church, but that doesn't really apply here." I said, shrugging.

"No, my god has no presence here," she said wistfully, "and telling you about him could be disastrous. One Sister flying around is one thing, but I've seen your forms of mass communication, this entire world would be infected with my god in a matter of hours if the wrong person was converted."

"Um, thanks for not telling me about your god then, I guess?" I said, confused. I'd never heard of someone referring to being converted as being 'infected' before, not even with the more dangerous gods.

"Why can't she just apply for a patrol, and take the option for new or unregistered gods and goddesses?" Forica suggested.

I looked over at her, surprised she knew about something like that. "Wait, what do you mean?"

She looked unsure. "You know, like, if you prove you have holy power, you legally *have* to be allowed to register as a Chosen if you want. So she could go to the GGDS office, be declared as a Chosen by showing her powers, put down a fake name as her god, and then apply for an area to patrol? They'd have to put her up in a base as part of the payment for the patrol since she legally needs an address. It'd be a shitty apartment or an office room or empty building or whatever, but it'd be something?"

Seraphim finished tying her bandages, but I could see her grin under them. "Ah, that's so... semantic." she hissed "I love it, come, let us go to the office!"

"I- I gotta do a job, and I have to go check in with Debbie." I said, not convinced.

"Well, let's head back and see what your bosses say, maybe you can go with her anyway?" Forica offered, "It sounds like you two are friends, so I'm sure if you explain, they'll let you head out for a few minutes."

I really didn't want to, but... I almost felt bad about leaving her here to be homeless. Almost. Still, this could be used to my advantage if i was smart about it. "Forica, could you follow us to the office and get some shots of me helping her? Maybe do like a 'helping the Chosen community' thing?"

She frowned. "Well, I was thinking you'd just, like, help your friend, but... I can do that, yeah."

"Perfect!" I said, "Let's head back and talk to Oori and Debbie!"

~~~

I stood in the line at the GGDS office and grumbled. Forica stood behind me, her mouth a thin line, not wanting to speak up.

"Now Miss Candy..." Oori said, "We knew there'd be a line when we headed out, there's no reason to complain like that, work with dignity, I say."

It wasn't the *line*, it was that there were no photos allowed. And and that Oori had tagged along to file our paperwork at the same time, and that he'd had the 'wonderful' idea to have Seraphim request to be assigned to our section too, so I'd 'have connections with the other heroes in the area'. This was *not* going how I planned at all, I'd
~~~

have just stayed at the square and done loops if I'd known it'd be like *this*.

"This card says my god's name is 'Lorem Ipsum', I don't wish to anger my god with false worship, could I scratch that part out?" Seraphim asked, looking at her ID card.

"No, just- it's not a real god, it doesn't mean anything, your god won't get mad." I said, exasperated, "It's a placeholder god, it means you're between gods at the moment."

She glared down at the card, but slipped it back into her sleeve anyway.

"So what's this line for?" Forica asked, "Is everyone here applying to the same section?"

"Oh, no, this is the line to be assigned a hearing." Oori said "We'll go to a separate room to present why we should be assigned that area, and we'll be compared with other hero teams who have requested to be assigned the same area. We're a shoo-in though, we have a headquarters there, and we don't need any additional funding from the GGDS."

"And myself?" Seraphim asked frowning, "I have neither of those things, and my 'god' is listed as a 'placeholder'."

"I'll, ah, put in a good word." Oori said, winking, "You *are* Candy's friend, after all."

There was that word again... I wish I'd said something, clarified that I didn't actually *know* this insane, scary, giant, glowing lady with a sword, but it was too late now. I folded my arms and sighed. The line couldn't go fast enough for me, and I was just so frustrated at even having to *be* here. I needed to be out there, getting more fans, every second I wasted was another second Alele was getting ahead of me.

Finally, after what felt like hours, we were called into a small room in front of a couple older agents with notepads. Oori showed them photos and diagrams of the building, our financial statements, as well as an example of our powers in action. He handed them the file and sat down giving me a small wink as he did, pointing at his foot. I was confused, what did- oh. 'shoe'-in. I groaned quietly, but gave him a polite smile. He really was kinda fun, when he wasn't being his usual work mode self.

"So, Mr Oori, From these documents, it's very clear that you'll be taking over as the primary patrol group from Creamy and Sliz in section 247, no questions there. They've been double-patrolling for months, they'll welcome the break. However, your companion, Miss, ah, 'Phim'? *She* is another matter." The agent on the left said, frowning at Seraphim's made up "real name'.

"Well, I was under the impression that since the current patrols would be leaving once there was a permanent solution, we *would* need more than just our team if we're going to patrol around the clock." Oori pointed out, "It'll be months before we can cut down to sporadic shifts, and we only have five members, so we can't do a full twenty four hour rotation without at least one person solo patrolling."

"Yes, I understand we need more help for 247." the agent sighed, "It's just she doesn't have any funding. We'd need to provide her a base of operations, and the *other* magical girl team that's going to be patrolling the area *also* had no funding or a base, so-"

"Wait, wait, *what* other magical girl team?!" I said, standing up partway from my seat. Oori pulled me back down by the skirt of my dress and frowned at me.

"I'm pretty deep into the MG fandom, and I wasn't aware there *were* any other new teams." Forica said, tilting her head, "Is this a transfer?"

"Ah, no. 'Magical girl' is a bit of a misnomer, really." the other agent said, "They call themselves 'The Unchosen', from what I understand, none of them are backed by a god or goddess, so they don't have any funding. They're part of a new movement by the city to show that anyone, not just Chosen, can be a hero."

"How did they even pass the test?" I asked, "Don't you need to have at least 3 D rank powers to form a team? How did they pass without powers?"

"That's classified," the agent on the right said, "I can't discuss their abilities, but I can say that they all tested well into the C rank range *without* any Chosen powers. We were quite impressed."

"So like," Forica cut in, "what about Sera? If she ends up testing as a C rank too, would you approve her?"

"That's the *minimum* rank required to be a solo hero, I personally would say she needs to be a B rank before we considered funding her, because of the two full teams already in the area." the left agent said apologetically.

Seraphim stood up and placed a hand on the hilt of her sword. "Well then. Let us start the tests! Who am I facing?"

Oori stood up and patted her arm. "Now, Miss Sera, they just need to get an idea of your powers, it's just going to be a few tests, no combat."

She frowned and shook her head. "I would rather face someone, but I can pass any test you present me with. I will outclass the heretics with ease."

One of the agents scrunched up his face. "Don't use the word 'heretics', if you please. And we can do the tests here on site, if you can just follow me..."

As Seraphim was led off to the tests I checked the clock in the room. If we got this over with fast, I could still get back and have 30 minutes of air time before we needed to get ready for the fancy dinner tonight...


~~~
~~~

Oori beamed and slapped me on the back, making me stumble slightly. "Wow, an A rank Chosen, in our pocket! I'm so glad you brought her to us, Candy." he said, nodding, "She's going to be *very* useful, I'm glad she's in our section of the city!"

I felt frustration and anger inside me as I walked with him back to city square. She'd gotten an *A rank*? Really? Just for being kind of strong, having a beam attack, and being good with swords? I was only officially C rank, but I was *pretty sure* I was almost as strong as her. Of course, with my power I was confident I could have tested as high as A too. Maybe B on a bad day, but I couldn't exactly *show* that to them to prove it unless they had someone on death row, and I was supposed to be keeping it a secret anyway. I could take Seraphim in a fight though, I knew it. She had to get close to use that sword of hers, and she had a lot of exposed skin on her hands, around her sides where her robe had holes in it, her midriff, I'd just need one touch and-

I blanched and shuddered. Was I really thinking that? She was supposed to be our ally, and I didn't even want to *use* my power in the first place. I felt a sick feeling of guilt. Was I that focused on my own fame and popularity that I'd fantasize about using my power on someone I was supposed to be helping? A lady who was obviously in need of support? I folded my arms across my stomach and looked around the square for Forica as we walked up. She'd headed out first, while me and Oori were finishing up our application, and she should be here by now. I spotted her talking to Galorna over by the Valley Nurses' tent, and I made my way over, feeling too drained and guilty to fly.

"Oh, Angel Rouge! We were just talking about you!" Galorna said, smiling at me as I walked up.

"Oh... you were?" I asked, unsure if that was a good thing.

"Yeah, I hear the fans love you, gonna get some more pictures? We've got a few minutes before we need to head into the church!"

I thought about it, and glanced over at Forica, who gave me a thumbs up.

"Um, no, we got a lot of photos of me already." I said. I really didn't want to be photographed while I was feeling this mixed up. "Do you think you could get photos of the other girls?" I asked Forica "Just get a nice picture of each of them, so all the fans remember we're all on a team, and we're working together."

"Oh, uh, yeah! I can do that, no problem. Uh, Miss Angel Saffron? Could you pose?" she said, mildly confused.

"Hey, no problem!" Galorna said, grinning "And you'll find Angel Verdant in the tent behind me, she got a little power fatigued, so she's resting. Angel Cobalt and Angel Sable are both in the square somewhere, you might have to track them down!"

Forica took the picture, and ducked into the tent to find Drizti. Galorna leveled a look at me and pulled me aside around the tent and spoke in a low tone.

"Candy, I get that you're trying to build a brand, but you can't just leave for half the mission like that, we *all* needed to be here and be seen."

"I-I was with Oori, at the GGDS office." I said, blushing. I had originally *gone* there to build my brand, yes, but it didn't work out, so Galorna didn't need to know that.

She glanced over at Oori, who was on the phone and directing a van that had just pulled up where to park.

"Did he need help? I'm glad you went, but-"

"No, I'm sorry, I met up with one of my-" I hesitated, then pushed through, "-friends, and she needed help registering, I think she's a new Chosen. She needed somewhere to stay, so I helped her get set up with the GGDS and get a patrol and a small building..."

"Oh..." Galorna said gently, "I'm sorry, that's sweet of you, I didn't know. I'm sorry for getting onto you about being gone. Helping the less fortunate is always the first priority."

"Well..." I said, "She *was* living in a storm drain, but she's also an A rank, so I'm sure she'd have gotten help soon, I shouldn't have blown off the first mission."

Galorna whistled. "Gods, an A rank? You don't see those often. But I think you still did good. If you hadn't helped her, she could have been helped by a fallen and gotten recruited, and then we'd have a new A rank threat in the city to deal with. You did the right thing, Candy, as a friend, and as a hero."

She carefully side hugged me and gave me an encouraging look. I felt worse than I did before, to be honest. I'd *lied* to her. I was still upset at Seraphim being so much higher rank than me, I was upset that I was upset. My plan had failed, I'd blown off the mission, I'd been selfish, I'd fantasized about basically killing someone who trusted me, and here Galorna was *praising* me for it all. My stomach was tight and there was a lump in my throat, what was I becoming? Was being this selfish and petty really necessary to be a magical girl?

"I- I need to go sit down, I'm sorry." I said to Galorna, giving her a polite, small smile, "I'm feeling a little tired."

"That's fine, head over to the church, we're almost done anyway, go ahead and rest up or get changed." she said, nodding.

I jogged out of the square and down the road the church was on, seeing it loom over the other buildings around it. It was a massive, tall cathedral with ornate carvings of flowers all over the walls and a three story stained glass picture of Lorgiaia on the front. It was the main church for Lorgiaia's Followers, but there were other, less impressive churches in her name spread all over the south west.

I stepped through the big double doors and was hit with the rush of cool air and the smell of cleaner and a vague scent of burning spices. I took a deep breath and relaxed. I hadn't been to the church since me and my mom visited to introduce me to the leaders a couple of weeks ago when I told everyone I was a Chosen. I should be going here once a month or so, to be seen in the congregation, but I still didn't know all the rules about the religion, and I didn't want to look like an idiot. A member of the church walked up to me and leaned in.

"Hello, Miss Clenson?" he said softly, as a question more than a statement. I nodded, and he waved me along. "Right this way, we have one of the study rooms set up as a changing room, and your clothes are already in there."

"Oh, th-thank you." I said. He'd recognized me on sight, that was kind of a strange feeling, but I'd have to get used to it as I got more famous. He led me alongside of the auditorium to a side passage to the room he'd set up for me, and I let myself in. I was going to wear my red dress with the flared skirt I'd bought with Alele and Drizti tonight, but I had a few hours to go before the big dinner, so I sat down in a large chair and un-transformed. I looked down at myself and sighed, stood up, and took off the dumb fake magical dress, draping it over the rack of clothes. I sat back down, the cool leather of the chair feeling good on my skin, and rubbed my head. I had a killer headache, but with the corset off, my stomach didn't feel as tight. The guilty feeling still stuck though.

I got a bottle of soda out of a little basket and sipped it while I looked at my reflection in the mirror that had been set up, and pulled at my cheeks. I looked worn out, tired even. Not a good look for someone about to go to a fancy dress ball. I stared into my own face, tracing the red on my lips with my eyes, the faint pink eye shadow, the blush on my cheeks. There was so much red on me, so much 'rouge'. I probed my lipstick with my tongue, but it didn't smear; it was waterproof and made to look and feel like it was a part of me. I thought of the blood pouring from the bite I'd taken out of Homicide, and imagined it staining my lips. If I ate him up whole, would I fill up with blood?

I lay my head back against the chair and thought about myself. I wanted popularity, I wanted to be loved, but did I really want to be the kind of person who wanted to be popular? I'd grown up being taught by movies and TV shows that 'popular girls' were stuck up pricks, but I'd been taught by real life that they were actually just people who you craved being around. The way I was going, I was going to be a TV popular girl and not a real one, and then I'd be everything I'd hated while growing up. I reached for my phone to check CirNet before remembering that it was still in the van, and sighed. I'd need to work on my public image later, but I really did want to be the kind of person people wanted to be around. Was that selfish of me though? Wanting people to want to be near me while knowing that it's actively dangerous to let them get close?

The door banged open and I jumped, covering my chest and pulling my legs up into the chair.

"Oh, hey Candy..." Drizti said dazedly, closing the door behind her, "I think me and you are sharing this room..."

She looked awful, her gray skin was more gray than usual, she was slouching, and she was moving like her muscles were killing her. I remembered what Galorna had said about her getting power fatigue and I got up out of the chair in front of the mirror and waved her over.

"You look really rough, were you helping with the clinic?" I asked, "I didn't know if you'd be doing much with them with how your power works..."

"Mm, no." she said, climbing into the chair and curling up on the seat, "I was making shapes with my powers, remember? Turns out making and moving the little orbs takes a tiny bit of energy from me directly, so doing it hundreds of times builds up, and suddenly I was on the ground, no mana left."

I pulled my party dress off the rack and stepped into it, pulling it up around my neckline and wiggling my arms in.

"I thought Lorgiaia powered our actual powers? Didn't Saara say that?" I asked, "How does that even work?"

"She does power them, I think." yawned Drizti, "But making the connection to her to use them still takes mana from us too, at least that's what the Valley Nurses told me."

"That sucks," I said, looking at her while I tucked my gloves under the sleeves, "were they able to help you at all?"

She shook her head. "No, they gave me an energy drink, but their powers don't really work like that. Field Dress said she could help me if she had leeches, but she'd been forced by their PR team to stop bringing them on missions with her."

I shuddered at the idea of leeches, and slid my tights off under my dress, replacing them with pantyhose.

"Can you dress yourself?" I asked, "If we're really really careful, I think I can help you, but..."

"I'll be fine." she said, sitting up and stretching, "I'm just tired and sore. I'll be sleeping in late tomorrow and skipping practice, but I'll be fine tonight for a few hours I think, as long as no one asks me to do math."

I snorted. "Why would anyone ask you to do math at a charity dinner?"

"I don't know, I just hope they don't. I couldn't even begin to think of how to do it." she said, smiling at me slightly.

"Ok, so... say... four times twelve?" I said as I passed her the forest green cocktail dress she'd picked out.

"I'd just guess." she replied, "A hundred and two, I don't know, don't make me think, Candy."

I felt myself smiling for real, just a bit. She always made my days a little bit more lighthearted, just by being herself. It was easy to see my teammates as rivals for my popularity, or just my supporting cast, but they were supposed to be more than that. Here was a real person sitting in front of me, someone who'd tried so hard to impress people that she'd passed out. Someone who was trying to respond to every single fan, no matter what, someone who was still brand new to the world outside her clan, and giving everything she had to be the best magical girl she could be. I felt my sense of self diminish, looking at her. She wasn't just another member of the team to plan around or analyze, she was a friend, they *all* were, and I needed to remind myself that through all the training and rehearsals.

"Hey, Driz?" I said as I put on my red dress flats. I never could walk in heels, hopefully no one would notice.

"Yeah?"

"You're a great magical girl, you inspire me. I just want you to know that." It felt cheesy and stupid saying it out loud, but she beamed at me anyway.

"We gotta inspire each other, friend!" she said, with more energy than she'd had since she walked in, "You inspire me too, that follower count, your dedication, making allies already from what I hear, I think *you're* an inspiration too!"

The feeling of guilt came back, and I tried to ignore it. "That's a good system, I think. I'll inspire you if you inspire me, ok?"

We shared a smile, and I thought about how shitty a magical girl I was as I finished getting ready.

~~~

"...and that's why I can say, with confidence, that Lorgiaia's Angels are going to take the city by storm! We're working hard and doing our best, and we've got a good team dynamic that brings us closer and closer together, every time we train or hit the streets!"

As the rich people around us cheered, I lightly sipped my champagne and rubbed my head. The headache hadn't stopped yet, but I was doing my best to hide it. Galorna's speech was... not the best.
~~~

She'd been in debate in high school, sure, but the speech sounded like it'd been *written* by a high schooler, to put it politely. I watched the crowd and picked at my food, some kind of fleshy flower with too much spice on it, hopefully dessert would be better. The others here were all wearing the face paint and ribbons, and I felt self conscious that me and the other girls weren't. Looking over at the crew's table, even Oori and Debbie had their paint on, but Oori at least still had his sunglasses on over it.

As Galorna's speech finished up, the room broke into applause, and she gave a thumbs up as she walked off the stage. She'd Chosen to wear a loose fitting white top with low cleavage tucked into yellow dress pants that flared around the ankles. When she walked off stage, she fluttered, giving her an almost ethereal look that clashed with her stocky body and muscles. I felt myself blushing, and looked back down at my food before my mind wandered.

"Awww..." Alele whispered to me, "Someone's getting all flustered, what's the matter, do you *like* girls that are stronger than you?"

I made myself smaller and shot her a look. "I think everyone likes that, Alele, it's not weird."

She giggled and shook her head. "You'd be surprised. That said, since you confirmed it, you know *I'm* stronger than you, by a lot, I have that elven strength.~"

I shook my head back. "I don't know what you're trying to do, I literally can't even touch you, flirting or teasing or whatever you're doing is pointless."

She sat back and pouted. "We could figure something out. It's been like, over two weeks, and no one is dating anyone yet. Most importantly, no one is dating *me*."

Galorna sat down just as Lucy looked over. "What are you two talking about?"

"Alele wants me to date her." I said bluntly.

"Hey- wh-" Alele sputtered, "No! I was- it's a thing we do, it was a callback!"

I narrowed my eyes at her. "So you're saying you're *not* interested?"

She glared at me, but didn't answer.

"I don't know if dating Candy is a good idea, Alele." Galorna said in that motherly tone she took when someone got hurt during training, "You wouldn't be able to do any of the things you'd want to do with her, you know."

"Oh for the love of the gods..." moaned Alele, "It. Was. *Banter.* Besides, I'm not JUST into people physically, I have emotions too, you know."

"You know," mused Lucy, "if Candy wore a wetsuit, like the kind divers wear? I bet-"

"Ok, shut up, everyone, drop it. I'm not about to listen to people speculate on my future 'love life' while I'm at the fanciest dinner I've ever attended." I snapped.

Drizti opened her eyes for the first time in a while and sat up off the arm of her chair. "Candy has a love life?" she said sleepily, "I'm so proud of you..."

"Lay back down, Driz" Galorna said, "She doesn't really, we're just talking."

I slid down in my seat, blushing hard. I didn't want or need this kind of attention right now, I was already all mixed up. Still, in a masochistic sort of way, the 'banter' was making me feel more at home, more like I belonged here with them. I needed to plan another get-together, the watch party had gone well, and I was surprised to realize that I actually wanted to do something like that again. Maybe I could have them over to play a racing game or something?

"I just wanted to thank you ladies so much for your hard work and dedication today!" an older man's voice said, disrupting my thoughts. I jumped, and slid back up into my seat, looking around.

A tall balding man in his 50s, dressed in black robes was standing next to Galorna, one hand resting on her shoulder.

"We were so happy to see such lovely, hard working girls Chosen to represent us." he said, "and seeing so many different lifestyles and backgrounds represented at this table! I truly think it'll bring a lot more unique followers to our church."

I felt a little awkward at that. After all, as a cis human woman I was the exact stereotype of a follower of Lorgiaia, so that last part obviously wasn't directed at me, but I still felt lumped in with the statement somehow. I wanted to say something, to let the others know that I wasn't trying to pretend that I was helping draw in new eyes as much as they were, but somehow saying anything would almost certainly make things *more* awkward than they already were for me.

Who was this guy anyway? He was acting like he was in charge, but I'd never seen him before, and he wasn't one of the priestesses, was he the event planner? I looked around to see if anyone else was dressed like him, but he was the only one in those strange robes. I'd ask Oori later, when I saw him again.

"Who are you, anyway?" Lucy asked, beating me to the punch, "Are you with the church?"

The man laughed, and smiled slightly. "You could say that, yes. You could say I've 'been with the church' quite a lot! You see, I'm Lorgiaia's current husband."

My eyes widened and I had to try not to gasp. "Her *husband*?" I asked, "I didn't know she was married."

"We try to keep it within the church, but yes!" he said, nodding, "She takes a new partner every thirty or forty years or so. I help her with the parts of being a goddess that require a human touch, I keep her grounded, so to speak. I was the one to convince her to finally choose heroes! She'd wanted to put it off until the 'fad died down', but I told her if she kept waiting, she'd just be left behind."

"Well, thank you for that?" Galorna said, unsure how to respond.

"No problem, girls. I'll leave you to your dinner now, I just wanted to personally thank and congratulate you." he said, "Oh, and save room for desert! It's some wonderful candied rose petals on an absolutely fantastic white cake! I think all of you will really enjoy it!"

As he walked off, I looked back down at my food and frowned. At first it'd seemed like the girls and I had been chosen for *who* we were, when we were first chosen. After his little revelation though, I wondered if we'd been chosen for *what* we were instead, in an effort to draw more people in. It was a gross feeling, like I wasn't really good enough by myself, like I'd only been chosen to fit the current demographic so the others' 'different lifestyles' wouldn't alienate the current members of the church. Was *that* why I was more popular than them? Not because I was more appealing or working harder, but because I was soaking up the preexisting demographic, while they were having to forge whole new paths?

I felt the guilt coming back, and I leaned back in my chair, my appetite gone and my mind full of worries and hurtful thoughts. I had a whole team around me, but I was still alone, still alien to them and their problems. I didn't fit, I was just the template Chosen to give boring kids a favorite hero, and nothing I could do would fix that or get rid of the gap between me and the other girls.

Chapter Ten

I walked a bit behind Lucy and Galorna, looking around for any 'crime' happening nearby. There was none, as it was 9AM on a Monday morning, and we were on the main road. The two ahead of me were chatting about an anime they were watching together, and not paying too much attention to their surroundings, but I didn't blame them. It was our first 'official' patrol of our new territory, so it was mildly important, but honestly, due to the low amount of patrols prior to us taking over (and us being in a generally outdated part of the city) there weren't usually people around here too often. We passed the corner story I'd gotten the food for the party at and I remembered that I still needed to buy more snacks if I wanted to have the girls over this Wednesday like I'd planned.

"Her, I'm gonna pop in here and pick up a few things, k'?" I said, interrupting their conversation.

Galorna looked confused. "We're on *patrol*, we're not supposed to be going shopping..."

"Well, we got snacks earlier, right?" I pointed out.

"I think that's different, we got bagels at a shop we were patrolling to eat while walking around. Carrying bags of groceries while looking for crime is unprofessional." she said, still not convinced.

"I guess so..." I muttered.

"Hey, I need to get food too," Lucy said, "I've been ordering out every day Saffron hasn't cooked for us, and that *can't* be healthy."

"Well, we can stop in here on the way back, but for now, we need to be on the lookout for crime." Galorna said, shaking her head.

I looked around, seeing a guy standing next to the building smoking a cigarette.

"Hey, you! Stop loitering!" I said sarcastically.

He flipped me off and shook his head. "That's how you new heroes are gonna be? Just out here harassing us?"

I sighed, annoyed at his attitude. I was here to *help* him, why be a butt to me? "No, I'm just- sorry, I was making fun of my teammate, I don't care what you do."

He glared at me, but didn't say anything else as we walked past.

"That *was* pretty rude. He was just minding his own business." Lucy pointed out.

"Yeah, well, whatever." I rolled my eyes. I looked down at the chai I'd gotten with my cinnamon sugar bagel. It'd gotten cold a while ago, and it was starting to taste bitter. "I need a trashcan, let me know if you see one."

"There's one over there, outside that pink building." Lucy said, pointing.

Pink building? I looked up, and saw that sure enough, there was a small warehouse painted bright pink with purple highlights. It looked garish and flashy, but there *was* a trashcan in front of it.

"Huh, I wonder what business that is," Galorna said, "we don't have public trashcans in our section yet, so they must be providing it themselves, that's nice of them."

"I'll check when I throw this away, let me see." I said, heading that direction.

I crossed the street, and dumped my tea into the road, dropping the cup and teabag into the trashcan after. I looked at the building. It had a small glass door covered in patterned paint, and a roll up door with tinted windows on it. There was no branding, no hours of operation, nothing to indicate that this building was anything more than a public art exhibit.

"I think it's privately owned?" I called back to Galorna.

I heard a chime, and I glanced back to see the door swung open, and a slightly chubby human witch peeking out. She looked like a character from an old cartoon, but not quite in a good way. Her hat was pink, rounded at the top with a lavender bow on just above the brim. She was wearing a pink cape over a white button-up and lavender pleated shorts, with white tights coming up her legs, ending halfway up her thigh, just under the hem of the shorts. Her chunky brown loafers completed the look of 'I wanted to look like a character from a kids show', bringing it all together.

"Hey, you're Angel Rouge!" the witch said, excited, "And that's Sable and Saffron!" She pointed across the street.

"Uh, hi, you are?..." I said politely.

"Oh, I'm Warrior Mage Blinding Crystal!" she said, "But you can call me Crystal! Or Kiri, if you like, my identity is public."

Ah, the fake magical girl team the GGDS told me about, ok.

"I'm guessing you're one of the other magical girls in the area?" Galorna asked as she and Lucy joined me on the curb.

Crystal beamed. "Yeah! We're not the *first* heroes to be un-Chosen, but we *are* the first team to made up of only un-Chosen members! Come inside, I'll introduce the girls!"

The four of us stepped inside and I stifled a frown. The interior was a work in progress to say the least. It'd *very* clearly been an auto mechanic's shop before these people moved in, and the layer of black dust on everything let me know they'd focused on making the outside of the building look nice first. Still, it'd only been a while since they were approved, so I'm sure they'd have it fixed up soon. She led us through the reception area into the garage area, which was broken into two sections and was brightly lit and open, looking naked without shelves of car parts or lifts in it.

"This is the base!" she said proudly, "We're all going to be donating a third of our paychecks to fixing it up until it looks like a real HQ!"

Lucy looked around. "Hey, I like how tall the ceiling is, that's cool."

"Yeah, we're planning on putting in a second level, for storage and stuff." a new voice said. I looked over to the other section, seeing a dryad walking out of the door to the other section, tying a top on around her ribs. She was shaggy, branches and what looked like vines growing off her limbs like overgrown hair, the foliage on her head looking similar to gray-green dreads that covered most of her face. She was wearing very little, just the tied top, and cutoff shorts, no shoes or accessories.

"Oh, this is Mourner!" Crystal said, pointing, "She's a weeping willow, so she can grow fast and use her branches to whip people, she's really good at it!"

"It's nice to meet you, Mourner." I said politely. I didn't see how a regular dryad with no extra powers could pass the certification test at a C rank, but if she *could*, I had to be impressed.

"Hey, everyone out, the competition's here!" Mourner yelled over her shoulder into the other room.

"No, we're not anyone's competition, we're looking forward to working with you, actually!" Galorna said, unsure of herself.

"Aw, she's just being dramatic, it's fiiine!" Crystal said, "We want to work with you too! Magical girls are the BEST, which is why we registered as that instead of a standard team!"

"So, is that why you're dressed like that?" I asked, "Is that your team's uniform?"

"No we each make our own uniforms, we- oh!" she perked up. "Here's the others!"

I glanced over at the other 2 members that'd walked in and jumped, gasping. One of them was a literal *cockroach*, her proportions stretched and twisted into a humanoid shape, with an almost human face other than the spines and cheek ridges, all black, brown, and shiny. Her mouth split vertically and horizontally at the same time, sharp needle-like teeth poking out from under, with a clicking set of mandibles over top the opening. Her 'skin' across her whole body was shiny and segmented, broken up with dull green lines, and covered in sharp bristly spikes along the backs of her limbs.

She had two sets of arms, both bent at impossible angles, and her legs had too many sections, bending backwards at one point before ending in clawed, splayed 'feet'. Her 'shell' started around her neck-line, the joint hidden by her stringy, greasy black hair, and continued across her whole back, ending around her butt. It fluttered slightly, letting me know there were wings inside, but at this size, I doubted they were functional. Her antenna curled around her face and twitched as her wide, impossibly large eyes watched us with an uncomfortable number of pupils forced into the irises.

She was wearing a short, tattered gray denim skirt, a necklace with a heart on it, and several chunky bracelets on each arm, the plastic and cheap metals clinking with each movement. It took me a second to realize she was technically topless, as you don't usually expect a roach to wear any kind of clothing, but aside from a slight curve in her carapace, she was featureless up top.

I couldn't look away, my eyes were locked onto her, soaking up every detail. It was a struggle to remain calm, insects were one of my biggest fears, and to have one walking around at *this* size, twitching its parts and watching me, I could feel my heart rate going up.

"Oh, Amaryllis, you forgot your mouthpiece again, you're scaring them." the second new member said, pointing back through the door. The lack of a 'mouthpiece' wasn't why I was on the verge of freaking out...

As 'Amaryllis' left, I was able to tear my gaze away and look at the other member, and was equally confused, if not far less disgusted. She was... artificial, in some way. Her body was made up of mismatched parts, mechanical or similar, with her torso and thighs being smooth pink plastic of some kind, and her lower legs being more rugged yellow construction grade limbs. Her left arm was raw gears and wires, moving and clicking constantly, ending in a clumsy three handed claw, and her right hand looked like one of the higher grade prosthetics I'd seen models use in photo shoots. She had large round pipe-like objects sticking out of her upper back, two on each side, the same tone and shade as her torso.

Her face looked like a porcelain mask, but emoted the same as a real face, and her metallic elven ears jutted up and out to the back instead of to the sides, like the art I'd seen made of fairies from before they went extinct. That, coupled with her small nose, which didn't extend out into a point like an elf's would, made her seem alien, almost uncanny. Her 'hair' was in a bob, and was a hard shell of metal, shaped to curl under her chin and stay off her neck. I noticed with some embarrassment that she wasn't wearing *any* clothes. Although, she didn't really need any, being... some kind of robot?

"I-I'm Angel Rouge." I offered, looking at the robot, "It's nice to meet you?"

She looked us over. "I'm Maud, but my 'hero name' is Mod, it's nice to meet you too! The lady who had to step away is Amaryllis, but she goes by Panic Attack in the field."

"Panic Attack?" Lucy asked, "So does she have the power to make people panic?"

I knew she had the ability to make *me* have a panic attack...

"None of us have powers!" Crystal said proudly, "We're all just us! I use magic that I learned from my grandmother, Mourner uses her natural dryad growth skills, Panic Attack is fast and can fly a little and is very good at close up combat, and Mod was built to be a next-gen military robot, so she's got all *kinds* of useful tricks!"

"Wait, like, one of the drones you see going into the folds?" Lucy asked, "That's badass. But I thought humanoid 'bots weren't *allowed* to have sentience?"

"We're *not*." Mod said, "That's why my creator was killed by the cops, and I was left unfinished. I was just a head, torso, and spare parts rotting in a warehouse until Amaryllis found me while out for food."

"So... Amaryllis... What- how- I mean, I don't-" I said, trying not to be rude, but desperate for answers.

"I was in Canyon City when the attacks hit." an artificial, hollow voice said. I looked at the door to see Amaryllis with a metal mask over her mouth, the words coming from a built-in speaker. Somehow, it sounded more robotic than the actual robot's voice... "I was a shut in, I didn't evacuate in time. I didn't even know about the dimensional rift until after the leaking energy field had blended my body with the roaches in my apartment. Couple other things too, but mostly roaches. I found Maud and fixed her up with whatever I could find, then we got out of the city and over the walls with her jets."

"Oh, fuck, you were IN Canyon City?" Lucy said, shocked, "You *stayed* in canyon city? Holy *fuck*, I'm surprised you lived, *that's* badass."

It explained a lot, that's for sure. I had *thought* she was a mutation experiment gone wrong, or an abomination at best, but to have survived Canyon City? I wondered if her name was on the memorial, or she'd gotten out before it went up. I tried not to look directly at her as she walked up, but tried not to let it look like I was avoiding eye contact. It was a tricky balance.

"So... this is us!" Crystal said, posing, "We'll be giving you support in the area, and that other hero who's around here too!"

"Well, I think it's more accurate to say 'we'll be working together', I'm sure you're going to be just at important to the area as us, you're more than just our backup!" Galorna said encouragingly.

"We'd better be." said Mourner under her breath.

"Oh, while you're here, can we get some advice? We have a patrol tonight, after six." Crystal explained, "We were discussing who should go out on it, we wanted two members out, and two here to rest up for tomorrow morning's patrol, how did you guys pick who to go out?"

"We just kinda took volunteers?" Lucy said, "We didn't think about it."

"We really *should* have though." I said, looking at them, "I mean, Saffron could patrol on her own, but even together, Cobalt and Verdant would have a tough time if there's trouble. You should have stayed home on this one, Sable, gone out later with the other two."

"We're just doing a general sweep for now, I'm sure it's ok." Galorna shrugged, "Anyway, as for *your* team," she waved at Crystal. "I think pair an attacker with a tactical to start off, right?"

"We aren't classified like that." Mod said, "We're all just 'whatever'. No powers, remember?"

"I think we should just flip coins..." Mourner said, shaking her head, "We're tough enough by ourselves, any two of us is a good combo."

"Well." I said, anxious to leave the room with the giant talking cockroach, "You guys figure that out, it was nice to meet you!"

Crystal looked at me, concerned. "Oh, are you leaving? I wanted to show you my magic..."

"Well, we *are* on call!" Galorna said, backing me up, "We'd love to meet up sometime though, you know where we are, and I'll get our agents to get in contact with you about any team-ups!"

"Well, um, bye, then! It was so nice to meet you!" Crystal said, disappointedly waving.

"I look forward to seeing you again, and I hope we can work together soon." Amaryllis followed up, her voice box making the words sound flat and insincere. I tried not to flinch, and I think I was mostly successful.

We stepped out of the building and walked a ways away in silence. I waited until we were a block away before I spoke up. "Ok, so that was *horrifying*, right?"

Galorna made a humming noise "Mmm, well, it was unexpected. I'm surprised the roach abomination and the android were even allowed to take the test, legally I think they're not supposed to be heroes?"

"Well they can't kill someone for existing, and *I* thought they were *all* super cool." Lucy said defensively, "They survived Canyon City?! Are you kidding me? That alone makes them cooler heroes than us."

"They're *not* cool." I said, "They're a poorly put together collection of second rate misfits that'll get ignored at best, and actively scare people at worst."

"That's unfair, only uhh Amyrellis? was scary, the others were fine." Galorna said.

"It's 'Amaryllis', it's a flower name, and no, the robot was scary too?" I pointed out, "All the wrong parts, and exposed insides? I'm just saying, I vote we avoid them."

"I liked Mourner and Maud a lot..." Lucy said, "I was looking forward to getting to know them."

"We don't even know Mourner's *name*, or anything about her," I protested, "I'm just saying, we need to stay away from those girls."

"Rouge, you're being dramatic." Galorna said, "We're going to get to know them better, and we *will* be working with them, we're in the same section of the city, you can't just decide you're 'not ok' with them."

I huffed. They creeped me out, they felt off, and I didn't want to be anywhere close to Amaryllis, ever again. I could just imagine her needle sharp teeth biting into my neck, her weird arms with the jagged hook things on the backs tearing into me, her *twitching* and *chittering*. I felt nauseous just thinking about it. I didn't even know if my powers would work on a bug, so I'd be at her mercy. Mod was ok, my powers absolutely wouldn't work on her though, and the whole team made me feel uncomfortable, like I was being judged or something. Regardless, they were too weird and too freaky to get any traction, so they'd just fade into the background, and end up being forgotten by people as a whole, just our backup patrollers. Speaking of other patrollers, I wanted to check in on something while we were out.

"To change the subject, do either of you know where we can find Seraphim?" I asked, "I wanna see where she's located, and see if I can get any contact information from her."

"Why the fuck would *I* know where your friend was?" Lucy asked, confused, "You're the one who took her to the GGDS office, right?"

"I- well, I didn't stay to see where she's stationed." I said, not wanting to admit I'd left in a huff after hearing her test score.

"Uhh, I think it's in our files, but I can't check them from my phone." Galorna appologized, "I didn't think about checking up on her."

I pulled out my phone from my pocket. That I had. In *this* dress at least. Gods, I loved my actual magic dress, I couldn't wait until I could stop wearing the fake one. "I'll call Driz, she'll be awake by now, I'm sure."

I dialed her, and waited on her to pick up. After a few rings, a groggy, confused Drizti answered the call.

"Candy? W-what's the issue? Uuhg, hang on..."

I heard her slurp something, and get back on the line.

"I just woke up, is everything ok?"

"Yeah, sorry, we're all good, I thought you'd be awake already, sorry."

"Mmm, I was up late arguing with some of the fans on my phone. They were saying some very nasty things and the ones who weren't nasty still wanted attention..."

Yeah, social media wasn't treating her well at all, and I'm betting she was still under the weather from Saturday, too.

"Hey, listen," I said, "we were wondering if you could maybe go to the main computer and pull up Seraphim's new place? We were gonna stop by while we're out, and try and find a way to communicate with her."

"Oh, sure, I can do that." Drizti said, more awake now.

I heard the sound of her power activating, and doors opening and closing. I waited, and before long, she read me the address the GGDS had given us for Sera's new HQ.

"Thanks, babygirl, you should go back to bed now though." I said, "And maybe stay off CirNet?"

"I would, but I've got over a hundred new things to check since I went to bed." she said sadly, "Maybe after I reply to them all I'll get a nap?"

"Mm, yeah, maybe so." I wasn't about to get into this with her right now, I had my own stuff to do.

We said our goodbyes, and I hung up, waving at the girls to follow me. "We're not too far, it's a few blocks over."

"We're like, a couple blocks from everything in our section, honestly." pointed out Lucy.

"Well, it's a section, so... it's 20 blocks by 20 blocks, so it could have been *kinda* far, if it was on the other side of the section." Galorna countered.

"It's pretty close to the middle, it looks like we'll pass our building, actually, or close to it." I said, "A few streets up, but I think they flanked us with Seraphim and The Unchosen?"

"Shit, they really *do* consider her a full team by herself then, I guess." Lucy said in an impressed tone.

"Ok, whatever, she's strong. Can you transform so we can fly over there?" I said, turning to Galorna, mildly annoyed.

"I'd rather have boots on the ground for our first walkthrough." she said, "Really understand our area, we can do fly-overs another time."

"Ugh, look, there's a dumpster, there's graffiti, a few faded fliers, there's a boarded up building, there's a clogged storm drain, there's a scary alley that looks like someone's waiting in it to murder us." I pointed stuff out as we walked "This is 247, it's just an empty, run down, mostly abandoned part of the city. The road our building is on? The one that leads to city center? That's the only road with anything worthwhile on it."

"That's the road with the bagel place, yeah." remembered Lucy, "Hey, the grocery place isn't on that road though?"

"There's a lot of work to do here, yeah, but once we're here constantly, people will feel *safe*, and they'll come back." Galorna growled, "I know it's a shitty part of the city, I'm sorry we can't have a giant building in the square like the Queens, but this is what we got. Do you actually *want* to do your job, Rouge?"

I flushed. Not really, I wanted to get famous, get popular, and stay out of danger.

"Of course I do!" I protested, "I was just saying there's nothing here, not even like, people selling magic goblin herbs or anything."

"I thought those were legal now, anyway?" Lucy said "Shit, are they not? I might have to delete a couple posts..."

"They're legal, they always were, for goblins. They're just legal in general now, it's fine." Galorna said, "Rouge, I know none of us are the best at this yet, but I think you need to stop making everything feel so... I don't know..."

"Urgent?" Lucy offered.

"No, but something like that." Galorna said, "You just seem to want something, so bad, but I can't figure out what, or why. I *thought* you wanted to be the best magical girl you could be, you were great at the meet and greet, but you feel hard to get close to, and you keep pushing, but no one is pushing back. Like when you left the first patrol to register Seraphim, or when you hired your own social media person, or just now when you told us not to work with The Unchosen. You're trying so hard to push ahead of something, but there's nothing there, just please, calm down, stop *pushing.*"

"What do you mean 'pushing'?" I asked, "I'm just trying to get through all this, I'm not in an ok place right now."

I was pushing? No, *she* was pushing, pushing *me*. She needed to just shut up and let me do my thing, not poke at me, not try to figure me out, just leave me alone, and let me do things my way, and it'd all work out.

"You come off as closed off sometimes..." Lucy murmured, "And you *do* maybe do stuff without talking to us about it. You feel aloof, to me at least, like you're keeping us away."

That was it, time to use my trump card.

"Yeah? Well maybe I try to keep everyone away because if I touch them *they die*." I said, loud and angry, "I have a full grown man in my fucking mini fridge who'll never get to live life again, and you wonder why I keep people away? Why I do my own thing? Really?"

"...I- fuck..." Galorna muttered, "Ok, yeah. I'm pretty torn up about that night too, but I get it, at least I can still touch people, I get it."

I decided to drive the point further. "You know I'm still a *virgin?*" I said coldly, "I'll never know a lover's embrace, I'll never have a real kiss, just a dumb prom kiss from some guy I was only pity dating."

"Maybe if you used a plastic bag, you could-" started Lucy.

"Sable, hush, not the time." Galorna said softly, "I'm sorry Rouge, I was putting too much weight on your actions and not enough weight on your situation. I'd love to help you get through this, any way I can."

I was glowing inside, the guilt at using my 'condition' to get away with being called out for being a manipulative, selfish bitch clashed with the knowledge I'd gotten away with it mixed into a shitty pool of satisfaction. I wallowed in the feeling of being a bad friend, letting the self pity and loathing fill me up, hot and burning inside. I thought about Drizti, so sweet and kind, and how I barely let her in, about Alele and her obvious crush on me, about Lucy and her gender issues I was pretending didn't bother me, and about Galorna, who was just trying to be the best team mom she could be. I thought about how I wasn't a part of their group, I was just a faker, a pretender who'd slipped in and *used* them, and my eyes filled with tears. Why was I so shitty? Why was I being shitty now? I knew it, I wanted to stop, could I stop?

"Oh... Candy..." Galorna whispered, "It's ok, it's ok, I got you..."

She'd noticed my tears, and assumed they were for my loss of human contact, which they were, in a way, but I'd lost *that* before I even got my power. She rubbed my shoulders, being careful not to touch my skin, and tried to say comforting things to me. The fact that I was 'tricking' her into thinking I was upset about my power even more than I had been before made me cry harder, and I felt even worse. I clung to the feeling of rot inside, and for a second, considered messaging Forica to take down the photos, to just let me fade away, but a chill went through me at that. Even in this state, I was still desperate to be popular, to be famous enough to limit my hero work to 'selling merch and inspiring little girls'.

"Uh, I'm not great at this stuff yet, but like, I still think you're cool, I didn't mean to be mean..." Lucy said awkwardly, "I'd keep people away too, if I did what you do."

"I-I'm *trying* to get closer" I sniffled, "I was going to have another party on Wednesday, I want to be closer to you all..."

I really, really, did. I didn't want to feel so alien and outcast, but I couldn't help but seeing myself as an outsider for some reason. I saw them as equal parts rivals and teammates, and that just wasn't fair, especially after what I'd realized at the dinner, about the 'demographic choices" that got them on the team.

"Let's just finish up our patrol, we'll go see Seraphim, and head back to the base, ok?" Galorna said, "And I'd love to see you host another party, that was a blast."

"Uh, me and Galorna watch tv almost every night..." Lucy said "Maybe you and Driz or Alele could start a show?"

"Hero names, Sable." reminded Galorna, "Scheduling will be harder now with our patrols, but you could do something like that, yeah." she said encouragingly, "I'd invite you to join us, but we're already over a season into our show."

"Y-yeah, it's ok." I said, wiping my eyes. At least I knew magical makeup couldn't smear from crying. "I can figure something out. I'm sorry I lost it there."

"You're going through a lot, you're ok." Galorna said, taking her hands off me, "Now come on, let's go see your friend, ok?"

We walked in silence towards the area Seraphim was supposed to be in. I felt good, I'd cried it out, and I was pretty sure I could stop being so much of a bitch, I hoped. I really, *really* needed to work hard on it though. I'd been mostly closed the whole time I'd been here, and opening up to anyone other than Drizti was going to be hard. I needed that connection though, the team needed me, kind of. Maybe not as much as they needed the rest of the group, but I *was* the one who was drawing in the largest audience, and- Fuck, there I went again. I needed to sit at home and think things over a lot after this.

Before too long, we stood in front of a standalone building, an abandoned house by the looks of it. I walked up to the gray, peeling door and knocked. There was a loud crash, and the sound of running feet, and the door burst open, Seraphim standing in the doorway. She was wearing a kind of white tunic instead of her usual robe-skirt thing with the holes and slits, and her face was un-bandaged. She looked me up and down, and her nostrils flared as she hissed in air, her third eye moving seemingly at random.

"Angel Rouge! You've found me once more, and you're in distress, how can I help avenge you? Who hurt you and made you weep?" she said, peering around me at the others waiting on the sidewalk.

"N-no, I was just- I was having emotional problems with the other girls, I'm ok now." I explained, "Can we come in? We wanted to talk."

She looked back over her shoulder, then shook her head. "No, I have already set up the altar, and it's blasphemous and dangerous to let nonbelievers into one of these churches. We can speak here."

I looked past her into the darkness, other than the light of a computer- one probably given to her by the GGDS, there was nothing visible, just the slight sound of something wet dripping slowly, and... low, heavy breathing?

"Ah, yeah. Hm. That's fine. Look, we were just looking to get your schedule, and exchange info for team-ups or emergencies. You didn't answer me about CirNet last time, but-"

She lit up. "Yes! I have a document for you!"

She ducked behind the door, letting it swing open slightly, letting the light in. Red vines and branches spread across her floor, leading to something just out of sight. I felt a sense of sickening allure, and leaned in to get a better look.

"No heretics in the church!" Seraphim said firmly, stepping in front of me to block my path and my view, "Here is the document I was told to give you."

I looked at the sheet of printed paper she'd given me. It was weirdly dirty, but it came from the GGDS, and it explained her schedule, her CirNet profile, and let me know she'd been assigned an agent who I could contact. Apparently Sera herself currently refused to use anything with a screen.

"Ok, so I text this person, and they call you?" I asked, "Couldn't I just call you?"

She looked at the paper and frowned. "I do not have a calling utensil, the machine receives the calls, and I speak to it."

"The machine?" I asked.

"The round one that glows and tells me a countdown to my next quest, yes."

She must mean her computer, it sounded like they'd put it into some kind of baby mode and set it to auto answer calls once they realized she had no idea what it was.

"*I* can't call the machine then?" It'd be very annoying to have to call the GGDS, then be transferred over to her every time we needed her for something.

"That is something to ask the person, I'm not aware." she said, sounding vaguely embarrassed at her lack of knowledge.

Maybe I could help her learn technology in my spare time, have her over and train her while- I pushed the idea out of my head for now. I needed to focus on *my* team, not this lady.

"Ok, um, I'll call then, and figure it out. So do you have a patrol soon? Or...?"

"The next quest is..." she looked behind the door, "...in two hours. Then I'll take to the skies and slay anyone who tries to harm the sanctuary of my domain!"

"Ok, so, don't slay them, just like, beat them up? Slaying is usually frowned upon." I said. Was she really planning on killing people?

She frowned. "Even the cursed ones?"

I shook my head. "I have no idea what a 'cursed one' is, but no, please don't kill anyone."

She pointed at Galorna. "She is a type of cursed one. A rare one to be fair, but I can still smell her cursed blood."

Ohhh, she was *racist*. "Nnnnno, people like that aren't cursed, they just look different, people used to think they were evil, but we found out they weren't actually, like over a hundred years ago."

She hummed. "Well, I'd never *met* a cursed one before I came here, so I will defer to you. I will not kill any evil people, even if they're cursed."

She didn't quite get it, but as long as she wasn't killing...

"Ok, whatever. I gotta get back to *my* quest, but I'm sure I'll see you around, ok?"

She gave me a sharp toothy grin. "Very well, I'll see you in the skies, then!"

I gave her a thumbs up and headed down the stairs.

"Oh, Angel Rouge?" She called out.

I turned around. "Yeah?"

"You mentioned having issues with your team. Please be careful, where I'm from, Sisterhood is the most important thing, the most valuable treasure to cherish."

I nodded, and walked back to the others. 'Sisterhood'. Made it sound like she was from a cult or something instead of just a weird church. Actually, thinking about it more-

"Hey, how's your friend?" asked Lucy, jarring me out of my musings "I saw her pointing at us, did she want to meet us?"

"Uh, no, she's just new to the area, and hadn't seen anyone like Saffron before." I explained. I wasn't *lying*, I was just avoiding a tricky topic, that still counted as me trying to get closer, right? They'd like me even *less* if they thought I was friends with a racist.

"Ah, ok, that's fair." Galorna said, "We should have her over sometime, I want to meet her, from what I've heard, she's pretty cool." She looked at the sheet of paper in my hands "Did you get her info?"

"Yeah, she won't use a computer or phone for some reason, so she gave us a printout of the schedule, and a number to call so someone can get in contact with her if we want to talk."

"That seems annoying, I'd just fly over here..." Lucy said, "Why can't she use a phone or whatever?"

I shrugged. "I don't know, she's from 'far away', and doesn't understand a lot of stuff. Anyway, it's been like, four hours since we got those bagels, can we get a snack or something? There's a tea shop around here somewhere..."

"Absolutely, and I'm impressed with you two, holding your transformations that long!" Galorna said, "You can de-power any time though, it's up to you."

I thought about my pockets; my phone, my mints my commonplace book, my earbuds, my wallet, the gun I still hadn't turned in yet... There was too much useful stuff that'd be stuck in hammer space if I turned back.

"I'm good." Lucy and I said at the same time, for totally different reasons.

We made eye contact, and started laughing, it wasn't *funny*, but it felt nice. I left the smile on my face as I led them back to the main road, I was already doing better, right?

Chapter Eleven

"I'm just saying, I'm still not sold on this idea..." I complained, kicking the water reservoir I was leaning on

"Well, me and you can't really hold our own if anything serious comes our way, so we kinda need her to run backup?" Alele pointed out. "There's been three fallen fights in the city so far tonight that ended wrong for the Chosen, we don't know if they'll show up here. I think having her on patrol with us is fantastic."

"I just don't want to have our two teams mixed like this." I yawned, "Also, I should have ended the video game party *way* earlier last night, I forgot I was on night shift tonight..."

"I think *you* should have pulled an all-nighter, and slept during the day." Alele said, "That's what I did, and I feel fine."

"You're *also* drinking your third energy drink of the evening and we've only been here for half our shift." I pointed out "What if you need to pee? There's no public bathrooms around here."

She shrugged. "I'll head back to that 24/7 corner shop I guess. Buy a stick of gum or something."

"I still think you should pace yourself..."

She snickered. "Oh, pace myself like you paced yourself last night?"

I glared at her. "What?"

"I lapped you like 3 races in a row, hell, *Verdant* lapped you once, and she didn't even know how to hold the controller."

"Look, I invite you into my home, let you play my video game, use a character and kart I'm not used to using to be nice, and all you can do is make fun?"

She lightly punched my shoulder. "Pretty much. Never take a handicap, if you race, you race for blood."

"...Next time, I'm using my main and kicking your ass."

"Yeah, but good luck kicking Sable's ass, gods, I was kind of expecting her to be good? But it was still impressive."

"Saffron mentioned she used to be a streamer, I think. She played a lot of games..." I said, watching the streets below us, "Anyway, we should go find Kiri and do some more actual patrolling. It's been over an hour since we told her we would do a flyover."

"Fiiiiine, if we have to." Alele said, dragging out the word and waving one hand as she crushed her now empty can with the other

"I thought you *liked* her being on our patrol?" I asked, flaring my wings and lifting up off the roof.

"Yeah, but it doesn't mean I like *her*. She's all... bubbly and innocent. I try and flirt and she just looks disappointed in me, and makes me feel kinda creepy."

"Maybe you should take that as a sign to not flirt with everyone you meet then?" I suggested.

"I know, but it works sometimes!" she said, poking me pointedly as she joined me in the skies.

"What, with me? It didn't work, we're literally not dating." I said, gliding forward as I looked for Crystal's pink hat.

"Just because we can't snuggle doesn't mean we weren't made for each other, Rouge." Alele pouted.

I sighed. Her flirting had been getting less and less joking the longer we knew each other, and it ramped up when we were alone now that she wasn't scared of me anymore. I didn't *mind*, I liked her, but I needed to get things straight between us. "Look, Cobalt, I know you're-"

She grabbed my arm and yanked me down to her, my body clashing into her as we spun in the air. My mind jolted, was I touching her? I didn't *think* I was, my gloves went all the way up, and my head was pulled away, but still why was she risking so much for a hug? She *knew* what I could-

A blue blast of light blew past us, chasing us through the air as we fell before trickling off into wisps and fading away. We were under attack, out of nowhere, who takes pot shots at heroes? I pushed away from Alele and looked around for the source of the blast, it'd come from a few streets over, and I couldn't see what had caused it from this angle. I flew up to get a better look, and felt a hand grip my leg through my tights. I glanced down, Alele's face was stricken, and she had tears in her eyes.

"I need to see where it came from, Kiri could be in danger!" I said, annoyed.

"N-no, Candy, it's too dangerous!" Alele said, "It took the entire top half of your body clean off!"

I dropped back down in shock, even the Fallen usually didn't have powers like *that*. Sheer destruction was rarely something the gods wanted, and those that did want it were turned on by the others.

"Oh... this is round two?" I said, stupidly trying to wrap my head around the fact that I'd apparently just died.

She nodded, and pointed away. "We need to get back, we need to call the Queens or the Children of Battle, we can't do *this*. Whatever did that, it tore through you like you weren't there, and you're *transformed*, this could level *buildings*, it's easily a B rank threat!"

I thought about dying, and how little I wanted to do that. I shuddered, and shook my head. I was trying to be *better*. Running away and ignoring the threat was about as shitty of a thing a hero could do... And anyway, it'd look *terrible* to my fans.

"No, come on, Alele. We've gotta go." I said firmly, "You stay back, stay safe, I'll use my earpiece, and go in. If I die, rewind, and tell me how to avoid it, got it?"

She blanched. "Oh, gods, I don't want to have to watch you die like that..."

I gritted my teeth at her. "I'll be *fine* if you tell me what to do, look, do you want to be on the morning news? Or do you want Lady Cleaver or someone to be on the news, in *our* territory, showing off *her* latest kill instead of us?"

"Being on the news isn't worth-" Alele started.

I ignored her, taking off around the buildings at an angle, hoping to catch the mystery blaster from the side. Alele shrieked and took off after me, following a ways behind. I heard her mic pop in my earpiece as she switched it on, and I tried not to think about the other versions of me that were most likely about to die. The blast sounded again, and a blue glow flashed from behind a couple of the buildings to my right, but I didn't see the beam. Was the person shooting at random? Or...

I rounded the corner, and Alele's voice shouted at me. "Up, up! Fly up!"

I instantly changed course as the beam shot under me, slamming into a building behind me and melting a hole in it. I looked down to see a man in a blue outfit with a large gun, hooked up to a massive, glowing battery pack on his back. I didn't recognize him, so he was either new, a lower rank nobody, or he was un-Chosen using a super scientist's tech. Across the street from him was a pink dome, cracks branching out from the center, burn marks splashed all over the ground around it. Inside it was Warrior Mage Blinding Crystal, her hands on the ground, coughing up pink, oozing slime that flew to the walls of the dome to patch the cracks.

Well, *she* couldn't survive another hit. I didn't want another one of her team to start patrolling with us instead, so I had to act fast. I shot straight down towards the man in blue, picking up speed, and I aimed for his face.

"Left!" Alele yelled, and I ducked as a beam blew past me, taking a little of my skirt with it. It would heal itself after a few minutes, but that was *much* too close. He lined up another shot, and I flipped over, my glossy, hard black Mary-Janes feeling like a better option than my hands at this point. I didn't want to stain my gloves, after all.

"Duck down!" Alele commanded. As I did, she continued, "...and don't let him fall on the battery pack!"

Fuck. I re-adjusted my angle as the beam flew over me, and I felt my shoe slam into the side of his face, and I drove him downwards, slamming him over sideways onto the asphalt. His head smacked the ground with a popping noise, and I stepped off him as we landed.

He wasn't moving, so I quickly grabbed the backpack battery and yanked, pulling it off him, and dragging the gun away with it. A shattering noise sounded out from across the road, and I looked up to see Crystal stepping over the remains of her shattered protective shield to come over, bits of pink shards still on her hat and in her hair.

"Who *is* this guy?" she asked, walking up, "I saw a blast from a street over, and ran up to see him aiming this gun at the sky. Was he shooting at you two?"

I felt for a pulse, but didn't feel anything. Which, admittedly, didn't mean anything; I was wearing gloves, and had no idea how to check a pulse.

"I know as much as you, Kiri." I said, "I was looking for you, and apparently this guy killed me, Alele saved me."

Crystal's eyes widened. "Ohmigosh you *died?*"

"Four and a half times so far." Alele said shakily, landing behind me and carefully patting my arm, "*My* job is making sure she doesn't *stay* dead."

"Half? What was the half time?" I said.

Alele pointed to the backpack. "The last shot he got off. The first time it killed you, the second time you dodged it, but the backpack exploded when you slammed him into the ground and burned you up really bad. The third time is what this version of you experienced."

"Wait..." Crystal said, "Is it like pre-cognition?"

Alele frowned. "No, it actually happens, I just send my mind back in time. So I just watched her die for real, like, maybe 5 times."

I really, really didn't want to think about that. Drizti had been killed once before already, and she seemed fine about it, so I was sure the sick, tight feeling in my stomach over it was just an overreaction.

I rolled the guy over and poked him with a foot. "Did I kill *this* guy? He's not moving."

Crystal looked sick. "*Kill* him? Oh, gods, oh gods... This is my first week on the job, please, *please*, tell me I didn't just watch someone die..."

I shrugged. "It's part of the job."

I'd watched 3 people die so far, and one of them was currently living in my fridge. She was going to see someone die sooner or later. That said, I *really* hoped he was still alive, I didn't need that extra guilt.

Alele bent down and felt the man's neck. "I *think* he's alive? He slammed his head into the ground though, so-" she perked up and stood, dashing over to the backpack and dragging it to one side. "Incoming." she announced causally, pointing upwards

An explosion rocked the air and a bloom of yellow orange and red shot across the sky. A humanoid shape slammed into the ground where the backpack had been a moment before, a flash sparking around her as she hit the pavement. I got glimpses of the woman who'd just cracked the ground around us through the smoke and haze of her impact. Her chunky, round, polycarbonate purple boots, the tiny blue shorts, the round forearm guards that matched the boots, I was looking up at one of the Downtown Queen's founding members, Miss Missile. I'd never seen her up close before, and I was shocked at how tall she was, easily seven feet tall, although her boots could have platforms in them, it was hard to tell.

She looked around at us, pulling her fried blonde hair out of her face, and then looked down at the prone man at her feet. "I take it you're the heroes of this section?" she asked sternly.

I stepped closer to her, waving away the smoke between us with my wings. "I'm Angel Rouge of Lorgiaia's Angels, this is my teammate Angel Cobalt, and this…" I waved towards Crystal, trying not to wince at her stupid name, "...is Warrior Mage Blinding Crystal, of The Unchosen."

She looked us over, then around the area, noticing the scorch marks and blasted buildings. She slowly reached into a pouch on her backside and produced a set of handcuffs, rolling the man over and snapping them on him.

"Thanks for the takedown." she said, "This man was a witness to a fight with a super scientist earlier in the square. He stole *that*" she pointed at the gun with her chin. "from the super scientist's mobile lab. I guess he thought he could come out here and set up shop as a villain with no resistance."

"He just started taking shots at us as soon as he saw us." I said, "He killed me 4 times before I stopped him."

Miss Missile jerked her head over to me, her gaze hard and unreadable. "I... wasn't aware there was a new immortal around, how long have you been?..."

"Ah, no, that was me." Alele said quickly. Too quickly, like she'd rewound time to say it. I needed to ask her about that... "I rewound time to keep her alive, I have limited time manipulation."

Miss Missile's expression relaxed, "Oh, ok. Thank the gods, I thought I was about to have to bring you guys in too."

Bring us in? I didn't know of any heroes that were actually *immortal*, but it sounded like a big deal if she was willing to arrest other heroes just for having that power. I'd have to ask Lucy about it later, if I remembered

"Thank you both for helping with this guy." she said, picking him up in one arm and the weapon in the other like they were made of packing peanuts, "Sorry to drop in and run, but we've got a full night tonight, multiple A rank fallen out and about. I'll send some news crews your way though, I'm sure they'll be waiting for me back at the tower."

"Ah, it was all three of us, actually." Alele said, "Warrior Mage Blinding Crystal drew fire with her magic, she helped too."

I was annoyed at that, all Crystal had done was stay alive, and barely succeeded at that, but I pushed it down. I was trying to be nicer, and her team needed all the good PR it could get. Having Crystal's bubbly, cutesy vibes on the morning news would be sure to get them at least a few fans.

Miss Missile gave a half salute with the hand holding the backpack, and glowed slightly. "I'll tell them to keep an eye out for you three then, thanks again, girls."

At that, she exploded upwards with a blast of energy, streaking away into the sky at speeds almost too fast to follow with the naked eye. I watched her go for a while, and felt something odd. Not a feeling of admiration towards her, or a sense of pride at having won our first super-fight, but the feeling something was off, something was wrong with the interaction, I just didn't have all the pieces yet. There was also something bugging me about how things went down, not only did the guy go down extremely easily, minus the deaths, but the city around us didn't respond to the fight at all.

"Wow... She's such a hero, I'm honored just to have been here next to her." Crystal said dreamily, watching the glow fade into the night sky.

"That was, like, a really weird fight, right?" I asked, looking around and ignoring her fan-girling, "There's damage to all these buildings, and it was *super* loud, so why don't we hear anyone making any noise? We should hear sirens, screams, dogs barking, something."

Alele floated up and peered in the hole the man had melted into the building. "Well, this part of the city is mostly abandoned, right? So..."

Crystal looked back and forth between us. "Are you two not even a little excited you got to meet *THE* Miss Missile? She spoke to us, even! She *thanked* me! Me!"

"Kiri, we're heroes now too, you just have to get used to meeting other heroes." I said, mildly frustrated that she was ignoring my concerns. I floated up next to Alele and glided into the hole.

"Hey! That's trespassing!" yelped Crysta,l "Get out of there, it's against the law to enter a building without an invitation or approval from the GGDS!"

"Well, or like, reasonable suspicion." Alele said, "I'm gonna say I'm suspicious, sooo..." She floated in after me.

I found my flashlight in my pocket and switched it on, shining it around the interior.

"Oh, shit." Alele said, "It's like, a movie prop or something?"

The entire inside of the building, a 5 story office building with windows on all sides, was fully hollow. No floors, no furniture, just one empty square box with support beams going back and forth to hold the walls and ceiling up. I shone my light along the walls, looking for evidence that the floors had simply collapsed or been removed, but the walls were smooth, save for the tinted windows. I noticed something else, and shone my light downwards, to the bottom floor. The windows started on the second, so the whole wall all around was made of textureless gray concrete, with no breaks, not even one for a door. There was no way in or out of this building, unless you blew open one of the walls like we had. Why would anyone build a full fake building like this? It's not to hide drugs in, or there would be a way to get the drugs out, it wasn't under construction, and it wasn't a half-job either, it was high quality construction.

"Oh, hey, Rouge, come look at this." Alele called from down on the floor.

I looked down, she was crouching in the center of the floor, her hand on the smooth surface. I dropped down and walked over to her

"What is it?" I asked.

She pointed. "There's a joint here, like, I think the floor opens up? I think this building is entered from underneath..."

The joint in question ran the length of the floor, wall to wall, and cut back and forth like blocky, jagged teeth. I flew to the side of the room and saw that the edges of the floor were rounded as they met the wall, implying the floor did, in fact, open up. I sighed in frustration. There was no way I was figuring this out on my own right now. I glided back over to Alele and pointed back the way we'd come.

"Let's get back outside, we can figure this out later. The news crews will be here any minute to interview us." I said, heading for the hole.

"Yeah, it's just... so weird." she murmured, looking down as we exited the building.

"Hey! Why did you do that?" Crystal called up to us as we drifted over her, "I told you it was illegal!"

I ignored her, and looked at the other buildings around us. A few had lights on, I saw a shadow in the window of one, but most were cold and dark. I went up to get a better view, and circled the area quickly, coming back around to where Alele was waiting for me in the air twenty feet above Crystal.

"So what do you see?" she asked, "Any other fake buildings?"

"...Yeah." I said, "At least a third of the buildings in this immediate area don't have doors to get in."

Her eyes widened. "A third?!" she looked around, checking for herself. "So this isn't just a weird building in the abandoned part of town, this is like, something big?"

I shrugged. "It could be something big, a secret drug running tunnel or something, but whatever is down there can get up, but it can't get out of the buildings, just into them. So it shouldn't be a *threat*, right?"

She groaned. "Are we gonna have to do something about this?... I feel like it's something we need to be looking into or something, it *is* in our section..."

"Gods, I hope not. I'll ask Oori about it in the morning, I guess." I grumbled.

It couldn't be that bad, they needed building permits and stuff, right? There had to be city oversight to these things, somewhere. Oori might even just know what they were, off the top of his head. I needed to think about what to say when the news showed up anyway,

"Damnit..." Alele whispered.

"Hm?" I looked over.

"I gotta pee, and the news trucks could show up at any time. We're at least 5 blocks from the shop, and I gotta buy a thing, and go in, and-*fuck*, I'm gonna miss the interview..."

I sighed. "Godsdammit, just go. I'll stall, I'll tell them you're scouting the area for other threats or something."

"Thanks..." she said, sounding slightly embarrassed, and flew off.

I'd warned her. Or I'd tried, at least. I should have said something before her third drink, though. Thinking about it now, I was a little thirsty myself... I hated night shift, because it meant the tea shop and the nice deli near our base were both closed. The only option was a soda or bottle of water from the convenience store, or going all the way to the diner me and Forica had eaten at for coffee. I glanced around at the businesses around me, the ones I could see that weren't boarded up or fake buildings and I shook my head, there *really* wasn't much around here. Tattoo parlors, auto shops, a CPA's office that looked like the place you'd need to ask proof of license at before trusting the CPA in question. Nothing worth coming all the way here for.

There were a *couple* of places to buy food at, but nothing open at 3-4 AM, and nothing worth writing home about. There was a pizza shop nearby called Pizza Pallor that was 'just ok', not as good as the one on the main road that we usually ordered from, but *this* one did Second City style deep dish, which was *my* favorite, so I could see myself getting it again. There was a dwarven pub a street over that had pretty good roast meats, but Oori had said they used 'sub-par minerals' to cook it, and swore that we shouldn't eat there again until he could get us 'some *real* dwarven roast brush pig'.

In all honesty, the nicest place in our section by far was our base, with our cafe and snacks and open lobby policy. If I was around in Valley City as a tourist, it'd be the only thing I'd come to this section for. It wouldn't be the 'luxury day spa', down the road from us that's for sure. I hadn't been myself, but Alele had tried it the first week we'd been here. She had ended up buying a ton of home-spa stuff the same day and setting up camp in the single bathtub we shared in the showers rather than go back. I'd have to see if I could borrow some of her stuff later, I'd never tried spa things, but it seemed like a very 'celebrity' thing to do. I didn't know if I *needed* it, I'd found any traces of acne and dry skin *did* vanish when I transformed, but the way Alele practically drifted out of her little mini-spa when she used it made me want to try it once at least.

Speaking of, she was taking her sweet time. I looked around to see if she was coming back, then begrudgingly dropped to the ground, letting myself fall and dropping right in front of Crystal.

"Hey, don't ignore me!" she snapped as she folded her arms at me, "I was trying to talk to you, we're supposed to be following the laws, if we don't, we're no better than the bad guys!"

"We were checking for injured people, it's fine." I said. If there *had* been people in that building, not going in to check on them would be a bad thing, why was she acting like this?

"You knew there weren't any! You just wanted to poke around!" she accused.

"Something weird is going on, it's our job to figure it out. Your job too." I didn't really want to drag her into this, I'd wanted it to get blown over, but I really didn't like being fussed at.

"What do you mean 'weird'?" she said, glaring up at the building in question.

"It's a fake building, it's hollow, no floors, no way in, and the foundation has joints in it to open up."

She looked at it and back to me, then back at the building. "Oh... That *is* weird." she shook her head "But it could just be an abandoned project, like, they were going to put a hero team there and it fell through or something? It's probably nothing, just a weird building."

I pointed to a couple of buildings we could see from the intersection we were on. "See those? They're the same, and there's a lot more around us too, it's more than just one weird building."

She looked nervous, like she wanted to say something, but wasn't sure what. Finally she asked, "So, what, our section is full of hollow buildings, what do *we* do about it?"

"Hollow buildings with massive tunnels leading down" I corrected her, "I'll talk to our strategic lead about it later, I really don't know. It might just be a city planning thing, who knows. He'll get our guys working on it either way."

She looked at the ground and kicked at it with her loafers. "...I feel so out of place here..." she muttered, almost too quiet to hear

I wasn't expecting *that*.

"What do you mean?" I asked her.

"I'm just *me*, I'm the one leading the team, I get my patrols, I go out, I go back, we work on the base. You have a small tower, a custom cafe, a head of PR, an agent in charge of strategy, a whole church backing you, 'guys', *money*. I look at us, and we have barely enough to *live* on once we put our pay towards fixing up that janky garage."

"Well that's how it is, when you're an independent." I said, "Chosen deal with that stuff too, ones with smaller gods, I mean."

"They still have a support group. A couple dozen people who worship the same god, who think they hung the moon. I don't- none of us even have *family*. We mostly all met in an online chatroom for people who just needed someone to talk to, to listen."

"That's pretty sad." I said. I wasn't trying to be mean, but it *was* a pretty pathetic thing to admit.

"We're ok now..." Crystal said, misunderstanding my meaning, "We have each other, but I see the other heroes, I see you guys, and I just feel like I don't belong here. It's a feeling of 'everyone else is here for a reason, and you're just tagging along, pretending you're like them'."

I felt a pang, that hit something in me, the feeling of not belonging. I didn't want to admit it to *her*, but she was getting close to the way I felt around my team.

"Well, what about Sera?" I said, deflecting the conversation, "She's got no one, and her religion is *weird*, I think she's the only one in it, from what she told me."

"She's on a quest, though, this hero stuff is just a way to get money and a base so she can 'hunt for the heretics' or something." Crystal pointed out, "She's been constantly going all over the city looking for something and getting into trouble all week when she's not on patrol."

She had a point, Seraphim seemed to barely care about the attention she was getting, focusing entirely on looking for someone else, someone she called 'the heretic'.

"That's fair." I said, "I don't know, it's like, sometimes you want something, right? Or- I guess you *need* it, you know it's you, but the universe tells you no. *You* weren't told you were a 'Chosen' by some god, *you* weren't declared and brought up to be one. You looked inside, and said 'I'm a hero', and made it happen yourself, you knew who you were, and you made the changes you needed to in order to make the you on the outside match the you on the inside."

She looked at me funnily. "Yeah, I guess I did?"

"So," I continued, "that means that even if your team doesn't look like a regular one, and you don't have all the stuff a regular team does, the fact that you're *still* heroes after the universe tried to tell you no means you've earned your spot here, right? I'm like, a hero nepo baby, I was *given* this stuff. You're self-made, the real deal."

I felt good, telling her that, I was helping, right? I was proud of that little speech, I was just disappointed she was the only one around to hear it.

"Wow, I guess that's one way to look at it?" she said, looking at me with a softer look, "I hadn't thought of it like that, thank you."

"No problem." I said, giving her a small smile. Maybe she'd be closer to me now, and she'd want to patrol with me. That way I'd have a smaller chance of getting paired up with *that* one...

"You said 'it's part of the job' before." she said quietly.

"What?" I asked.

"The seeing dead bodies, you said it was just part of the job, when I was worried for that man."

"...oh, yeah, I did." I let my words hang.

"...You've seen a dead body?" she asked.

"I'm not allowed to discuss it." I said, turning away.

"So you *have*." she confirmed, "I keep thinking about that, since you said it. How long will it be before *I* see a dead body? Or even cause one? My spells aren't all safe after all..."

I stayed quiet.

"I'm sorry, I know I should have thought about this before I signed up, and I'm sure I'll be fine, but I'm sorry." she rubbed at her face with her hands. "Listen, can I give you a hug? You seem like you need one, and I'm still all worked up."

I shook my head quickly. "Absolutely not."

She looked hurt, and stepped back. "O-oh, no, I was- I'm sorry..."

I looked at her for a long second then pursed my lips. I'd need to tell her eventually if we were going to be working like this.

"I have a condition. If you touch me, it could kill you." I said, "It's a secret, and no one can know outside of the heroes I work with, but you really, really can't touch me, ever."

Her eyes went wide. "Oh, oh *gods*, the dead body you saw-"

"Can we not?" I interrupted her, "I don't want to talk about it."

"Talk about what?" Alele said, softly touching down next to me.

I glanced over, she had *another* energy drink in her hand. Of *course* she did. "I was explaining to Crystal that I can't be touched or bad things happen, and I don't want to go into details."

Alele winced. "Ooh, yeah. *Real* bad things." she looked at Crystal. "Don't touch her or I'll kick your ass, she's mine."

"No-ugh, it's serious." I growled, frustrated.

"Are you two dating?" Crystal said, looking between us.

"No!" I barked, at the same time Alele chirped, "Yes!"

Crystal frowned and glanced back and forth between us.

"It's complicated." Alele said.

"It's not, she flirts with everyone, and I'm part of everyone." I said flatly.

"Yeahhh, but it's personal with you." Alele said, "After all, there's a 40% chance of teammates-"

"Oh *gods*, Alele, we know the statistics, we get it." I said, cutting her off.

"What?" Crystal wrinkled her nose, "What statistics?"

Alele's face lit up. "Well! According to team dynamic studies-"

"Oh, look, the news is here." I said dryly.

A single news van pulled up, and stopped in front of us, a lady and a cameraman getting out onto the pavement as the doors slid open.

"Ok, you three are the junior heroes who helped stop the thief?" the lady asked, holding up her mic.

"We're the three *regular* heroes who stopped him by ourselves, if that's what you mean?" I said, offended. Junior? Did I really look like a teenager to her? I supposed the Mary-Janes and puffy dress didn't help, but still, I was *obviously* an adult.

"Mm, we'll just roll and you can tell your story, however you like, ok?" she said, waving at the cameraman to get the camera the camera running.

"Shouldn't we be waiting on the other new crews?" Crystal said, "I'd like to get back on patrol, and I don't want to give the story over an over."

I nodded, it wouldn't make sense to do it six times for each of the major news companies if we could just do one group interview, we'd be done way faster.

"Oh, hun, this is it..." lady said, gently, "We've got multiple other cases going on tonight, bigger than this. We'll put you on air, of course, but we're only here because no one else is. We thought it'd be good to get some footage the other newsgroups don't have of the aftermath of the fight the Queens had earlier."

"But- this is our first thingy, right?" Alele said, "Don't we get like, special attention or something because of that?"

The lady shook her head. "Sorry, hun, but there's hundreds of other heroes in this city, we can't give special treatment to anyone but the bigger teams. Can we get you three together a bit more so you all fit in frame?"

We all stepped in closer, my arm bumping Crystal's, causing her to yelp in fear. I took a step back, standing between and behind the other two.

"Ok, and three... two... oneeee, and..." the lady counted off, looking at the camera, "Hello, my name is Raquel Pikelle, and I'm here with the three girls who helped apprehend a dangerous criminal this morning!" the camera panned to us, and Raquel held out the microphone to us "Would you three mind giving your names for the camera?"

"My name is Angel Cobalt, of Lorgiaia's Angels, and this is my teammate!" Alele said jutting her thumb at me.

"Hello, I'm Angel Rouge!" I said, with fake cheer in my voice.

"...And I-I'm Kir- Cry- uh, I'm- I- I'm-" Crystal's voice shook and she tried again, louder, "I'm Warrior Mage B-Blinding Crystal, of the Un-Ch-Chosen!"

"And what was your part in the takedown?" Raquel asked us.

"Well, Me and C- Rouge were flying around looking for Crystal," Alele started, "and a big beam just blew Rouge's whole top half off, so I used my power-"

"And what *is* your power?" Raquel prompted.

"Oh, um-" Alele was thrown off, "Time manipulation, so I used that, and rewound time to before Angel Rouge was killed, then we took off after the source."

"I d-drew fire!" yelled Crystal, "I chased him down and got him to shoot at me too!"

"Yeah, and while she was drawing fire, I drop kicked him, and knocked him out, and we held him until Miss Missile came to pick him up." I finished for everyone.

"Wow, it sounds like a well executed takedown! Thank you so much for your hard work!" she turned back to the camera, panning us out of frame. "This has been Raquel Pikelle, here in section 247 of Valley City!"

The camera turned to the ground and shut off, and Raquel turned to us.

"Thank you very much, you can see this on the morning news, around 7, and probably again at 9!"

"That's all?" I asked, "That was... nothing."

"Well, you're supplementary footage, so it's just a quick blurb. You did great though!" she turned to Crystal, "I would recommend getting some public speaking lessons to get used to talking on camera, but you all did great!"

She climbed into the van. "Ok, have a good rest of the morning!"

As the van drove off, Crystal stepped back and looked at me, her face pale and her hands shaking

"Am- am I going to die?" she whimpered.

I blinked, then snickered, remembering the arm bump. "Oh, no, it's only skin to skin contact, it's fine, you're fine. It'd already have happened, anyway."

She sagged in relief. "Ohhh gods, I could barely focus on the interview, I bet I sounded like an ass."

Alele patted her, causing her to jump. "We all sounded like asses. Let's forget about it. Me and Rouge will do one more fly over, and meet up with you at the diner on Sky Street, ok? Victory breakfast and all that."

"But our patrol doesn't end until 7, it'll be like, 5:30 by then, the section will be left undefended!" she protested.

I groaned inside, seriously? She expected us to be actively hunting for crime the whole time? I wanted my victory donuts, *this* is why we ditched her earlier...

"The bad guys don't *know* it's undefended, though." I pointed out.

"Oh, hm." she said, thinking, "...Alright, but we gotta be fast while we eat, ok?"

"Yeah, yeah, we'll be fast, now let's hurry, ok? My power makes me super hungry." Alele said, shooing her to start her walk through.

"Ok." Crystal murmured, "I'll see you there, then."

As she walked off, I looked over at Alele. "So, race you there and pretend we just finished the flyover when she shows up?"

She laughed. "Yeah, ok. We gotta get there quick either way."

"Why is that?"

She crunched up the can of her fourth energy drink. "Nnnno reason, but let's make it quick."

As we tore off into the sky, I couldn't help but admire her form. While I beat the air to rocket forward, she had a lot less wing control, so she focused on gliding and cutting through the air instead. She really *was* pretty, if she'd stop aggressively flirting with me, she might have a chance. Maybe. I pushed the thoughts out of my head and blew past her, spinning her over behind me as I rocketed off at top speeds.

It *was* a race, after all.

Chapter Twelve

Oori frowned and stroked his beard.

"Well... I can't say I heard of 'fake buildings' before, but... if you saw them, then I'll take your word for it?"

"It looked like they had tunnels under them and stuff, I don't know." I said, mildly embarrassed.

"I see, we know the street you were on for that fight, so I'll get some of our people to check in with city hall, see what we can find out."

"Thanks, I'm sorry if it's nothing, but me and Alele noticed it, and we just wanted to be safe." I said, taking my order from the orcish guy with shaggy hair at the cafe.

It turned out we *didn't* have to pay for cafe food, and it turned out I *did* take advantage of it. I swear the guy was going to memorize my order at this point

Training made me very hungry, dammit. I needed my sweets.

"No problem, Candy, I appreciate your concerns. And congratulations on your first villain takedown!" Oori said as we walked to the front of the lobby.

"Well, second, really. First *official* one though." I corrected him.

He furrowed his brow and nodded. "Ah, yes, hm..."

He looked at me with a sideways look for a moment, then nodded slowly. "So, where are you off to? You're not on a patrol until tomorrow afternoon, gonna take advantage of your 'day off' so to speak?"

I held up the bag in my hand "I'm just going to the park, the good one, with the ducks. I want to sit in nature, I miss it."

"That's understandable, you did come from a pretty rural area of the city." he said, "Sometimes I like to go into the basement and stare at the concrete walls, it reminds me of the mountain back home..."

I blinked at him. "Oh, really? I- I hadn't thought of that..."

He looked at me seriously. "No. I'm messing with you, Candy."

A half laugh slipped out, and I shook my head. "Whatever, I gotta go, I'll be back later!"

He gave me a short salute and stepped back as I walked out of the building. I was glad to have him around, when I'd met him, I'd thought he'd be a hardass, and he *was*, sometimes, but usually he was one of my favorite people to interact with. He reminded me of my dad, and I felt like that was important, somehow.

I transformed and took off as I walked, something I was getting better at as I practiced it. I couldn't quite keep my transformation up for a whole patrol without swapping back for a few minutes yet like Lucy could, but I could still transform on the fly. The lights and swirling colors wrapping me up and lifting me as I moved along. I liked to imagine it was intimidating to see me snap into 'battle mode' without slowing down. I did look a *lot* more severe with my new hair, but realistically I knew my puffy dress and child-friendly appearance were far from 'intimidating', no matter what I did.

As I flew, I watched the people below me wandering around, their days full of work or shopping, and I smiled. They had no idea what it was like to be up here, flying over it all, seeing them as ants... I could drop down and grab one of them up, bringing them up with me, and they'd just scream and flail. I could just imagine some fancy business lady, yanked out of her life to be drug around the sky for a while by a hero, it'd be the single most interesting thing in her life to ever happen, by far. I slowed, absently looking for someone to try it with, or at least to imagine trying it with. I wasn't about to risk the negative PR if they ended up hating it and tried to sue or something, but it was fun to imagine.

A flash of light caught my eye and interrupted my thoughts, and I floated over the alley it came from, curious. A tall, muscle bound human woman in a tan skirt with a matching sweater vest was beating up a shorter man in black combat armor, each hit blasting light and shock waves out from him as her blows landed on his face and chest rapid fire. I sighed, and lowered myself to the ground behind them. I didn't really care about what was going on, but... one of them HAD to be a hero, and *that* meant post-teamup selfies and media traction.

"Hey, which one of you is the good guy?" I asked over the sound of the shock waves.

"Fuck off!" The man yelled, smacking the woman across the jaw with a shock baton. She made a strangled sound, but didn't fall as she kept hitting him.

Call me old fashioned, but *good* Chosen didn't usually tell other Chosen to fuck off. I stepped up and popped myself forward with my wings, driving my knee into the soft spot on his lower back, right under his armor. He arched his back and turned, swinging the baton at me with a speed I wasn't expecting, but I'd managed to step back before it made contact, and I smirked as his swing went wide.

"Oh, fuck this all to hell..." he panted, "I'm not being beaten up by a fucking cosplayer and a life-sized doll, I'm out."

He flickered, and his clothes fell to the ground, empty and limp.

I looked up at the woman, mildly surprised. "Did he teleport? Why didn't he do that before?"

She stood up straight, easily six feet tall, and stretched her arms, massive and well toned, over her head. I didn't stare, because that would be unprofessional, but I *did* watch her carefully, for... tactical reasons. Her outfit looked vaguely like a school uniform, if the school didn't requite you to wear shirts under vests. Her lower legs and forearms were covered in some kind of loose disconnected 'sleeves' that matched the color of her her 'uniform', and every inch of her clothing and silver blonde hair was covered in pins, clips, and stickers, in all shapes colors and sizes.

"He's one of my main arches," she said, shaking her head, "he can 'rewind' to whatever place he had sex at last, but in the state he was in when said sex happened. His name's Morning-After, if you can believe it."

I grimaced. "Oh, ugh, what an awful name..."

The woman laughed. "Yeah, no kidding. Speaking of names, I'm Genki, are you new in this section? Or are you poaching?"

I shook my head. "My name is Angel Rouge, I'm from section uhhh 240-something, not poaching, I was just on my way to the park to eat and I noticed the flashing lights from your punching."

She nodded. "It *is* very impressive."

"Yeah, he looked like he could take a hit very well though, those shock waves were going right through him, and he barely flinched, should... we be looking for him or something?"

"Nahhh, my punches are mostly sparkle, and he was wearing his stupid padded outfit. He's not as dangerous as he looks, he's *supposed* to be in jail for petty crimes, and refuses to stay in."

I kicked the outfit in question with my foot. "So... does he come pick this up later? Or...?"

Genki scooped the clothes up into a ball and tucked them under her arm, grinning. "I'll bring them home, I collect them. I have like, 10 sets of this guy's clothes, it's hilarious."

I ignored the potentially creepy side of what she'd just said, and glanced around the alley. "Ok, uh, well I'm not going to lie, I mostly just came to help so I could get a selfie with another hero, is that ok?"

She wiggled her eyebrows. "Oooh playing the social media game, huh? I play that game too, gotta get those brand deals! I'm working on one right now? Oh. My. Gods. They wanna put me on a literal cereal box! *That* is how you know you made it, girlie."

"I mean, my team has our own themed cafe, not to brag or anything." I said, bragging.

She looked at me more closely, her eyes narrowing. "Wow, I'd have thought I'd recognize someone who was famous enough for their own cafe."

I wilted slightly. "...My church is huge, we debuted with the cafe, full disclosure."

Genki laughed, and lightly punched my shoulder, a small shock wave and flash going off when she did so. "Thought so, but hey, maybe I'll show up there sometime, and get you *real* popularity by tagging it for my fans."

I felt a twinge of anger, but I squished it with a small smile. "Oh? And how many fans do you have?"

She dropped the clothes and pulled her skirt up a few inches, fishing her phone out of a pocket on her shorts, tapping at it and turning her screen to me proudly.

I stared at the number in awe, taken aback.

"You have fucking one point six *million*?" I gasped.

"Totally!" she chirped, beaming at me, "It's soooo easy too, I just flex, do dances, and wear outfits that show off my muscles!"

I looked down at my own body. While I *did* have tone and muscle in my transformed state, I was not nearly as strong as Genki was. *Galorna* looked small compared to her, and she was, well, *Galorna*.

"I guess I could try doing dances?" I mumbled, fumbling for my own phone.

"You'll get there, what are you at right now, girlie?"

I opened CirNet and glowered at my profile. "...Seventeen thousand..."

"That's a good start! I bet you pick up at least another five kay from our selfie, and once you hit about thirty, the followers just roll in!"

"I- I have a public relations person, and someone helping me with this stuff, but I'm not growing fast at all, could you help me?" I asked, keeping my voice from sounding like I was overwhelmed.

"Uhhh." Genki said, her eyes narrowing again, "I don't really *do* that, but umm, if you like, I can like, follow you back? How long have you been trying to grow your following?"

I sighed and shook my head. "*Days*, since like, last Saturday? Since my debut"

She frowned. "Wait, you've been a hero for less than a week and you're complaining about having seventeen kay?"

I shrugged. "I'm seeing stupid fan accounts for other heroes with a hundred thousand, it's logical to get frustrated."

Genki pointed to her phone. "Look girlie, I don't know if you're not into Chosen culture or something, but like, I've been one for like, *gods*, eight years? Since I was a teenager, at least, and it took me that full amount of time to get my fans. I'm internationally famous, yeah, but I worked for *almost a decade* to get there, so... sorry for not being surprised you didn't hit the trending page in a week."

"I've never even heard of you, to be honest." I admitted, "I didn't know anyone outside of like, the big teams or the founders could have that many followers. I was aiming for around two hundred and fifty, max. Enough to justify being an angel."

"That's realistic, yeah. You'll flatline around there, I'm guessing." she said thoughtfully, "You said you're on a team? That tends to split interest, there are members of the Children of Battle with less followers than me, just because with *them* everyone has a favorite, I'm just me."

"Oh, fuck." I said, "I just realized I'm only following D Gunn from that team."

"Exactly!" Genki said happily, "If you were solo, you'd be doing *way* more numbers, every member of your church would follow you automatically, for one. That's why I have so many, I'm the only Chosen in my church! Heck, the official Spacegirl account has over two mil, and she doesn't even *have* a church, as far as anyone knows, and the account just reposts other people's posts *about* her, it's not even her making the posts."

"I'd hoped the church would all follow me anyway..." I grumbled.

"You're just not everyone's favorite! It's natural." she said, bending over and putting an arm that could bend steel girders around my shoulder, "Now let's get that selfie, we can at least get you some of *my* fans, right?"

I posed, and pulled my own phone out, snapping a picture with me looking serious and hopefully mysterious and Genki crossing her eyes and sticking out her tongue throwing a peace sign with her free hand. I looked at the picture and frowned. It looked odd, something less than professional

"Oh, trust me, people *love* that face for some reason." Genki said, "Plus it like, clashes with *your* expression, so it stands out!"

"I guess so." I muttered, "Uh, thanks, I'll tag you in it, and you can share it?"

"Will do!" she said with a fake salute, "Now, I gotta get back to my patrol, Morning-After isn't the only lawbreaker around!"

I waved goodbye and picked up my bag. My slushy was mostly melted by now, but I didn't really care, Genki had given me a lot to consider, especially concerning my team...

~~~

I drank my watered down mango juice and fiddled with the Galorna cookie in my hand. My sandwich had been soggy from being in the bag next to the slushy covered in condensation, but I'd eaten it anyway. I was in my base form in jeans and a t-shirt-people's comments about my sweaters were starting to bother me-, and I was on a bench overlooking the water.

What was I even *doing?*

I felt torn between going back to home and sitting in my room, and going back *home* and sitting on my childhood bed. I couldn't focus on enjoying the nature, I was too worried about my stupid fucking phone and the stupid *fucking* implications from what Genki had said. I wanted to go out and find more Chosen, to get *out there* more, to be seen, but I knew that Chosen who butted in on other people's areas were seen as 'unprofessional' and I *desperately* wanted to be a professional. It was also technically against GGDS guidelines to 'poach', if I got reported...

I'd added up everyone on our team's followers, it came to just under forty-five thousand. If Genki was right, that's about how many I'd have by now if I was solo.

I leaned back and looked up at the sky, letting the bright blue air fill my vision with haze, and thought about my needs. I *needed* to be famous, to have people see me and to fawn over me. I wasn't *just* doing it for attention, there was *money* involved, and political power. If I could get to be famous enough, I could help fix our section, or help sway public opinion about things that really mattered, I wasn't trying to get famous for *selfish* reasons, right? And then there was-
~~~

I thought about one of my childhood crushes, a hero from Bay City named Anchor Drop. I'd had posters and figures of him, I'd watched his TV specials over and over, I'd followed him in his journey for most of my childhood until I was almost 17, and there was an announcement from the pantheon. Anchor Drop was going to be ascended, he was leaving earth, and moving across the veil to become one of the gods. His following was *so* big, *so* many people worshiped him, that his spiritual energy was equal to that of a small god. I'd been devastated at the time, I'd lost my idol, the man I imagined holding me as I fell asleep for years on end, to the great white cloud in the sky. Or, the great white cloud in a fifth dimensional space overlapping earth, I guess. And I was *part of why I'd lost him.* My worship of him *directly* helped him get the energy to ascend, so in a way, I was the reason I lost my favorite hero.

It was nothing too 'unusual' for him to leave like that; on average at least three or more people rose to godhood per year, but for me, no one else ascending ever mattered, until it happened to *him.*

Over time though, as his old church fell back into obscurity, and Anchor Drop's *new* church, The Church of The Humble Hero, rose to become one of the number one churches in the country, I understood why he'd done it. Every city across The Union had at least one of his Chosen; a 'Humble Hero' in it; someone with a calm, soft demeanor and a quiet strength. I met one of his Chosen, once. They looked at me with eyes that spoke to my soul as they helped me find my classmates when I got lost on my senior trip. Looking into those eyes, I felt myself realize what I wanted from my life, however I could get it.

I wanted to ascend, to become one of the gods. To be able to do what he'd done for the world, myself.

It was stupid, a pipe dream, a fucking joke I tried to ignore. I didn't like to admit it. It felt like the kind of thing that would get you put on medication or *worse.* Especially when you're just a farm girl who missed more days of high school than she went to, whose dad was a missing person, and whose mom was so emotionally distant and exhausted that she might as *well* be a missing person. I'd held onto that hope, that *desire*, to become a goddess, for years, holding it close, imagining it in my head as I worked on the farm and lay in my bed, thinking of all the ways I'd influence the world, what powers I'd give my Chosen, who I'd choose...

Part of me wanted to choose my 'friends', and give them wonderful powers, like lasers and sparkling shields, while the *other* half wanted to pick the people I hated. The people at school who surreptitiously judged me for taking days off for farm work, for not having a dad. I was never really 'bullied', no one stole my lunch money or anything, but when someone thinks little of you, you can *tell*. It hurts. I wanted to choose *them*, and give them a power like 'frog senses' or something, and send them off to the folds to do rescue missions, never to return.

I tried not to dwell on those desires too much.

Still, here I was, a Chosen myself, and part of one of the biggest churches in the region. I still had to think about my team, of course, but I wanted- *needed* to get far, far more popular than I was right now if it meant I had even the slightest chance of becoming a goddess. I needed people to *worship* me. Genki had more followers than I could imagine getting and still wasn't even an angel, I knew I needed *way* more than that to ascend, but how *much* more? Anchor Drop had left before CirNet was the de facto form of communication and news sharing, so I couldn't look at *his* numbers, but there *were* others to compare myself to.

I pulled out my phone and sorted the people I was following by the numbers of followers they had, and checked the top one. As I'd expected, it was Chap, the leader of the former Arena City team "The Knights of The Abyss". Following the attack on the city, and after loosing so, so many Chosen to it, he'd stepped up as the 'face' of Chosen everywhere. He'd spoken on Chosen law, and fought for the rights of any Chosen to pick their *own* battles, instead of being forced into a suicide mission with no hope of winning, like his team had been.

He was by *far* the most famous and most popular hero I'd ever seen, and his roguish grin and sparking eyes peeking out of his half-helmet made it easy to see why, political power aside. He was sitting firmly at four hundred and thirty six million followers. Almost a third of the planet's population had eyes on him, saw every post he made, and cared about him. Why hadn't *he* ascended yet? Had they offered and he'd declined? Was his god being difficult about it? If that many followers wasn't enough to ascend, then how many *was*?

I slurped my drink and put my phone away again. This was frustrating. I needed to focus on my original mission; get rich, get famous, get power. I could worry about rising to godhood later.

...Not that I'd have a chance with 4 other teammates hogging the spotlight.

I needed them, of course, I couldn't do anything on my own, especially with my shitty power, but still, hearing that *they* were the reason I wasn't seeing as much growth made me almost feel jealous of them. I was *just* starting to get closer to them, too... I tossed my mostly empty cup in the trash next to the bench and took a bite of the Galorna themed cookie. The lemon-y tang was really nice, and I wished I'd kept my drink now to pair it with. I glanced at the trash can, it'd most likely fallen in straw up, I could...

I violently took another bite, angry at myself for considering *digging through garbage* for a drink and grumbled. I was distracted and full of too many thoughts, if that's where my mind was going. I needed to lay down some priorities, instead of making guilt induced promises to myself and thinking vaguely about how to improve. Let's see...

Step one, get more followers and therefore fame, of course

Step two, define my brand as distinct from the other girls, make myself stand out in a way that makes *me* appealing aside from the team.

Step three, meet and greet as many other Chosen as I could. Networking was hard, but I already knew, what, ten? eleven? I just needed to keep going, keep making myself known.

Step four, train harder. *Actually* train, not just go through the exercises and dodge glowing lights. I'd mostly given up after I got my power, but Genki... I got the feeling her build had very little to do with her *power*, and everything to do with her *training*.

Step five...

I stood and started the walk back home. To the base, at least. I did miss my mom, but I didn't want to *see* her yet. I still didn't know how she'd react to the hair...

Step five... It'd have to be to keep getting closer to the girls. I really *did* like them, even if they annoyed me at times and they were holding me back from my true potential. I needed to find a way to actually maintain the bonds with them. When I was actively bonding, I was having a great time, I was engaged, I liked them. I could laugh and feel good about myself, but as soon as I was alone or had time to think, I couldn't help analyzing them, *judging* them. And *now* I was going to be blaming them for my lack of fame. Great.

I had my list of tasks, or 'goals' or whatever, I should write them down or I'd forget, but I didn't think I would. I passed in front of the square, and looked up at the Queen's skyscraper, my mind wandering to 'meeting' Miss Missile. Did she even remember me? It'd been all of a few moments, but she *had* gotten alarmed when she'd thought I was immortal for some reason, was that enough to make me stick?

I'd never asked Alele about her reaction to that, now that I thought about it. It probably wasn't important. What *was* important, was that every single one of the buildings I was walking past had a front door or garage door or *some* way of getting in. The weird fake buildings must only be a thing in areas further from the center or something. Or were they just better disguised here?

I finished my cookie and put my bag in a trashcan as I passed. Trashcan... It sure was nice to be on a street with fucking trashcans. It *should* be a standard thing everywhere, but nooo, there's 'budget problems' in our area. Which made sense, if there was no one in the fucking buildings, then there was no one to pay the taxes, but the fact that we had *one* street trashcan in our whole section was just embarrassing. I couldn't even be mad about the random garbage and stuff in between the buildings, it's not like there was anywhere *else* to put it.

A random sign caught my eye, a poster for a diamond ring, advertised by a crystalline gnoll Chosen looking sultrily at the viewer, their hand in front of their mouth like they were gasping. Fuck, they were practically *made* to advertise diamonds, with that body. I wondered if they could change back and forth between 'that' and normal flesh like Homicide, or if they were just stuck like that...

I thought about what items I could try and sell that'd have the same effect as this one had one me, something that made people think 'Oh, she's *perfect* for that!' Makeup maybe? Transformed, my makeup was always perfect, but it wasn't like I could claim I was using theirs or anything, it was magic makeup. Maybe hair dye? I wasn't sure if I was supposed to pretend my hair was red because of my power or something yet, but Forica had already posted a 'before' picture, so the cat was out of the bag either way, I supposed.

My feet scuffed the pavement, and I pulled up the map on my phone to see how much longer I had to walk to get back to the base. The timer estimated 40 more minutes. I stared at my phone for a few seconds. The walk would do me good, and I was trying to get more exercises, like I had just said...

Fuck it, I crouched, and jumped, transforming and flying into the sky before my feet hit the ground. Fuck walking, fuck sidewalks, and fuck the map, Flying just felt *so* much better.

~~~

I sat on top of our building, looking around at our section. It really was a piece of shit, when you looked at it. I needed to find a good
~~~

bar or someplace close by to hang out at, this 'day off' was so, so boring. Alele was off grocery shopping with Lucy, Galorna and Driz were on patrol, Crystal was at her base with the rest of her team... Was that my entire friend group? Really?

...Did I just include Crystal in my friend group?...

I groaned, and stood up. I could sit and poke around, or I could *do* something. I thought about building my dioramas, but lately it'd felt like I was having to push myself to work on those, like, every second I spent making them was a second I was wasting not doing... something else. I wasn't sure what. I still liked it, I still wanted to finish the one I was working on, and I felt guilty that I *wasn't* doing it, but I felt guilty when I WAS doing it too. It was confusing and I didn't want to think about it right now.

I looked along the streets towards the main city, my eyes tracing the buildings for anything to do, an advertisement for a store, a fun looking shop, but there wasn't much worth paying attention to, here. I saw a familiar figure float by over the buildings, and I smiled as I recognized Sera, back from one of her 'heretic hunts'. Her white and gold figure glided across the sky towards her run down house, and she faltered, her wings buckling. I started as I saw a large red smear across her stomach, and I lifted into the air, had someone gotten the best of her? I didn't know if she was a regenerator or not, but just in case...

I took off from the roof, closing the gap in no time, and flying up alongside her, reaching out and taking her shoulder in my hand. She hissed, and turned, her rings collapsing into her mostly human face as she saw it was me.

"C-Candy, I s-seem to have overextended m-myself, please, if you would..." she pointed to the street her house was on, and I slipped my arms under hers, feeling her wings go limp as I carried her to her porch.

I lay her down, and stared at her stomach; there was a large hole, scorched around the edges, with her internal organs exposed, her hands pressing them in, holding them back. I noticed with mild interest as I started to panic that she was missing most of her digestive tract, was that due to the injury? Or did... whatever she was just not have intestines?

"I need- I need some medicine, please, Candy, I c-can tell you where it is..." she groaned.

"In your house?" I asked, "I can go get it, where is it?"

"T-two paces in, f-four paces left, turn left, one p-pace forward." she whispered, "*Please*, keep your eyes closed, it's in a sack..."

I stood up. "I think your safety is more important than a religious tradition, let me-"

"No!" she coughed, "It's for y-your own g-good, please..."

I looked at her, the blood pooling under her and held back my panic. If it was really *that* important, I could do it. I closed my eyes and opened her front door. A smell like a sweet, fruity blood hit me, and the humid, hot air felt sticky on my skin. It wasn't that hot outside, did she have working heat? Or was whatever she had in here *making* heat? I stepped carefully, my feet touching the wood floor, a dripping sound towards the center of the room making me feel slightly nauseous. My shoe hit something soft and limp, and my first thought was that it was a limb. I cringed, and stepped over and past it, pretending I didn't notice, and swung my arm, feeling for the sack I was in here for. My fingers touched something fleshy that sloshed, and I gasped, it was warm and smooth, like leather over a water balloon. This must be it. I used both hands, and lifted the sloshing sack off of whatever it was sitting on, and backed up, retracing my steps until I felt the cool outside air hit my face.

"P-perfect, close the d-door." gasped Sera as I felt her take the sack from me. I found the handle, and slid the door closed, finally opening my eyes.

"Are- is- we need to get you to a hospital..." I said, my head spinning and my vision slightly blurred. Was there something in the air in her house? Why was I so fuzzy?

Sera had put the mouth of the sack to her lips and was sucking deeply, drinking whatever was inside in gulps. She pulled away and gasped for air, much calmer now.

"No, no hospitals, I'll be fine now, thank you." she scooted back until she was against the house.

I looked at her wound, expecting it to heal over or seal up now that she had her medicine, but nothing happened.

"You don't *look* fine." I said, "What happened? Were you fighting crime?"

She shook her head, a light smile on her face. "No, I was seeking the heretics, I was asking questions of one of the ruffians on the other side of this city, and asking about them, but he didn't seem to understand."

"And, like, he, what, had a shotgun or something?" I asked, looking at the wound and wincing. It didn't look like any wound I'd heard of, it was clean, almost cauterized, and looked more like an explosion than a gunshot did it.

"Mm, nay, my fair maiden..." Sera said, drinking more of her medicine, her eyes looking heavy "A lady made of silver accosted me and hit me with some type of magic crossbolt. I shot her with a beam, but her glimmering armor reflected the blast into the walls and the young man I was attempting to get information from. She missed her second shot, and my sword hit her arm, barely scratching that damned armor. I flew off at that, and in the sky, noted that her first shot had opened my stomach..."

I gaped at her, my head still spinning. "Holy FUCK, you fought Spacegirl? And lived?" I looked at her guts, "Well, lived for *now*..."

Sera snorted, and laughed lightly. "I am in no danger of dying, Candy. I presume you know my accoster?"

I shook my head. "No, but everyone knows OF her. She's untouchable, no one can hurt her, and she never talks or anything. Do you know why she'd attack you?"

Seraphim hummed as she kept drinking. "Well, she may have been attempting to get me to let go of the man, but if that was her goal, then she failed utterly. His bones are smoldering on the stones now."

I shuddered. "Maybe don't mention that you accidentally killed someone, if this comes up again... It's not like Spacegirl can tell anyone, after all."

Sera laughed louder and punched my leg, pulling me down by my gloved hand to sit next to her. I winced as the blood pooling on the porch smeared on my white tights, but it'd be fine, it'd be clean next time I transformed anyway.

"Candy, I appreciate your dedication to my cause, you know not what it is, and you *still* devote yourself to keeping my secrets, I am truly blessed by Elmaem to have a companion like you." she snickered, "Well, more blessed than we Sisters are already."

I frowned, I hadn't even *considered* reporting her for killing a guy, was that a sign of friendship? Or just of me not caring?

"Elmaem?" I asked, to get my mind off it, "Is that your god?"

She held a finger up to her lips. "Shhh, you're not supposed to know that..." she passed me the sack of fluid, and I noticed with mild interest that the leather was the same exact tone as her skin.

"Why- why can't I know that?" I asked, holding the sack up to smell it. It smelled like raw meat, yule cookies, alcohol, and a hint of... vomit? Somehow, that mix, that combination smelled so, so good to my still slightly fuzzy mind. Like a feast in every sip. I felt my mouth watering at the smell...

"If I let you know *too* much" she said, resting her head on my shoulder, "My god will worm his way into you, then spread to everyone else in the city, as quickly as any virus."

I looked down at her, her eyes were closed, but she was breathing and not bleeding anymore, so whatever this liquid was, it must have stabilized her? I lay my head on top of hers, using my hand as a shield so I didn't touch her directly. I'd stay here until she woke up, then we'd talk about the hospital again. I took a tentative sip from the sack, to see if it was as tasty as it smelled, and the world exploded.

Colors streamed out of my eyes, everything bled together, the universe sang, a giant, fleshy thing towered over the world, hugging it with arms miles long, branching into worms that fed into every living thing, into Sera, into me, into Oori and Drizti, stroking us, inside us but not fully part of us. The vision spun, and it faded as soon as it'd arrived, and I was left in a gray, boring world again, lying against Sera on the porch. I looked at the sack, and licked my lips, the residual liquid on them sending my mind into sparks for a moment.

With a great effort, I put the stopper back in, and set it next to me on the floor. Whatever that wonderful stuff was, I should stay away from it until I found out if it was addictive or not. I slid my free arm around Seraphim, weaving it under her top set of wings, making sure my glove and sleeves were between us, and pulled her sleeping form over me a little more, closing my own eyes. I felt... drunk wasn't the right word, but something. Cozy, at least. I caught sight of Sera's organs, still exposed, squirming and pulsing inside her torso, and I giggled, closing my own eyes to fall asleep.

Chapter Thirteen

I felt Sera shift under me and my eyes cracked open. It was later in the evening, the sun was going down, and the sky was lit up in an orange glow. I yawned and lifted my head, looking down at Seraphim to see how she was holding up. Her wounds had been pretty bad, and while she'd seemed ok after having that drink, I was still worried that she'd appeared to be missing some of her organs. She rubbed her face, her fingers tracing her third eye as she woke up. Her hand found the sack of juice I was holding and took it back, taking another swig of it.

"Are you feeling ok?" I asked, "I *really* think we should get you to a hospital. Even if it was a fight against another Chosen- or, I *think* she's a Chosen- because you're registered, it'll be totally free."

She hummed, and rubbed her stomach. "I'm fine, I don't need any sawbones or snake oils, I'm alright, now."

I glanced down, and jumped as I saw her wound. Where she'd *had* a gaping hole in her gut, there was now a monstrous mouth, teeth jutting out over the lipless opening. I watched as it opened slightly, a slimy tongue flicking out, the shallow maw shiny and pink inside.

Seraphim saw me staring, and laughed, running her hand along the teeth in an almost loving motion.

"You like it? My god doesn't want his Chosen to die, Candy, we can live through *quite* a lot if we let our god have a bit of us in return." She held her arms over her head and opened her new mouth wide, there was a coiled tongue inside, and a throat that seemed to go past where her back should be, violating physics in the process.

"Holy *fuck*." I said, scooting away, "Wait, you *gave* part of yourself to your god? What does that mean?"

"I cannot give you *too* much information, but my god likes to have a physical form, and I'm willing to let him overlap *mine* to get that if it means I stay alive." Sera said smugly.

She pointed at her third eye. "It's not the first time he's saved my life..." she pulled down her neckline, showing a smaller mouth with more human looking teeth just above her right breast. "Or the second..." she stood and turned away from me, pulling her robe up to show a cluster of yellow slitted eyes on the lower part of her ribcage "Or the third."

I stood up and stared at her more closely "Does that mean you can't die? Because it looks like that extra eye on your face came from a headshot..."

"I can die same as any other, Candy." she said, "But I do admit to being harder to keep down. That's why I'm telling you this, despite the danger. If I *do* experience another encounter with 'Spacegirl', then I may need *you* to administer this medicine to me, even if I don't appear to be living at the time."

"I- Fuck." I said, "That's a lot of responsibility, this is a lot to take in..."

"Don't think about it too hard, please." she said, "It's not good for you."

"You-" I frowned. "Is this something *I* could get in on? If I die, can I drink that juice and come back?"

Sera shook her head. "No, my god doesn't know you, you'd need to be converted for him to even feel you, much less push into you."

"Oh, damn." I said, "I'll remember this, obviously. I- I just need to get you the medicine and put it in your mouth?"

"And some on the wound, if I'm very far gone." she nodded.

This was much different than any other Chosen power I'd seen so far. There were Chosen with multiple powers, of course, and lots of Chosen could regenerate large amounts of damage, but Sera seemed to be something else. Flight, transformations, a kind of healing that made her god manifest on her body, the beams of light, even her *sword* was some kind of blessed. There were plenty of Chosen with more powerful abilities than her, but it was *very* rare to see a Chosen with a variety of powers that all felt as strong as hers. No wonder the people at the GGDS gave her an A rank...

I felt strange, being trusted to be her lifeline, to literally be the one to bring her back if she died. She trusted me a lot, even giving the details of her powers to me in a way that most people would only tell their teammates. *Were* we teammates? We were in the same section after all, and we would be working together eventually, though all her patrols so far had been solo, due to her rank.

I watched her as she pulled her scorched robes off, leaving her in her under-wrapings, and started trying to clean the dried blood off of her legs and stomach. My eyes fell on a strange symbol burned into her chest between the breasts, just under where her robes usually fell around her shoulders. It looked like a tattoo, if it weren't for the texture, it made her already altered body look even more alien. Looking her up and down though, I was now 90% sure she actually *was* a human, or at least, was a human at some point.

Pushing her body out of my mind and looking at her trust of me reasonably, I *had* given her a name, gotten her a job and a house, and saved her life, so I was probably the most trustworthy person in her life right now. It made sense, but it felt odd too, like I'd tricked her into trusting me or something. I *was* trying to get closer to other Chosen and the girls, those were both parts of my 5 step plan. She didn't *quite* fit into that, but I still felt like I owed her more trust than I'd given her so far if she was putting her life in my hands.

"Hey, Sera?" I asked, leaning against the railing of the porch, "Have you ever wondered what my power is?"

She stopped rubbing at the blood and glanced over at me. "It's flight, and I presume a form of strength and durability, isn't it?"

"Well, all of us in Lorgiaia's angels have those, but we also have a secondary power too, a stronger one..."

"Oh?" she looked at me curiously. "I wasn't aware of that, do you try to keep that hidden?"

"Not exactly?" I said, "We're vocal that we have powers, but mine is unique. Right now, we're telling everyone my power is flying fast."

"I'm guessing it's not?" she said, looking me up and down, "Why tell me if it's not common knowledge?"

"It's not flying fast, no. And let's call it a show of faith, for you telling me how *your* power worked and trusting me with that medicine."

"Fair enough, so, if it's not flight, what power *do* you have, Candy?" Sera said, her arms folded over her chest.

"I..." I struggled to explain it, "I fold people into edible things."

"What?" she asked, her eyebrows bunching together, making her third eye squint suspiciously, "You fold people?"

"I can pull someone through themselves, and they end up looking like something to eat, like a slice of pie, and the universe *thinks* they're a pie or whatever they turn into, but if I eat them, I get stronger."

Sera's eyes widened. "Oh, I see... That's a *very* good power, how do you..?"

"I don't know, I just feel the pull when I touch someone's skin. It's why I wear gloves and stuff, if I touch people, I can feel a spark in them, and I don't know how not to pull it out, it draws me."

"Fascinating..." she said, "how many times have you used it?"

"Just once, I can't turn them back, so it's pretty much like killing them, and, um, I don't want to kill anyone."

"Candy..." she said gently, "being willing to kill in combat is very important, and getting familiar with your skills is a must."

"I just- I don't think I can do it again." I said looking at the blood on the ground, "I wanted to be a Chosen to be famous and to inspire people, not to kill them."

"Killing people is very inspiring, though!" she said encouragingly, "I think you should embrace this power. No one would *ever* stand against you if they knew you would *eat* them if they tried." she looked out at the twilight streets around her house. "If it wasn't such a danger to those around me, I'd be much more open about my own habits when it came to ruffians. Really scare them, make them fear me before they ever see me."

"...Maybe, yeah." I said, "It doesn't seem to bother you as much as I assumed it would, to be honest, maybe others would take it well too?"

Sera snorted. "I'm used to the idea. Not of 'folding' people, but the other part. I assure you, when other people find out about *that* part, they will see you as a monster, same as any of the others."

"We really don't like to use the term monster these days..." I reminded her.

"They'll still call you one." she said, "I say lean into it, be scary. You wanted to inspire, to be famous? Make people fear you and *everyone* will know your name."

I should have known she'd have this opinion, or a similar one, but she wasn't saying anything I hadn't already considered. I'd thought about how to leverage my powers to my advantage, what to do to make them valuable, but I'd come up blank aside from "Threaten to eat people and hope it went over well with the target audience". I could make it a theme, like, be super cutesy about it, and act like it was a silly, fun gimmick, and just pretend I wasn't dooming people to a fate worse than death. I'd felt *powerful* when I ate a single bite of Homicide, and another had let me crumple his desk, from what Alele said. I could maybe even get away with being too scary for my PR team to tell me no...

"I might try that later, but not yet. While we're setting up our team dynamic, I want to keep it under wraps." I said, pushing the idea aside for now.

"Very well, I will keep it a secret, but I still think it would help to use it." she said, "You could be a very, very powerful woman."

A sound from behind us made me flinch, and I spun to see Drizti and Galorna walking up the sidewalk towards us.

"Hey Angel Rouge! Hey Seraphim!" Drizti said, "It's nice to meet you. Saffron said you might be here, Rouge!"

I blocked their view of Sera with my body as she waved and ducked inside her house, hopefully they hadn't seen the extra body parts she had, I didn't really want to explain those...

"Uh, I guess she didn't want to meet you, Driz..." Galorna said.

"No no, she got, um, cut, and we were dressing her wound, she's getting new clothes, I bet." I said, glancing at the door.

"Oh, gosh, that's some cut..." Drizti said looking at the blood on the porch, "Were you two patrolling? I thought you were off until tomorrow."

"I was bored, and she was patrolling. We just ran into each other." I said. Telling them she tried to one vee one Spacegirl wouldn't endear her to them, Spacegirl was a city treasure.

The door opened and Seraphim stepped out again, wearing her casual robes and slightly damp. She must have washed the blood off her while she changed, I looked down at my blood covered outfit, and de-transformed into my normal state to clean up.

"Sera, I was just telling Verdant, she's the green one, about that cut you got, she was worried about the blood." I told her, stepping aside to let her out.

Seraphim nodded. "Yes, I was accosted by a ruffian, but I gave them what for. I'm more than fine now, though."

"Are you sure?" Galorna asked, "This much blood is concerning. We can take you to the hospital, Sera."

"She- she's a regenerator." I lied, "So it *looks* way worse than it actually was."

I didn't know why keeping Sera's secret was so important to me, I just got the feeling bad, bad things would happen if I told them too much about her. Was that an after effect of that juice I'd had? Or just me taking Sera's word that it was dangerous to talk about?

"Oooh, lucky..." Drizti said, "We'll have to remember that, I can transfer wounds to people, so maybe we can transfer people's wounds to you in a pinch!" she smiled proudly at Seraphim, who gave a forced smile back.

""Ah, well, I still scar, and badly at that..." she said nervously, "I'd really prefer to keep my body as un-marred as possible, if that's ok with you."

Drizti looked downcast. "Drat... I thought I'd found a cheat code for my power..."

"There are other regenerators, Driz." Galorna said, "We'll meet another one eventually."

She turned to Sera. "Speaking of, though, I hadn't even heard about you having that power, you really do have a lot of tricks, I'm happy you're in our section! You're very powerful, you'll be a huge help moving forward."

"I was just telling Angel Rouge that she herself could be a powerful Chosen, if she'd only allow herself to use her powers." Sera said, glancing at me.

"Uhhhh what powers?" Galorna said, her face going blank.

"I already told her about my thing, Saffron." I said, "She and I swapped some information about our powers, it's fine."

"I thought we weren't supposed to talk about your power without church approval..." Drizti said, "This seems like a bad idea..."

"It's my power, and it's in my body- or, soul or something, so I'm the one who decides who gets to know." I said grumpily.

"Still, the first person you told just encouraged you to start killing people." Galorna said sternly, "No offense Sera, it's just not PR friendly."

"I take no offense, horned one." she said, amused, "I don't know about 'peayar', but I do know that people will flock to follow her if she demonstrates her power." she looked at me and frowned. "If it works the way I presume, she could even best me in single combat, unless I stopped her from afar, and her flying abilities would make that *quite* difficult."

"Well, I don't think I'll ever fight you." I said, "I hope..."

"It's still fun to chat about it though!" Drizti said, "Me and Sable did that, we tried to figure out who'd win in a fight between everyone."

"That's- hm..." Galorna said, "Actually, that sounds like a good team dynamic exercise, I'd like to do that as a group sometime."

"So who would-" I started, "Oh, wait, yeah."

"Alele." Me, Drizti and Galorna said all at once.

"As long as she gets more practice in, that is." Drizti said, "But she brought you back a bunch, Candy, and me once, so I put great odds on her."

"Alele?" Seraphim asked, "I don't know this one..."

"Ah, Angel Cobalt, the blue one." I said, "Sorry, I guess we forgot to use code names, since it's just us."

"I see, and her power is to raise the dead?" Sera asked.

"No, it's time travel." Galorna clarified, "She can jump back in time three seconds and do stuff over again."

“I- hm. I can see how that would be difficult to counter." Sera acknowledged, "I think I could work around it though."

"You make it sound like you're planning on taking our team out or something." I said, "Don't get weird about it."

She laughed, and patted my back. "Don't worry, even if I have to go through your team to get to the heretics, I'll leave you alive."

"Oh, how *touching*." I said sarcastically, "Are you sure you're not scared I'll eat you?"

"The thought *had* crossed my mind." she said, a small smile still on her face, "I'd be honored to feed your power."

“Anyway, we need to be getting back to the base..." Galorna said, "It's almost time for the shift change. Cand- sorry, Angel Rouge, are you coming back with us?"

I nodded. "Might as well, I need to get in training today still." I turned to Seraphim. "Hey, I'll see you later, it was nice hanging out! Well, aside from the injury."

I was happy to notice that I really *had* enjoyed my time with her, and I was even looking forward to seeing her again soon. I really *could* make this 'networking' and 'friends' thing work after all.

"Ah, I enjoyed our time as well!" she said, curtsying, "We shall have to meet again, maybe for an ale, or training, or even for you to train me in the ways of this place's communication, those small circular machines with pictures!"

"You mean phones? Yeah, absolutely, I thought you said you couldn't have one though?"

"I will be very careful." she said, "I wish to explore the possibility, though. I am being recognized because others see me on their machines, and I would like to see myself on them as well."

"Oh, I've seen those videos!" Drizti said, "You get really rough, but people like how you look, I think you'd be pretty popular if you got on CirNet."

"Angel Rouge is great at that stuff, she's got almost twice as many followers as me." Galorna said, "She can hook you up."

I looked at Seraphim, an idea forming in my head. "...Yeah, I'd love to do that for you, I'll help you figure it out, no problem."

"Thank you for your grace, my friends." Sera said, "I must retire now though, I know you must leave, and I am very tired from the mer- mm. From regenerating."

"Ok, well, see you around, nice meeting you!" Drizti said.

Sera waved, and slipped inside her house, the smell of incense, spices, and something familiar wafting out to me as she closed the door. Dangers aside, I was so, so curious as to what could be in her house, was it a still for the juice she made? A pet? Was she making magic brews or something? I'd find out one way or another, eventually.

~~~

Drizti groaned and tossed the controller on the couch next to her, flopping back into the cushions. I gave her a half smile as she glared at me and shot me the finger, but her heart wasn't in it.
~~~

"This isn't fair, you know shortcuts and stuff, I'm still figuring out how to hold the dumb controller." she said.

"Hey, you're the one who wanted to come over after training." I retorted, unwrapping a piece of chocolate, "If you didn't want to get beaten, you shouldn't have shown up!"

"I was lonely, and you're the only person around to hang out with. I don't actually mind losing, I just never played these games before Wednesday." she sighed.

"So you're only hanging out with me because it's convenient?" I teased, "Wow, way to make a girl feel special."

"No, no. Candy, I was-" she caught my smirk and huffed, throwing a pillow at me. "Rude. No, I like hanging out with you, you're the only one who feels like you really take me seriously sometimes, I'd pick you over Galorna or Alele or whoever any time, I swear."

"What do you mean 'take you seriously'?" I asked.

"Well, like, Alele won't flirt with me like she does everyone else, Galorna keeps patting my head like I'm a pet or something, Lucy calls me 'shrimp' or 'shortstack', but you just hang out with me. I like it, I feel normal. No one making fun of me for being a gnome."

"Oh." I said, wincing, "Yeah, that's gotta suck."

"Right?" she said, sighing, "Anyway, I wanna get good at these games. It was really fun playing all together with everyone a couple days ago, no one was being judgy or rude, no one made fun of my size or past, it was all about the skill you had. I want to be skilled enough to *win*, then maybe they'll see me as a serious person."

"Maybe, yeah." I said, "I'm kinda in the same boat, in a way. I feel- I don't know." I considered not telling her, but I needed to stick to the plan, and this was step five in action. "I feel *alien*. I don't have a power I can use like everyone else, I don't understand the other girls' motivations, and I'm the only person on the team that *wasn't* Chosen because she fits an underrepresented demographic."

"Huh." Driz mused, "I hadn't thought of it like that, I guess. You're not alien to *me* though, I like you. My motivation is… I guess to not be in a cult anymore? And like, yeah you're not a minority, but that's a stupid thing to complain about, you're the normal one, just let yourself be yourself."

"I- yeah. I guess it is stupid." I muttered, "I just feel like I can't connect to the team because I'm not like, a former monster, or trans, or an ex-cultist, or an elf or whatever."

"Alele being an elf isn't that weird though, elves are rare, sure, but they're a lot more common than gnomes." Drizti pointed out, "She was probably picked more for her fancy, refined tastes than for being an elf, you can connect to her over that?"

"Fancy and refined?" I asked, "You mean 'stuck up and picky'."

Drizti giggled. "She's not so bad, she's just set in her ways."

"Yeah, I like her a lot." I admitted, "I look forward to patrolling with her these days."

"Oooh, but do you *like* her?" Drizti asked, leaning over and wiggling her thin white eyebrows.

"Nnnno?" I said, my voice less sure than I felt, "I can't touch her, so like, it's a moot point."

"You can still be sweet on her even if you can't touch her…" Drizti said, "Still, that does make it harder."

"It makes *everything* harder." I said, "I come into the rec room to see what people are doing, and Galorna is wrapped around Lucy teaching her how to play pool, or you're laying on Alele while you read. Even just after patrols I see you and the other girls hug, and- I miss that, I need that, I want to *touch* people…"

"That doesn't help the alienation, I'm sure." she said sadly.

"No, it really doesn't." I growled, more harshly than I meant to, "It hurts, but in a dull sense of loss way, I can't explain it."

"I get it, I'm used to way more touch than I'm getting now too." Drizti said, "Gnomes are very physical, so I miss that a lot. I know it's not quite the same as no touch at all, but I still want to be held."

I shook my head. "I can't help you there."

"Hm." she mused, looking at me closely "If we both wrap up in a blanket, we could at least sit *next* to each other?"

I thought about it. It'd be something real at least, not an awkward post-fight hug from Galorna or a drunken nap with Sera, just us, hanging out. I nodded silently and wrapped myself in the blanket I'd been using, keeping my hands in my lap. Driz scooted closer, and I felt her body heat against mine as she cozied up. This was nice, it was contact, even if it was muffled by blankets.

"Wanna watch something?" she asked.

"Yeah, I do." I said, "Here, get the remote, there's this great show I wanted to show you about a family of Chosen who were paid to let a camera crew in their house to record everything they do. It's totally wild, you'll love it."

As the reality TV trash started playing on the screen, I breathed out slowly, letting my body relax. I needed this. I was glad to have someone like Drizti who I could be around and be honest with, she was a valuable friend. Now if only I could connect to the *other* girls…

~~~

I stepped back into our building, waving goodbye to Crystal. It'd felt nice to patrol again, I'd gotten a good night's sleep last night despite my nap with Seraphim. My and Crystal's time out was uneventful and peaceful, *and* because it was in the afternoon, we'd stopped in at a couple of shops to 'inspect' them, and I'd gotten a nice, sweet ube roll for dinner.
~~~

My next time out would be tomorrow night, and it was a later shift, it'd start at 8 at night, and go until 4 in the morning. I wasn't looking forward to it, because I would have to stay up all night tonight and sleep in the day tomorrow and then do it *again* that night too. Plus it was a weird time to get off work, only the diner would be open, so my breakfast options would be limited. Apparently having our shifts end and start at different times was supposed to make them unpredictable for criminals, and make us more aware of our surroundings.

I found I was not usually very aware of my surroundings at 4 AM one way or another, to be honest.

I was scheduled to be patrolling with Lucy, which could be nice, and that one member of The Unchosen, the drone girl, whatever her name was. She could fly at least, so she would be more useful than Crystal at covering ground, but I didn't really know her past our introduction and a single 'hello' when we ran into each other at the shopping center once. Still, I was slightly apprehensive about it, and I was still dreading the day 'the other one' of The Unchosen would tag along with me on a patrol. I heard from Galorna the first time she'd run into a civilian on her route, they'd actually reported her as a threat to the GGDS. Galorna and Mourner had shown up, only to find the bug girl curled up in an alleyway sobbing, unable to handle the woman's screaming.

That pathetic display aside, I still was too afraid of her to be around her.

I looked around the lobby, I'd expected to see Alele and Driz here, heading out to meet up with Mourner for their shift, but it looks like I was alone. They must have already left? That was fine, I had stuff to do, anyway. I dug in my pocket and pulled out my commonplace book, tearing out the map I'd been marking on while I patrolled this afternoon, and headed for the offices on the far side of the lobby from the shop and cafe, and stepped inside. There was a drone of typing, printing, quiet talking, and the occasional phone ring, a collection of sounds I'd heard in the backgrounds of shows, but I'd never expected to hear in person. I was a farm girl, why would I ever step foot in an office?

As it was, I hardly ever came in here. This marked maybe the third time I'd been past the 'employees only' door, and it took me a few minutes of wandering to find what I was looking for, the executive offices. There was one for a church head that I'd never seen filled- they mostly just called in the orders and decisions- but the other one was a large office with a partners desk in it. Oori was on one side, and Debbie was on the other, an engraved nameplate reading 'Willa" covered by a sticky piece of paper reading 'Debbie' in front of her.

Oori looked up from his computer and smiled at me. "Hello, back from patrol? How'd it go?"

"Pretty good, I guess. Nothing weird, but I wanted to give you this..." I said, handing him the map "I marked all the buildings without a way in, the fake ones, I mean. Some are attached to others so maybe they just had ways in I couldn't see? But most of these are absolutely fake buildings."

"I don't see how a building can be 'fake'," Debbie said, "if it's there, it's got four walls and a roof, it's real."

I glanced at her. This wasn't her thing, I was talking to Oori, and she had no business butting in. "They're hollow." I said bluntly.

"Well, I'll get this to the research team," Oori said, taking the map, "they submitted a request on a couple of the other ones already, but we haven't heard back yet."

"Hopefully they figure it out soon." I said, "I looked around at other sections, and it seems like it's mostly around us, maybe two to four sections away from us will have these, but past that, nothing."

"You think it's something to do with the location, then?" he asked.

"I don't see why you're so worried about it," Debbie cut in again, "I can almost assure you it's just zoning or city planning or something."

I ignored her. "I don't know if it's the location as in, just the area we're in? Or as in, someone around here has something to do with it, but yes, it's very locational."

"And your other teammates consider this odd as well?" he asked.

"They do." I confirmed, "Lucy didn't really care too much, and Drizti didn't quite understand why it was so weird, but we're all interested overall."

"Hm, ok, well we'll put this on the board as our top priority." Oori said, "I'll let the others know to keep an eye on them during patrols, and I'll bring it up at our next team meeting. With any luck it'll be your first big breakthrough once you solve it!"

"How wonderful, publicity for looking at empty buildings..." Debbie said dryly.

"Thanks, Oori." I said, "It might be nothing, but solving mysteries and stuff like this is much more my speed than fighting people."

"Your 'speed' is going fast." Debbie said firmly, "And you're the only one of the team with an official takedown on your record, so fighting is your 'speed' too, like it or not."

"..." I bit my lip. She *was* still in charge, even if she *did* seem to be trying to hold me back and slow down my follower count with her stupid 'no selfies on patrol' rule. "I'm going to go, I've got a late night photo shoot later, because I'm staying up for my shift tomorrow? And I want to relax in base form so my mana's full for that."

"Alright Candy," Oori said, "thank you for your hard work, and if I hear anything, I'll let you know!"

"Just make sure to follow the rules, no brands, no panties, no violence." Debbie reminded me. For the umpteenth time.

I gave a tight smile, and stepped back out of their office to head to my room. I liked Oori, I just needed to find a way to get *just* him, instead of having *her* be there each time. I shouldn't hate her so much, but she'd been riding my ass a lot more since I hit twenty thousand followers, and being honest with myself, I kind of resented her for making me cut my hair. Even if I'd agreed, I still blamed her, overall.

I rode the elevator up to my room, and de-powered, leaving me in my lazy day clothes, a pair of sweat pants and one of my dad's t-shirts. It was falling apart, but I still wouldn't let myself get rid of it. The door dinged open, and I stepped out, almost colliding with Lucy, who was getting on.

"Oh, oop, sorry-" I said, catching myself on her shoulder with my hand. I instantly felt the connection, the spark worming into my brain, her essence, and it tasted like vanilla icing. I gasped, and threw myself to the side, crashing to the floor with a thump, scrambling away from her. Was I too late? Had I-

"Uh, fucking weirdo. Gods, you won't even touch my shoulder?" Lucy said angrily, "I stand by my choice to shower alone, gods..."

I sat up and shook my head. "N-no, L-lucy, no, I- I touched you..."

"Yeah, I noticed." she said darkly, "and you freaked ou- oooohhh *shit*, you're not gloved..." her face paled. "I was almost-"

I nodded. "Sorry, I- I *tasted* you, Lucy, it was really close." I shuddered. "You tasted really good, too, very sweet..."

"...I can't even make a joke about that right now." Lucy said, "Fuck, girl, glove up in public areas, gods."

"I'm sorry, I- I was just walking like 10 feet to my room, I'm *so* sorry." I said, "I transformed in my room before patrol, so no gloves, I just- fuck..."

Lucy looked at me for a second, and then made a face "It's whatever. Just be more careful. And- ugh, I'm sorry I implied you were like, I dunno, transphobic or whatever. It's just, like, easy to blame my problems on that, so I get a little sensitive."

"No, no, I get it." I said awkwardly, "I can imagine people are weird about it. I'm not. Weird. About it I mean."

"No, you're just weird in general." Lucy said, "I get weird vibes from you, like you don't treat me like, I don't know, like I'm real or something. I took it personally, like, I assumed it was because I was trans, but *fuck*, you do that to everyone. That initial impression of you though, it stuck in my head, I guess, sorry."

"I just- I'm really bad at people." I said, "I see you as real, I just- I have a hard time acting the right way."

"Are you like, autistic or something?" she asked, tilting her head.

"Oh, uh, I don't think so, I just don't understand people, or how they work." I said. I was pretty sure I'd know if I had autism, right?

Lucy shrugged. "Well, you're going to be dealing with people, like, every day from now on. You'll get better."

"Uh, yeah, I guess."

"Anyway, I'm going for pho, want to join?" she jutted a thumb at the elevator ,"Once you put on a pair of gloves, at least, seriously."

"Oh, uhh, no, I'm good." I said, "I have a photoshoot later, I need to get rested and ready."

Lucy pressed the elevator button with her keycard and stepped inside. "Fair enough. This shop isn't on the approved list, anyway, I wouldn't want to drag you into breaking the rules."

"Lucy, really?" I said, annoyed, "You got *shot* the last time we went to an unapproved place."

"What? Oh, damn, sorry, can you repeat that?" she asked as the door slid closed, "I didn't quite catch that last p-"

I watched the lights change, showing the floors as the elevator went down. The odds of there being another super villain owned shop in our area were pretty low, but not zero... I stood up, my hands still shaky from the panic at almost folding Lucy, and licked my lips. I could swear there was a slight taste still there, what *was* that? Cake frosting? I hadn't tasted Homicide until I'd bitten him, but I had tasted *something* minty when Alele touched me. That said, I'd had to fight to fold Homicide, and I'd just barely felt Alele's spark. With Lucy, it was like her spark was *begging* to be folded. Was my power getting stronger? Or was it something else? It was impossible to tell without testing it, but I almost felt like I was hungry, on a deeper level than physical, and I was craving cake, too…

That was concerning. That was also an issue for a later time, I had a photo shoot to get ready for.

~~~

I took another bite of my double chocolate fudge swirl cone with sprinkles, and kicked my feet against the old bridge, feeling very happy with myself, the buzz thrumming in my head. The night had gone great, and I thought the pics looked honestly amazing, with my natural glow shining slightly in the darkness.

"Ugh, I still don't know how you can *bite* it." Forica said, shuddering, "If I did that, my leaves would curl, gods..."

I took another bite, making a big show of putting my teeth directly into the ice cream. "Mmm, it's sooo much better this way..." I said as I chewed.

"I'll stick to licking." she said, "I heard people who bite ice cream are psychopaths or something."

I pulled the cone away from my mouth. "Do you really think I'm a psychopath?" I asked, curious.

"I have no idea." Forica said, "That's the point, you can't really tell if someone is one, right?"

"I don't know, I haven't really looked into it." I said, "You're the second person today to try and diagnose me with something, I don't care about that stuff, I just want to get CirNet followers."
~~~

"You know..." she said thoughtfully, "If you *did* get diagnosed with something, you could post awareness stuff and like, post tips and help for other people who have the same diagnosis. Those accounts do crazy well, especially when it's a more interesting diagnosis."

"Oh, sure, let me be the psychopath poster child, that's *great* for PR."

"You could show that maybe it's not so bad? Like, you could prove it's ok to be a psychopath, and still be successful."

"I- I'm not a psychopath though, or if I am, I don't care, I just want to have a normal CirNet account." I said, angrily.

"Ok! Ok, just spit balling. Pretty sure the 'bites her ice cream cones' diagnosis was thrown out years ago anyway." she said, "We got some great pictures tonight anyway, and I think it'll give you a big boost."

"Yeah, I think so too." I said "Hey, did you see I got a selfie with Genki?" I asked proudly, "That got me a *ton* of followers."

"I did see, yeah. She's super popular, but she's mostly a thirst trap poster, so you'll lose some of those followers as they realize you're not posting the kind of stuff she is."

"Oh, drat, ok." I said, disappointed, "Should I be?"

"It would help." Forica admitted, "But Debbie would murder us both, so no, don't do that, please."

"Fucking Debbie..." I muttered.

"Eh," Forica said, "she's a necessary evil."

"I can figure out my own social media, she should stick to public appearances and stuff." I said, frustrated.

"I've seen too many magical girls fall into being, like, not kid friendly if they're not managed." Forica said, "They're supposed to be heroes for kids, but one of them I know of even started a skintube account. Ended up being forced to *just* do that, her church cut her funding and she wasn't strong enough to go solo."

"Well I'd never do *that*." I complained.

"Yeah, I know. But it's good to have at least a little bit of rules." Forica said, "To make *sure* you never end up on skintube."

"What about you?" I asked, "You're a model or something, right? I'd assume you'd be all over that kind of thing. It'd get you a ton of followers, I'm sure."

"Angel Rogue, I am a *minor*." Forica laughed, "I'll do that when I hit eighteen, not before."

I flushed. "Ah, fuck."

This was *not* a conversation I should be having with a teenager. I'd forgotten she was 16. Was that on me for not focusing? Or on her for acting like an adult? It couldn't be on her, she was a kid, was I just that bad with people?

"Uh, I should... get back to base." I said, "I've gotta get ready for tomorrow night, by- uh, staying up, and I don't want to-"

Halfway through, I realized my excuse didn't make sense, and I stopped.

"Candy, look." Forica said, "You can run away at the first sign of controversy, that's fine. That's good PR. *Or* you can just forget about that dumb comment and let me show you some places that'll help you stay up tonight, *and* wear you out for the morning."

"I- I don't know." I said, "Like clubs? You can't go into clubs, you're a kid, and I really shouldn't be seen going into clubs with a kid."

"Yeah, clubs, I have a press pass." she grinned, "I won't drink or anything, we can go in separately or something, meet up inside."

"I- no, that's a cool offer, but no. I- I can't do that. Something would go wrong, or someone would take a pic or something, just- no."

"Fine, no problem." Forica said, "But they're *great* places to network!"

"Maybe a different day." I said, "Look, just give me the names, I just- I'm ok being friends, but going clubbing together isn't ok."

"Well, dang. I guess goodnight, then." Forica said as I floated up off the bridge, "Maybe I'll send you the names, maybe not. I just want someone to dance with is all."

"Yeah, well if you do send them, I'll check them out." I said, "I- I'll see you later, thanks for the pictures, I'll see you later."

I took off without waiting for a response. Going to a club and meeting new people, new Chosen, even, sounded amazing, but the optics of going clubbing with a 16 year old were *not* great, and the *morals* of taking a teenager clubbing were pretty much nonexistent. I liked the idea of the clubs though, I'd need to figure out a way to find them though.

And, I supposed, find a way to avoid skin contact in a room full of moving bodies...

Chapter Fourteen

I leaned against the outside of our building, waiting for the robot girl from The Unchosen to meet up with us so we could start our patrol. I checked my phone; it was still five 'til, so she wasn't *late*, but if she wasn't here at eight sharp, I was leaving Lucy to deal with her. I wanted to 'patrol' the tea shop before they closed at 8:30 so I could get snacks for the night. I scanned the sky, and thought about my plan. Oori hadn't been able to turn up *anything* on the buildings, they were all owned by separate companies, they all were zoned as 'office space' with some minor concessions, and they were all paid up on their taxes and utilities. If they weren't hollow, there'd be nothing odd about them at all, except they were marked as exempt from regular building and fire code inspections. But they *were* hollow, and *that* meant something was up. I hadn't discussed it with Lucy or robot girl, but I was planning on investigating a little more tonight, and I'd have some help, too.

"So, you excited?" Lucy asked.

I flinched. "Uhhh, why?" I asked, concerned. She shouldn't know about my plan, I hadn't even told *Oori* about it.

"I mean, *I'm* excited." Lucy said, "I know she's only like, half FolDrone, but still, a sentient *drone?* Most 'androids' are like, basic computer programs or copies of brains on wheels because of the stupid regulations. Her being a full on humanoid is pretty awesome, I can't believe we get to *patrol* with her."

"Oh, yeah, right." I said. Lucy *would* be excited about that. "I mean it's no big deal, she's just a person that happens to be made of metal, it's whatever."

"I appreciate your kindness, Angel Rouge!" a voice said from beside me.

I snapped my wings open and lifted off, backing away as I got my bearings. The robot lady was hovering a foot off the ground, the tubes on her back glowing blue at the ends, not making a sound. She smiled at me and Lucy, and I lowered myself down slowly, and crossed my arms, embarrassed at my reaction.

"Many people don't see me as a person, it's refreshing to know you think of me as such." she said

"Uh, yeah, I mean-" I hadn't really thought of it like *that*, but at least she was happy with me? "I just- you know, people are people."

"I think you're awesome, seriously!" Lucy said, grinning, "I *love* robots, they're like, one of my favorite things, and like, you *are* one!"

"Thank you!" she said, "I have to ask though, can you avoid using the word 'robot'? It used to mean 'slave', so it's a little weird to be called that."

"Oh, shit, I'm so sorry, I didn't know it was a slur, I wouldn't have used it if I'd known." Lucy said, appalled.

I frowned at her. "Lucy, I heard you use a slur two hours ago."

Lucy blushed. "No! *No*, you can't just *TELL* people that, I used a slur about ME, that I'm *allowed* to say."

"Whatever..." I said, turning to the other girl, "So what *can* we call you?"

"Well, just Mod, or Maud, either one!" she laughed, "But if you're *describing* me, then I prefer the term 'artificial life form', personally."

"Ok," I said, "I'll remember that."

I doubted I would, but I'd pretend to try at least. Step 5.

"So, do you have a pattern you guys usually patrol in?" Mod asked, "Or is it just easier to wander?"

"Well, I'm going to hit up the tea shop a few streets over, first." I said, "I need snacks and caffeine, but after that we just wander, usually."

"Mind if I stick with you two then?" Mod asked, "After what happened to poor Amaryllis on her first patrol, I've been trying to stay close to the 'normal' looking members of the patrol so citizens won't be afraid of me too."

"Oh, yeah, we'll all go as a group." Lucy said, "I heard about Amaryllis from Galorna. She said she was so stressed they could barely get her to uncurl and walk home..."

"She has severe agoraphobia, it's why she stayed in Canyon City until it was sealed." Mod said, "So going out in public and getting screamed at... It set it off again."

"Why is she a superhero if she's-?" I started, then thought better of it, "Mmm. Never mind. Sorry."

Lucy glared at me. "She's being the best person she can be, don't judge her."

"No, it's ok." Mod said, "It was a hard choice for her to make, and I *did* push her into it a little, but she's using it as a way to grow and become more confident."

"I get it." I said, "I just- I was just thinking out loud. I'm going to go hit up the shop, I guess."

I wasn't happy about the two of them following me all night, but I'd still do what I had to. This was my only lead on getting on the news and getting famous, and I was already having to share the spotlight with one other person if we found anything. I'd just have to make sure to be the most charismatic person there when we were in front of the cameras.

We made it to the shop in time for me to get a sack of pastries and a matcha tea, and a can of peach tea for later. I was craving sweets *constantly* these days, I'd ramped up my training in the past sessions, and I was pretty sure that was it, but I felt somehow empty when I wasn't eating or drinking something sweet. Lucy got a coffee and a muffin, and Mod politely waited outside for us. I sipped my tea as I rejoined her outside and tried to think of the best way to tell them about my plans for the evening.

"So..." I started, "I actually have plans tonight."

"Wait, we can just blow off patrols?" Lucy asked, perking up, "Fuck, me and G- uh, Angel Saffron need to finish the show we're watching, If I can just *leave*-"

"No, it's- I'm still on the job, it's a Chosen thing, in our section." I interrupted her, "I'm just- I won't be *patrolling*, patrolling. I'll be... investigating."

"Well, I think we should stick together still, what are you investigating?" Mod asked, crossing her arms.

I tried not to stare as her left arm's gears started clicking and shaking from being pressed against her smooth right one. Was that bad for her? Did she need to replace them from time to time? What was the maintenance on an 'artificial life form' like? Could she do it herself? I pushed it out of my head, I didn't really care about it, her body was just... interesting. I refocused, and tried to remember her question.

"Did Kiri tell you about the hollow buildings?" I asked.

Lucy groaned. "Ugh, *that* again?"

Mod nodded. "Yyyyes, I heard. We're going to try and find more?"

"No, uh... I already marked them all out on a map." I said, "We-we're going in one."

"I thought you and Angel Cobalt already *did* that..." Lucy grumbled.

"Yeah, but this time we're going to try and get through the floor, too." I said, pulling out my commonplace book to check the address, "Come on, I already picked out one to explore, but we gotta get there fast, a secret helper is waiting for us already."

"Will we be breaking and entering?" Mod asked as we all lifted up into the sky, me taking the lead, "I *can* override my programming, but it still makes me uncomfortable to break the law."

"The buildings are empty." I said, "It doesn't count. Plus we're using the 'reasonable suspicion' thing, the one that lets heroes go into fallen lairs even if they're not actively chasing someone."

"...I won't do any of the breaking, but I'll come along, then." Mod said, after thinking for a moment.

"This is *not* what we're supposed to be doing tonight, Rogue." Lucy said, "Breaking in, bending the law, maybe you're not as much of a stuck up asshole as I thought!"

I cringed, was *that* how she saw me? I was kind of rude, yeah, and I *did* look down on people a lot. I still had a lot of work to do on step 5 if she was willing to call me an asshole to my face like that.

I swallowed against the lump in my throat and pointed. "Um, t-that building, the one over there, that's the one we're going into."

I flew ahead quickly to hide my watery eyes, and dropped over the edge of the building to the ground in the alley between the building in question and another one. We'd chosen this building because of this alley, no windows pointed at the building from here, so we could get in without being caught.

"Ah, you've arrived!" Seraphim said, stepping out of the shadows, her face bandaged up again to hide her glow. How she kept managing to hide in darkness while wearing all white was beyond me.

"'Sup, we have company." I said, pointing up.

"Hey, uh, C-Candy?... I was just- *oh*, fuck, hi." Lucy said as she came over the building and saw Sera looming in the shadows.

"Oh, you're the other hero in our section?" Mod said as she lowered herself down next to me and extended her right hand, the prosthetic one, to Sera, "I haven't met you. I'm happy to make your acquaintance, my name is Maud."

"Oh, a wonder!" Seraphim said, lighting up. She shook Mod's hand gently. "I'd wondered if there were any mageworks craftsmen here, what manner of golem are you built on? I see you have glass, but also clockwork, you are surely a work of *fine* craftsmanship!"

"Aww, you flatter me!" Mod said, "Mh, yes, I'm- I suppose golem *could* describe me, in a way. A sand golem, maybe, on account of my computer chips? I'm an artificial life form, I was made of, well, whatever parts my friend could find, at the time."

Seraphim's eyes widened and her smile spread under her wraps. "I am curious to see what your friend could create if they had access to a full workshop, then! I am *such* an admirer of wonders, I'm thankful I get to see one here, so far from home."

I sighed and stepped in. "Mod, this is Seraphim, she's not on patrol right now, so we'll be covering for her if we get caught." I turned to Sera. "Ok, enough chatting, get us in."

Sera smiled, and put her hands on the side of the building and flexed. A flash of light exploded outwards and washed over the alley with a cracking noise and a shock wave, and the wall blew inwards, leaving a gaping hole in front of us.

"Holy *shit*..." Lucy said, "remind me to never fight you, Seraphim."

Sera looked at the three of us and smugly tilted her head back. "I could fight all of you, if need be, I have no reason to remind you to avoid a fight."

"You told *me* you'd lose against me." I pointed out.

"Only if you were naked, or close to it." Seraphim said, then glanced at Mod, remembering my power was a secret, "Ah, but *that* is not a conversation for this place."

I glanced at Mod to see if she'd picked up on anything, but she was just smiling knowingly at the two of us, her hand over her mouth as if to say 'that's so sweet!~'. I rolled my eyes, let her misunderstand, it kept my power secret all the same. I pulled my flashlight out of my pocket, and stepped into the hole, switching it on. The interior of the building was almost the same as the other one, no windows on the ground floor, but rows of them on the upper floors, nothing inside but metal and concrete support beams. I walked to the center of the room, keeping my flashlight on the ground to hide the light from the windows and ran my shoe along the ground until I found the joint.

"I got it!" I called out to Sera, "Come blast this, and we'll all drop down."

"I can stay watch?" Lucy offered, walking slowly into the room behind the others, "This feels, uh, I don't know, like something out of one of those cheap cash grab horror games."

"I don't play many games, so I don't know what you're talking about." I said, "But no, if you're here, you're coming down with us."

Sera stepped up and floated over the ground, her hands out, and I stepped back. There was a large flash, and the ground shattered and crumbled where she'd shot. Once the dust cleared, I saw there was still more concrete , she'd made a dent a couple of feet deep, but she hadn't broken through.

She charged up, and blasted again, the ground shattering and splitting open, hot air rushing up out of the newly opened hole. I drifted over and looked down, the floor was around three feet thick, and the cavern underneath was pitch black.

"Whoah..." Lucy muttered, kicking a rock into the hole, "It's deep..."

The rock hit the ground a second later, the sound echoing around in the empty building

"It's about 30 feet deep, sounds like." Mod said thoughtfully, "I can set up some anchors and some rope from my storage compartment so we can get down there."

"My dearest wonder, we can all *fly*..." Sera said as she unwrapped her face, her shine brightening up the whole building.

"I'd rather be safe than sorry, we have no idea what's down there." she said, driving a spike into the ground, "I have 4.46 hours of flight battery left, I want to be able to get out if I use all that up."

"Fair enough." Lucy said, "I've got my transformation up to almost twelve hours now, so I'll be fine."

"And mine lasts for- um. I'm actually not sure? It lasted until the end of last patrol, though." I said.

"Mine lasts for as long as my god breathes and the universe cycles, and maybe longer!" Seraphim said, laughing lightly. I didn't get the joke, but she was still smiling at herself when she jumped into the hole, leaving us in a much darker space, barely lit by my and Lucy's aura.

"Hang on- fuck." I said, and jumped in after her.

It was a good ways down, around 30 feet like Mod had said, and about as wide as the building itself. The ground we landed on was covered with the rubble from up above, and I picked my way over to where Sera was standing as the others made their way down too. The room was mostly empty, but the wall Sera was looking at had a desk, a sink, and a tall rack with bottles and jars lining it, full of liquids. Some had lumps floating in them, some had a slight glow. It looked like they hadn't been touched in a long, long time, based on the layer of dust on them.

"What's this?" I asked her, "Some kind of lab?"

"It's alchemy of some kind, I'm sure of it." Sera said, picking up a bottle and shaking it. The lump inside spun slowly and I took a step back when I realized it was a severed hand, with sharp claws and strange mottled skin.

"It's... body parts?!" Lucy said, coming up behind up, "This is *way* too much for me..."

Sera turned to look at Lucy, concerned, and the hand in the jar she was holding twitched, clenching the fingers slightly. The other body parts in the jars all wiggled slightly too, and one of the eyes squirmed its tail, bumping into the glass with a small 'tink'

"Hhhhh, yep, nope, I'm staying up top." Lucy said.

"I thought you were all goth and stuff," I groaned, "isn't this your thing? These are super old anyway."

"Being goth means I know enough *about* spooky stuff to stay away from rooms with moving body part jars, thank you very much." Lucy snapped at me.

"I support your decision, Angel Sable." Mod said, giving a small smile, "We'll contact you if anything goes wrong!"

"Yeah, whatever." Lucy gave the jars another look and shuddered. "Maud, I still wanna hang out some other time, hit me up..."

As she flew up and out of the hole, Sera sighed. "These parts are concerning, and have signs of *some* heretic mischiefs, but not the ones I'm looking for."

"Well this is just one building, we could go up and try the next one?" I said, "We know there's *something* in at least this one, so..."

"If I may," Mod said politely, "my sensors are showing a passageway to the north, and one to the south, could we try looking there before we break into anywhere else?"

I shone my flashlight in one of the directions she pointed. "Oh, sure enough." I said, thinking, "I bet they lead to other empty buildings, Sera, do you want to go south, and Mod and I will go north?"

"Hmm." Sera said, sniffing the air, "I'm fine with that, you go ahead, we'll meet back here after we investigate."

I waved at her, and we headed off in our directions. As we approached the passageway, Mod stopped, and pulled back a panel on her left leg, turning on an industrial construction light in her 'thigh'. I watched it bounce and flicker across the walls as we walked, and looked at my own flashlight. I'd known I'd need more light than my aura, but it almost felt pathetic compared to her giant spotlight. I tucked the flashlight into my pocket and let Mod pass me, so my shadow wasn't blocking our view.

"I'm surprised you didn't want to go with your friend, Angel Rouge. This was *your* mission after all." she said, glancing back at me.

"I mean, I know she can handle herself." I said, "I don't know if I'm much good in a fight, but I'm better than nothing, so I went with the weaker person. No offense."

"None taken, my strength is in my utility." Mod said, "Drone's weapon systems are mostly in their arms and legs, so while I *can* hold my own, I am of no disillusion about my real power."

"I mean, you *are* pretty helpful, though." I pointed out, "Rope, a light, that spike, it's handy stuff."

"Mm, and I can lift over a ton as well!" she said, "I have my uses."

I could only lift around 700 pounds transformed at full power, but I was pretty sure I could go way, way higher if I had a transformed sweet to eat first. I was contemplating if we could figure out how strong I was by comparing the strength needed to crumple a metal desk with people's max lift when we stepped out into another room. This one was dimly lit with red glowing lights, and Mod shut her light off as we entered, making the whole room feel oddly numbing.

The walls and ceiling were covered with thick, tan flesh, with thin mouths and wide eyes everywhere. The center of the room had a large hole in it, and a pillar of flesh poured out of it, seeming to be the source of the rest of the flesh, growing out of the middle of the room like a weird flesh mushroom. A strange smell filled the air, similar to the one on Seraphim's house, but sweatier, and unclean.

"Oh, fuck." I said, my skin crawling, "This isn't what I expected to find at all."

"It's alive, and it goes down, way, way down..." Mod said, "My seismic detectors are picking up a pulse from as far down as I can get a reading."

"What *is* it?" I asked, carefully walking around the pillar, noticing how the eyes followed me, watching my every move. One of the mouths opened up and a tongue slithered out, giving me a flashback to the mouth in Sera's stomach.

"I *think*." Mod said, her eyes flashing, "I thiiiink it's a part of The Northern Empress? It matches up with how her body looked the last time she left her cathedral, just, you know, not woman shaped."

"But-" I said, getting chills, "No, she's in the *wastes*, she *is* the wastes, we're an ocean away from her main body, and half a continent from her containment zone!"

"Then someone is growing a new one of her." Mod said grimly, "This is almost an exact match for her style and presence, even the pillar in the center could be the tail end of one of the tendrils that comes off her back."

"So- what, she just grew herself all the way here? Underground, across an ocean, from the northern wastes?" I asked, wondering if she was listening to us, "That's- that's *stupid*."

"She could be trying to set up branches in cities?" Mod said, "She might be looking to expand. We know she can make new bodies, her original avatar was a *fraction* of her true height when she first intro-duced herself last century, this could be the seed of a new cathedral."

"I *guess*, she did have that weird kid, recently." I muttered, "Fuck, this is like, a global threat, we need to report it, or something..."

"Let's keep going for now." she replied, "There's more passageway to investigate."

I looked over at the far wall and saw a hole in the flesh, leading deeper into the rooms. The first room had what looked like a serial killer's trophy case, the second had a part of one of the most dangerous physical gods on the planet, what could the third have? A space-time rift? I wanted to get as much information as I could before I went to Oori with this though, so I didn't have much of a choice here.

"Fuck, ok, fuck." I said, "Let's keep moving then."

I watched as some of the flesh on the pillar started to twist and shape, and I dashed ahead. Whatever she was doing, I didn't want to sit around and watch it happen. Mod used her jets and slid up next to me, turning her light on as we moved quickly down the tunnel.

"Drat. We have to go back through there, you know." Mod said, shaking her head, "And I'm pretty sure she noticed us."

"I don't want to think about that." I said, "Hopefully she's asleep again by the time we come back."

We walked in silence for a while, the clanging of Mod's construction feet echoing out around us. I felt nervous about this whole mission now, and I was *really* regretting not going with Sera. If *we* had run into The Northern Empress, she could have just blasted it. If it was me and Mod, I could hope god-flesh turned into pie like human flesh did, I supposed? I was screwed if it didn't, I only had the one trick.

Mod's light fell on a large steel door at the end of the hall, and I walked up to it slowly.

"Damn, if it's locked, we'll have to go back." I said, looking for a way in, "I doubt you're strong enough to get through this."

"I think its got an inset handle, there." Mod said, pointing to a small hole on the side.

It didn't look like any handle I'd ever seen, but I fit my hand into the oblong hole, and felt my fingers slide into place, each pushing in some kind of button. The door hissed, and swung open with a pop, flooding the small space we were in with the smell of dirt, rot, and old leaves. I gagged, and put my gloved hand over my mouth to block it out, slowly walking forwards into the darkness.

"This place *stinks*." I said, pulling off one glove to tie around my head. Mod was a robot anyway, so she'd be safe from me at least.

"Oh, dear, I'm sorry to hear that." Mod said, sounding almost smug, "I can't *imagine* what that must be like."

I grumbled and looked around. There were no lights in this room, and it'd been blocked off into small corridors that went off at random angles. The ceiling was much lower too, being barely higher than the one in the passageway we'd just left.

"Leave the door open, in case we have to make a dash for it." I said. I shone my light down the different passageways and tunnels, seeing strange grooves on the walls about waist high, and dirt on the floor instead of concrete.

I wasn't about to go wandering down one of the paths and get lost, so I kept to the 'main' one until it dead ended with a sharp right turn.

"Hey, I'm going this way." I whispered back "Bring your light."

Mod coasted up beside me, and shone her light down the hallway, the hall took another turn to the right, so we followed it cautiously until we entered into a large, open area with dirt walls and floor. It wasn't as tall as the other two rooms had been, but still taller than the tunnels. There were 2 tanks set up with humanoid shapes in them along one wall, the liquid filling the tanks too clouded to see into, a row of computer equipment along one side. To the right, there was a small living area with a bed, fridge, table, and a real floor, and the doors to an elevator set into one wall.

I crept forward to one of the tanks, seeing waving, twitching things coming off the humanoid's bodies in one, and a coil of something serpentine around the other. I shuddered, not sure what I was looking at. I turned to get Mod to shine her light into one of the tanks, and froze when I saw movement from the living quarters.

There, from on the floor, a strange, cursed, hateful thing was crawling towards me. It had the upper half of a human, with splotchy red and white skin where the top half met the lower half, and long blonde hair. The eyes were blood red, with yellow rings and black centers, and they slid into slits as it reared up. It was vaguely feminine in appearance, with two horn like antenna and two sets of arms, both hanging loosely as it scurried. The lower half, though, was my worst nightmare. It was a long, fat centipede body, black and red, with yellow legs that jutted out from the body, slightly transparent and moving too fast to see clearly. It hissed, and I saw that its mouth was full of human teeth, except for the two sharp fangs that slid out from the cheeks as it lifted up towards me.

My heart was racing, and I was about to scream, I could tell. Or- no, actually, I was *already* screaming, that must be why I couldn't hear it hissing anymore. I swung my foot at it and felt it thud as I punted it across the room, straight at the passageway we'd just come down and collapsed. It screamed and writhed, flopping around on the dirt floor before getting up and dashing off out of the room. I tried to catch my breath, even if it'd only been a couple of feet long, that was one of the most terrifying things I'd ever seen.

"No- my baby!" a voice yelled and I turned to see a halfling man with a white beard and a stained tank top stumble out of the bed, reaching for where the horror had slipped off to. Had he been *sleeping* here? With that thing in the same room with him?

"Baby?" Mod said, whipping her head around to look where it'd gone, "Angel Rouge, what *was* that?"

"It- b-bug thing..." I stuttered, trying to get my words out.

Mod looked at me for a moment, then nodded, and stepped over to the man while I collected myself, my skin still crawling. I swear I could feel it crawling up my legs and over my wings...

"Sir, you said that was your *baby*?" she asked.

"Why-why are you in my home?" the man asked, a far north accent slipping through, "You scared her, she'll be in the tunnels for *hours* now, please, why did you come in here?"

"We're investigating criminal acts, and we stumbled across your home." Mod said plainly.

The man looked her up and down, then looked over to me. "Oh- oh gods, *no*, you're *heroes*?"

"We are, yes." Mod said firmly.

The man nodded slowly, then spun, slamming his hand on a box next to the computers. All the lights on them lit up, and a red light flashed on the walls.

"Fuck you!" he screamed, "I was told I wouldn't be bothered!"

I stood up, "Uh, Mod, I think he just did something, we should-"

At that, the floor buckled, and a huge centipede, as big around as I was and as long as a bus- luckily without any human parts this time- burst from the floor, followed by another, and another.

I screamed, and bolted, charging down the exit, soaring around the turns and covering my face in case the little insect girl was still there, pushing myself to get to the door. If I could get to the door, I'd be safe, I just had to get to the door. I swished through it, and turned, slamming it on Mod with a clang as she flew up behind me, pushing, trying to get it to latch.

"Damnit, Candy, let me-" She shoved the door open, knocking me over, and turned, slamming it herself on the horde of approaching insects.

She turned and glared at me, her drone face not quite built for the action. "Really? We're in this together, you know."

"Sorry- I-I, I mean I-I" I stuttered, "No, I was panicking, I just-"

She sighed as the metal door banged and shook behind her "Look, I know you're entomophobic or something. I noticed when you met Amaryllis, your heart rate was sky high, but- you can't let *that* make choices for you. If I hadn't been stronger than you, I could have been torn apart just now."

"I- hhh, sorry..." I said, "Please don't tell Panic Attack, I just, gods, bugs set off my *brain....*"

"I think she knows." Mod sighed, "She's not stupid, and you screamed when you saw her."

"Oh, yeah." I said, listening to the scratches coming from the other side of the door. It wasn't so bad when there was all that steel between us.

"I guess it's time to go back then?" I said, "I wanted to check out that elevator, but, uh, I'm not going back in there."

Mod nodded. "Yeah, come on, let's try and get through The Northern Empress's room quickly. If she grabs you, say something, I have a couple of tricks that might help at least."

I braced myself and took off, flying blind as Mod zoomed behind me, having trouble keeping up. As I saw the red glow from the flesh-room I slowed down enough to let her catch up, and then went ahead, taking a wide arc to avoid the pillar in the center of the-

I stopped, and Mod pulled up behind me. The entire room was empty, not a trace of the flesh that had covered everything, the hole

in the floor being the only proof she'd ever been here. There was a slightly sticky coating on the walls, and the smell lingered, but not an inch of flesh, no mouths, no eyes.

Me and Mod exchanged looks, and I lowered myself to the ground. "Is she *hiding* from us?" I asked, "She's *way* stronger than us though."

"No, she's not here at all?" Mod said, "My sensors don't detect anything, as far down as the tunnel goes. What the heck?"

"So much for being able to show off my findings to Oori, I guess." I grumbled.

"Angel Rouge, it's a *good* thing that she's gone, we don't want her anywhere near our city." Mod said.

"Who's gone?" A voice from the entrance asked. I looked up to see Sera walking in, sniffing the air.

"Just- one of the terrestrial goddesses." I said, "She was in this room the first time we came through, or *part* of her was, and when we came back, she was gone."

"I see." Sera said, her face in a deep frown, "A goddess you say?"

"Yeah, one of the ones who lives on earth 24/7, The Northern Empress." I explained, "She's why the top third of the planet is an icy wasteland."

"I see." Seraphim said again, "We may need to speak to her, eventually. Her scent calls something familiar forth."

"Well, good luck with *that*." I snorted, "She eats almost half the people who go to see her. Anyway, what did *you* find?"

Sera looked back at me, her train of thought breaking "Hm? Oh, I found a room full of weapons and strange tools, with a testing area where they'd been used on something alive. There was a lot of sour blood, some fresh, some very old." she tapped her crown as she thought "The *next* room was one full of magic tools in cases. I didn't recognize the symbols on them, but by the smell, I'm guessing they were useless cursed items, no reason to take them with us. The room after that was locked, and my blasts wouldn't get through the door. What did you two find?"

I started down the hallway to the hole we'd made. "We found the goddess, like I mentioned, and some old guy who was making giant bugs."

"And person bug hybrids, I think." Mod added.

I shuddered. "Yeah, those too."

"I fail to see the connection between all these things, but I can tell there must be one." Sera said as we walked through the doorway and started flying up to the hole, "They are all unconnected, are they not?"

"They're all frowned on?" Mod said, "They're all things that would get you thrown out of polite society, right? Testing weapons on living things, curses, genetic modifications, bringing a horrid goddess like that into the city, collecting body parts... Those things aren't strictly *illegal*, aside from the weapons testing, but they're still *bad*. The old man implied someone gave him the space, could they be renting the areas out?"

"What, like, someone who only rents underground spaces to weirdos?" I asked and we came out of the hole. "That's a *terrible* business practice."

"What kind of weirdos?" Lucy asked, coming over, "There was a little weirdo that came out of the hole a while ago, but she was too fast, and I lost her."

"Oh *fuck*, the little bug girl?" I moaned, "That thing is loose up *here*? I'll never sleep again..."

"What *happened* down there?" Lucy asked, looking concerned.

"Here, let me catch you up..." Mod said, taking Lucy aside to explain what we'd seen.

"Angel Rouge, I don't mean to be contradictory, but the theory the wonder put forward isn't correct." Sera said quietly, "These rooms may be things that are frowned on, but there's a thread here, I know it."

I nodded. "Yeah, and they're all linked up, too, with the tunnels. There's got to be three dozen of these fake buildings around here, and we only looked at 5 of them. I think we need to branch out. I'll get my map, and we'll mark which ones we've looked at, and then try and hit all of them over time to figure out what's going on."

"You said you wanted to take it to the authorities, do you still want to?" Sera asked.

"Yeah, of course, I want that sweet, sweet clout." I said, "Getting followers is the only reason I'm *doing* this, but unless *I'm* the one who exposes what it is, whoever they send in will get all the credit. Probably the Children of Battle, they're the most tactical, and it's all underground. Freedom Fighter's powers would thrive down there."

"Well then next time we're both out here like this, let's find a new one, and keep investigating." Seraphim agreed, "I felt something important down there, and I think I can get closer to the heretic I'm hunting if I can just figure out what was setting off my bells..."

"Hey so like, giant bugs, huh?" Lucy said, stepping over to the conversation, "I bet you looooved that, huh Candy?"

"Shut up Sable." I said, "What time is it? Is our shift over yet?"

"It's about midnight." Mod said, "We have a few more hours."

I picked up my bag of snacks from where I'd left it and dug in it for my can of tea. "Well, let's do some flyovers, then I guess keep an eye out for a tiny thing with a centipede body..."

I pulled out my tea and frowned. "Wait, I got 3 of these cream filled donut things, it was buy two get one, where's my other one?" I looked up at Lucy, "Did you eat my fucking food?"

"I mean, they must have forgotten to give you the free one, I guess?" Lucy shrugged.

I stifled a groan. I was almost *positive* I'd counted them when they put them in, but if she *said* she didn't eat it... Step 5... I was very hungry, but two could tide me over. I'd have to watch the lady behind the counter next time I went in though, just to be safe.

I pulled down my makeshift mask and shoved one in my mouth whole and gulped some tea to wash it down, shivering at the wonderful, grainy sugar filling oozing into my body, making my brain buzz. Mmm, sugar just did a body *good*. I must have burned more calories down there than I'd thought.

"Mmph, ok, let's head out." I said, wiping my mouth and swallowing.

I flew over to the hole in the wall and lifted up, reaching over the top of the building and into the open air. I spread my wings, and-

I felt something slam into me, wrapping me up and dropping me like a stone. I let go of my snacks and rolled. I couldn't hold my transformation as the weird net that had hit me tightened around my body. I flickered, and went back to my base form midair as I fought to pull the weird fleshy metal mesh off me, the netting feeling like it weighed a hundred pounds. It slammed me into the roof of the fake building with a force hard enough to stun me. I screamed, and I saw Lucy and Sera zip up to find me.

Lucy got shot out of the air the same way as me, going down limply without a twitch, but Sera refused to go, struggling with her net, and trying to pull her sword out. A dart hit her in the side, then another, then another, then one hit her in the neck, and slowly, finally, she sank to the roof beside the two of us. Mod, for her credit, shot off down the street below us, staying away from the skies, running for help most likely. She made it almost a whole block before she was hit with a glowing ball that made her spasm then clatter limply on the street.

I lay there, trying not to hyperventilate. What was going on? Were the people who shot us out of the sky the same people who were running the fake buildings? Were we going to die? How did they un-transform us, and why couldn't I feel my powers at all anymore? Was Mod *dead* or was she just de-powered too? I strained against the cords, feeling them dig into me, and I sobbed, I couldn't move, I couldn't even thrash...

A figure walked up to the three of us on the roof and I stared up at her. She was 'human', or at least she had human ears, and was fairly short, maybe twenty five or thirty years old, with teeth sharper than Sera's. Her skin was a swirled pink and dark gray reminding me of the hand I'd seen in the jar below us, and her hair was a very dark gray, hanging straight and limp around her plain, unremarkable face. She wore a light gray pinstripe business suit with a large, flat gold necklace around her neck, a symbol of some kind; religious, from the looks of it. She exuded both grace and power as she loomed over me, seeming much bigger in my mind than physically in front of me. She bent over, and stared at me with her pink and black eyes, and spoke to me in a raspy, quiet voice.

"Hello, 'Angel Rouge'. I think it's time your group and I had a little talk about *privacy*, and I've been meaning to talk to *you* personally since your secret debut. Won't you come back to my office with me?" Her words were careful, as if years of talking through razor sharp teeth had made sure she enunciated every word.

I couldn't do anything but shake as she smiled and stood up, snapping her fingers. Three strong people in matching suits climbed up onto the roof with us, each taking one of us over their shoulders and heading back down the fire escape.

"Put them in the back, and put the android in the trunk." the lady said coldly.

I whimpered as they tossed us in a pile in the back of a limousine, the lady getting in the front. At least with my powers turned off, I didn't have to worry about changing my friends as I lay on top of them. I felt almost guilty about enjoying the physical contact, but I had to take it where I could get it at this point.

Not that that would matter for much longer, if this lady was planning on killing us...

Chapter Fifteen

I sat in the chair, my arms and legs tied with the strange sinew-y metal rope and I tried to regulate my breathing. Lucy was to my right, and Sera and Mod were to my left. Lucy was tied up the same way I was, while Sera was chained with thick heavy chains. Mod seemed to be in some sort of electrified cage, and was sitting very still in the middle, not moving. She hadn't moved since she was captured, I wasn't even sure she was awake or alive.

We were in another one of the large underground rooms, but this one was well furnished, with tapestries, fancy furniture laid out like an old feasting hall, and what looked like a lavish one story house talking up one side of the room. We were sitting in front of a throne of sorts, high backed and wooden, and the lady sat in front of us primly, looking down at us from her seat, a cigarette in one hand. She took a draw, blowing the smoke towards us as she stared us down.

"I suppose you wonder why you're here, aren't you?" she said, watching us.

"No, I figure it's because we broke into your building." Lucy said sullenly.

"I'm sorry about that, we- I didn't know they were full of stuff." I said, trying to look innocent.

"If you didn't expect to find anything, then why break in?" the lady said calmly.

"We- it's our- *my* job." I stuttered, "I'm supposed to- to, I don't know, find problems in the area, and fix them, I'm a hero. I thought there might be a problem."

As much as I wanted to get out of this alive, it *had* been my idea and my mission, if I could draw attention away from the others, they might be able to get out of this alive...

"*I* was hunting for heretics." Sera spat, "And *you* smell like nothing I've ever come across before. Starting to wonder if I found what I was looking for after all."

"And you're not any kind of *Chosen* I've ever seen, 'Seraphim'." snapped the woman, "I'd be careful with your tone or I'll send my men to search your house, see if they can find anything that can identify your god. Trinkets, symbols, *books*..."

Sera paled at that and went silent, her head ducking as she bit her lip.

"...I thought so." the lady said. Did she know something about Sera? It almost sounded like she did, but it could also be an empty threat that happened to hit home.

"We won't tell anyone!" Lucy said, "About the weird stuff I mean, I didn't even see it, I stayed up top, I have no *idea* what's down there."

"I know you won't tell anyone." the lady said, "But even if you *did*, it wouldn't matter. All you saw were legal, legitimate businesses. A company laboratory, an office chapel, a testing facility for a licensed weapons manufacturer. Nothing you saw was breaking the law."

"Ok, that's what Mod said, so there's nothing wrong then!" I said, nodding quickly, "We didn't see anything bad, we were acting under the reasonable suspicion excuse, so you can bill the GGDS for the repairs, and-"

"There *is* something wrong, though." the woman said, standing and walking over to me, her shoes clicking on the floor as she approached, "You are inhibiting my business ventures, and you are digging into things that aren't any of your concern." She leaned in, her smoky breath mixing with the air around me face as she looked deep into my eyes "There's a *reason* there hasn't been any permanent Chosen in this area for almost a year, Candy Clenson."

"My real name is public, you're not scaring me with the whole 'I know who you really are' junk, I'm *registered*." I said, blowing the smoke away from my face, eyes watering.

"I don't make a habit of 'scaring' people." she hissed, "I simply operate, and people fall in line."

I leaned back, turning my face as she got closer. I looked at Sera, her face scrunched in a pained expression, the ropes leaving deep bloody marks on her wrists and legs. Was she tied tighter than me? Was she straining that hard? We needed to get out of here, whatever it took to do that.

"So, what do you want from me then?" I said, not looking at her.

She leaned back. "I'll forget about all this, in exchange for three things. One, you do not speak of this to the public, *any* of you. Two, you do not investigate any further. Lastly, Candy, I wish to see you in private, for a few moments of your time."

"Ok! I agree!" Lucy said quickly, "That sounds great, No problem with me."

I glared at her. This wasn't her call to make, but she still tried to throw me under the bus like this? Maybe I shouldn't have been so quick to try and claim the blame.

"What about the wonder?" Sera said, her voice ragged, "Will she be ok?"

"The wonder..?" the woman said, looking at us and frowning. Her eyes fell on Mod and she nodded. "Ah, the android, yes. She's aware, but her motor functions are locked down. As long as she keeps quiet, she will be restored to her normal function upon release."

"Then that is amenable to me." Sera said, "As long as Angel Rouge is ok with the meeting."

I swallowed. I didn't really have a choice, did I? I *could* refuse, she hadn't said she'd *kill* us, but we were tied up in an underground chamber with no powers, the implications were heavy.

"I'll, uh, yeah, I'll meet with you in private." I said, my voice shaky.

"Perfect." she said, "In that case, I'll retire to my quarters. My men will untie you and escort you there."

She dropped the cigarette at my feet and tapped it out with her foot, stalking away to the small house. My stomach turned, her quarters? Was this a sexual thing? I knew people had 'things' for powered individuals, but there were a number of things she could want from me, it didn't have to be *that*. It could be information, or exchanging CirNet follows, or... something... I just hoped I wouldn't have to do anything that would jeopardize my morals.

~~~

"Candy, I want you to kill me." she said, a fresh cigarette in her mouth.

We were in her sitting room, the whole thing done up in hand carved oak with ancient books lining old shelves. There were tall backed plush chairs, a full bar, and paintings of a young girl dressed as a nun of some kind hanging on the wall. The plush, ornate rug and yellow lamps on the walls made me feel like I was living two hundred years ago, and the mounted animal heads didn't help that impression. Taxi-
~~~

dermy had been banned for so long, I didn't even *know* how old the heads must have been. I couldn't imagine she'd found someone to stuff them in the modern day, but where else would she have gotten them?

Her words caught up with me.

"Wait, wait, what?" I asked, shocked, "I don't *kill* people, I don't-"

"I've *watched* you kill someone." she said plainly. She pulled a wall panel down to show a small computer screen that clashed with the design of the room, and pressed a button. It began to play a video, and with shock I realized it was of *me*, in Homicide's office, his arms around me, gun to my head.

I watched in horror and awe as the me in the video folded him, and the chaos started.

"I- I don't-" I started.

"No excuses." she said, "Like I said, I've seen you kill someone."

"I smashed everything, all the videos should have been gone!" I shouted, my body cold.

"I have access to his cloud files, stored off-site. We've worked together for a while, in a professional sense. I erased the videos of you and your 'friends' at his establishments as a matter of professional courtesy but *this* one I thought was worth saving."

I stared at the screen, watching as I took a bite of him- biting his *legs off* if I remembered right.

"I don't understand..." I said, "Why- why would you want *that*?"

"Because I've tried all the other options." she said coldly, "I've been trying to die for over five hundred years, and nothing *works*. The gods don't want me in Samsara *or* the afterlife, but I've got people to see on the other side, martyred people who escaped the cycle, waiting on me."

"Five *hundred*? What the fuck..." I mumbled.

This was the person Miss Missile mentioned, she had to be. I shuddered, five hundred years was a long time to want to die.

"What all have you tried?" I asked. Maybe if I could find a way for her to do it herself, I wouldn't have to do *that* to her...

"I've been stabbed, taken apart, poisoned, drown, burned alive, starved, everything." she said, making a face "Five hundred years is an eternity to try killing yourself, I've gotten quite 'creative' over the years. With the advent of Chosen last century, I was hopeful that one of them could put me down, but..." she sighed, "Powers that kill outright are usually **PR** unfriendly, so they don't show up much." she glanced up at me. "You, though, *your* powers come from a goddess who's never Chosen anyone before, who's got a big enough following that she can ignore the bad press. A goddess who's slightly out of touch with the mortal world."

"Oh, yeah..." I said softly. My head was full and I was feeling the pressure of my lungs against my heart, I'd been trying to *avoid* my power, and now she was *demanding* I use it? Every time I touched someone, I got closer and closer, if I used it here, would I even be able to stop myself next time I bumped into someone?

"I *really* don't want to do this..." I said, "And you disabled my powers, anyway, so... I can't even do it if I wanted to."

"You have your powers back now, you were only powerless when you were bound by the net made of my flesh." she said coldly, "You can transform and use your ability on me as soon as you stop *deliberating* about it."

I dipped inside, and felt the familiar hum of my magic deep inside me. Ropes made of her blocked powers? That didn't make sense, but it'd worked. I tried to think of a way out now that I had my powers back. I could transform, punch her in the face, bust through the door, free Sera and drag Lucy and Mod out of here, no killing required, I could just-

Get caught again by the immortal lady with power canceling ropes the second I let my guard down. I didn't see a way out, even if I left

the area and flew out to the folds, she could just capture my family and I'd have to come back.

I belatedly realized that the family implication was most likely why she'd used my full name.

Chosen, even the *fallen* Chosen, weren't supposed to go after families. Doing so was a good way for the Chosen with *real* power, to drop the PR friendly act and smear you across the pavement in a split second to make an example out of you. This lady wasn't a Chosen though. She'd said the gods hated her, so whatever she was, she wasn't following the same set of rules as me. And from what she'd said, being smeared across the pavement would just be a mild inconvenience for her at worst.

"Well?" she asked, lighting a fresh cigarette, "Are we going to get this over with already?"

I took a breath and transformed. I didn't know if she knew I didn't strictly *need* to be transformed to use my power, but I thought I should be careful anyway. I looked around for something to stall with, my heart beating hard against my ribs.

"So, smoking, is that an attempt to die too?" I asked, pointing at her cigarette, "You know, cancer and stuff?"

She frowned and glanced down at it. "...No, it simply makes someone close to my heart very upset when I do it. So I do it as frequently as I can."

"Oh." I said. That wasn't an answer, that was a riddle, and I didn't really care about her enough to try and figure it out. "So, these stuffed heads-" I started, pointing at the taxidermied animals.

"Candy." she said, her eyes flashing with anger, "Take my hand."

I looked at her hand as she reached out, and down at my own hand, still bare from when I had used my glove as a face mask. I swallowed hard.

"It's- you remain aware and awake the whole time, it's not death, it's-"

"So you'll *eat* me." she growled, "I doubt I could survive *that*."

"Are you sure you want to die? I know you've been around a while, but if you talked to someone, maybe-"

She hissed smoke out of her mouth, and reached over snatching my hand with hers. My mind exploded into sensation, sweet, sour, sticky, all of it flooding my mouth as I felt her hand in mine. The 'spark' that I usually saw when I touched people was more like a night sky full of stars, hundreds if not thousands of sparks flickering and bounding against each other, spinning and writhing. I couldn't comprehend all of them, but as I felt her hand in mine, something folded anyway, and my hand pulled away, the familiar feeling rushing into me as my power activated.

I opened my eyes, and stared at my hand. In it, was a single blue and green gummy worm. I took a shaky breath. I hadn't felt anything like that before, it was like I was touching a thousand people all at once, all connected into one.

"Well, fuck."

I snapped my head up at the curse, jumping as I saw the lady still in her chair, still humanoid. I looked from the gummy to her, and back again, and I blinked.

"Wh- how are you still here?" I asked, "I folded you!"

"You folded a *piece* of me." she said, "A very small fragment. And it's already grown back."

"So you're *not* this worm?" I asked, holding it up.

She grimaced, "I *am*, but in the same way you're the hair on your hairbrush."

"Oh thank the gods…" I was so relieved I hadn't been able to kill her, I felt calm and cool, with my legs feeling weak under me.

"S-sorry I couldn't kill you?" I said, not sorry at all.

"We're not done." she snapped, "It took a moment for that part of me to grow back, if you use both hands, and you pull constantly, you may be able to outpace my healing."

I felt the pit return to my stomach. "Uh, m-ma'am, it's kinda traumatic for me to use my power, it's like, I *killed* someone with it already, it's kinda stressing me out to think about having to try and kill you over and over..."

"Well, I'm sure there's many, *many* more things that are much more traumatic than *that*, wouldn't you agree?" she said, holding both hands out to me and glaring.

I read the unspoken threat, and suppressed a shudder, taking off my other glove. "I- I just- if I do kill you, will your men know to let us go?"

I probably should have asked that before the first attempt, actually.

She sighed. "They know why you came in here, yes. You'll be fine. Hurry this up, please. If it doesn't work, I have meetings to go to later."

I bit my lip, and reached out with both hands. I felt her skin, her sparks, and I pulled. One side came away into another gummy worm, then the other, then the first one again. I pulled at the sparks as quickly as I could, alternating between them, watching them wink out and reappear as my hands filled with candy. I pulled and pulled, and tried not to think about how I was actively trying to help a woman I'd just met kill herself.

She pulled her hands away, and I stopped, opening my eyes. My fists bulged with gummies, and my head felt light and buzz-y. I fell back into my chair and dumped the worms into my lap, my eyes full of spots.

"It's not working." she said, her voice cold and distant, "I'm regenerating too fast, and *you're* already almost out of mana."

"Oh, is that what this is?" I said, my voice warbling and my head lolling back.

"You're experiencing power fatigue." she said, "Try eating one of the worms."

I rubbed my head as a headache came on, and pulled up one of the worms, looking at it nervously.

"It's fine." she said, "It's not going to hurt you, just eat it."

I took a tentative bite, and tried to hold back a gag as a drop of blood formed and pooled at the end of the gummy. It tasted good at least, sour and sweet, and just the right amount of chew. My teeth worked into the sugary meat, and I felt the sensation of dizziness fade slightly. I ate the other half, licking the tangy blood off my fingers and I felt much better, a good buzz of energy. My headache was fading, and while I didn't feel the sense of being too much stronger like when I'd eaten Homicide, but the worms did *something* at least.

"This was a disappointment." she said darkly, "I was *sure* you'd be able to bypass the worms."

"You *knew* you'd turn into gummy worms?" I asked, confused. Was there a way to tell?

"No, the *worms*." she said, "The gummy worms were just a cruel prank by your power. Look."

She pulled a knife out of her suit jacket and dug it into her palm, dragging it roughly, gashing open her skin. I screamed, and she gave me a dirty look.

"Shut up, look." she snapped.

Her wound bubbled with off-colored blood, and small pink worms oozed out, spreading a thick goo on her cut, pulling it together and gluing it closed. I watched in awe as the worms used their bodies to patch the cut, sealing the gash in a matter of seconds, the pattern of the worms and the goo matching the rest of her body.

"The worms." she said, "They stop me from dying. I can't figure out how to get rid of them."

"Ohh, I could feel them, when I touched you." I said, "It's like there were lots of people I was touching at once, I think that was them."

"Probably." she said, "I'm showing you this because I want you to think about it. I want you to think about how to use your powers to get past them, and I want you to think about how people you meet could use *their* powers to get past it. If *you* can't kill me, you need to be on the lookout for someone who can."

"I can look for someone, yeah." I said, "There's got to be someone though, I saw the Northern Empress in one of the chambers, maybe she could-"

"*NO*." the woman said, shuddering, "She will not have another chance at my life. Her methods are... unpleasant. She can try again when she has new ideas."

"So she's actively trying to think of a way to kill you? Is *that* why she's down there?" I asked thoughtfully. I gasped. "Wait, I just realized, holy *shit*, are all the empty buildings, the stuff under them, is it *all* just people you hired to find a way to kill you?"

She raised her eyebrows at me, and a hint of a smile played around her cigarette, "You're quick on the uptake, Candy. I'm almost impressed."

"Why are they trying so hard to kill you?" I asked, "Isn't it like, murder?"

"No, I'm considered a nonperson." she said "I made sure of *that* when I helped write the laws concerning monsters and inhumans. I can own property, but no crimes against me count as real crimes. A few experiments, constructs, undead, and 'others 'also count as non-people as an unfortunate side effect, but legally speaking, I'm a colony of worms. The people working for me are working to kill me because there are no consequences, and whoever kills me gets all of my wealth and all of my companies, outright."

"Wait, I could have been a millionaire if I'd been able to do it?"

"No, you'd be much, *much* richer than that." she laughed dryly, "But you still could be."

Her voice turned serious. "I need you to go out and actually fight crime, Candy, or other heroes, if you prefer. I need you to *earn* the rank of Angel, earn your name."

"Why?" I asked, dreading the answer. I didn't want to *fight*, I wanted to get *popular*, to take it easy, to be a mascot, why did everyone keep wanting me to fight?

"Whatever your power evolves into when you become an Angel, it'll almost certainly be enough to take me out." she said, "It was almost enough now, if you were a just little faster, and you didn't have to worry about mana draw."

"Oh." I said, "I really just want to be popular, ma'am, I can't fight, I don't have any useful powers, I can't-"

"You have those, right?" she asked, pointing at the large pile of gummies in my lap, "That's more than enough to fight with for a while. Keep some in a bag in your pocket, and eat one when you find someone to fight. I saw what eating that pie did, you'll do fine with those."

"Ok, but what if I accidentally find and fight crime that *you're* doing?" I asked, "I already did, kinda..."

"My type of crime isn't the kind that you'll see on the streets." she said, "You'll need to look in the skyscrapers, courtrooms, and banks for what I do."

"There's no one *in* my area, though." I said, hoping to convince her to drop it, "No people means no crime, right?"

"Then step on some toes." she snapped, "Go to other areas, poach fallen fights, make yourself *known*."

"That won't make me very popular..." I said, feeling panic starting to rise panic.

"Well, you'll do it anyway." she said, "I am demanding that you fight, so you *will* fight."

Again, the unspoken threats sounded louder than her words. I blinked back tears, this wasn't how I wanted my career to go at *all*. I was basically working for a super villain at this point if I did what she said. Granted, the job was 'be the best hero you can be and stop crime', but it still felt sour to work for someone like that, even if what they asked you to do was a good thing.

"I'll do my best." I said, gathering the worms off of my lap and standing up.

"Here." she said, handing me a cloth bag from a drawer under the bar, "Put them in here."

I dumped the worms in, and took the bag from her, my hand brushing hers. I saw stars again, and tasted sour. I blinked, and she was holding a gummy worm, looking at it thoughtfully. She pushed it into her mouth, past the sharp teeth, and chewed slowly, her eyes narrowed. She looked at me for a moment, then swallowed.

"Interesting." she muttered, "You should put your gloves back on. It's time for you and your companions to leave."

I nodded, and held the bag in my teeth as I slid on one, then untied the other from around my neck and put that on too. I looked at her and felt a chill as she watched me. I felt like a monster being eyed up by an adventurer, except I wasn't in danger of dying, I was in danger of being enslaved. As long as I did what she said though, fought hard and tried to earn Angel, it sounded like I'd keep my freedom. Still, I got the feeling that as long as I was in Valley City, me and everyone else here were, at least in some way, under her thumb.


~~~
~~~

The four of us sat on the roof, legs hanging over the edge. Our shift wouldn't be over for another hour and a half, and none of us really felt like going out and patrolling at the moment. The bag of worms felt heavy in my hands, and I moved it to the rooftop behind me. I glanced at Lucy, who was being quiet for once, her legs drawn up to her chin as she stared out over the city. I felt bad she'd had to get wrapped up in all this. Mod was an adult in her own right, and me and Sera were a lot older. I was at least four years older than Lucy, and Sera was in her... maybe early 30s? It was very hard to tell with the way her face shone. Lucy was still a teenager, and one who *felt* like a teenager too. This was weighing heavily on her, and I wanted to say something, to be the person who could help her through it and make her see me in a better light, but I was still going over my own thoughts and ideas, still stressed and sick over having to work for *her*, even if it wasn't anything too bad.

"On the bright side," Lucy said, finally breaking the silence, "you got some free candy out of all this at least, huh Angel Rouge?"

I looked back at the sack of worms and bit my lip. "It's not- well, I guess so."

"Why did she give you sweets, anyway?" Mod asked, her eyes glowing dully as she looked over at me.

"It's complicated." I said, not wanting to tell the others that I repeatedly tried to kill someone just a little while ago.

"Is it because of your name?" Sera asked, looking up from rubbing the deep gashes on her wrists where the ropes had burned into her flesh.

"...Huh..." I said, thinking about it, "That would be pretty stupid, but maybe."

We sat quietly for a few minutes more, and once again, Lucy broke the silence.

"You're not, by the way." she said, looking at me.

"What?" I asked, giving her a funny look.

"A stuck up asshole. I called you one earlier, but I was trying to make a joke, I wasn't serious."

"Oh." I said, unsure how to respond. I'd forgotten about that in all the chaos.

"I just kept thinking, like, while you were in that weird house, like, if you were being killed or something, you'd die thinking I thought you were a stuck up asshole. I don't know, it was stupid, but it felt important to tell you that you're not, it was just a bad joke."

I looked at her, her cheek resting on her knee, looking at me with a defiant, worried look.

"Well, thanks for telling me that. I try *not* to be a stuck up asshole if I can help it." I said.

"I don't get an asshole vibe from you, not much at least." Mod said encouragingly.

"I do." Sera said, "I think you need to embrace your asshole self more, use it to grow stronger and more brutal."

"I saved your life, Sera, you don't get to call me an asshole." I muttered at her.

"I think that means I can tell you the hard truths, and I know you won't be upset." she said, smiling smugly, "You have a mean streak for sure; remember when I got my results back from the GGDS? I thought you were going to fight me then and there, you looked so full of hate and anger at my ranking... Not that I'd have minded the challenge if you had."

"I'm working on it. I have a whole thing I'm working on right now, being less of an asshole is one of five things I'm working on." I said, embarrassed.

"Self improvement is important!" Mod said, "I won't pry, but the other four, they're not unhealthy for you, are they?"

I frowned. "What, like a crash diet or something? No, you've seen me eating sweets all night long, I'm *not* on a diet."

"Ok, I was- I just wanted to make sure you weren't straining your-self." Mod said, "I know Ki- someone I know struggles to balance her goals and her health from time to time."

I sighed. She was being helpful, but I didn't *ask* for help, especially not with *that.* I was doing fine on my own, and that's not even related to the stuff on the list anyway. Or, I guess it could help with steps one and two. And it was kind of related to step four, but- I didn't want her help, dammit.

I reached for my snacks, and stopped, remembering they'd been dumped on the roof we'd been kidnapped from. I wilted slightly, I wanted my sugar fix. I considered the gummy worms, but those had power in them, it'd be a waste to eat one just because I wanted something sweet. I *always* wanted something sweet these days, if I ate one every time I had an urge, I'd be out in a couple days and there'd be none left to augment me for when I needed to fight crime. Maybe I could get the girls to go to the convenience store with me, get some other stuff? Explaining why I couldn't eat the perfectly good candy sitting behind me instead would be a pain, though.

"So what *was* in that little house, anyway? Besides gummy worms?" Lucy asked, "You never told us what happened in there."

I didn't really want to tell them, I wasn't *going* to tell them, it wasn't any of their concern, really. Still, they needed to know something. I thought for a moment, and sighed.

"She wants me to start branching out, fighting crime outside our section, seeking it out." I said. Which was technically true. "I think it's about getting rid of her competition." That was... less true.

"That's *very* against the rules..." Mod said, "That violates the whole idea of having sections in the first place. Unless someone agrees to let you join in an existing fight, you need to report the crime to the GGDS hotline and let them dispatch someone."

"Well, the scary lady who knows where my family lives wants me to fight crime outside my zone, so I can't really say no." I said.

"You could just ignore her." Sera pointed out, "We could take her on if we knew to look out for her."

"No, trust me, we couldn't." I said, shaking my head, "She showed off a little in that house, she's... I don't even know how *anyone* could stop her."

"I bet *you* could stop her." Lucy said, giving me a look.

"Let's not take that bet." I said firmly, "I'm going to be, I don't know, I guess gaslighting as a hero, while also being a different hero?"

"Moonlighting, not gaslighting." Lucy snickered. I rolled my eyes, they all knew what I'd meant.

"Why not just be a hero?" Mod asked, "Just go out as yourself, right?"

"Because I'd lose popularity and followers for breaking the rules, duh." I said.

"Well, I'm pretty sure they'll notice the massive fuck-off wings either way." Lucy pointed out.

I grimaced. I hadn't thought of that...

"I won't transform." I said, "I'll just fight in my base form, I'm still pretty strong."

Plus I'd have the gummies to help out a little too, if I needed them.

"Our powers are made to work as a team, Candy." Lucy said, "Driz is the combat healer, Galorna is ranged, Alele is tactics, and me and you get up close and personal while the others distract the bad guys and support us. Just me or just you doesn't work."

"Then why the fuck are *we* on patrol together?" I asked, annoyed at her logic.

"If you like," Mod said, "I'm mostly tactical, so, I can offer the support for you two?"

"Debbie wants us all to go out together, paired up with the others equally, to build bonds or whatever." Lucy said, "It makes sense for us to like, know how to work together."

"Well, I guess I'm going to be going solo anyway." I snipped, "At least off the clock."

"I'm just saying, if you had more than just *you*, it'd be-"

I cut Lucy off. "Well it can't be *you*, because you'd never be seen dead in public untransformed, so it doesn't matter."

She stopped talking, looking at me hard, her eyes watering. I looked away, folding my arms as she kept staring at me. I felt the creep of guilt ease into my brain and I internally groaned. Maybe I *was* a stuck up asshole after all.

"Ok, whatever." I said, "Sorry, I get it, I didn't mean it like that, but you can't be seen with me with your wings out anyway."

"I was more thinking you and Alele, anyway." Lucy said quietly, "For the tactical advantage."

"Oh, maybe." I said. Alele was fine, I think she'd be a good choice to patrol with if I had to have someone. "I'll have to explain the situation to her, then."

"Were we not going to tell our teams?" Mod asked, "I'm going to tell *my* team, at least the basics."

"I am my team," Sera said smugly, "and I'm all caught up."

"No- yeah, ok, whatever, we tell our teams, but only that we got got, nothing about me being two heroes or anything." I said, "And I'm *not* explaining it at all to Oori and Debbie, it'd just get complicated."

"Ok, yeah." Lucy said, "I guess we'll have to text the team? We won't have another chance to all sit down for another two shifts."

"No, I want it verbal." I said, "No writing."

"Writing can be very dangerous, and it can fall into the wrong hands so, so easily..." Sera said, sounding somber.

"Yeah, exactly." I agreed, "We can wait sixteen hours or so. I'll be sleeping most of that anyway."

"Aaanywho, changing the subject a little, I guess we need to find a new name for you?" Lucy asked, "For your disguise."

"Ah!" Sera perked up, "I can name you! To return the favor from when you named me Sera!"

"Wait, is Sera not your real name?" Mod asked.

"It is *now*, my old name is sand on the shore, I am now and forever, Seraphim." she said proudly.

"That's fine, I guess?" I said reluctantly, "Just don't make it anything weird, ok?"

"Of course!" she said, "I'll call you... Comfit!"

"Did you say 'comphet'?" Lucy asked.

"No no, Comfit! Comfits are my favorite candy, and Candy is my favorite person, and she's *named* Candy, so I named her Comfit!"

"Aw, I'm your favorite?" I asked in a fake sweet tone, "Huh, I feel like I knew that already. Anyway, I guess that's ok, it's only a *little* weird. I've never even *heard* of a 'comfit' though, what is it?"

"It's a ball of spices, a bit of fruit, or a seed, covered in a sugar shell several times over." Mod said, "At least, that's what the dictionary says."

"You have a built in dictionary?" Lucy asked, "Nice, do you have a calculator app too?"

"I'm an artificial life-form, not a *phone*." Mod said, sounding insulted, "...but yes, I can compute math problems, if you must know."

"Dang, ok, what's the square root of-" Lucy started.

"Stop, Lucy." I said, rolling my eyes at her, "You wouldn't even know if she got it right."

"Oh, yeah... Sorry, Maud." she said, "I still think it's cool."

I looked up at the stars in the sky as we sat in silence for a minute, watching the city around us twinkle as the various flying Chosen dipped in and out of the buildings in the distance, doing what we *should* be doing right now. I yawned, it was late, I was tired, and there was no point in staying out of we were just going to be killing time instead of doing our patrols.

"Ok, let's just go ahead and get home." I said, "No reason to sit out here all night."

"We'll get in trouble though, I don't want to-" Mod said.

"No, we won't, *Sera* is covering the last part of our shift, because we asked her nicely." I cut her off.

"I never agreed to that, if anything *I* need to get home myself and get medicine on my wounds before they scar." Sera said, frowning.

"You don't actually have to cover for us, babygirl." I said, "It's just our excuse, and if anyone asks, you covered, ok?"

"Ah, I see, very clever." she said, "I'll be your alibi, Comfit."

"Don't call me that in public." I said "Only in my Comfit outfit. Which I guess I have to make, now."

"So many names to keep track of..." Sera said under her breath, "Well!" she continued in a normal tone, "I must away! I'll see you on the morrow, most likely, although whether you see *me* or not is another matter. Fare thee well!"

She took off into the skies, heading for her house on the northern side of the section, her glow lighting up the buildings as she passed them.

"That leaves us." Mod said, "I'm running low on fuel anyway, that energy ball thing drained most of my reserves, I actually *do* need to get home early..."

"I'll see you later then, Mod." I said, "It's been a pleasure."

It had been, actually. Not the 'getting kidnapped' part, but she wasn't as bad as I thought she'd be when I first met her.

"I still wanna hang out soon, hit me up, ok?" Lucy said to her as she lifted off.

Mod smiled and nodded, zipping off into the darkness toward the east.

I glanced to the left, I could just barely see our building poking up over the other buildings around it. It wasn't too far, but I was suddenly feeling very tired, which made it feel so much farther away.

"Ugh, I can't believe I have to take *another* shower when I get home." I moaned, "I'm covered in dirt and stuff under my transformation thanks to that stupid rope canceling my power."

"Do you not usually take a shower after patrol?" Lucy asked as we floated up and towards home.

"No, I shower before, so when I de-transform I'm still all fresh and clean under all the magic."

"That's *genius*." Lucy said, impressed, "I never thought about that, I always just shower after I get home."

I realized that meant she'd need one too, and I groaned inside. I was trying to be better though, step five...

"Uh, you can take first shower tonight, if you want." I offered, "I can wait a while, we're off early anyway."

Lucy looked at me, then down at the ground, her face scrunched in a complex frown.

"Uh, if it's all the same, there's like eight showers in the locker room, I guess I could just... use one at the far end, and you could use one close to the door, nothing weird about that, right? we'd be like twenty feet apart, with walls between us."

I looked at her in mild shock, was this progress for her? Or was it her being more comfortable around me specifically, trying to show me trust? Either way, I needed to encourage it.

"Yeah, that's a good plan." I said, "Nothing weird about that at all."

We flew in silence, and I thought the night over. All in all, despite being terrified for the future, I think I was still making good progress on my list, and even if the lady had tried to risk my chances at popularity, I'd still found a compromise. The hard part would be getting the rest of the team to understand.

Chapter Sixteen

Alele sighed "You can't just wear a balaclava to fight crime in, Candy. That's the most 'bad guy' thing to wear, you'd be attacked on sight by like, half the heroes in Valley City."

I glared at her and stuffed the mask in question back into my pocket. "I don't exactly have a lot of options here, I need to cover my hair *and* my face if I'm going to pull this off."

"Yeah, so wear a domino mask and a wig, like I said." she said, rolling her eyes.

"I'm not wearing a wig to fight in, it'd get torn off instantly, and then it'd be obvious I was trying to hide my identity. Plus, I don't even *have* a domino mask or a wig." I pointed out.

"Uuuuugh why are you so difficult?" she moaned, "Can I *please* just take you to a custom shop?"

"I'm not trusting some random shop with my secret identity, and therefore my *popularity*, I need to keep my two personas separate until I'm famous enough as both to make Angel, or at least get away with breaking the rules."

"Gods, have you never heard of identity exposure laws? These places *thrive* on Chosen business, and if they ever leak a name, they get sued for everything and go to jail."

I shook my head. "I know the laws, Alele, I just don't think I want to risk it."

She glared at me. "What if I let you wear the balaclava during the fitting? Would you go then?"

I thought about it. I knew I was being difficult, and part of that was because she was being so pushy about this and my natural instinct was to push back. I couldn't really do much with the clothes I had though, if nothing else we'd end up having to go shopping for duplicates of whatever we went with, in case of tears and damage. A custom shop would have better quality stuff than a random store, true, and getting a custom outfit would help with steps one and two, but did I really want to risk giving away my identity like that? I held back a snip and let myself calm down. I was just being a bitch to be a bitch, I'd wear the mask to the fitting, it'd be fine. I needed Alele on my side anyway, she was basically doing double work with me for no pay, after all.

"I *guess*, if I can wear the mask." I said, "I *do* need a costume that'll make me look nice for photos. A black turtleneck and cargo pants aren't really going to get me a lot of followers on CirNet."

"Yeah, plus that's already the signature look of Freedom Fighter, from the Children of Battle." she said.

"Well, he wears that little hat, too." I muttered.

"I need a new costume for myself if I'm going to be tagging along with you for these, and I'd like to match you at least a little, so really a private shop is our only option here." Alele said as she transformed, "Here, if we go now, we can get our order in before lunch, ok?"

"This isn't going to be expensive, is it?" I asked as I transformed and opened her window to leave.

"Not everyone gets magic clothes when they get Chosen, think of it as getting to learn how the other half lives!" Alele said, pulling me out the window into the sky. "Here, this way!" she yanked on my arm as we sped towards the shopping hub.

The city spread out below us, zipping past as we rocketed through the air. I let her pull me, staying behind her just enough to let her lead, but keeping up enough that she wasn't tugging on me. I watched the ground below me melt into a blur, and looked up to scan the skyline. Flying Chosen weren't rare, but I did rarely see any when I was in the sky. I wondered if it was because of the buildings being in the way, or if other flyers had tricks to stay out of sight. I didn't need any of those tricks myself, if anything I wanted ways to be *more* flashy in the air. Alele banked towards a side street, slowing down as we approached.

"You already have a place picked out, I'm guessing?" I asked.

"When you told us about your dilemma last night, I started looking! I think I found the best fit for us, they're the same shop that made the outfits for The Lacerations and The Dropkickers!"

"Isn't one of those groups made up of mostly *fallen* Chosen?" I asked as we started dropping to the ground.

"Yeah? That's how you know they can be discrete, duh." Alele said, giving me a look.

We hit the ground, and I looked up at the building we'd landed in front of. It *wasn't* what I expected.

"This is a burger joint, Alele." I said, deadpan, "And it looks like a grease trap."

"Oh, it *absolutely* is, that's why this is where we're going for lunch after." she said with a grin, "The shop is another block up the street."

"Why didn't we just land *there*?" I asked.

"Because you didn't want anyone to know- gods, really?" Alele asked, raising an eyebrow, "I *swear* you're smarter than that."

"Whatever, I just want to get this over with..." I said, de-transforming. A few people glanced over at us, eyes wide, but I ignored them and pulled the balaclava out of my back pocket where I'd stashed it, slipping it on.

Alele glared at me. "Just come on..." she grumbled

We walked up the street, and I tried to ignore the looks I was getting as we approached the shop Alele had picked out. It was a two story building, connected on both sides to other shops, and it had a big sign reading "Milton's Handmades" on a glass window. The window featured a display case with a couple fancy dresses, a nice stylized blue suit, and interestingly enough, a Chosen's hero outfit, one with a hood that had yellow wings on it, with a red body and silver boots. There was a 'SOLD' tag on it, so I assumed it was only on display for advertisement's sake, to let everyone know that they did hero costumes. Alele opened the door, jingling the bell, and she waved me in.

Stepping inside, I saw that the interior was lined with fabrics on racks and drawers built into the walls, with even more outfits and Chosen costumes in nooks and on podiums through the store. A halfling man behind the counter with a small mustache and smooth hair looked up and jolted in alarm as he saw us, his hand reaching for a phone on the counter in front of him. He looked under dressed for this place, just a white button-up and gray slacks, but he carried himself well, like a relic from an earlier time.

"No, we're Chosen, put down the phone, we're not here to rob you, we're just here to get costumes." Alele said, pointing at the man as she came in.

"I, um, just don't want my identity getting out." I said, slightly embarrassed.

"A lot of folks don't, but there's *laws* for that, missy." the man said in an affected old-time-y accent, like they used to use in black and white movies, "We tend to get a lot of Chosen types around here, and we don't get a lot of them wearing that kind of get-up. You're liable to get taken in, looking like *that*."

"It's- ugh, I just need something to wear when I fight crime, can you help with that?" I said, getting frustrated.

"I *can*, but what did you have in mind?" he asked, pulling out a pen and paper, "You can't just walk in off the street and demand a costume, I need *details* missy."

I huffed, not liking his tone. "Something lightweight, easy to move in, and durable. I'll want to punch people and stuff, but I don't want to risk making skin contact, my skin is, uh... poisonous, so tight and tough, I think."

"That narrows it down exactly none." the man said snappily, "Themes, powers, moods, what are you wanting out of this?"

"We want it to be cute, and to have marketability, mostly." Alele stepped in, "As for a theme, hers needs to be candy themed, maybe bits of candy in the design? Her name is Comfit, like the sweet, and she's got enhanced strength and durability. *My* costume is going to be psychic themed, I'm a combat precog and my name is Trigger Warning. I'll need more armor than her though, by a lot. I was thinking we could contrast our outfits a little? Maybe have hers be bright and flashy and mine a little subtle."

"A combat precog?" the man asked, "That's rare, do you girls have a team yet? I can hook you up with several who'd-"

"No, we're doing this as a duo." I interrupted, "And we'd like to be kid friendly too, no boob windows."

"Ok, I think I got it." the man said after a moment of looking over his notes, "For Comfit, I'm thinking an olive leotard over a white body suit to cover your skin, with pink frills on the arm and leg holes to add the kid appeal, and small bits of fake candy on the leotard itself to fit your theme. Masks are kinda hard, but if we go with *helmets*, we can have matching ones for you two, even though the outfits themselves look different. What about a darker pink motor-cycle helmet for you, Comfit, with a digital face that mimics your real one, and a solid black one for you, Trigger Warning, with three eyes on it that mimic expressions?"

"Can mine be dark blue, actually?" Alele asked sweetly, "And what were you thinking for my costume?"

He tapped his pen against his mouth. "What about, hm, if you like dark blue, maybe a dark blue leather jacket and matching leather pants with purple highlights? You mentioned subtle, so it'd be close to street wear. I could put combat armor into them, not enough to stop a bullet, but enough to stop a punch or a stab, at least."

"Ohh, *I'd* be the badass one, then?" Alele said, perking up, "The sweet one and the scary one, and *I* get to be the scary one! I like that!"

"Something like that, yeah!" he grinned, "Not that you're that scary now, but costumes do wonders. Now, the helmet, would you like an elven helmet? It'd have a longer face-piece for your nose, like an air filter, and it'd poke out at the sides for your ears. Alternatively, we can just use a standard one and you could bend your ears and nose to fit, if you'd like to hide the fact you're an elf."

"Ick, nnnno, I'll take the elven helmet, please and thank you." Alele said, shaking her head, "I want to be comfortable, *she's* the one who cares so much about her identity."

"It's a valid concern!" I glared at her, "Anyway, uh, you." I said, addressing the man, "Milton?"

"It's Romanson, actually." he said with a throwaway smile, "Milton is retired these days, I took over."

"Oh, congratulations, then?" I said, "I was wondering how we'll do a fitting for this, my skin is, like I said, poisonous."

"No problem! Give me your shoe size, hat size, and general waist, hip and leg, and it'll be fine. The material will stretch, so you should be ok if it's not exact." he said, making a few notes.

"Well, *I* want a full fitting for mine..." Alele said, "Leather needs to hug the right places, and if it has armor under it, I need it looking sexy and not bulking me up in the *wrong* places."

"Of course, do you want an estimate now? Or after the fitting?" Romanson asked.

"Now would be great, please." I said, dreading his pricing.

"Just the outfits themselves come to..." he tapped on his phone, adding up the notes from his notepad, "About five thousand blessings for both."

"Oh, that's not bad!" Alele said "I was expecting more!"

"Well, the helmets have to be hired out, I don't do tech." he said, "That's going to be three thousand each easy for the two way coms, voice changers, the expressive screens, and an awareness mode that lets you see around you as well as in front of you."

I winced. "Ah, *fuck*... That's, what, fifty five hundred blessings from each of us total? That's insane..."

"I've had people pay upwards of six figures for their suits, this is a *very* good price." Romanson said, sounding hurt.

"How the hell did the price go up so high?" Alele asked, "Was it made of gold?"

"Super science built into the suit, every feature, more armor, anti-Chosen measures, it adds up." he explained, "I'm not even one of the more expensive designers out there. There's several people who charge twice what I do here in Valley City, just for the brand recognition. If you go somewhere like Sound City or Archipelago City where all the heavy hitters are, you can expect to see people running around with seven figure outfits."

"Gods..." I muttered, "Well, we're happy with our four figure outfits, thank you very much."

"Let's pay and get me fitted already, we can afford this, right Can-Comfit?" Alele asked, pulling out her bankcard.

"Yeah, I guess so." I said, frustrated. It was still over a full paycheck for me, and I'd thought I was doing pretty well for myself.

We paid, and Romanson locked the door and led us upstairs to a small room where I gave him my sizes and Alele got undressed for him to get her measurements. I wasn't *too* upset about the new outfit, I liked the helmet idea, the leotard sounded cute, and I'd get to show off the tone I'd been building up via my training these past few weeks. I was pretty sure I was putting on muscle and toning up way faster than people usually did now that I was chosen, but I couldn't really *tell*. I'd always had a little muscle just from farm work, but I still felt like I was getting stronger anyway. My transformation was a strength multiplier, so I wanted to be as strong as I could be in my base form, because that strength was exponentially boosted later.

I thought about how I'd go about actually fighting as Comfit, and I realized I'd just have to get my hands dirty. Throw punches, nothing special, no air support, no dive bombs, no gimmicks, just my slightly stronger than normal fists and "Trigger Warning" in my ear giving me heads ups. She hadn't really gone over that name with me before she blurted it out to Romanson, and I was a little annoyed at her. It was a funny name, which could get us more followers if we played up the goofy side of things, but it also made us sound edgier than I wanted, like a tongue in cheek joke about society or something. Still, she did want to be the 'cool' one while I'm playing the 'sweet' one, and it did kind of fit a kind of borderline antihero. I liked my theme a lot more, though, I'd even be able to eat the gummies in view of the bad guys, as part of my 'sweet' gimmick if I played it up enough.

Speaking of...

"Hey, Romanson?" I asked as Alele put her clothes back on, "I was wondering, I want to eat candy while I'm fighting crime, and play it up, make it part of my character. Could I get a little pouch on one hip for the candy? And some kind of hole under the helmet to poke candy into?"

Romanson frowned. "Aren't you worried you'll choke?" he asked, "I can add that, it shouldn't be a problem, but make sure Trigger

Warning here knows how to get the candy unstuck from your air pipe..."

"I can do that, don't worry!" Alele said, "She eats sweets constantly out of costume as it is, I think it's her metabolism or something."

"It's not *constantly*." I objected.

"It's pretty much constant, how many sweets have you had today?" she asked.

I thought about it. I'd had a fancy tea with flavor and cream with breakfast, which was french toast, then I'd gone out for donuts, and gotten a peach slushie, then while hanging out in Alele's room I'd helped myself to her bowl of mints. That wasn't too much, right?

"Not a ton, I guess. Maybe like, five or six sweet things, depending on if you count the donuts separate." I said, crossing my arms.

"Comfit, it's just past noon. I usually eat one or two sweet things a *day*, maybe. If that." she retorted.

"It's "not a big deal," I said, my voice trailing off, "I just get cravings, and I train a lot, anyway, so whatever, shut up."

"Hm, well, if you need your outfit altered later, don't be afraid to come in!" Romanson said, "We do it for a small fee, and we can be sure to make it look good too!"

"I- no, I'm not going to get my outfit altered." I said, glaring, "If I start seeing my body change, I'll stop eating the sweets, gods."

"No worries, just letting you know!" he said amiably.

"Anyway..." Alele said, "Speaking of eating, we gotta go get lunch, thank you so much, Mr. Romanson! When can we expect the outfits?"

"Oh, they should be done by next week, no problem!" he beamed, "They're not too complicated, me and my assistants can pop them out in no time, and I have a super scientist on retainer for the helmets."

"Oooh, super science? You didn't mention that!" Alele said, perking up.

"Ah, no, mundane helmets, just made by someone who can work at triple the speed a regular person can, sorry to get your hopes up!" he clarified.

"Aw, well, I'm sure they'll be fantastic anyway!" she said, once again pulling my hand as she led me down the stairs, "Bye, and I'll be back soon to check in on the order!"

He waved at us, and started making notes on his notepad as we left the room, heading downstairs. Alele crashed into the front door before remembering he'd locked it, then opened it up and we were on our way. We walked the street the way we'd come, and after checking for anyone looking, I pulled off the balaclava and tucked it away, leaving me once again just plain old Candy Clenson instead of secret hero Comfit. It felt almost nice to have a secret identity, most heroes didn't bother with them, but a third or so did, and they defended them to the last breath. I had always wondered why they *wouldn't* want the fame and fortune in their private lives too, but some people just weren't up to being in the spotlight, I guessed.

I was looking forward to the build-up of the Comfit character, though, the secrecy, the new social media account, the mysterious way I'd have to do things, there was an allure to it that I couldn't deny. Sure I'd be doing double work, but I'd also be getting double the fans, and when I made the big reveal that I was both Comfit *and* Angel Rouge? My follower count would double, at least. It wasn't a good idea to play my hand too early though. If I didn't have enough total supporters, or if there was too much overlap between the two fanbases, then I'd be wasting my hard work without actually getting to angel like I wanted. That said, would Alele make angel too? I couldn't imagine her power evolving into something better, it was already fantastic, but I was interested to see. Maybe she'd be able to time travel back even further?

"I need you to eat some real food here, ok?" she said, breaking my train of thought, "I know it's not as fancy as the places I usually like, but I've heard *great* things about it."

I looked up and saw we were standing in front of the shiny metal grease trap we'd landed in front of earlier. I could practically smell the oil oozing out of the rivets and cracks in the building. The whole place screamed 'dive', and I highly doubted they'd have what I really wanted right now, which was a brown sugar boba and a lemon bar... My mouth watered just thinking about it.

"I'd rather go back to the base and eat there, Alele." I said, wrinkling my nose as someone left, the smell of fried 'something' wafting out the door.

"Yeah, sure, so you can get treats from the cafe and avoid actual meals, *again*." she said, "Even when Galorna makes us her protein meals for training these days you eat half of what everyone else does if that, and I *know* it's not because it's bad; the girl can *cook*."

"I just like the quick energy rush sweet stuff gets me, I get a lovely brain buzz too, I haven't eaten non sweets in days, it just doesn't appeal to me." I said, "I *kinda* wonder if has something to do with my power."

Alele made a horrified face. "Like- like your power is trying to make you want more and more sweets so you use it again?"

"Something like that." I admitted, "It wants to be used, I think."

It wasn't too much of a stretch, when you were chosen a small part of the god or goddess's spirit was imparted into you, into the mana connection that linked you to them and gave you your powers. The gods could always just tell you in person that they wanted you to use your powers more if they wanted, they had that ability, but from what people could *tell*, the will of the gods trickled through the connection like whispers into your mind, pushing you subconsciously to act in one way or another. At least, that was the conspiracy theory.

People claimed it could change someone's personality, or make them do things they otherwise wouldn't, but the existence of fallen Chosen proved that at least, if nothing else, the influence was minor enough to push past and defy. The idea that Lorgiaia, in all her infinite wisdom, was trying to get me to *eat* people? It just didn't sit well with me, it didn't make sense. Still, she *had* given me this power in the first place, she *did* expect it to be used somehow.

"That settles it, we're eating here to get rid of those urges, and you're not allowed to get *anything* sweet, got it?" For the third time that day, Alele grabbed my arm, yanking me inside the metal diner, my glove bunching up under her hand.

As we walked in, I tried not to wince. The whole place was full of a strange spicy smell that made me think of that dwarven bar we'd tried overlayed on top of the smell of cooked meat and sizzling oil. It was the kind of place that made me afraid to see the kitchen to be honest. It was cute enough though, the checkered floor was stained, but not dirty, the shiny metal tables and countertops matched the exterior, and the creme colored walls were doing a good job at hiding any yellowing from the oil in the air. I was mildly surprised to see it was almost full, a myriad of different people were at the tables, all kinds of abominations and former monsters, and I couldn't even see an open booth, just spots at the counter.

"Are we sure this place is on the up and up?" I whispered, "I don't want people to see us here if it's shady."

"Does *that* answer your question?" Alele asked, pointing at a booth in the corner.

I followed her gaze, and saw a tall woman in a purple jacket with slightly fried fluffy blonde hair and a short, brunette, gray-green half-goblin in a green vest made from a torn up hoodie. Her arms were bare and covered in tattoos, one arm looked like it had flowers, the other, some kind of goblin runes. I stared at them for a moment, wondering what Alele was trying to show me, when the blonde met my gaze, and narrowed her eyes. After a split second, she perked up, and waved at us, beckoning us over to her booth.

"Ooooh, we're getting *recognized*!" Alele said under her breath as we walked over.

The brunette got up and moved to the other side of the booth to sit by the blonde, giving us the other side, and I noticed her outfit seemed... uncoordinated. Her brown combat boots had fluffy lace socks poking out the top, she had a large black bow behind her head, and her cargo capris had flowers embroidered into the spaces between the pockets. Even her makeup was off, with dark red lipstick and teal eyeshadow but no foundation or mascara. If these were people Alele knew, she must respect them a *lot* to not have gone off giving her fashion advice as soon as we walked up.

The blonde grinned at me, and I sized her up. She was wearing a white t-shirt that had "DTQ" on it in college font, and she wasn't wearing any makeup at all.

She lounged back and pointed at the menus behind the napkin holders. "We just ordered, go ahead and pick something out, we'll pay for it." she said casually.

Hearing her voice, I had to stifle a gasp. The lazy, raspy, crackly, smokers voice that everyone had heard a million times on the screens in the square, on TV, in movies, that I'd heard *in person* like a week ago. This was Miss Missile, out of costume, at a burger joint with- I snuck a glance at her companion and mentally superimposed a flowery gas mask over her- Fem-Butch, the Queen's resident commando, the rarely seen girl who usually stayed with the ground troops on missions, and almost never made public appearances. I tried to hide my shock as I reached for a menu and looked down at it, feeling a little confused at the situation.

"It took me a second to recognize you two, but Angel Rouge's hair is pretty unique. Thanks again for the takedown last week. It made things a *lot* easier, I rarely get to bring people back in good enough condition to question." Miss Missile said.

"I saw you on the news after." Fem-Butch said, "That witch girl was bugging out, huh? My name is Elma, by the way."

"It's lovely to meet you, Elma!" Alele chirped, "I'm Alele, and this is Candy!"

I waved, and gave a small smile, still feeling in over my head.

"Oh, shit, yeah, you can call me Gianna, it's nice to see you off the clock, I love getting to pick new heroes' brains." Miss Missile smiled at us, and sipped her drink.

"I- yeah, thanks for picking up the guy for us, and sending the news van, too, that was nice of you." I said.

"Sorry it was just the one, but that night was busy. Hey, I wanted to ask about your powers, the two of you said something about time manipulation?" she said, tilting her head.

"Gods, I'd *love* that power..." Elma grumbled, "My power is just 'be better than the people around me at stuff'. I can't even go and patrol out by myself."

"Wellll it's just basic time travel, *mental* time travel. I can send my brain back in time up to three seconds!" Alele explained, "And that lets me get kinda creative, like rewinding after Candy here dies and retrying."

"That sounds like it'd be a good party trick." Gianna said "I'd use it to cheat at cards, as it is, my power just blows the cards up."

"I can kinda cheat at cards." Elma said, "I'm just better than anyone I play with, so I'm more likely to win. Luck still can be a bitch though."

"I can do more than cheat at cards!" Alele said, "Here's a game I like to play with the girls, Fake Psychic. I ask you one question, you answer truthfully, and then I tell you about yourself!"

"Ahhh, I see how this works." Gianna said, smirking, "Ok, go ahead, one question."

"What... is your favorite color?" Alele said dramatically.

"Purple, duh." she responded, arching an eyebrow.

"Ok, fair, are you ready for me to... reaaad your miiiind?" Alele wiggled her hands as she said it, and I held in a snicker.

"I guess so, yeah, go for it." Gianna nodded.

Alele wiggled her fingers and spoke slowly and with a spooky voice "You... are thirty two years old! You are lactose intolerant, but took a pill for it so you can drink a milkshake with your lunch. You have no less than five girlfriends, but *might* have a sixth, labels are confuuuuusing! Your favorite food is lasagna, but only if there's no meat in it. You once accidentally blew a side table through a plate glass window at the Queen's headquarters when you stubbed your toe on it! And... the most dark secret of all... you have a parasitic twin living in your lower torso!"

Elma's head whipped around to stare at Gianna, her shaggy hair spinning as she turned. "You have a *what?*" she said, her voice cracking.

"That last one wasn't true," Gianna said, laughing, "but the rest were, good job! I can see how that's a pretty fun trick, very useful."

"Yeah, I'd be dead without it." I said, trying to contribute something to the conversation.

"You told me." Gianna said, her smile slipping, "It's gotta be rough, knowing that."

"I-" I'd been trying not to think about it, to avoid it as much as I could. "I'm just happy I'm alive right now."

"So, have you guys had any other big interactions?" Elma asked, "Maybe not fights, but like, other stuff?"

"We- uh," I trailed off, "it's complicated, we were investigating something, but we ended up closing the investigation, it was over our heads."

"We might be able to give a hand with it," Gianna cut in, "I'd be happy to help, give you guys most of the credit."

"It's- it was- it wasn't technically *illegal*..." I said, "There were loopholes and stuff, we couldn't go anywhere with it. It's not a big deal."

Gianna's expression hardened for a split second before relaxing again. "Ah, one of *those*. We've been dealing with that stuff for years ourselves. We can't break the law for justice, but sometimes the laws are made by the unjust, it's a bitch."

"There's one lady in particular." Elma grumbled, "She's so *fucking* smug about it too, like, we can't just fucking punch her over it because she's not doing crime that can be fought. I got her on back taxes once, hired a whole firm of CPAs to sit in the room with me so I'd get my accounting skills high enough to do it. She paid the taxes all off instantly, and got away without any backlash, like it was nothing to her."

"May I take your orders?" a new voice asked, and I glanced up to see a dwarven lady in a white and red dress holding a clipboard by our table.

"Yes! We'll both have the double bacon cheese burgers with fries, and water, please!" Alele said with a smile.

The lady smiled and made a note, walking off to the next table.

"I hadn't even finished looking at the menu!" I said, mildly annoyed.

"Well I knew I needed to order *for* you before you saw they had an option to replace the buns with donuts, that maple syrup glaze was a topping, *and* before you noticed their selection of milkshakes." Alele said, holding her nose up.

"Wait, are you on a diet?" Elma asked, "Dude, don't do that, we're *Chosen*, we shed the pounds without even trying, you'll starve."

"No, my power might be making me crave sweets, she's trying to help me break that." I said.

"The fuck is your power that it wants you to eat sweets?" Elma asked, confused.

I stared at her for a moment. "...Flying fast?" I said unconvincingly.

"I don't buy that." Gianna gave me a look, "Listen, one of our most popular members' power is being an eldritch mass of body parts phasing in and out of reality, whatever your power is, it's not worth hiding. Use it and embrace it, it's what Janna did."

"Janna?" Alele asked.

"Lady Lunge." offered Elma, "She accepted she was scary, and now people love her for it."

"My power is less 'scary', and more 'impossible to use in moderation'." I explained.

"Come on, it can't be *that* bad." Gianna said, "Give us a hint?"

"I can't talk about it too much because of church orders, but..." I thought of a way to say it. "If I use my power, someone dies."

"Oh, gods." Gianna whispered, "I mean, *my* power has a pretty high chance of killing, but I train super hard to avoid that, you can't do that at all?"

"No." I admitted, "training it would lead to people dying."

"Oh, fuck." Elma muttered under her breath, "Oh, *fuck*, you like, can't stop using it, can you? It's on right now, that's why you're all gloved up..."

"How- what?" I asked, "That's- how did you get *there*?"

"There's someone here in the diner who's good at reading people, and someone who used to be a private investigator, as far as my power can tell. Might be the same person" Elma said, "Anyway, you've got like, an *actual* unstable power, don't you?"

"It's not 'unstable'." Alele said, rolling her eyes, "She's got it under control! Look, just don't touch her."

"*You're* touching her." Gianna pointed to our elbows.

"No, I'm touching her *glove*." Alele said, "It's different. She's fine, honestly, it's not a big deal."

"I hadn't heard about anyone being killed by heroes lately." Elma said, "Did you cover it up?"

"Cover *what* up?!" I asked in alarm.

"Well, you found out how your power works somehow." she pointed out, "Someone had to die for that. We all go too far sometimes- well, *I* haven't, my power sucks, but *still*, Chosen can't always pull their punches, shit happens. I just want to know if you hid it well enough, or if it's going to come back and bite you."

"No- I'm- The GGDS *knows* what happened, I reported it." I explained, "We're trying to- *I'm* trying to reverse the effect, but- it's hard, because I can't practice, but I did *NOT* cover it up, it's all above board."

"Hm." Gianna said, thinking hard, "I- well." she looked at me sadly. "I just- *please* be careful. You have *so much* future in front of you, you just started, and I really think you and your team can breathe new life into the 240 blocks. I know what it's like to have a shitty power. Before I had my boots and gauntlets to direct blasts, and before I learned how to store impacts for later instead of just exploding, I used to take out whole *buildings* every time I was shot or hit on the head." she sighed. "I don't know if you'll be able to figure things out, it took me *years*, and a lot of blood on my hands before I was able to be the public hero I am today, but at least try?"

"I can't relate to you, my power has the opposite problem." Elma said, "Unless I'm around someone who's the peak of humanity in whatever I'm copying, I'm just a normal person who's really good at stuff. Not even superhumanly good, just- better than anyone else currently in the room. I *hated* my power. I almost lost my faith and went fallen over it, but I stuck it out, I met people who cared for me anyway. I found that with a good team, a support group that cares for you, and the ability to forgive yourself as you grow, almost anything can be overcome. You're *more* than your power, that power is just a small part of you and your journey, *not* your defining feature. I believe in you, Candy, and I hope you find what you need for you *and* your power to bloom."

"Just *had* to do it, huh?" Gianna said, a mild glare on her face.

"Hey, I can't help it if I'm better at being motivational than you, it's just how I work." Elma said with a smirk.

"Here you go, girls, enjoy!" the waitress said, walking over with a cart filled with food. Miss Missile got two cheese burgers, a basket of fries, a side of onion rings, the vanilla milkshake Alele mentioned, and a bowl of beans. Elma got a salad, a double bacon burger, some chili and a small bowl of fried cheese. I looked at my single burger and fries and felt like I'd been beaten somehow, in a contest I didn't even know I was having.

"You gotta eat more than *that*..." Elma said, "We're Chosen, we have magical god powers burning fat and building muscles while we sleep, *live* a little."

"I do!" I said, "It's just usually sweets, not... I don't know... this stuff."

"Real food?" Alele offered around a mouthful of burger.

"Yeah, that, I guess." I picked up my own, using napkins so I didn't stain my gloves.

"I still don't understand why your death power is telling you to eat more sugary stuff." Gianna said.

"Church secret, can't explain." Alele said before I could speak up, "Honestly, we said too much already."

"Fair enough, I won't pry." she said, digging into her spread of grease.

I took a bite, and tasted the meat on my tongue, the gray, congealed grease coating it, the taste of something dead in my mouth. The bacon was sweet at least, but it still made me feel mildly sick as I chewed. The texture was all wrong, it was lumpy, and springy, and *weird*, my mouth didn't like it. I washed it down with some water, and forced myself to take another bite. *This* bite was worse somehow, I was expecting it now, but the way the fresh pickles and lettuce clashed with the sickening animal flavor felt like a bastardization of food itself. I thought of the gummy worms back home, of Homicide in my mini fridge, of all the wonderful foods we served in our lobby.

I could be eating *anything*, and I was eating this? I felt the wetness of the oil ooze out of the sides of the flesh on my next bite and I had to dissociate to get it down. I was almost done, just a few more bites... I swallowed, and bit again, barely letting the taste hit me as I mashed it with my tongue and swallowed, taking a sip of water to clear my mouth. There was easily another two or three bites left, but I didn't care, I pushed the rest into my mouth and forced it down my throat, using my enhanced strength to stop myself from gagging or choking, and felt the hateful, slimy thing work down to my stomach. I took another gulp of water, finishing the glass, and wiped my mouth on my napkin.

"Would anyone like my fries?" I offered, looking around the table.

Three sets of eyes stared back at me, horrified. Alele reached out and pet my arm gently. "Uh, yeah, we'll eat those for you, it's ok..."

"What the *fuck* was that?" Gianna muttered, looking queasy.

"What was what?" I asked.

"You just kinda went blank and force fed yourself a double decker burger, in like, 5 bites, it was pretty weird to watch." Elma said.

"I didn't- oh." I said. That *had* happened, hadn't it? "I just didn't really enjoy it, it kinda made me uncomfortable to eat, so I just got it over with, I guess."

"Candy, I don't care what I said earlier, eat all the sweets you want, just never do *that* again, ok?" Alele said, looking mildly worried.

"Here, I haven't drank out of this yet, will it help?" Gianna asked, handing me her milkshake.

I took a sip and felt peace wash over me. "Oh, gods, thank you, that helped a lot..."

I drank the milkshake, letting the sweet creamy goodness fill me up and replace the taste of animal in my mouth. I felt myself lay back against the booth as I sipped. I was trying to think of the last time I'd had 'real food', and I was drawing a blank. It'd have to have been one of the times Galorna cooked, but that was last week. Had I really lost the ability to enjoy 'real food' in the past few days? I didn't mind too much, sweet stuff was better anyway, and if I didn't have to worry about my figure or health, there was no harm, right? I finished the milkshake with a slurp and set it down licking my lips. The others had mostly stopped talking after my display, but they all looked up at the sound of the milkshake being emptied.

"Better?" Alele asked.

"Yeah, *way* better." I said, "I don't think I can eat burgers anymore, but that milkshake was great."

"…Here, I want you to take this." Gianna said, writing something on a napkin.

"An autograph?" I asked.

"I- we- look, it's a private power management company." she explained, handing me the napkin, "They helped me get in the right form to join the Downtown Queens. Get church approval, and see if they can help you."

"Thanks, I'll look into it!" I said politely as I took it.

"No, I *mean* it, I've never seen someone *that* affected by their own power before. Changing what you can eat? Mental shutdowns when you're in situations your power doesn't like? Not being able to turn the power *off*? It's bad, Candy. These people can help you."

I looked at the name on the napkin, 'Hero Helpers' and felt myself wilt. I doubted they could help, and they had a stupid name, but I'd talk to Oori about it anyway. *Oori*, not Debbie, screw her. I nodded and put the napkin in my pocket, smiling gratefully at Gianna.

"Thank you, Candy. Now, *I* still want a milkshake, wanna get another one for yourself and we can race?" she asked her green eyes sparkling.

If I had to bet, she was one of those people who were immune to ice cream headaches... They were always the ones to suggest milkshake races, in my experience. Still I *did* kind of want more milkshake, my tongue kept finding bits of that horrible burger behind my teeth.

"Ok, you're on!" I said, flashing her a wide, put-on smile.

As the waitress brought out our milkshakes, I realized with a small twinge of joy that I was working on steps three *and* five right now. If I could get Miss Missile and Fem-Butch to trade selfies with me, I'd be working on step one, too! As much as I hated that burger, I was glad Alele had made me come here after all, it was turning out *very* productive.

Chapter Seventeen

As we walked back to the base, I felt the napkin in my pocket and thought about what Gianna had said. If my power really *was* hurting me, I needed the help, but was it *really* hurting me? I didn't mind eating candy, I preferred eating candy to anything else, it *was* my name after all, why shouldn't I like it? Gloves weren't so bad, yeah I couldn't have a *physical* relationship, but I'm sure there were other fulfilling ways I could have fun with any partner I had that didn't involve skin to skin contact. I might check them out if I ran into any problems, but for now, I was going to focus on Comfit.

A loud crashing noise sounded out, jarring me from my thoughts and my head snapped towards the sound. It was coming from the direction of our section, wasn't it? We were almost there, should we wait and see if the people on patrol would take care of it, or should we-?

"Candy, transform already, we gotta go see what that was!" Alele yelled, smacking my arm and deciding for me.

I glanced at her, she'd already transformed, her navy blue dress flapping as she kicked her legs in the air impatiently. I nodded and let myself feel the pull, the lights covering me, and my clothes and body shifting to my magical girl outfit. I followed her to the sky, looking around for the noise. I *really* didn't want to fight right now, I was still feeling sick from that burger, and I just wanted to go home and curl up until later this afternoon when my next patrol was scheduled. I saw a cloud of dust billowing up from an area of the city that was well inside our section and I groaned. This *was* my responsibility after all.

I zipped forward, using my speed to get ahead of Alele and cut around to the dust-free area on the street next to the commotion and landed hard. I looked around, Drizti, Lucy, and Mourner were already here, Driz was behind everyone, holding her hands out like she was bracing something, with the other two in battle ready poses. There were a few onlookers, but most of the civilians, the smart ones, had run off already.

"What's the situation?" I asked Mourner.

"This fucker just busted out of the ground and started attacking us." she said grimly, "He's all wound up, and he's not in a 'talking' mood."

The dust cleared enough for me to get a glimpse of the man in question. He was a shorter, white bearded man with a white leather full-body coat and a golden helmet on his head, spikes shaped like pincers cutting just in front of his eyes. Beside him was a young woman not much older than me, dirty blonde with green pants and a top that had the 'pincers' from the man's helmet printed on it. She was wearing a cheap green domino mask and a headband with childish green antenna on it, and crying as she tried to make herself small behind the much shorter man.

I could have sworn I'd seen the old man before, I just couldn't place it. He had that look though... His eyes met mine, and his face turned from determination to rage.

"*You!*" he roared, "Give her back!"

He held up a hand and huge, spiny shaped rose into the air behind him, snaking forward, each as long as a bus. I realized with horror that they were the giant centipedes from the basement room, and this man must be the old halfling who lived with them.

"Give *who* back?" Mourner yelled, "We haven't taken anyone!"

"You stole my *daughter*!" the young woman said, her voice rough and raw, "I just need to know she's ok, please!"

"Who is 'we?'" Drizti said nervously as the massive centipedes encircled us, "I've never *seen* you people before!"

"Her!" the old man barked, pointing at me, "She took my progeny! She broke into my home and took the child I was raising!"

Lucy glanced at me, her eyes widening in realization. "Oh, shit, you totally did that."

"That's not *helping*, Sable." I growled, "Old man, look, I saw your daughter-"

"*My* daughter!" The woman corrected me, "My fucking child!"

"Ok, the- the whatever, the child, I saw it- her, like, one time, I kicked her, and never saw her again, I don't have her!" I said, holding my hands up.

"I saw her run off into the streets, actually." Lucy said.

"Then I will tear the streets apart until I find her!" the old man said, waving his hand.

There was a hiss, and the centipedes thrashed, tearing into the surrounding buildings, smashing a small doctor's office and a long-closed bakery, glass exploding into the streets. Mourner yelled, and lashed out, the vines on her arms snapping forward and catching one of the centipedes around the 'neck', slamming it into the ground. Lucy flickered, and appeared in front of the other one, driving her fist into an eye, a spray of goo bursting out of it. I dashed for the lady, raising my fist to put her out of the fight. I could leave the others to the rest of the girls, I wanted the easy target. Alele landed in front of me, catching my blow in a hand and pushing me back, putting herself between me and the lady like a wall.

"No!" she yelled, "She's a *minion*, a non-combatant, focus on the other one!"

I gritted my teeth, *technically* I could get in serious trouble if I fought a noncombatant, but she was *right there*. Why couldn't Alele focus on him? It wasn't like I had a more useful power than her, I couldn't even *use* mine. I bit back my argument, and charged the old man, swinging my foot at his head. He blocked with a gauntlet, then switched to a grab, and punched my inner thigh with his free hand. I grunted, and he swung me around, slamming me into the ground stomach first, hard.

The air shot out of me and I struggled to breathe, I looked up to see Mourner twist her body, landing on the back of the centipede she was fighting and turn, so the vines around the neck tightened. She screamed, and flexed her arms, and with a snap, there was a spray of fluids, and the head of the centipede was ripped off by the noose she'd made. I made a mental note to never underestimate dryads again, and rolled over just in time to see the old man head butt me, the pincers on his helmet driving into my torso, cutting deep. One went into a kidney, and the other in my intestines, the pain lancing through my body. He pulled back sharply, and the teeth on the pincers cut and tore as he wrenched himself free of me, my insides hanging off of his helmet.

I writhed, screaming as blood pooled under me, the pain was more than anything I'd ever felt, why hadn't Alele rewound that? Was I in the 'bad' timeline? Could that happen? Every time I died, was there a timeline she'd failed to save me? Another me that had to suffer?

I tried to tighten my muscles to stop the bleeding, to stop the oozing guts from leaking out, but I couldn't. I was feeling cold, and I gasped for air, I hadn't been hit in the lungs, why was it so hard to breathe? I tried to sit up, but my gloved hand slipped in my own blood and I went back down. The old man stood over me, what I could see of his face twisted in rage, and he lifted his gauntlet to hit me again.

A green light shone over my face, and another joined it, connecting together into a bar. The bar stretched, one end touching my stomach, the light hurting and causing pressure on my wounds, and the other end shot forward with a speed I wasn't expecting, hitting the old man on the mouth as he swung, the only exposed skin on his body. He roared and collapsed, and my world came into focus. I sucked in air, my body shaking. I looked down, the guts weren't hanging out anymore, there was a lot of blood still, but no wounds, and there was barely any lingering pain. I backed away quickly, crawling out of the sticky pool of blood and scrambling to my feet. The man was holding his own stomach, curled up in a ball and moaning, blood staining his white coat, seeping out of the button-holes and seams.

I looked around, still shaking and dizzy. Was it over? Mourner and Lucy were smashing the last centipede into a pulp, it was twitching but not thrashing anymore, and Alele was on her phone, looking around the fight scene and describing it to someone. It *should* be over, right? The two combatants stopped their punches, the sound came back to my ears, and the scene felt tired, like all the urgency had rushed out of it at once. It was over. I rubbed my stomach and staggered over to a side rail on the sidewalk, leaning against it. I hated fighting, I'd tried to take the easy path and *still* gotten hurt. I'd need to be sure and avoid *any* power or super science enhanced crime as Comfit, un-Chosen criminals only...

"Sorry about that..." Drizti said, coming up beside me, "I wanted to do it faster, but I needed him clear of you first, or he'd just attack again."

"N-no, you're- I- no, it's ok..." I said shakily. It was a weird feeling, being disemboweled and standing up just fine a few seconds later.

"I was surprised when I saw you take the hit, I thought Alele was getting better about that." she said, looking over at her, still on the phone.

"I think Alele was planing on you doing what you did, making him take his own hit." I said, pointing at the old man.

"That's a good strategy, I guess?" Drizti said, frowning.

"I guess." I said, shuddering, "I'd rather *not* get my guts pulled out again though."

I could still feel them, like lumps of wrongness sticking out of me, an emptiness inside that felt final. I knew I was healed, but I kept finding my hand reaching for my stomach, like I needed to try and push them back in.

The young woman was on her knees over him, crying harder now, her hands hovering over him but not touching him. "Please, he needs healing, are any of you a healer?" she said, looking at the group, her eyes scared.

"Um, my healing *made* him like that" Drizti said, "I think my team-mate is calling medical care, though?"

"He did that to *me*, and *he* didn't have a healer handy." I muttered, feeling guilty and annoyed all at once.

"I just wanted my daughter back..." the woman sobbed, "I need her, I love her so much..."

"You keep talking about a daughter, is this guy the dad?" I asked, pointing to the now-unconscious man bleeding out on the cracked pavement.

"No, he's- he helped make her, I gave the genetics, he made her in a tube." the woman sniffed, "I was trying to get him to let me adopt her from the lab, I just-" she broke down into tears again

"I'll, uh, keep an eye out for her?" I said, "I did see her at the lab, she didn't look, uh, humanoid? She honestly might get picked up by the monster crew and taken to the wilds..."

That made the woman cry harder and I bit my lip. Not the right thing to say, obviously. Imagining your baby daughter trying to survive the wilderness full of slimes and gryphons and skeletons and *worse* was enough to scare any mother.

"Um, look, are you a fallen Chosen?"

She shook her head.

"Are you a super scientist?" I asked.

"No, I'm- I'm *nothing*, I'm an intern who donated genetic material, that's *it*, and now my life is ruined..." she said, holding her head, "I just need to know she's ok..."

I looked around at the others. They'd gathered close enough to hear our conversation, and I was feeling a little on the spot.

"Well- ok, look, um." I tried to plan my words carefully. This woman didn't need this mess. I got the feeling if we let her go, she'd quit forever, and I *really* didn't feel like locking up a young mother as one of my first arrests. "If you're not a real, paid, minion, and you aren't any kind of villain, then we can't legally hold you here as anything more than a witness. How about you, like, leave and go look for her, before anyone shows up?"

"We're letting her go?" Mourner asked, "But-"

"She didn't actually break any laws." Alele said, hanging up her phone, "It's fine, but the GGDS will be here in a few minutes to collect the bodies and the old man, soooo..."

The woman looked at us, her face confused and stressed. Without saying anything, she stood up, and dashed away, her shoes slapping on the pavement as she tore off down the street. I watched her go. It was the kind of thing that either could end in a returning threat, or a grounding moment that I'd look at to remind myself that I *was* a good guy in a moment of self doubt. I was hoping it was the latter. Not that I *wanted* to have a moment of self doubt, but that was the kind of things Chosen just seemed to have, according to the movies, so it'd be nice if I could look back on this when it happened.

"I don't feel good about that." Mourner said, "She was *obviously* a minion, just because she was unpaid doesn't mean she's not going to go back to his lair and gear up to bust him out of the GGDS lockup."

"Honestly, if we took her in it'd just end up with the GGDS trying to intimidate her into confessing to a crime. We didn't see her do anything but cry and ask about her kid." Alele pointed out, "The GGDS could get a goddess of childcare to confess to tossing a baby off a building though, so it's better that she's free, for her sake. If she breaks the law for real, we'll get her."

"Well," Drizti said, "I just hope she's smart enough to quit the business after this. Being a minion sounds so *dangerous*."

"I considered being a minion for a while, actually." Lucy said, "There's a super scientist in what's left of Arena City, goes by Pressure Cooker. She's a feminist type, super into queer rights. If you go join up with her, she pays for all your transition stuff as long as you're on the payroll. Even does top surgeries for her minions herself."

"So there's a super villain who is specifically recruiting trans people?" I asked, "That seems like bad optics for trans people."

Lucy shrugged. "The optics aren't great from the good guys either, and at least *she* helps people transition. Rotten Fruit is *still* trying to get their team to let them present more masc and promote trans visibility, most people don't even know they're enby."

"*I* didn't know that." Alele admitted, "I'd *never* consider being a minion, but if you need help, sometimes you turn to bad people I guess."

"Is this a common thing?" Mourner asked us, "*Last* time I was on patrol with Angel Sable all our conversations turned queer, is that just a thing with her?"

"Yeah, pretty much." I said, "It's her favorite topic."

"No, it's not *every* time!" Lucy protested, "I talk about a lot of stuff, this is just the biggest part of my life right now, it's important to me. Fuck you, whatever..."

"I'm not saying it's *bad*, I just noticed it." Mourner said, "There's a guy bleeding out, we just tore up two huge bugs, we should be talking about the *action*, the *fighting*, how we did, not politics."

"My identity isn't 'politics'." Lucy said dejectedly.

"How the world reacts to it *is*, though, and *that's* what you're talking about." Mourner said, "Look, I'll talk about it all you want later, but like, the fight? That just happened? Can we talk about that now please?"

"I liked how you used your vines as lassos!" Drizti said, trying to move the conversation along, "I thought that was really clever."

"Branches, actually." Mourner said, waving the tendrils on her arms in the air, "I like to keep 'em long for that reason, down to my feet. I can extend them about four times the resting length, which is great for takedowns."

"I thought dryad's limbs were their branches?" I asked.

"No- well, I mean,- we have lots of branches." Mourner said, giving me a look, "My fucking *hair* is branches."

"I was pretty impressed with how I punched straight through that one's eye, and then I just like, went nuts, My fists tore through the shell like paper. It was pretty great!" Lucy said, regaining her enthusiasm.

"Yeah, I can't help but think of you doing that to a person next time." Drizti said, "If you hit a *person* that hard, I'm giving you the injuries and making *you* deal with it."

"Ooh, harsh." Mourner said, grinning, "I'm guessing you guys don't have regen?"

"Nah, barely any, enough to heal bruises and scrapes in a day or two, nothing more. We mostly just have Angel Verdant here." Alele said, "We're strong, but as you saw, just a guy with knives strapped to his head can still hurt us. We're trying to get a contract with the Valley Nurses though, for when we don't have a handy bad guy to send our injuries to."

I heard a noise and glanced up to see the GGDS cars pulling up to the other side of the hole the centipedes had crawled out of. I had to act fast.

"Ah, shit, quick, Angel Cobalt, get a picture of me next to the centipede missing the head before they dissolve it!" I said, holding my phone out to her.

She glared at it disdainfully, "Do a selfie, I'm not helping you boost your follower count any higher, miss 'target demographic'. You're already beating me by twenty three percent, by *cheating* I might add."

I looked at the others. "Come on, I need a picture, please?"

Lucy sighed. "Fine, do it quick..."

"Can I join?" Driz asked, "I'm doing *super* well on my social media, I'm getting so many sparkles!"

"Sure, just look cool and do pose, umm, 5b, ok?" I said, rushing to the best spot and getting into pose 2c. Driz floated over and joined me, doing a cute pose as the picture took. I relaxed and flew back over to Lucy, taking my phone back. The GGDS troops finally got to us as I did, and began work on melting the corpses with their acid sprays and blocking off the streets.

"Thanks, do we look good?" I asked.

"You're covered in blood, so, I mean, yeah. You look great" she said sincerely.

I winced, I'd almost forgotten about that. I checked the picture. It was a lot bloodier than most magical girl pics, yes, but that's what made it *real*, right? Fans liked real, I'm sure it'd be fine.

"It'll be nice to have an action picture to share for once!" Driz said as I sent her the picture, "I keep having to take pictures of myself for the fans, and they keep asking for really weird ones."

"Verdant, no!" Alele gasped, "*Never* do photo requests! What kinds of pictures?"

Drizti looked surprised at Alele's outburst. "Um, silly ones?" she said, unsure.

"Let me see." Alele demanded, stepping out of the way of a medical team moving to check the old man.

Drizti handed Alele her phone, and she flipped through, her expression getting darker and darker as she went through the photos.

"Oh, Driz..." she said, "Almost all of these are fetish pictures."

Drizti gasped, shaking her head. "No, it- they're *not*! I made sure it was nothing sexual, I ignored all *those* requests!"

"Uh, sometimes it's hard to tell." Lucy said, "I've absolutely seen one of your pictures on- uh, a website for 'specific' stuff."

"And you didn't *tell* me!?" she shrieked, drawing the attention of a few troopers.

"I thought you knew?" Lucy said shrugging, "It was such a specific picture, I figured it was your thing. It was the one with the high heels and the balloon, and you're-"

"I'm not into *that*!" Drizti said, flapping her hands, "I'm into- into-hugs, and snuggles, and blankets, and sharing cookies and milk!"

"Is that a fetish?" Mourner asked, "Shit, I might have that one too, then."

"It's not a-" Driz looked like she was going to cry.

"Hey, look, let's go to my social media friend, ok?" I said, "I can call her right now, and she can help get all this under control."

"I think we need to call Debbie about this, really." Alele said, "This is really serious, it could hurt the whole team. I'm shocked there's not a trashy magazine already talking about a 'child friendly magical girl doing adult photo shoots!' with how the media likes to jump all over this stuff."

"Well, we're not big yet, so, maybe they aren't following her?" Mourner pointed out.

"We're on different teams, there's no 'we'." I reminded her, "'We', as in, Lorgiaia's Angels, actually *are* kinda big thank you very much."

"We sleep in different buildings, yeah, but I mean, we patrol together, we get the same GGDS documents, we're in the same section, we're all magical girls," Mourner said, "I think it's fair to say we're all one big team."

"*I* think you're stretching that word, 'team'." Lucy said, "We do team-*ups*, we're not one team."

"So I'll need to talk to *two* of you then?" a GGDS agent cut in, holding up a recording mic and a notepad.

"Yeah, those two." Alele said, pointing at Lucy and Mourner, "They'll debrief you, we have to be somewhere. We'll be back when the news vans show up."

She grabbed me and Drizti's arms and pulled us down the street to a side road with no noise or people. I was getting used to her pulling me, but I had to wonder why she kept doing it so much, it's not like we were going to *willingly* sit in on a debrief we didn't need to.

"Cobalt, I'm on patrol, I really should be helping, what are we doing?" Drizti asked.

"We're going to call Angel Rouge's friend, get her opinion, and then go to Debbie." Alele said, "And we're doing it as soon as we can, because the longer we don't get ahead of this, the worse it could be."

"Oh..." Driz said sadly, "I just- I was just trying to make my fans happy, they were all so nice and sweet to me, and *some* sent gross stuff, but I blocked those like you showed me. I just don't know how those pictures could be anything like *that*."

"People *like* people with powers." I said, "It's a thing, anything you do will be seen by someone as sexual because of that. A lot of people like gnomes, too, most for, uh, not great reasons, but *that's* something to consider as well. And like, you're attractive, you're *adorable*, all those things come together into a perfect storm of 'there's going to be a lot of creeps who are interested' and you'd never even *seen* a smartphone before, so they can take advantage of you easily."

"I did kind of wonder if maybe we should be like, helping you more with it." Alele said, "I just don't know how I didn't see any of these pictures come up on my feed."

"Well, I didn't post most of them to my page." Drizti shrugged help-lessly, "I usually sent them directly to the people that asked for them."

"Oh? That's good! That's a good thing!" Alele said, "That means that there's no public evidence, just DMs, right?"

"I did post a few I thought were extra cute, but yeah." Drizti said.

"Can we see what you shared publicly?" I asked, "Or- no, wait, here, let's see what Forica says first, hang on..."

I reached into my own pocket for my phone, and only found the gun and my commonplace book. I sighed, I'd forgotten to keep my phone out when I transformed. I un-transformed, and got my phone out of my jeans pocket where I'd left it, and dialed Forica

"Hey boss, what's up?" she asked, answering on the first ring.

"We have a bit of a social media situation..." I said carefully.

"Oh, shit, is it the video of your flyover? I was trying to edit it to look faster like you wanted, but I think I overdid it. The comments are turned off now though, so we should be-"

"No, no, it's my teammate, Angel Verdant." I explained.

"Mm, yeah, there's been some rumors about her." Forica hissed, "Something about photo requests?"

"Yeah, that's- that's what I'm calling about. She's been doing photos for fans not realizing they were fetishes." I said, "We're concerned it'll hurt her image and we need to get ahead of it and end the rumors and scrub the evidence."

"And you're concerned it'll hurt *your* numbers by association, I'm guessing." she extrapolated.

I glanced over at the other two to make sure they hadn't heard. "I won't say that's not part of it."

"'K, have you talked to the lady running your PR? The rude one who yelled at me in the square?"

I shook my head, then remembered she couldn't see that. "No, we haven't. She's the last line of defense, I don't want to go to her just yet."

"I do *not* blame you. Lady is a queen bitch." Forica agreed, "Ok, I can help damage control, and I'll help spread counter rumors too. I'll need extra though, this isn't included in our deal."

I wrinkled my nose. "How much extra?"

"This is a career changing mistake, and I'll need to call in favors to make enough noise to drown out the current discussion over it, so all in all, 'bout two thousand blessings?"

"Oh, for- that's two *months* of what I'm paying you!" I said, frustrated.

"Yeah, I know, you're getting a great deal because you boost my pages. She gets the regular rates."

I sighed and turned to Drizti. "She said it'll be two thousand blessings to do what she needs to do. Is that ok?"

"Yeah, whatever, that's- I don't care." Drizti said, flapping her hands and pacing, "I just want to fix this."

I turned away and spoke to Forica. "She said it's fine, can we meet you at the diner we ate at the one time?"

"Sure, I can come over now, or..?"

I thought about it. "Uhh, we're expecting a news crew soon, give us thirty minutes? It'll be me, Alele, Driz, and I guess our team leader, if she's free."

"Ok, cool, I'll be there."

She hung up, and I looked at the phone for a moment before dialing Galorna's number.

"Hey, what's up Candy? Everything ok?" she picked up on the third ring, out of breath and panting.

"Hi, uh, nnnnot really?" I said, "We're in emergency mode here."

"Was there a fight? Did anyone get hurt?" she said, snapping into her leader voice.

"Oh, uh, yeah? We fought big bugs, I got stabbed a little, but that's not why I'm calling..."

"You getting stabbed *isn't* the emergency?" she asked, her voice hard and urgent, "Where do I need to be? I'm leaving right now."

"Well, I wanted us to meet at the diner on the main road at the edge of our section, the one I met my social media friend at? We need to talk about Drizti's social media."

"The emergency that's more important that you getting *stabbed*- is Drizti's social media?" Galorna asked incredulously.

"Well I'm not stabbed *anymore*." I said, "And yeah, she's been sending almost any picture of herself to anyone who asks for it."

"Candy, sometimes I- I don't- We're supposed to-..." Galorna tried and failed several times to start what she wanted to say before she gave up, "*Fine*, this *is* something we need to address. Are we meeting alone?"

"No, Forica is helping us, and we're gonna get ahead of this quickly, I hope."

"Transformed or untransformed?" she asked tiredly.

"I'll be transformed, it's up to you." I said, "We've got the news vans coming soon, so you've got time."

"Ok, I'll see you there, bye, Candy." Galorna said, and hung up.

I glared at my phone. What was with people not giving me a chance to say goodbye to them? I peeked around the corner to see a couple of news vans on the other side of the hole in the ground, but they were still setting up.

I turned to the other girls. "Ok, let's get this interview done. Drizti, everything is normal, do *not* act weird, ok?"

"This is my first interview, how do I not act weird?" she asked, looking panicked.

"Just pretend it's your hundredth interview." Alele said, "You'd be really good at them if you had a hundred of them, so just act like you have, got it?"

"Uh, I guess?" Drizti said.

I finished transforming and noticed with a little annoyance that the blood and tearing had already started to fade and repair. I'd wanted to look battle-worn on the news, make myself look like I was doing more physical work than I really was. Still, the bloodstains were there, faded as they were, so it was something. Lucy and Mourner were covered in brown and green bug guts, so I was the coolest looking one of our group by far. We walked over and made it to the other two as they finished talking to the GGDS officer, and they turned to greet us.

"Oh look, Angel Rouge showed up just in time to be on the news, what a coincidence." Lucy said dryly.

"We told you we'd be back." Alele said, "We needed to set up the meeting to take care of-" she glanced at the two news crews coming towards us. "-normal business."

"Hi, we're the Valley City Anchor," the first new man said, stepping up, "We'd like an interview?"

"I'd like to do both at once, please." Alele said, "I have an important date."

"Not a problem, hi, Stew with the Local 12." the other man said, waving the crews over, "Now, some of you are a mess, do you want to do a shoulders up interview? Or do you mind the mess being in frame?"

"We *can't* do a 'shoulders up' interview." Drizti said, "I'm only waist high to the rest of them."

"Yeah, I'm ok with the blood on me being seen." I said, "We fought hard, no reason to hide that."

Mourner nodded, and Lucy frowned, but nodded too.

"Perfect!" The VCA man said, " Just get in position, and we'll get rolling, we already got shots of the hole, and we'll explain through voice over, just answer the questions, ok?"

We set up, and the cameras started rolling. The VCA man nodded at Stew, a signal of who would start, and Stew stepped forward, holding his mic parallel with the other.

"Hi, I'm Stew with Local 12, would you mind introducing yourselves?"

We took turns telling him our names and team affiliation, and he smiled like he already knew. I guessed he didn't but it was nice of him to at least act like we were worth knowing about on a larger scale.

"Can you tell us about the villain? He seemed to have a goal in mind, what was it?" he followed up with after we were finished.

"He was looking for his baby, it went missing." Mourner said plainly.

"And he thought the best way to find it was to tear through the streets of section 247?" the other man asked with a fake laugh in his voice.

"I'd met him and the... child before, while in costume." I explained, "The child went missing shortly after, he attributed the disappearance to me."

"And is there any truth to that claim?" Stew asked pointedly.

"No, none." I said, "I was investigating another incident, and the child became afraid of me, I'm assuming it must have run off shortly after I first saw it."

"Do you feel any responsibility for the missing child?" the VCA man was being neutral in his tone, but jabbing in his questions.

I kinda *was* responsible, I'd scared it, I'd kicked it, I'd left the door open, but I couldn't *say* that.

"No, I don't believe so." I said. Was that too harsh? "But I will be searching the area to make sure the child is safe and gets to a secure location."

That's better, less cold.

"And the giant bugs that were used against you, has the team seen them before?" Stew cut in.

"We've been aware of them for a while, a few days at least." Alele said, glancing at me and Lucy, "Unfortunately, due to legal restrictions on the actions of Chosen, we were unable to help keep the city safe until they acted first."

Now *that* was harsh. She wasn't wrong, but straight up blaming the regulations like that made it sound like we were standing up for *less* restrictions on Chosen? I didn't know if that was a stance we wanted to take. After what Miss Missile had said, having 'a lot of blood on her hands' while getting used to her powers, was that really a good idea? New Chosen were made every day, and not all of them could be as good at their jobs as us.

"I see, well, I have no further questions, Stew?" the VCA man said.

"Just one, the two quiet ones, what are your thoughts one the fight? We've heard from the other three, do you have any comments?"

Drizti looked up at the camera and I saw her shake slightly as she nodded. "Yyyes, I was very happy to be able to help the community and see my first live combat. I was able to use my healing powers in ways I'd only imagined, and I look forward to helping protect others more in the future."

She said it clearly and without any hesitations, except for the very start. It sounded planned, rehearsed almost, but it was still very polite and well mannered. Very 'Drizti'. It was hard to imagine the little professional getting up to the stuff we'd seen on her phone just minutes before, hopefully that'd help the plan as we moved forward.

"And you?" the cameras focused more on Lucy.

She gave a throwaway smile and shook her head, the fluffy blonde hair waving as she did. "Hey, I'm just glad I got to save the day, fight some monsters, and keep my friends safe, y'know?"

Was- was she going for 'teen heartthrob'? It worked, a little, but she was acting less like the angry bitch she usually was at events and more like she was trying to impress a girl at her first high school party. I cringed, and tried not to look.

"Fascinating, ok, well thank you all for joining us! I hope we see many more wins from your teams!" the VCA man said.

"Great getting to chat, thank you!" Stew said, and with that, the cameras shut off and the crews turned to go.

"That was fast." Drizti said, "I thought they'd want makeup and lights and all kinds of stuff."

"That's for staged TV." Lucy said, "This was a street interview, so they want it to look natural."

"Plus, like, they gotta do like, thirty of these today, right? There's like thirty Chosen fights a day on average here, right?" Alele pointed out.

"I'm heading out to finish my patrol, catch up whenever." Mourner said, walking off without waiting on us to respond.

I checked my phone. "Ok, looks like Forica is already at the diner, I'll be by in a few minutes, I need to walk part way there so my clothes aren't all bloody when I get there, see you then?"

"Sounds good, we'll wait on you to start." Alele said.

"You know what she looks like?" I asked.

"Yeah, dryad, orange and yellow leaves, kinda bored, I got it." Alele snapped.

"Close enough, now go!" I said, un-transforming so my clothes would continue the self-repair.

This was fine, I was getting on top of the problem, it'd be fixed, I'd have another stream of fans soon, it'd all be fine. I kept telling myself that as I thought about the pictures I'd seen, and tried not to imagine them leaking...

Chapter Eighteen

I slid into the booth, folding my wings as best as I could. They still overlapped Galorna's a little, and she gave me a look. I ignored her, my wings didn't trigger my power, she'd be fine.

"Why are you so late?" she asked me as I picked up the menu.

"I had to wait on my transformation to repair so I wouldn't be covered in blood from the stabbing, duh." I said, raising an eyebrow.

She opened her mouth then closed it again with a slight sigh. What was her problem?

"Ok, so we're all here, right?" Forica asked, looking at the four of us. Drizti was next to her, on her left, and Alele was on her right, nearest to the wall.

"Yup, this is all of us." I confirmed, "Sable is staying behind with Mourner to patrol more, she's got a few hours left on her shift."

"So did I..." Drizti muttered.

"Right, but you're the woman of the hour." Forica said, "Now, phone out, show me what you sent so far."

Drizti sighed and pulled her phone out, holding it in both hands and flipping through the bubbles with her forefingers, her thumbs pointing in the air.

"These are all my fan-requested photos I've taken. Of these, I've posted maybe five of them to my main page, and the rest went to people in DMs." she said sadly.

Forica whistled and shook her head. "These are weird ones, for sure. I think most news coverage would have trouble proving to the masses that they're fetish content though, it's a lot of niche stuff."

She pointed to a specific picture. "This though, and stuff like it, that's a common enough kink that people will believe it."

"I *thought* that was a weird thing to ask for a picture of." Drizti admitted.

"We didn't come here to look at Driz's porn, what are our options?" Alele asked.

"I'd like to get Debbie in on this ASAP." Galorna said, "I really don't like that we're going to a third party here, no offense, Forica."

"None taken, and we'll loop her into the ordeal once it's solved. She can play cleanup." Forica said, "It's a tricky situation, and her go-to would be to make a public statement, I'm sure, which would cause more damage than good."

She drummed her wooden fingers on the table. "As for our options, I think we go through and delete every DM manually, then block the people who got them. As for the ones posted to the public page..."

She opened her own phone and typed quickly, then flipped through Drizti's home page. "There's only two that are really suspicious on here, the one with the whipped cream on her face and crossed eyes, and the one where she's upside down trying to drink milk. The rest are innocent enough to regular people. I'd just hope no one notices those ones in particular, and post even more pics to your page, every day."

"More pics?" Drizti asked, "I thought I wasn't supposed to-"

"More pics." Forica said firmly, "The weirder and sillier, the better. We need to make these look like just you being yourself instead of fetish requests. Mix it up, get your friends to take pics of you, I don't know, chasing the ducks at the park, or sitting on top of things taller than you, or wearing costumes, just being weird in general. From here on out, you're the quirky one."

"That's a whole rebranding, do we really need to do all this?" Galorna asked, "Can't we just delete the photos and be done with it?"

"Absolutely not." Forica said, "There's a site devoted to tracking deleted posts, as soon as a post gets deleted, it's mirrored there, and a *lot* of trash news people know that site. If weird photos of Verdant started popping up *there*, it'd draw *way* too much attention, it'd prove we knew about it and tried to cover it up."

"I know that site." Alele said, "I've used it to stalk some people I used to like."

"Ok, ok, I don't know how to delete the messages to people though, can you help me?" Drizti asked.

"I can show you how, yeah. I'll also need your login for some of the stuff I'm doing, so I can do some myself too." Forica said, "I want to make sure you're thorough, and I'll need to have access to your blocked list afterwards so I can go through and actually check to make sure if these guys reposted the pictures."

"What if they have?" I asked, "Wouldn't they still post to the other site even if they *were* nice and took them down?"

Forica smiled smugly. "Ah, this is where my help becomes *extra* valuable. See, I can use the anti-revenge porn laws to get re-posts from other people taken down because they were shared in DMs instead of publicly posted. Drizti's no longer in that 'relationship' with them, nor did she give permissions for them to share them. If *that's* the takedown reason, it gets marked differently on the backend, so the other netsite isn't accidentally hosting illegal content."

"Is this something you've done before?" Galorna asked.

"Yeah, I had an ex who got mad when I dumped him and, oof, well, let's just say he broke more than a few laws that day." Forica said rolling her eyes.

"I'm starting to feel better about the whole thing!" Drizti said, "I think I'm doing ok now. I was really worried I'd ruin the team, but if all I need to do is delete messages and be silly in public, I can do that."

"It's unfortunate that you've got to be the goofy one now though..." I said, reaching out to pat her hand, "I know you wanted to be a role model for young gnomes."

"I think I still can be." Drizti said slowly, "I *wanted* to be cool and fashionable, but we gnomes are known for being very traditional in lots of ways. Goofing off and showing people gnomes can be silly too might help break some of the stereotypes?"

"That's a great way to see it, yeah." Alele agreed, "We needed a silly one anyway. Sable is the angry one, or maybe the romantic one? She was acting weird in the interview. I'm the sexy one, obviously, Galorna is the tough mom mode one, and Rouge is the relatable one. Before this, Driz, you were honestly the innocent one, so it's an upgrade."

"Wait, why do *you* get to be the sexy one?" I asked, "I'm plenty sexy, and I'm not 'relatable', I'm the fast and reckless one, my trading card prototype says so."

"I have sexy *energy*, Candy." Alele said, "You're more of a sexy *vibe*."

"My trading card just said stuff about my cult and being a healer." Drizti said, "I hadn't approved it yet, maybe I need to ask them to change it to say I love having fun or something?"

"Yeah, for *sure* have it changed." Forica said, "And see if you can get art of you doing a funny pose on it too."

"Well they already started the art of me in pose 2a surrounded by my orbs." Drizti said, "I wouldn't want them to waste all that work."

"It's just a sketch, Verdant." Galorna said, "Mine had me yelling and flexing like I just stubbed my toe, I had them fix it to be me hovering and in a boxing pose, they'll fix it."

"Ok, I'll email them later..." she said shyly.

"This went well!" Forica said, "I'm happy with this. Driz, jot down your login for me, and I'll call this meeting done! Who wants a snack?"

"I'm starving..." I admitted, passing Driz my commonplace book for her to write her login info, "All I had for lunch was a couple milk-shakes and a terrible burger."

"The burger wasn't terrible." Alele said, "Mine was amazing and juicy, your brain is just broken because of your power."

"What?" Forica asked, "Your power made burgers taste bad?"

"Don't ask." I said, "I just want something to get my mind off all the stress that's happened today. Maybe a nice, sticky stack of waffles, with whipped cream and cherries and chocolate chips and butter-scotch drizzle and some sprinkles, and a nice tall glass of syrup to wash it down..."

"That's- *gods*, I know Chosen don't have to worry about their diets as much, but *gods*." Forica said, "I can't imagine enjoying that much sugar."

"Am I going to have to learn to bake?" Galorna asked, "We need to have a talk about your powers after we're done here, Angel Rouge. What you just said was concerning."

I grumbled, I was fine, I just had a sweet tooth, nothing more. I needed the energy anyway, I was starving. I wasn't sure exactly how Driz's power worked, but even after the old man had been hit with her power my guts had still been hanging on his face, the guts with my lunch still in them, I bet. I didn't feel anything *missing*, but I was feeling very empty now, much more than I was before the fight. Forica waved the waiter over, and we made our order, the waiter's eyebrow raising at mine, but he didn't say anything, and we were soon left alone, waiting on the food.

"So, Drizti, doing anything after this?" Forica asked, "I can help you get some of the funny pictures if you like. I'll charge you... hm, let's make it forty blessings per picture we decide to post?"

"Forty- oh." Drizti said, "I'm paying you two thousand already, that doesn't come with any freebies?"

"She charges me roughly twenty five per pic." I said, "It started out free, and then she jumped the price, be careful."

"Yeah, but you *know* it's worth it." Forica said, "I even have my nice camera with me, and I'll share them on my page, really sell the rebrand!"

"Ugh, fuck it, fine." Drizti said, slightly annoyed, "I know it's too much, and you're overcharging me just because I make a lot of money, but I don't really have anyone else to ask."

"I could always do it!" Alele said, "Free! Well, free and you share every picture I post for a week, and none of Candy's."

"Hey!" I protested, "That's- why?"

"You're still beating me, and I don't like that." Alele smirked, "I like having *all* the power over my little pets, so I'm going to pass you in followers and then make you mine."

I gasped and spluttered, shaking my head. "You- no! You can't just declare me your 'pet' in public like that! We haven't even dated or anything! You don't even know what I'm into!"

"We *are* on the same team though, and statistics show that-"

"No! No, look, why do you never flirt with Saffron? Or- or Sable? I'm sure *she'd* love it."

"They're literally dating each other." Alele said flatly, "That leaves you or Driz, and no offense Drizti, but I'm not about to take advantage of you being clueless to get you in bed, it'd be too easy, and pretty fucked up."

"No, that's fair, I get it." Drizti agreed, making a face.

"Wait..." I looked at Galorna, "You and Lucy?"

"Nnno, not really." Galorna sighed, "It's complicated. She's too insecure to admit she likes me, and I'm not going to push it, so... we're just playing the 'friends who cuddle too much' game for now. Please don't talk to her about it, she needs time."

"Told ya, forty percent, and it goes up from there." Alele said, smirking at me.

I shook my head. "I can't even- you know we can't- I'm not- ugh."

"You guys are cute." Forica said as the waiter brought her eggs and bacon, "If you make it official, let me take the announcement pics, kay?"

She pointed at Galorna. "You too, missy."

"I'll join in the fun soon." Drizti promised, "I just need to get my feet under me first."

"You don't have to 'join' anything, it's- this is..." I looked for the words, "Relationships are serious, not a game."

"No, relationships aren't a game to *humans*." Alele said, "For us elves, they absolutely are."

"They're usually arranged for gnomes, and *fuck* that." Drizti said, "So, they're whatever to me."

"I'm with Rouge on this one." Galorna said, picking up her fork and cutting into her southern fried steak, "Relationships are very serious and need to be respected."

"Is that why your last one ended up being so messy?" Alele joked.

Galorna gripped her cutlery and I watched it bend. "Please don't mention Saara again, please."

"Oh, *shit*, Galorna dated the heretic hunter?" Forica asked, "When?"

"No, S*aa*ra, she's a sorceress, not Sera, the hero." I clarified, "Saara is an un-Chosen human."

"Ah, boring then." Forica nodded.

Galorna's lips were tight, but she held her tongue and let out a slow breath, returning to her steak a moment later. Still a sore subject, it seemed. Honestly, it didn't seem like too big a deal for the two of them to date, but if the one who could look at the future said it was a bad idea, then who was I to butt in?

"So, any of you girls like dancing?" Forica asked, "I'm looking for people to go to clubs with, and I don't have a lot of adult friends."

"I like dancing!" Drizti said, "I don't know much about it, but I like watching the videos of people dancing on CirNet!"

"Forica, we talked about this." I said, "We can't be seen in a club with a 16 year old, we just got on top of one potential PR nightmare, we don't need another."

"I agree, I think you're a nice girl, Forica, and I appreciate you helping us, but it's not a good idea." Galorna said, nodding, "If you like though, we could look into hosting a teen dance night at the cafe? You could invite friends your age, and we'd be there to dance too."

"That's kinda lame compared to a real club." Forica complained, "I like watching people get drunk and stuff, be adults. Plus the music is better at real clubs, teen dances all have songs from forty years ago."

"My offer still stands, if you'd like, you can pick the songs and I can get Debbie to go through them with me and approve them?" Galorna offered, "We can put paper on the windows, get a fog machine, put lights up, it could be cool."

"Oooh, maybe we could get the cafe to sell mocktails based on us!" I said, "That would actually be *really* cool."

"Oh, oh!" Drizti said, "I could do a light show! My power glows, I could do tricks! I just gotta remember not to do too much this time."

"I could see this being really fun, I know a DJ who could host it, he owes me for something, too." Alele said thoughtfully, "We'd need a draw though, a contest maybe?"

"Like a dance competition?" Forica asked, "That could be pretty fun to watch, like, people go up and dance one by one and we all vote?"

"Sure!" Alele said, "And we could offer a prize! Something to draw a crowd..."

"Cash, cash draws a crowd." I said, "I'd say merch, but if they're teens, do they really want merch of magical girls?"

"If the party goes well enough they might?" Galorna rubbed her chin, "I think this could be a great outreach, we'd have to be sure the church doesn't make it sanitized, it needs to feel free and cool or no one will care."

"Lorgiaia's husband seemed to understand that stuff pretty well, he helped pick us all to target different demographics, so he understands the need to be flexible." I reminded them, "I could ask Oori to talk with him, let us head it up ourselves? Sanctioned church event, so we have funds and people, but the church stays hands off."

"As long as it's not going to be like the last day of a church camp. Like where they try and hype everyone up for the god they follow by giving them pizza and telling them it's a 'party', then I think it could be ok." Forica reluctantly admitted.

"Would you be interested in promoting it?" Drizti asked her.

"It's my rep on the line, so, like, pay me, but yeah, I can spin it to my followers. I'll get my friends to post about it too, I guess." she agreed.

"I'm glad we all had this sit down!" Drizti smiled, "We started off trying to avoid disaster, and ended up throwing a party!"

"I want to see if we can get some guest stars," Galorna said, "Rouge, do you think you could try and get some other Chosen to come and be 'judges' or something?"

"Me? Why me?" I asked.

"You're mutuals with like six other Chosen, not including us." Alele pointed out.

"No, I'm mutuals with Genki and two of the Valley City Nurses." I said.

"Nope, Miss Missile and Fem-Butch followed you back after we left the diner." Alele showed me her 'followers you follow' page on my profile, and sure enough, they'd added themselves. I also had the rest of my team, and The Unchosen, but they didn't really count.

"I don't know if I can get *the* Miss Missile to come to a teen dance, Alele. I've met her twice." I pointed out, "Plus, her god is Ransandus, and he's in a different faction than Lorgiaia."

"Just see what you can do." Galorna said, "After we get the date and time set, of course."

"Ok, I'll see if they respond." I said, not expecting much.

"This has been very productive!" Alele said, "Now, I do want to end it here though, I have patrol later tonight, and I'd like to get some rest in case we run into that minion from before."

"Oh, that won't be a problem." Drizti said, "She's over at the counter crying, I don't think she's the 'revenge' type."

I glanced over and saw a young human lady in an inside out green shirt with a chicken sandwich in front of her, wiping her tears and holding back quiet sobs.

"Uh, Drizti, that's not the minion." I said nervously.

"What? No, it totally is, she just turned her shirt around and took off her mask and headband." Drizti said, confused.

"No, it's absolutely not her." Galorna said in a tone that left no room for argument, "Even if it *was*, as soon as she took off that mask, she's a different person, legally speaking. Never forget that."

"...Oh, I didn't know." Drizti said, lowering her head.

"It's ok, we don't have masks, so we didn't go over those laws." Alele said, "You had no way of knowing."

"Anyway, I need to rest up for patrol too." I said, "I *was* stabbed after all."

"Actually, meet me in the sitting area on the top floor." Galorna told me, "We need to chat."

"Ooooh, girl's in trouble!" Forica said, grinning.

"No, she's not, I just... need to understand a few things." Galorna said, "It's nothing bad, I hope."

I rolled my eyes, and drained the rest of my syrup, licking my lips, enjoying the sticky taste coating my mouth and throat. I had an idea of what we were going to talk about, and I was already dreading it.

~~~

"Candy, you *drank a glass of maple syrup*." Galorna said, throwing her hands up, "How do you not see how that's a problem?"

I leaned back in the leather chair and crossed my arms. "I can't control my cravings, if I want a glass of syrup- which, it wasn't even *real* maple syrup by the way, it was the thick, fake stuff- then I'm allowed to get one."

"No- look, you've been eating sweets constantly, it's concerning." she sighed, "You're drinking a slushie right now, even! Did you stop at the cafe on the way up?!"
~~~

"Lorgiaia will help me stay in shape, I just gotta train" I pointed out, sipping my cherry slush, "I've been getting way stronger lately, faster than the others, and I'm pretty sure it's because of all the sweets."

"You need to get back in the habit of eating real foods again, this isn't healthy. What you told me about the burger almost making you sick is very concerning."

"Why is it concerning?!" I said, annoyed, "I'm just eating what my body wants me to!"

"No, you're not." she said, "You're eating what your *power* wants you to. And your power makes people into sweets, so your power is... I don't know, trying to push you to eat people?"

"I thought about that already." I said, "If I keep eating sweets, I won't have to worry about my power convincing me to eat someone, it's fine."

"Have you had any... urges?" she asked, "In that way?"

"..." I didn't want to validate her concerns, they were stupid and pointless, but... "Yeah, I bumped Lucy and tasted frosting a few days ago. I was craving... I guess *her* for hours afterward."

"So- you tasted frosting when you touched her?" Galorna confirmed, "You bumped her and you think you tasted what she'd turn into?"

"Yeah, something with frosting. The good kind, not the oily kind? The stuff that's creamy and has just a little tang, and it's soooo thick, and...." I trailed off, my mouth watering, "...Gods, I need to find a good bakery, not a donut shop, a bakery. Do you think there's one closer than downtown?"

Galorna stared at me, her face in a slightly horrified expression, slight disgust leaking through.

"What?" I asked, "I'll check the registry, I'll make sure it's good guy owned, I just want to see if they'll deliver me cakes."

"It's not *that*, Candy." Galorna said, her voice taking on an angry tone, "You just described the *taste* of one of your teammates and were so overwhelmed by the desire to *eat* her you had to think of a way to get a, I don't know, a proxy?"

"Ugggh" I moaned, "It's not 'her' taste, that's gross, it's the taste of whatever treat she turns into. They're good treats, Galorna. Homicide was the best piece of pie I've ever had."

She rocked back and took in a breath of air sharply. "Oh, gods-. you haven't... you haven't *eaten* him, have you?"

"No, he's still locked up." I said, "I took a bite of him day of, remember?"

"Did your power make you take a bite back then?" she asked.

"No! I was just trying to figure things out." I snapped.

"Most people's first idea wouldn't be to take a bite of a person is all I'm saying." Galorna shook her head.

"I don't know where you're going with all this." I said, "I am doing my job- I got *stabbed* doing my job- I'm moonlighting to do my job extra well as Comfit soon, I've been fine around the girls, and I'm growing my followers. Eating sweets won't change any of that."

"I'm saying this happened fast, I remember you loving my cooking, now you barely touch it, and-"

"Ohh, so *that's* what this is about, you're sad you can't be my *mommy* and give me your special protein breakfasts anymore, huh?" I taunted.

She growled, a deep and rumbling sound. "No! Godsdamnit Candy, it's got nothing to do with that! I'm saying I've *watched* you change over the past month, you're getting more and more self-focused, you're losing your ability to enjoy things you loved before, you're blind to obvious problems, it's a legitimate concern."

"It's literally not." I said, "It's causing no problems, at all."

"It *will* though. If you keep getting stronger cravings, you'll end up eating someone, if you keep focusing on yourself instead of the team, you'll push us away and we'll lose cohesion, if you keep ignoring your problems, they'll consume you."

I stood up. "Galorna. I know you're the team leader, but just back off and let me eat my gods-fucking-damned sugar, ok? Can you do that? If these fake problems you're trying to force on me happen, whatever, we'll deal with it then, but I think my relationship with the team is *fantastic*. Alele trusts me again and wants to *date* me, Driz sees me as her big sister, Lucy fucking *showered* with me, the only one I'm not getting along with is *you*."

"I- dammit Candy, let me connect to you, please, look, if you need sweets, let me *make* you something, I connect to people by feeding them, let me get close and we can work *through* this."

"You should connect to people by actually connecting to them." I retorted, opening my door.

"I just want to help you, I'm concerned. I'm trying to help and I'm *worried*." she looked up at me, her shoulders slumped.

"If you really want to help, get the stick out of your butt and relax, just fuck off and let me eat what I want." I glared.

"I'm cool! I'm fun, I watch anime and play games! I make jokes, I like to have fun and relax, I've even started smoking goblin weed with Lucy sometimes. I'm not this hard ass bitch you seem to think I am. I'm fun..." she protested weakly.

"All *I* ever see is the you that tries to tell me what to do," I said coldly, "that punches me with her power to 'train' me, who whines about her ex, and who doesn't even have half the followers I do. You try to boss me around and tell me how dangerous I am, but *you've* killed people too, and I'm sure as *hell* a lot less dangerous than an at-range brain crusher."

Her eyes filled with tears. "I don't know what I did to you, Candy, I'm just trying to be a good leader, I- I held you when you cried, I supported you, we drank together, what did I do to make you hate me?"

I stared at her. What *had* she done? She was bossy, sure, she fussed at me like a child more than once, she was always acting like she was the most mature person in the room, was it just all building up over time? I couldn't end on a weak note though.

"Think about it, you'll figure it out." I said, "Now if you'll excuse me, I have a patrol tonight that I've been dreading, and I'd like to rest up for it. And *now* I have to find a bakery that delivers sheet cake to the fucking 240s too, so thanks for *that*."

I slammed my door and stalked to my bedroom, feeling the anger and pent up feeling of something ready to burst inside me. I didn't understand where this frustration came from. I flopped on my bed face down. I wasn't usually that mean, was I? I didn't think so, but somehow I couldn't manage to feel any kind of remorse. I just didn't, I felt like I'd won a fight and gotten away with something, not chewed out my team leader for- What had I even lashed out at her over? Being worried? Trying to tell me to be more aware? I knew I was in the wrong, but I still couldn't feel any kind of guilt over it and that worried me.

I lay there stewing in my emotions, waiting to calm down and the anger to fade. I felt something, underneath the anger and cloudy, sour lashing. Something that made me feel bad, it was something I wanted to fix, was that the guilt finally showing up? I felt relieved almost, I'd started to worry I'd lost my empathy or something. I focused on that feeling, and pulled it out to see what it was and how to fix it. If it was guilt, I'd apologize, if it was regret, I'd find a way to rephrase what I said in a nicer way to make her think I'd apologized.

With a chill, I realized it wasn't guilt at all, or regret, or even shame.

I was hungry.

~~~

I took a bite of the chunk of sheet cake I was holding as I walked slowly down the street with Alele. It wasn't as good as I'd hoped, but it was fresh and it was sweet, and I wasn't hungry now. I slowed down further and looked up at the street we were about to turn onto and sighed.

"What's up?" Alele asked, glancing at me, "You ok?"

"I'm just not looking forward to this." I admitted, "I haven't patrolled with her yet, and, ugh, I'm just dreading it."

"I've patrolled with her before, it's annoying because we have to stay on the ground with her the whole time because of the incident, but she's cool. Weird, but cool."

"She's a *cockroach*" I said, "She- ew, ok, whatever, yeah. Let's just get it over with."

We turned the corner and saw the brightly colored building, the pinks and teals clashing in a way that made it stand out in a garish way. In front of it, leaning against the roll up door, was Amaryllis. I held back a shudder as she turned, her metal mouthpiece gleaming in the late afternoon sun. Her shell looked shiny and inky at the same time, her front a lighter, sicker color than her back, her limbs all turning the wrong way. I tried not to gag and I shoved another bite of cake in my mouth to distract me as we walked up.

"You're late, were you held up? Or did you just stop for a snack?" she asked, eyeing the last bit of cake in my hand. Her voice was robotic and harsh, and I could hear furious clicking as she spoke, her teeth and tongue working the mechanics to craft words from movement instead of air.

"We just underestimated the walk, sorry!" Alele said chipperly.

Amaryllis nodded. "I understand, it's a big section. I'm considering building a bike of some sort to get around."
~~~

"Oh, you build things?" Alele asked, "Are you a super scientist?"

"Not quite, no." Amaryllis said, shaking her... head? The top of the shell? Whatever her 'face' was attached to. "I have a talent for building and creating, I went to a school for super science back in Canyon City, but I failed out. I don't have the spark that lets me build things that defy logic, unfortunately."

"Is that why you became a shut in?" I asked, finally getting the courage to speak up, "Flunking out made you depressed or something?"

She looked at me and a clicking sound sounded out from behind her mask before she answered. "Yes, that is what lead to my self imposed imprisonment."

"Weellll uh, let's head out then, shall we?" Alele said, "We have a lot of ground to cover!"

We headed out from there, making our way out from the center of the section to the far edge, making our way inwards in a zig-zag pattern. We tried to mix up the direction and order we did our rounds every patrol, to make sure we didn't get predictable, but as a result, I'd usually get turned around on foot. My wings itched to be used, but I plodded along, unsure of where we were going or even what direction we were headed. I saw more shops, a couple of bars with people inside who watched us as we passed, and a few more of the fake buildings that hid... something dangerous. I did my best to avoid looking directly at Amaryllis. I'd run out of cake, and I worried if I looked too closely at her, I'd scream, vomit, or run away, and I wanted to at least *pretend* to be friendly.

"So, Amaryllis, how are the renovations coming along?" Alele asked, "I heard you guys were donating portions of your pay to fixing up your base, right?"

"It's coming along well." she said, her artificial voice making me jump, "My room is mostly finished. I have a bed and my own bathroom now."

"Did you not have a bed before?" I asked, "Did you sleep in a box or something?"

"I had a sleeping bag." she said, glancing at me.

"Must have been a big sleeping bag." I said, looking at her shell and then quickly looking away.

"It was two, zipped together." she explained.

"...Mm." I said, not sure where to take the conversation from here.

"Oh, hey, check this out!" Alele called back to us from slightly ahead, "I found a thing!"

I jumped on the distraction and walked over to the building next to us, one of the fake ones. Taped to the side was a poster with big bold words on it: "MISSING: MY DAUGHTER, REWARD AVAILABLE FOR ANY INFORMATION". Underneath the words was a picture of the weird bug human hybrid from a couple of days ago, the one I'd been stabbed over earlier. It was wearing a fluffy sweater and holding its arms out to the sides with a big grin on its face.

I stared at it in the darkening evening, feeling odd over it. She'd had this printed and hung it up sometime in the last couple hours, the woman *really* wanted this thing back. The contact information at the bottom of the page was a local code, meaning it was her actual, traceable information. She'd get tracked down over this by the GGDS if she kept it up. Amaryllis stepped up and stared at the poster for a few seconds before reaching out and taking it off the wall, folding it up and tucking it into her skirt.

"Hey why'd you do that?" Alele asked, "Someone might know something and see the poster."

"I think I know something." Amaryllis said, "I need this."

"Did you see the thing on the poster somewhere?" I asked, "It's kinda small, and it's fast, so I imagine it's hiding behind or under some of the trash littering our section, ready to slither away at a moment's notice. Well, if it's not been *killed* by someone already, of course. It's kinda terrifying, freaked me out when I first saw it."

She stared at me and her limbs moved, twitching and shaking slightly. She hissed a low, quiet noise, it sounded like air escaping from a tire, and I stepped back away from her, feeling a chill go through me. I swallowed, she seemed upset, was she angry at me? I glanced at Alele, and felt a cringe as I saw her glaring at me, her jaw set hard. I blinked, why was *Alele* mad? I wasn't even talking to her, I was just trying to get used to talking to Amaryllis...

"I believe I must return home." Amaryllis said, "I'm sorry I cannot finish the patrol, but I have begun to feel unwell."

She turned, and walked quickly in a direction. I assumed she knew where she was going, but I still had no idea where we were. I turned back to Alele as she walked off and frowned. "That was weird, right?" I asked, shaking my head, "She saw that poster and instantly felt ill."

"Gods, Candy, you're so *oblivious* sometimes." she muttered, "Now we have to do the patrol *alone*, and her whole team is going to ask her why she went home early."

"So? She can explain to them whatever she wants, why do we care about that?" I said, shrugging.

"Because if she tells them about how you've been a bitch to her all night, and how insensitive you were, it'll make the rest of us look bad too, gods."

"*Insensitive*?!" I asked, shocked, "I was *so* polite, I didn't call her a bug or gag or anything, I stayed calm! I didn't even scream this time!"

"This time?" Alele asked.

"Well- I screamed the first time we met, gasped, really. I think tonight was a great improvement." I said, nodding, "I even spoke to her, at least twice."

Alele stared at me for a few long seconds and her frown deepened. "I want to give you the benefit of the doubt here because you're usually better than this, so remind me to look up some of the tenants of our church later, I need to check some things."

"What?" I said, shaking my head, "Ok, sure, whatever, what does that have to do with our patrol member fucking off?"

"I just want to check on some stuff." Alele said, "Ugh, look, can we just get in the skies? We've still got over half our section to cover."

"Yeah, I've been itching to fly this whole time..." I said, flaring my wings, "I hate being stuck on the ground."

"Just fly, Candy..." Alele said, sighing.

I didn't need any encouragement, and I rocketed up into the air, the ground spinning below me as I swooped and dashed, covering the section way better and way faster than we had been doing. I got the feeling Amaryllis had gone home because of the bug human baby thing somehow, but I couldn't imagine why. I pushed it out of my head though, she was off the patrol, and that meant I could fly and be free, and that already made the night better than it had been a few minutes ago.

Chapter Nineteen

I pulled my blanket burrito tighter and shook my head "I just don't understand, I honestly don't." I growled, "I was so nice!"

"Were you *nice*?" Drizti asked absently watching the TV, "Or were you polite? There's a big difference, you know."

"I think I was both? I asked questions about the stuff she was saying, I tried to engage with her on her level, I don't know, I just know Alele was mad about it the rest of patrol."

"It sounds frustrating, I know Alele really likes you too, so for *her* to be mad like that is odd. Are you *sure* you didn't do anything bad?"

"I don't know…" I muttered, "I'm just tired and mixed up inside."

"That's a fair way to be feeling." Drizti said, "I'm still all torn up over the whole fetish photos thing. One of them was just a funny face, how is a *face* a fetish?!"

"Some people are into weird stuff, Driz." I sighed, "One guy in my school had a thing for making people sneeze, he carried powder around and would blow it at other students. Once the admin found out it was a sex thing for him, he was expelled."

"I wonder if *I* have anything like that…" she mused.

"Like sneezing?" I asked.

"Kinda, or like, something that I'm super into that I've just never experienced before." she shrugged, "Honestly, I'm pretty sheltered, there could be loads of stuff out there I might have a thing for, and I'd just never know, you know?"

"I kinda get it." I said, "I don't know if I have anything like that personally. I like being held, or having someone lay on me, but not in a weird way, just like, it feels safe and cozy."

"That might still count?" Drizti said, "Forica was saying a lot of these things aren't actually sexual, they're just stuff people 'like', but I don't know why they'd like them like that if it *wasn't* sexual."

"Who knows, maybe it's like, a memory from their childhood or something." I said, "Hey, pass me another slice of cake, would you?"

"You've had like four already!" Drizti squeaked, "Gods, Candy, you're going to be sick."

"Still hungry." I said, shrugging, "Anyway, how much longer are you going to stay up? We've only got two more episodes in this season, if you're up for it."

"I *am* off tomorrow…" she frowned, carefully passing me a plate of sheet cake, "I guess I can watch two more, yeah."

I smiled and pressed play on the next episode. I wasn't sure if Drizti was enjoying this show, it was a little trashy and loud for her tastes- mine too, really- but it was teaching her a lot about the world outside her cult. Chosen culture too, now that I thought about it. The main family, the Sinsais, were neck deep in Chosen drama constantly. The dad was dealing with brands dropping him as he got older, the mom was trying to keep her fans as she 'lost her looks', the daughter was struggling with online bullying because of her collabs with a company that donated to anti-abomination campaigns, and the son was so violent on patrol he'd almost been marked as a fallen twice just in the first season.

It wasn't a perfect show, but it was a fantastic one to just turn your brain off to and relax. I'd been trying to get Driz over to watch it with me more frequently lately, and since this afternoon's 'revelation' about her CirNet, I was determined to double my efforts. She needed a crash course in the modern world, fast. I ate a bite of my cake and felt the buzz going through me as I shivered. This was *good*, I needed more of this, all the time. Who gave a fuck if I didn't like Galorna's rice and meat dishes anymore? If she wanted to feed me that bad, she needed to learn how to make sweets.

~~~

I trudged through the waterfront section and my nose wrinkled at the smell of rotting fish and the wafting sticky-sweet scent of Bilge-Ooze's sap floating on top of the water. Hopefully she wouldn't surface while I was here, I'd rather not have to pretend to be nice to the giant walking, breathing, rotting, poison factory. She *was* the reason I was here though, in a roundabout way. If I could track down some crime in the areas around where she lived, pretty much no one would care if I poached it as Comfit, it's not like anyone *else* came around here after all.

I was still waiting on my Comfit uniform to be done but it shouldn't be long now, just two more days and I could go out in costume as her for the first time. I was nervous about it, but I needed to get used to the idea, it could only help me in the long run, more fans, more attention, more power, networking, the works. Sure I'd have some issues with poaching laws here and there if other Chosen complained, but once I was popular enough, no one would really care about something trivial like that. I hoped.

The docks and warehouses of section 78 looked like shit in the midday sun, the rusted metal and rotting wood giving the whole area a run-down look. There was a reason Alele and I were planning on starting around here. The only heroes who even patrolled
~~~

these sections were basically just warm bodies to fill a schedule on the wall of the GGDS offices, most didn't even have combat powers. I couldn't name a single hero *or* fallen from the docks area off the top of my head, not counting Bilge-Ooze herself, and I'm pretty sure *she* was technically just an abomination. Not many gods would choose a dryad and risk alienating Turganth and his bigoted followers who believed you needed flesh to be considered 'alive'.

Peeking into the window of an abandoned building, I held back my frustration. I was poking around the 'bad' part of town, where was all the crime? I'd assumed I would find a drug den or a smuggling ring or something like that by *now*, but there was just more and more ick and abandoned buildings.

Maybe I needed to go further north up the coastline, away from the toxic water? If no one could dock here without the bottom of their ship rotting off, no one could smuggle stuff or sell drugs or anything, duh. I kicked myself for not thinking it through and turned to go. I wanted to go farther inland for a snack, then I'd go north until I couldn't smell the rot anymore and pick up my investigations there.

A crashing of waves jarred me out of my thoughts, and my heart rate spiked, fuck, she was surfacing *now*? Right when I was about to leave, too… I turned and looked out at the water over the pier, and sure enough, the water was swelling up and breaking around the concrete wall, two massive hands made of driftwood and seaweed slamming into the street. She was just popping up for some air, that's all it was, she wasn't here for *me*, she just wanted to see the sun, right?

She lifted herself out of the water, the smell of rotten plants, brine, and sap flooding out into the streets as she lifted her form up onto the road. Water gushed off her body and running towards me along the sidewalk. I took a step back, if she ruined my shoes, I was going to be *so* mad…

Her eyes slid open with a pop, and she looked directly at me, her face fifteen feet over my head even though she was sitting on the edge of the road with her legs in the water. Her wooden face was carved with half a decade of water currents and salt, her leaves were long gone and her mouth was full of sea-glass teeth. She'd been normal-sized once, I'd heard, before the experiment that made her... this. She smiled at me, her wood creaking as she did, and she waved.

"Hello, are you here to see me?" she asked, her voice sounding more like wind than spoken words.

"N-no, I'm a hero." I said, keeping my eyes on her carefully. If she touched me, I could die in minutes...

"Oh? Here to fight me, then?" she asked, "I can't say it's a good idea, but if you like, we can work it out. I'd prefer a better battlefield though, there's a beach to the south we can visit? Lots of sand to dilute my poisons."

I shook my head furiously. "No! No, never! I was looking for crime! I want to fight crime, and that's all! I know this area is... abandoned, I thought there might... be... uh, crime."

She nodded, the seaweed draped over her swinging back and forth. "Ah, very good of you. I don't know of any crime here, aside from myself, polluting the ocean, but I *doubt* you're asking me to climb out on dry land to be arrested, hm?"

"Oh, gods no, I'm not- that's not even a crime! You're fine!" I said, laughing nervously. The *last* time she'd been fully on land was right after her escape, and the path she'd taken to the sea had been blocked off for weeks until the toxins were neutralized enough for people to go near.

"I tend to scare off everyone who comes around here, criminals too, you know." she sighed, "I don't *try* to hurt them, but what can one do?"

You can go back in the ocean and leave me alone, who knows how many air born spores you're sending my way? I didn't say *that* though, instead I laughed again and jutted a thumb over my shoulder. "I guess you just… gotta deal with it, huh? Uh, anyway, I gotta head out, I'm going to a place, I was just about to leave."

She looked sad, but slid back into the water, splashing the divider with more polluted seawater. "I understand. I hope to see you again, hero! I feel no one ever comes to talk anymore, if not for the vibrations of your footsteps, I may have slept for several days before seeing someone…"

"W-well, that's sad." I said, "You're kinda scary to talk to, so maybe that's why?"

Her face fell and she sank lower, and I winced.

"Like, scary like a god! I met my goddess a couple of times, it's like that, you're like a goddess!" A goddess of rot…

She shook her head. "I know what I am, hero, but thank you for your words. If you don't mind, please come see me again?"

"Sure, yeah, absolutely." I lied, nodding quickly, "I'll just get out of your branches now though, uh, I'll see you later?"

She gave me one last sad smile and dropped fully back into the ocean, the waves splashing and the water rippling. I let out a long low breath and quickly stepped away from the ocean water that was still threatening to melt my shoes. She could sense vibrations from people walking around up here while she was *sleeping*? I highly doubted anyone would be dumb enough to do any kind of crime anywhere near her, this was a waste of time, and bad for my heart too. I needed a snack…

~~~

I closed my eyes as I savored the fruity tang of the pie, the firmness of the peaches, the stickiness of the syrup, it was *heavenly*. I slid my eyes open and picked up my dark chocolate mocha, taking a deep gulp of it, the slightly bitter sweetness clashing and complimenting
~~~

the fruit in a way that made my brain *writhe* with pleasure. I'd have to remember this place, the cafe at headquarters could *never*.

I swallowed and picked up my next treat, a coco dusted ladyfinger, and bit it delicately. The slightly crisp exterior broke way into the airy, spongey middle, and I toyed with the idea of dipping it in my mocha. It'd be a good blend, but would it get crumbs in it? There was nothing worse than drinking a creamy, velvety drink and having the texture of the silky chocolate broken with a soggy crumb, it ruined the whole sip. I compromised, and took another drink while the ladyfinger was still in my mouth. Perfect.

This cafe was expensive, my snack was costing me almost fifty blessings, but *gods* if it wasn't worth it. I'd just ran into Bilge-Ooze anyway, I *needed* something like this to 'cleanse the palette' so to speak. I turned back to the peach pie and carefully cut another bite with my fork. I'd savor this, take my time with it, and later, I'd go back out and look for a *better* area to make my debut as Comfit in. I wasn't supposed to be home for hours and hours, so I wasn't in any rush. It'd been stupid of me to bounce around looking for crime on an empty stomach without even a smoothie or something to tide me over. Now I knew better.

I eyed my 'dessert', and bit my lip. I still had ladyfingers and more pie, to eat first, but it looked so, *so* good. It was a gigantic strawberry, thrice dipped in milk chocolate, covered in candy nuts, and drizzled with caramel and dark chocolate flakes and sitting in a nest of mint leaves over a chilled bowl of frozen cream to ensure the chocolates didn't melt. It looked perfect, and it was the whole reason I'd picked this cafe, but the other food was more than enough to ensure I'd come back. I had to wait though, I'd told myself I'd eat my 'meal' first...

There was a sharp rapping on the wooden privacy wall of my booth and I jumped, almost transforming on instinct. I got on my knees and poked my head up, glaring over the wall at the person that *dared* to interrupt my lunch. I flinched as a wide set ogre in a pinstripe suit glared back at me. I felt the color drain out of my face and my mouth went dry, I recognized that suit, *fuck*. I swallowed and nodded to the other side of the booth for him to enter, and sank down into my seat again, my heart racing.

He slid the partition open and got in, the seat flexing under his impressive size. I sat straight, not moving, not giving any indication that I was terrified. He cleared his throat and waved a hand at the table in front of us.

"Celebrating yesterday's fight, I see." he said, his voice deep.

"This is just a regular lunch, actually." I said calmly, "It's not for any reason in particular."

"Then you won't mind stepping away with me to meet with my benefactor." he said, sneering at me.

I felt a flash of anger, who did this guy think he was? I was in the middle of eating, I was enjoying myself, I wasn't about to just leave all these treats on the table like that, it was disrespectful to the food! Someone put care and effort into these sweets, and fuck anyone who tried to stop me from appreciating them. I twisted my mouth into a snarl and leaned across the table, pulling my glove off to stare him down.

"So *help* me, if you try to order me around, to force me to *abandon my lunch,* just to talk to that weird lady, I'll turn you into a mille-feuille and have *you* for dessert." I hissed, and his face twisted into one of fear.

Good, he knew what I could do, and he was adequately scared. I was bluffing- at least I *thought* I was- and there was no way I could know what he'd turn into, but *he* didn't know that. I sat back and took a sip of my lovely, silky mocha and licked my lips, drawing myself together.

"Go outside, I'll be along once I finish my meal." I told him, "If you bother me again, I won't hesitate to transform you, understand?"

The man glowered, but he stood up, and without a word, left the booth. I sat there, feeling the thrill and panic of having told off a minion for one of the scariest people in the city. I'd *done* that, why had I done that? *How* had I done that? I felt bolder than usual, the buzz of my brain bouncing with excitement.

I looked down at my food and scrunched my forehead in thought. I got a buzz when I ate sweets in general, and I felt stronger when I ate sweets made out of people, was I getting a mental boost just from eating what I wanted? I took my bite of peach pie and traced the feeling over and over in my head, the little flicker of fun that snaked through my skull and rewarded me for having sugar. It *was* doing something, I felt clearer, sharper as it danced. This was big, I'd need to be eating something sweet *constantly* from now on. If the 'sugar buff' was strong enough to sharpen my brain and give me the confidence to stand up to a walking phone booth, I couldn't afford *not* to have it.

I smiled to myself and kicked my feet under the booth, my power wasn't so useless after all! I just needed to change how I thought of it a little, being rewarded for eating candy was downright fantastic, even if I didn't eat people. I picked up another ladyfinger, I'd enjoy my lunch, then go meet whatserface after, making people wait on you was a power move or something, right?

~~~

I stepped out onto the street, my tummy full of treats and my head full of buzzing energy. I could still taste the slight minty aftertaste of the strawberry, it'd been just as juicy and flavorful as I'd hoped. This was a good day, Bilge-Ooze aside. I glanced around for the ogre, and saw him across the street, arms crossed and leaning against the wall of a taco shop, still glowering. I waved at him, and started over to see him. Hopefully the lady wasn't too mad at having to wait, I'd only been ten minutes, maybe fifteen, so it wasn't a huge deal.

I was halfway across the road when the car hit me.
~~~

~~~

My eyes fluttered open and I moaned, my head throbbing. I remembered lunch, then… I hissed in a breath, I'd been hit by a car? Who runs someone over in broad daylight? Did they not see me? I looked down at my body and cringed at the sight. My chest was bloody from a bad nosebleed, my hands were scratched and raw, my leg looked like it was turned the wrong way, and my clothes were ruined. Oddly enough, that was the part I was most upset about, I only had a few pair of jeans that fit right and this sweater was a birthday present, both covered in tears and blood now.

I coughed and tried to roll out of the cot I was laying on, but I couldn't move yet, my legs weren't responding. I took a few breaths and looked around the room while I mustered the strength to get up. I was in a small concrete room, a single light hanging over the cot I was in, and there was one door leading out, steel by the looks of it.

Who would want to capture *me*? Was this a plan by the weird lady to get me more attention? If I was missing, she could have a whole campaign about me, missing posters, news highlights, vigils, the lot. If she did it right, I'd get so much attention and energy Lorgiaia would have no *choice* but to make me angel once I was 'found'. It was genius, why had no one tried this before? I just wished the first step didn't involve me being hit by a car…

I'd heal eventually though, my healing factor was slow and weak, but it *was* complete. From what the GGDS had said during power testing, as long as I was alive, I'd heal to full eventually. The only issue was, with the shape I was in now, 'eventually' could mean months. I needed Drizti and a body donor, *someone* would be fine taking these injuries, right? I was kinda pretty, depending on who you asked. I could play it off like a sex thing or something.

The door clicked, and I sat up as quickly as I could, holding in a yelp as something pinched in my chest. I grabbed my right glove in my teeth and yanked, I wouldn't be caught off guard, I'd fold
~~~

anyone who tried to fuck with me. I'd play along with their kidnapping, but I wouldn't stand for being treated poorly.

The ogre from before stepped in and placed a folding chair in the middle of the room, looking me up and down as he did. I watched him closely, teeth bared and hand ready to snap out if he so much as twitched, but he didn't come near me, just finished setting up the chair and left. I let my breath out and winced as my lungs caught on something hard and a spike of pain went through my body. Fuck, it'd been a while, I couldn't feel the buzz from lunch anymore, was I late for my patrol yet?

The door swung open again, and I sighed and slumped as the lady herself walked in, turning the folding chair around and sitting in it backwards, facing me. Her expression hard and angry. I still didn't say anything, better to be thought a fool and all that, I couldn't afford to say the wrong thing here and put my foot in my mouth. She watched me and I watched her, the silence heavy in the air around us. Finally, after what felt like hours, she broke the standoff.

"I don't like being made to wait, stupid girl" she said calmly.

"You hit me with a *car* because I made you wait ten minutes?!" I blinked, "I thought you had a plan or something!"

"My *plan* was to talk to you." she said, pulling out a cigarette and lighting it, "Once you made me wait, the plan changed to me hitting you with my car."

"That's- you're a fucking psycho!" I shouted, and instantly fell into a coughing fit, holding my chest in pain. That was a broken rib, I was sure of it…

"I get what I want, simple as that." she said.

"Wh-what *do* you want?" I said, still coughing.

"I wanted to congratulate you on such a successful fight, for one." she said, "But that's past us now. No, what I *really* want is to know how you're planning on leveraging yourself into a better position to be made Angel. The fight against… what was his name, Dr. Half-root? was quite impressive, but as a result, one of my best poison crafters is stuck in a hospital room waiting to heal so he can be locked up in Queens Tower."

"*He* attacked *us!*" I protested, "I know he's yours, but honestly, he tried to ruin our section just looking for his little centi-baby thing. Some abomination he made, I guess."

"I'm familiar with it, yes." she said sourly, "I'm not happy he made it, and even unhappier he ruined his place in my company over it. Still, *you* were the one to put him in the hospital, according to the reports."

"No, it was Dri- uh, Angel Verdant," I explained, "he stabbed me, and she transferred the wound to him, I didn't do more than grapple a little."

"I don't care who *did* it, I just care that you *replace* him, so tell me, have you made a plan on how to achieve Angel yet?" she snapped.

"I- yes, I have one..." I said nervously, "I was going to make a new hero character called Comfit, one that wasn't aligned with a specific god? I'll wear a helmet and eat the gummies you gave me to get stronger, and go outside 247, and... um, fight crime, I guess..."

"How will *that* help you make Angel? You're not supposed to just fight, you need to be getting power for your stupid goddess." she glared at me, "It's useless if *you're* not getting the attention."

"I'll unmask!" I said quickly, "I- I was going to use the Comfit character to like, you know, do stuff outside of the church and get lots of followers, then I'd unmask and combine the followers, and I'd be *really* popular, enough to make Angel!"

She drew in on her cigarette and breathed the smoke out of her nose slowly, looking at me closely. "That might work." she admitted, "I don't know if it's as good as having one of the best bio-geneticists in the south-west on call, but it could work."

"I'm going out on patrols with a friend, too." I told her, "She's helping me, she's a combat precog, so she'll make the fights look really flashy, I swear!"

"…Alright, I'll trust you on this, for now." she said, "I'll be watching you closely though, and if you try and fuck me over, I'll hit you with something a lot bigger than a car." she flicked her ash at me and waved at the door. "You may leave now, Farnson will drive you home."

"Uh, oh." I said, "I kinda can't really move very well right now? I was just hit by a car, you were there."

"Don't get smart, brat." she snapped, holding out her hand, "Eat some gummies then fuck off."

I took her hand and felt the sparks, and I came away with five worms in my palm. I wrinkled my nose at them, but shoved them in my mouth, the blood gushing out and bursting out my mouth, dripping on my chin and mixing with my own dried blood. My body spasmed and I forced myself to swallow, they tasted *good*, it was just the idea of eating that much blood that made me shiver. I coughed again and felt the familiar boost of energy, and clenched my teeth as the effects kicked in.

There was an unfamiliar feeling, like pins and needles under my skin all over my body, and my chest clenched, making me cough up a blob of congealed blood from my lungs. I felt something pop inside me and I whimpered, my organs shifting, my leg twisting painfully back into place, my ribs clamping back together, all surrounded with that weird tingle, my brain wiggling back and forth. I dropped my head in my hands to ground myself and found them to be smooth, no trace of the road rash from before, and I hiccuped, something along my lower back twisting and making my legs kick involuntarily.

I looked myself over, the sparks and stars in the air filling my vision. I was healed, but I felt like I was floating, was I floating? I couldn't tell, everything was so soft… I wondered where my friends were, weren't they supposed to be here with me if I needed them? Or *were* they my friends? Drizti was my friend, even if the rest weren't.

That must mean Drizti was here, right? I looked around for her, but she must have been under the bed, because I didn't see her. She was probably scared of how big my thoughts were right now, I didn't blame her, they were pretty powerful!

"I- healed, we're- I wanna- mmm…" I said, perfectly encapsulating my thoughts.

"Fuck. That's new." someone said, a pink and gray blob that smelled like an ashtray, "Don't eat more than one worm at once next time, got it?"

I reached out to hold the ashtray, she was full of stars, she could help me to find Drizti! "My friend, she- we, I need to touch…" I explained to her.

"We're not friends, and you've had enough touching for one day. You're healed up, so we're done here. Farnson!"

I slid my legs out off the bed, my powerful legs that could walk through anything, and I stepped towards the ashtray, but it'd already gone. When had *that* happened? I looked around to see if there was any sign of my friends- no, of Drizti, but there was only a phone booth walking towards me with a blanket. I laughed as the blanket went over my head and I tipped over. I wasn't tired, I was full of bees and lightning. I wanted to hang out and run around and fly in the sky, but since I was already laying down and had a nice blanket on, it'd be rude not to at least take a *little* nap. I slipped away into the stars, Drizti would help me back once I needed her, I was sure of it.

~~~

I slammed into the sidewalk outside Lorgiaia's Angel's headquarters and groaned. My floaty feeling was starting to leave, and the impact hurt more than I thought it would, was my pain tolerance lower now? Or had I just gotten used to the nice, numb feeling the worms
~~~

gave me? I sat up and licked my lips, tasting the dried blood from the worms still on them, mixed with the blood from my nosebleed earlier. It was gross, but it still cleared my head enough to gather my thoughts.

She was a bitch, that's all there was to it. Only a real asshole would run someone over and interrogate them like that, she could have called, or just sent an email, why did it need to be face to face anyway? And why not heal me *before* she asked all her questions, did she just want me to suffer more? And where the fuck had Drizti gone? I could have sworn she was there with me, did the lady still have her?

I growled and clambered to my feet, still dizzy from the… worms? Did the worms make me dizzy? That couldn't be right, they made my head clear and focused me, like all sweets did. She must have drugged me when I wasn't looking, or put something on the worms she gave me or something, fuck. I leaned against our building and blinked slowly, my head still full of fluff. I needed more sweets, something to get this fog out from between my ears. I looked at the door, but it was so, so far away… I just had to go in and get to the counter, that's all, I could do that, right?

I took a step, and pitched forward, collapsing on the ground as soon as I didn't have the wall holding me up anymore. *Fuck*, was I still injured from the car accident? A concussion maybe? I heard a gasp from in front of me and lifted my head, seeing a familiar pair of old-timey shoes in front of me. There she was! She must have slipped away when no one was looking. I rolled over and smiled up at Drizti, Galorna towering over her, both looking down at me with horrified expressions, both holding kababs. Yyyuck, those were all covered in meat and spices, I couldn't imagine ever wanting to eat something like *that*, weirdos.

"Holy shit, Candy, are you ok?!" Galorna asked, shoving her food into Drizti's hand and crouching down.

"Aw… I'm okey." I said, patting her leg, "I was just hit by a car, nothin' serious."

Galorna froze and then jumped back, pulling Drizti with her. "Candy you're not wearing your glove, did you change someone?"

"Oh, gods, is that even your blood?" Drizti asked, her voice shaking.

I sat up and looked down at myself, shrugging. "It *was* my blood, but I got healed, I guess."

"How did you heal? Who healed you?" Galorna asked me, her voice hard.

I thought about it hard, I still didn't want her to know I tried to kill that one lady, but I *had* told her the lady existed, I could use that…

"The weird lady, the one who made me be two heroes?" I said, "She had a healer, but I'm all drugged now, I think."

Galorna relaxed and sighed. "You're sure you didn't change anyone?"

I shook my head. "Not a one, far as I know."

"You look pretty bad, your clothes are all ruined, how did she find you?" Drizti asked.

"Uh, I told you, she hit me with a car?" I said, waving at myself, "Pretty obvious."

"She- what the *fuck*?" Galorna muttered, shaking her head, "She hit you with a car, then healed you?"

"Yyyyes." I nodded, "I'm doing pretty great, peachy keen, even." I giggled, remembering the peach pie I'd eaten earlier.

"Why would she want to do *that*?" Drizti asked, handing Galorna back her kabab.

"Just to talk, I guess. Make sure I was doing my job." I said.

"And… were you?" Galorna asked, "Or do we need to stay with you so you don't get run over again?"

"I'm doing a great job!" I said, grinning, "I even scoped out a few places to patrol as Comfit before she hit me, but Bilge-Ooze was already there. I'll find new places though."

Galorna looked at me sadly and shook her head. "I'm sorry you have to go through this, Candy. You said she threatened your family if you didn't fight crime for her?"

"Yeah, basically." I said.

"This whole situation is horrible, is there any way we can help?" Drizti asked.

I thought about it. "Umm, yeah! Get me a piece of cake and a slushie from the cafe!"

"You need to go lie down, not eat sweets." Galorna said firmly. "Do you have your other glove?"

I patted my pockets and shook my head, it must still be in the car I was brought here in. That's fine, I had lots of spares.

"Ok, well… Put your un-gloved hand in your pocket, I'll guide and support you with your other one, we'll get you to your room."

"But my snacks!" I said, "I'm hungry!"

"I'll get those and bring them up, it's ok Candy." Driz said sweetly.

I sighed, but I guessed another nap couldn't hurt. I stood up, wobbling on my feet, and Galorna took my hand in hers.

"It's ok, Candy, you'll feel a lot better once the drugs wear off, ok?" she said gently, "I've been there, just gotta sleep it off."

She led me into the building, and I hoped Drizti wouldn't be too long with the sweets, I felt empty inside…


~~~
~~~

My eyes slid open painfully and I stared at the ceiling of my apartment. I still hated how the walls were that dark red color, it just made everything feel so dingy and dim, it even made the ceiling look darker. I sat up and checked my bedside clock, just past nine at night, which meant I'd missed my patrol by a full hour, damn. I hoped the other girls understood, I hated letting people down. Still, as long as I was already late, I might as well be a little later. I stood and went to my dresser to get my pajamas so I could take a shower before I headed out and flinched at the girl in the mirror.

I looked like shit, dark rings under my eyes, stains and rips all over my sweater, blood all around my mouth and nose. My hair was-well, it was too short to really be a mess, but it still looked bad, especially with the light blonde roots starting to poke out. The memories of the afternoon rushed back to me, the docks, Bilge-Ooze, the expensive lunch, the lady…

I coughed and winced as I tasted blood. Was that left over from before I healed? I couldn't tell. I hoped I wasn't still injured, I hated doctors. I felt mostly fine, aside from a tingly feeling across my skin and a headache, if I was bleeding in my lungs, I'm sure I'd know it, that's not something you could just ignore.

I finished getting my pajamas out and put them in my bag to bring downstairs. I could honestly get away with skipping patrol completely if I wanted. I was *hit by a car* a few hours ago, but I didn't want to be 'that person', and I was sure I'd run into even worse situations in the future when I started going out as Comfit. I'd do my patrol today, and I'd do the next one after that, and I'd do patrols as Comfit too, every chance I could. I just needed to push myself, hit my limits and never let up.

I took a deep breath and looked at myself in the mirror again, taking in every detail. I was tall, I had a pretty good figure, I wasn't beautiful but I had facial definition, I was strong and determined, I could *do* this. I was going to be the best fucking hero the city had seen. I'd get popular, get my name out there, and kick the ass of anyone who stood in my way.

My power might be shit, but it still had its uses, I could rise to the top and become an Angel for *real* in no time as long as I focused on myself and played the game. I could do that, I had support from Forica, Alele, Drizti, and even the other girls if it came down to it, I could make it, I'd take the world by storm, I knew I would.

And when I finally *did* make Angel? I was going to kill the bitch that ran me over with a car, and I was going to fucking enjoy it.

End

Sweet Touch will continue in Volume 2: Mango Smoothie, a collection of short stories that help bridge the gap between the two volumes of Candy's story. Coming soon.

About the Author

Erica H. Campbell is an up-and-coming queer author in her late 20s. She lives in the southeast US with her sister and a turtle named Inertia. In her free time, she enjoys tabletop games, board games, and cooking vegan meals for her friends. You can contact her directly at SylifiPublishing@gmail.com

The original draft of this book, and other upcoming novels by Erica Campbell are all available for free on https://sylifi.neocities.org